NECESSARY AS BLOOD

DEBORAH CROMBIE

AVON

An Imprint of HarperCollinsPublishers

A hardcover edition of this book was published in 2009 by William Morrow, an imprint of HarperCollins Publishers.

HarperCollins books may be purchased for educational, business, or sales promotional use. For information please write: Special Markets Department, HarperCollins Publishers, 10 East 53rd Street, New York, NY 10022.

FIRST AVON A EDITION PUBLISHED 2010.

Library of Congress Cataloging-in-Publication Data has been applied for.

ISBN 978-0-06-128754-1

12   13   14   WBC/RRD   10   9   8   7   6   5   4   3   2

NECESSARY AS BLOOD

BOOKS BY DEBORAH CROMBIE

Necessary as Blood

Where Memories Lie

Water Like a Stone

In a Dark House

Now May You Weep

And Justice There Is None

A Finer End

Kissed a Sad Goodbye

Dreaming of the Bones

Mourn Not Your Dead

Leave the Grave Green

All Shall Be Well

A Share in Death

FOR GIGI

Illustrated map by Laura Hartman Maestro ©2009

NECESSARY AS BLOOD

PROLOGUE

Umbra Sumus—"We are shadows."

—Inscription on the
sundial of the
Huguenot church,
now the Jamme
Masjid mosque, on
Brick Lane

That Sunday began like any ordinary Sunday, except that Naz, Sandra's husband, had gone in to work for a few hours at his law office, an unusual breach of family protocol for him.

Having pushed aside her initial irritation, Sandra had decided to use the time for one of her own projects, and after breakfast and chores she and Charlotte had gone up to her studio on the top floor of the house.

After two hours' work, Sandra stepped back, frowning, from the swatches of fabric she had pinned to the muslin stretched over the work frame in her studio. The carefully shaped pieces of material overlapped, forming a kaleidoscope of images, so that at first the whole appeared abstract, but on closer inspection, shapes appeared:

streets, buildings, people, birds, other animals, flowers—all representing in some way the history and culture of Sandra's particular
part of London, the East End, in and around Brick Lane.

Sandra's love affair with fabrics had begun as child, with the acquisition of a tattered quilt from a market stall on Brick Lane. She
and her gran had pored over it, marveling at the intricacy of the pattern, wondering which bits had come from an Auntie Mary's best
pinny, which from a little girl's Sunday dress, which from an Uncle
George's cast-off pajamas.

That passion had survived art college, and the pressure to join
the vogue for shock art. She had learned to draw and to paint, and
gradually she'd translated those skills into what she still thought of
as painting with fabric. But unlike paint, fabric was tactile and three-
dimensional, and the work fascinated her as much now as it had
done when she had haltingly composed her very first piece.

Today, however, something wasn't quite right. The piece wasn't
generating the emotional impact she wanted, and she couldn't quite
work out what was wrong. She moved a color here, a shape there,
stepped back for a different perspective and frowned again. The dark
brick of Georgian town houses formed a frame for a cascade of
color—it might have been Fournier Street, or Fashion Street, with
the women parading in their gowns, intricately worked iron cages
held high in their hands. The wire cages held, however, not birds, but
women and children's faces, dark to light, a few framed by the hijab.

Late-morning sun poured through the great windows in the
loft—a blessing for the warmth in midwinter if not in mid-May—
but it was the clarity of the light that had drawn her to the place,
and still, even when the work wasn't going well, had the power to
hold her transfixed.

She and Naz had bought the Fournier Street house more than a
decade ago, when they were first married, disregarding rising damp,
crumbling plaster, and minimal plumbing, because Sandra had seen
the potential of the studio space. And it had been affordable on Naz's

solicitor's earnings while Sandra was still in art school. They had worked hard, making many of the repairs themselves, to create their vision of a home, not realizing that in a few years' time they would be sitting on a property gold mine.

For the town houses on Fournier Street were Georgian, built by the French Huguenot silk weavers who had come to London's Spitalfields to escape persecution in Catholic France. The weavers had done well for themselves for a time, their looms clicking in their spacious lofts, the women congregating on the front stoops in their lustrous taffeta gowns, while their canaries sang in the cages they carried as marks of status.

But cheap calico imports from India had threatened the weavers' livelihood, and the invention of the mechanized loom had sounded its death knell. New waves of immigrants had followed the Huguenots—the Jews, the Irish, the Bangladeshis, the Somalis—but none had prospered as the Huguenots had done, and the houses had sunk into a long, slow decay.

Until now. Despite the recession, the City was moving relentlessly eastwards, encroaching on Spitalfields, bringing a new wave of immigrants. But these were yuppies with fat pocketbooks who were snapping up the houses and warehouses of the old East End, pushing the lower-income residents out as they came in. For the present bled into the past, and the past into the present, always, and to Sandra it seemed particularly so in the East End, where the years accumulated in layers like the fabrics on her board.

Sandra sighed and rubbed her fingers over the scrap of peacock-blue taffeta she held in her hand, contemplating its position in the overall design of her collage. It was inevitable, she supposed, change, and she had friends now on both sides of the economic divide—and if anything, she owed her ability to make her living as an artist to those on the upper end of the scale.

She glanced at the pile of fabric scraps under the loft casement. Charlotte lay nestled among the silks and voiles, drawn like a cat to the pool of sunlight. She had settled there when she tired of a long and one-sided conversation with her favorite stuffed elephant—Charlotte, like her mother before her, would have nothing to do with dolls.

Graceful as a cat, too, her little daughter, even asleep with her thumb in her mouth, thought Sandra. At almost three, Charlotte had held on to her thumb sucking a bit too long, but Sandra found herself reluctant to deprive her precocious child of a last vestige of infant comfort.

Her frustration with the collage-in-progress momentarily forgotten, Sandra grabbed a sketchbook and pencil from her worktable. Quickly, she blocked out the spill of fabric, the small French panes of the casement, the curve of Charlotte's small body in dungarees and T-shirt, the delicate and slightly snub-nosed face framed by the mass of toffee-colored curls.

The sketch cried out for color and Sandra exchanged her number 2 for a handful of colored pencils pulled from a chipped Silver Jubilee mug—a flea-market treasure kept for its accidental misspelling of the Duke of Edinburgh's name.

Red for the dungarees, pink for the T-shirt, bright blues and greens for the puddled silks, warm brown for the polished floorboards.

Absently, she went back to the silks, her hand attempting to reproduce the half-formed memory of an intricate silk pattern she had seen. It had been sari silk, like those spilled on her floor, but an unusual pattern, tiny birds handwoven into the apple green fabric. She'd asked the girl who wore it where it had come from, and the child had answered in soft, halting English, saying her mother had given it to her. But when Sandra asked if her mother had bought it here, in London, the girl had gone mute and looked frightened, as if she'd spoken out of bounds. And the next time Sandra visited, she had been gone.

Sandra frowned at the recollection and Charlotte stirred, as if unconsciously responding. Afraid she would lose her opportunity to capture the tableau, Sandra reached for her camera and snapped. She checked the image, nodding as she saw Charlotte's sleeping face framed by silk, timeless now.

Timeless, like the faces in the cages in her collage . . . A sudden inspiration made her glance at the collage. What if . . . What if she used photo transfer for the faces of the women and girls, rather than fabric and paint? She could use the faces of women and children she knew, if they would agree.

Charlotte stretched and opened her eyes, smiling sleepily. A good-natured child, Charlotte was seldom cross unless tired or hungry, a blessing Sandra was sure she had not bestowed on her own mum. Setting down her camera, she knelt and lifted her daughter. "Nice nap, sweetie?" she asked as Charlotte twined her arms round her neck for a hug. Charlotte's hair was damp from sun and sleep and her pale caramel skin still held a faint scent of baby muskiness, but she didn't give her mother much chance to nuzzle.

Squirming from Sandra's arms, she went to the worktable. "Duck pencils, Mummy," she said, eyeing the empty mug. "I want to draw, too."

Sandra considered, glancing at the clock, at the sun-brightened windows, and once again at the half-finished collage on the worktable. She knew from experience that she'd reached the point where staring at the board wouldn't provide a solution, and besides, she wanted to try out her photo idea. A break was in order.

It was not quite noon; Charlotte had been up early and Sandra had let her fall asleep before her usual nap time. They'd agreed to meet Naz for lunch at two, that is, if he could drag himself away from the office. She gave a sharp shake of her head at the thought. He and Lou had both been working much too hard on an upcoming case, and Naz was showing uncharacteristic signs of strain. Family

Sundays had always been a priority for them, especially since Charlotte's birth, as they both were determined to give her the secure childhood neither of them had had.

Naz had been orphaned, his Christian parents murdered in Pakistan by the swell of fundamentalist Muslim violence in the seventies. Sent to London in the care of an aunt and uncle who felt themselves burdened by the charge, he had grown up adjusting to the loss of both family and culture.

And Sandra, well, her family didn't bear thinking about.

But as for her husband, no Bangladeshi restaurant owner's troubles with the law were worth damaging what they had so carefully built. She would have to have a word with Naz. In the meantime, it was a perfect May day, and there was still time to go to Columbia Road.

"I have a better idea," she told Charlotte, putting the pencils firmly back in the cup. "Let's go see Uncle Roy."

Sandra held Charlotte's hand as they made their way up Brick Lane through the bustle of the Sunday market. Fall-off-the-lorry day, Naz always called the Sunday market, with a hint of disapproval. He was right, of course. Half the things hawked by the traders had either fallen off a lorry or been smuggled across the Channel in the back of one. But Sandra loved it—loved the tatty chaos of it, the vendors with their makeshift trestle tables selling everything from French wine to cases of oranges (no doubt rotten at the bottom) to old car batteries.

When they passed the Old Truman Brewery, Charlotte tugged at her hand. "Roots, Mummy," she said, pointing into Ely Yard. In the car park behind the brewery, an old Routemaster bus had been turned into a vegan restaurant called Rootmaster. Charlotte didn't understand the pun but loved to eat in its top deck. The bus rocked with the wind and with the waitress's tread on the curving stairs, and Charlotte would shriek with joy at every sway.

"Not now, sweetie." Sandra clasped her hand more firmly. "We'll meet Daddy there in a bit. And when we get to Columbia Road, I'll buy you a cupcake for after."

She waved at her friends in the vintage-clothing shop where she often bought things to use in her collages, but resisted the temptation to go in. The window gave back a distorted reflection of her mop of blond hair, and of Charlotte's, a few shades darker but just as curly.

It was only as they neared the railway line that Sandra slowed, then stopped. When Charlotte tugged at her hand again, she scooped her up and propped her on her hip. In one of the recessed brick arches under the old railway bridge, an anonymous artist had pasted a black-and-white photo image of a young woman. She was nude, shown from the pelvis up, her torso almost as slender as a boy's. The shape of the surrounding brick arch suggested an icon, and the subject gazed out at the viewer with such a serene grace that Sandra had mentally dubbed her "the Madonna of Brick Lane."

But she was fading, the Madonna, the paper wrinkling, the edges beginning to peel and curl. Soon she would disappear, in the way of street art, to be replaced by another artist's vision. Sandra pulled out her camera and snapped a shot. Now, at least, the Madonna would be preserved.

The inspiration she'd had in the studio suddenly crystallized. She would use photo transfers, yes, but fade them . . . They would vanish as had the women and girls held captive in so many ways over the years. Vanish like the girl with the sari—

Oh, no, surely not . . . Sandra tightened her grip on Charlotte. She'd heard the stories, of course, but not connected them with anyone she knew. It was impossible. Unthinkable. And yet . . .

She must be mad, she told herself, shaking her head. But now that the idea had taken hold, it grew, blossoming in all its permutations into something monstrous.

Charlotte squirmed. "Mummy, you're hurting me."

"Sorry, sweetheart." Sandra relaxed her grip and kissed the top of Charlotte's curls.

"I want to go. I want to see Daddy," said Charlotte, kicking her trainer-clad toes against Sandra's leg.

"We'll see Daddy. But—" Sandra glanced once more at the Madonna, then turned away, keeping Charlotte on her hip, hurrying now. The suspicion might be mad, but she would have to prove herself wrong. She had an excuse for a visit—she'd ask to take a photo, for the collage. It wasn't far. She'd just need to leave Charlotte with Roy for a bit.

She crossed Bethnal Green Road, then made her way through the quiet, council-estate-lined streets of Bethnal Green. Her hip began to ache from Charlotte's weight.

As she neared Columbia Road, she began to pass pedestrians going the other way. Some carried bunches of cut flowers, some potted plants; some even pulled wagons filled with shrubs or small palm trees.

She heard the market before she saw it, the noise coming in staccato bursts. At first it sounded like a foreign language, then, as they grew nearer, the words resolved themselves into English, bawled in a Cockney singsong patter. "Nice buncha daisies a five-a. Get yer tulips now, three bunches a tenn-a."

Turning a corner, she passed by the pocket park and plunged into the bottom end of Columbia Road Flower Market. Every Sunday morning at the break of dawn, the flower vendors set up their stalls here, hawking everything from flats of bedding flowers to small trees. It was only as an adult that Sandra had come to know the market from an outsider's viewpoint, as she had worked her way through school and art college here, helping Roy Blakely at his stall.

Sandra hugged Charlotte closer and pushed through the crowd, ducking away from the tendrils of a stall's climbing roses that threatened to catch in her hair. Roy stood beneath his green-and-white-striped awning, tucking a folded note into the purse he wore at his waist. When he saw Sandra and Charlotte, he winked. "Come for the best of the lot, have we?"

The vendors would sell everything before they knocked down, and Roy would let Sandra pay only a pittance for the leavings on the stall. Her loft was full of potted plants, her small garden riotous, and most weeks she took home bunches of cut flowers for the house, but not today.

"Cupcakes," said Charlotte seriously, eyeing Treacle, the shop near Roy's stall. "Lemon."

"Not just yet." Sandra let her slide to the ground. "Roy, can I ask a favor? I've something— I've an errand. Would you mind watching Charlotte for just a bit? It won't be long—we're supposed to meet Naz at two." She glanced at her watch, feeling the pressure of time.

Charlotte jumped over a flat of pansies and wrapped herself around Roy's knees. "Can I sell flowers, Uncle Roy?"

"That you can, love." Roy stooped to give her a hug. "Go on, then," he added to Sandra. "I can manage, now the punters have thinned."

Sandra hesitated just for a moment, tempted by the comforting familiarity of the market. It would be easy to slip on an apron and give Roy a hand. But she'd made up her mind, and now she must see it through.

Bending, she gave Charlotte a kiss. "Right. Thanks, Roy. I'll owe you."

Sandra glanced at her watch. It was five minutes past one. Waving to Charlotte, she turned away. When she reached the corner, a sudden impulse made her glance back, but the crowd had obscured her daughter as seamlessly as a closing zipper.

CHAPTER ONE

*Sadly, I have recently come to accept what I refused to accept
for so long: that the house may be only ephemeral.*

—Dennis Severs,
*18 Folgate Street:
The Tale of a
House in Spitalfields*

The streets were greasy with moisture. The air inside the bus felt
thick, almost solid, and in the damp August heat the personal-
hygiene deficiencies of some of the passengers were all too apparent.

Gemma James stood near the center doors as the number 49
lumbered south over the Battersea Bridge, gripping the stanchion,
trying not to breathe through her nose. The man in the seat beside
her stank of more than unwashed body—alcohol fumes came off
him in waves, and when the bus lurched he swayed against her.

Why had she thought taking the bus a good idea? And on a Saturday. She'd had a few errands to run in Kensington and hadn't
wanted to bother with parking—that had been her excuse, at least.
The truth was that she'd craved the mindlessness of it, had wanted
to sit and watch London going about its business without any assis-

tance on her part. She hadn't planned on having to protect her personal space quite so diligently.

When the bus ground to a halt just past the bridge, she was tempted to get off and walk, but her map told her there was still a good way to go, and a few sluggish raindrops splattered against the already-dirty windows. To her left she could see the rise of Battersea Park, an impressionistic gray-green blur through the smeared glass. The doors opened and closed with a pneumatic swish. The drunk man stayed resolutely put.

Gemma didn't know this part of London well, and as the bus turned from the fairly posh environs of Battersea Road into Falcon Road, the neighborhood quickly lost its gloss.

Surely, Hazel didn't mean to live here rather than in Islington? Thrift shops, video rentals, halal butchers, down-at-the-heels nameless cafés—and now ahead she could see the converging railway lines of Clapham Junction. Had she missed her stop? She jammed her finger against the red request button, and when the bus doors opened at the next stop, she almost leapt out.

Her feeling of relief was short-lived, however, as she stood on the pavement and looked round. She consulted her A to Zed, double-checking, but there was no doubt this was the street. It was, she saw, not even a cul-de-sac, but simply a short dead end. A square concrete building that announced itself in both English and Bengali as a mosque stood on the corner, and in the street itself a few young men in skullcaps and *salwar kameez* idly kicked a football.

Gemma moved slowly forward, searching for the number Hazel had given her. A rubbish skip stood on the pavement to her left, overflowing with what looked like the complete interior of the terraced Victorian house behind it. That was a good sign, surely, she thought, the area on the upswing. But aside from the short terrace, there were only council flats at the end of the street, and a high wall to her right.

The young men stopped kicking the ball and looked at her. She gave them a neutral nod, then straightened her back, surveying her surroundings with deliberate purpose. Police work had long ago taught her that it was not a good idea to wander about looking like a lost sheep—it marked you out as a victim.

She'd worn a sundress, in deference to the sticky weather, and although the persimmon-colored cotton skirt ended demurely enough at the knee, she felt suddenly uncomfortably exposed.

A bungalow, Hazel had said, with a charming garden and patio. Gemma had found the thought of a bungalow in London odd enough, but it seemed unimaginable here, and she began to wonder if she had somehow got it all wrong.

She had begun to contemplate asking the now obviously interested young men for directions when she saw the number, half hidden by the creeper trailing over the high wall. Beneath the number was an arched wooden door, its paint faded to a dull blue-gray.

Checking the address against the scrap of paper in her bag, she saw that it was definitely a match. But where was the bungalow? Well, no point in standing gawping all day, she thought, walking up to the door and pressing the bell beside it. Her stomach suddenly tensed.

She hadn't seen her best friend in more than a year, and so much had altered for both of them. E-mails and phone calls had kept them up-to-date, but Hazel had seemed distant these last few months, and had said little about the reasons for her unexpected return to London. Gemma had begun to fear that their close relationship had changed, and then Hazel had asked that she visit without the children, a very unusual request.

Toby had been clamoring to see Holly and had thrown a tantrum at being left behind, and Kit had gone silent, a sure sign that he was worried or unhappy.

As Gemma was about to press the bell again, the small door swung open and Hazel stood framed in the opening, her face lit with a smile. She gathered Gemma into a fierce hug.

"I'm so glad to see you." Hazel stepped back and examined her, then tugged her through the door and closed it behind them. "And you look fabulous," she said. "Engagement must agree with you."

"You, too. I mean, you look wonderful," answered Gemma, awkward in an attempt to cover her shock. Hazel didn't look wonderful at all. While she had never been plump, there had always been a bit of softness about her that made her particularly attractive. Now her cheeks were hollow, and her collarbone jutted above the neckline of the cotton sleeveless blouse she wore. Tan hiking shorts hung on her hips, as if they'd been borrowed from someone several sizes larger, and her feet were bare, making her seem oddly defenseless.

"I know, I'm pale," Hazel said, as if she sensed Gemma's reaction. "It's Scotland. We had no summer this year. I'm sure I must look as though I've been living in a cave. But enough of that. Let me show you the house."

Gemma took in her surroundings. The door in the wall had actually been a gate, and they stood on the brick patio Hazel had described, overarched by trees. Across the patio stood a white-stuccoed bungalow, its single story capped with a red tile roof. Yellow roses climbed up trellises on its front, and lemon trees in tubs stood at either side of the front door.

"It *is* a bungalow," Gemma said, delighted. "It's a bit exotic for London, isn't it?"

"I call it my *Secret Garden* house." Hazel took her arm. "I fell in love with it the minute I saw the photo online. I know it's not Islington, but the neighborhood grows on you, and I could just barely afford it."

"Those boys—"

"Tariq, Jamil, and Ali," Hazel corrected. "They've taken to keeping an eye on me. Tariq said he wouldn't want his old mum living all on her own. Quite took the wind out of my sails, I can tell you. Not that his *old mum* is likely to be more than thirty-five."

Hazel's brightness seemed a little forced, and Gemma wondered if she were really as comfortable as she made out. But this, she sensed,

was not the time to force the issue, and she followed Hazel obediently into the little house.

The front door led directly into a sitting room that ran the width
of the house. The walls were white, the floor tiled, so that the room
seemed almost a continuation of the patio. One end held recessed
bookshelves on either side of a brick fireplace, the other a dining
area and a small, fitted kitchen set into an alcove.

"It's still a bit bare, but I've raided Ikea, and I've got books on the
shelves, so that's a start," Hazel said. "And I've got tea, and wine in
the fridge. Life's essentials."

Gemma recognized the pink-and-red-floral sofa and red-checked
armchair from a recent Ikea catalogue. Hazel had added an ottoman,
an end table with a lamp, a rag rug, and baskets filled with magazines
and knitting yarns, a comfortingly familiar touch. The dining furniture was pale wood, pleasingly simple, and Gemma thought it, too,
had come from Ikea. A vase filled with red tulips stood on the table,
another familiar touch. Hazel had always had flowers in the house.

It was on the tip of her tongue to ask why Hazel hadn't brought
anything from Carnmore, her house in Scotland, or from Islington,
when Hazel said, "It's a doll's house, really. Reminds me of the garage flat. Do you remember?"

Hearing the hint of wistfulness, Gemma squeezed her friend's
arm. "Of course I do. It's only been—" She stopped. Had it really
been that long?

Gemma had rented the tiny garage flat behind the house in Islington where Hazel had lived with her daughter, Holly, and her
now-estranged husband, Tim Cavendish. It had proved both sanctuary and launching pad, allowing Gemma to regain the confidence so
badly damaged by her marriage, and to move on in her personal as
well as her professional life. Hazel had cared for Gemma's son, Toby,
who was the same age as Holly, and had provided Gemma with a
stability she'd never felt in her own home.

Then an unexpected pregnancy had propelled Gemma into a new life with Duncan Kincaid, and a few months later, Hazel's marriage had collapsed and she had moved to the Scottish Highlands to take over her family's whisky distillery.

"It will be two years at Christmas," Gemma said wonderingly. Two years since she and Duncan had moved into the house in Notting Hill with Toby and Duncan's son, Kit, two years since she had lost the baby.

"There's only the one bedroom," Hazel was saying. "But when Holly stays, she's comfy enough on the sofa. And of course she usually manages to creep in with me."

"When Holly stays?" asked Gemma, brought sharply back to the present. "What do you mean, when Holly stays? Isn't she with you?"

Hazel looked away, started to speak, then gestured towards the kitchen. "I'll just put the kettle on, shall I? And then we'll have a proper talk."

CHAPTER TWO

It was the summer we became orphans . . .

—Emanuel Litvinoff,
*Journey Through a
Small Planet*

He struggled up from the dream, grasping for consciousness the way a drowning swimmer gasps for air. For an instant he seemed to breach the surface, and with an effort of will forced his lips to move.

"Sandra." In his mind, he heard his own rasping whisper. But then the fog lifted a bit further, and he realized that he hadn't spoken at all, that even his plea had been part of the dream. "Wha—," he managed, and this time he was sure he had spoken, but his dry lips felt foreign, as if they belonged to a ventriloquist's dummy.

"Where—" It was only a thread of sound, but encouraged, he attempted to blink. The sudden flare of light seared his eyes, and the accompanying wave of pain carried him back into comforting dimness.

Hazel took the armchair, settling into the curve of it and tucking her feet up as if she needed the comfort. She'd brought a tray holding a red teapot and mugs, a jug of milk, and a plate of mixed biscuits from a supermarket package. It was the first time Gemma could recall Hazel offering something she hadn't made herself. Hazel had remembered, however, just how much milk Gemma liked, and poured for her before filling her own cup and cradling it between her hands.

Gemma felt the hint of a breeze from the patio windows, and thought she caught the scent of lemons. The voices of the boys in the street came faintly from beyond the wall.

When Hazel didn't speak, Gemma said slowly, "I thought, when you said you were coming home, that you and Tim might be getting back together."

"No." Haltingly, Hazel went on, "I had thought . . . but I'm afraid it's just too complicated. Even if Tim could forgive me, I'm not sure I can forgive myself." The look she gave Gemma held an appeal. "I had everything, Gem. Marriage, family, home, career—and I threw it all away."

"But you loved Donald Brodie. If things hadn't gone so terribly wrong—"

"Did I?" Hazel sat forward, sloshing her tea. She rubbed at the wet edge of her mug with her thumb. "Did I really love him? Or was I just bored, and desperate for attention? It was a fantasy. It would never have worked, even if—" She swallowed, shook her head. "But none of that matters. What does is that I was willing to hurt Holly, and Tim, and I can't take that back."

"And Tim, does he feel that way, too?"

"I don't know. He says he'd like to try, but I think once the novelty wore off, it would eat at him. How could it not? How could he ever trust me?"

Gemma was about to urge her friend not to be so hard on herself, but seeing Hazel's obstinate expression, changed tack. "Then why have you come back? I thought you loved Carnmore." The distillery, tucked away in one of the most remote regions of the Scottish

Highlands, had seemed horribly isolated to Gemma, but she hadn't been able to dissuade Hazel from staying.

"I did. I do. And I had an obligation. But the distillery is back on its feet now, and there are those better qualified to run it than I." Hazel set down her cup and leaned forward, the light from the patio window revealing the dark shadows under her eyes. "And I found I wasn't made of as strong a stuff as I thought. I was homesick, and I just couldn't face another winter. It wasn't fair to Holly, living like that, the two of us on our own for weeks at a time. She needs her dad, and a familiar environment, and a good school . . ."

Hazel seemed to hesitate, then said, "Holly's going to stay in Islington with Tim during the week, Gemma. We've worked it all out. She can go to school just down the street from the house, and Tim will be working at home, so he can easily arrange after-school care for her."

"But, Hazel, you're her mum—" Gemma's arguments died on her lips. She knew the decision would have been difficult for Hazel, and she knew Hazel's tenacity once she had made up her mind. Instead, she regrouped, trying to find something positive. "So Holly will spend weekends with you?"

"Yes, and we can always juggle schedules if it's needed. I asked Tim to keep her over today so that we could have some time together."

"But what will you do?" Gemma asked. Hazel, like Tim, had been a family therapist, but after the disintegration of her own marriage she'd felt she wasn't fit to counsel others. "Will you go into practice again?"

"No. I'm going to work in a café." For the first time since her greeting, Hazel's smile seemed to reach her eyes. "It's a new venture in Kensington. I know the chef, and she needs a general dogsbody. I can cook, or serve, or run the cash register. Right now it's only breakfast through tea, but if we open for dinner I'll be able to do evening shifts during the week. You'll have to come for lunch someday. It's just behind Kensington High Street. Now"—she refilled Gemma's cup and her own with a briskness that seemed more like her old self—"tell me about you. How's your mum?"

Gemma blinked back an unexpected and infuriating prickle of tears. Her seemingly indomitable mother had been diagnosed with leukemia in May. Ongoing chemotherapy seemed to have effected a partial remission, but they all felt as if they were walking a tightrope. "She's holding her own. Dad's had to get in extra help at the bakery, but his biggest job is keeping her hands out of things."

"I can imagine." Hazel smiled. "I'll go see her, shall I? One day next week." She gave Gemma an appraising glance. "And what about you? You haven't said a word about the wedding plans and the summer has almost gone by."

"Oh." Gemma's mind froze for a moment, then she felt the ever more frequent squeeze of panic in her chest. She forced a breath and a smile. "It seemed a good idea at the time."

"Gemma! Don't tell me you've got cold feet." Hazel looked so alarmed that Gemma gave a strangled laugh.

"No. Not about Duncan, anyway." The proposal had been hers, after all. She and Duncan had been partners, lovers, friends, and now, parents in their blended family, and the decision to commit to being together she didn't regret for a moment. She hastened to explain. "It's just the bloody wedding business. It's driving me mad. I thought we could just get married—silly of me, I know," she said, forestalling the comment she knew was going to accompany Hazel's raised brows. "But everyone's got involved, although I must say Duncan's family have been decent about it. Mine, though . . ." She rolled her eyes. "And it's not just Dad and Cynthia, demanding this and that for Mum's sake. The boys are even in on it. They want a reception at the Natural History Museum. Can you believe it?"

"Yes," said Hazel, laughing. "But I thought you wanted Winnie to perform the ceremony."

Winnie Montfort was the Reverend Winifred Montfort, married

to Duncan's cousin Jack, and dear to them both. But she and Jack lived in Glastonbury, and Winnie, nearing forty, was expecting her first child. "Her doctor doesn't want her to travel, and of course Jack's frantic with worry." Jack Montfort's first wife and their baby had died in childbirth and he had taken the news of Winnie's pregnancy with mixed feelings. "But even if she could come, she couldn't marry us in someone else's church."

"Why not just ask the vicar at St. John's to do the ceremony, then?" St. John's was the Anglican church near their house in Notting Hill. "That seems simple enough."

"Because it's high church. My parents were brought up chapel, and to them St. John's might as well be Catholic. My dad says it would kill my mum, which of course it wouldn't, but my mum says to try to humor him—"

"Then a civil venue—"

"Just as complicated. The boys want in on the choice, and if we hold a proper reception, the guest list turns into a nightmare. We'd end up having to invite everyone either of us has met since primary school."

"A register office—"

"Then we'll disappoint everyone." Gemma shook her head and looked out the window so she wouldn't have to meet Hazel's eyes. "I don't know. I've done this before—it seems now that the wedding was the beginning of the end for Rob and me—and I don't want to go through that again. I'm just about ready to chuck the whole thing."

The heart had gone from the house. Tim knew it, and Holly knew it, and there didn't seem to be anything he could do to fix it.

During the longest and darkest days of the winter, he had painted the kitchen. Not that he was very good at painting and decorating, but it gave him something to do to fill the seemingly endless evenings and weekends, and when he was finished he'd been quite proud of his handiwork.

Gone were Hazel's soft greens and peaches. The cupboards were sparkling white, the walls a deep maize yellow. A new beginning, he'd thought. Then Holly had come for a much-anticipated visit and burst into tears at the sight of it. "Where's Mummy's kitchen?" she'd wailed, and he'd been powerless to comfort her.

She got used to it eventually, of course, just as she'd got used to their routine, but he'd never stopped feeling he had to try too hard. Holly would be six in a few weeks, and he'd argued the case for her starting proper school here with him as persuasively as he could. Hazel, however, had capitulated more easily than he'd expected, and now he found himself wondering if he would be able to cope.

"Where's Mummy?" Holly asked for the hundredth time that afternoon. She sat at the kitchen table, kicking her heels against the chair rungs. He had given her one of the fizzy drinks Hazel didn't allow, and it had only made her more cross.

"I've told you, pumpkin. She's having a girls' day out with your auntie Gemma."

"I want to go. I'm a girl," Holly said with irrefutable logic.

"You can't this time. It's grown-up girls only."

"That's not fair."

"No, I suppose not." Tim sighed. "We could have cheese on toast," he offered.

"I don't want toast. I want to play with Toby." Holly's pretty mouth, so like her mother's, was set in a scowl that would have done justice to a troll.

"We'll arrange something."

Gemma and Duncan had gone out of their way to keep up the connection between the children, and they often included him in social invitations. Decent of them, but he was always aware that there was an element of charity involved, and it made him awkward. Their lives had diverged, the only point of contact the children, and making the effort to talk casually about Hazel exhausted him. But it was one of the few anchors in his life these days, and he was unwilling to let it go.

"Now," he said to Holly, "let's stop kicking the chair." Why, Tim wondered as he heard himself, did adults talk to children in the plural? It wasn't as if he were kicking the bloody chair. If the inclusiveness was meant to be persuasive, it didn't work.

Holly kept kicking the chair rungs. He ignored it. "We could go to the park after Charlotte visits."

"I don't want ta play wi' Charlotte," said Holly, and Tim heard the Scots accent that had been popping up intermittently since she'd come back to London. He found it both endearing and annoying, but on the whole wanted his daughter to sound like her old self. "Charlotte's a baby," she went on with disdain.

"And you're a big girl, so you'll do a good job of looking after her while I talk to her daddy."

Mollified by this appeal to her bossy nature, Holly's mouth relaxed. "Can we still go to the park?"

Tim glanced at the kitchen clock. Naz and Charlotte were now almost an hour late, and that was very unlike Naz. "We'll have to see, pumpkin," he told Holly. He tried Naz's mobile, but it went straight to voice mail.

He didn't normally see clients on a Saturday, and especially not when he had Holly. But Naz Malik was an old friend—they had been at uni together—and considering Naz's situation, Tim had been willing to juggle his own schedule to suit his friend's. He'd thought they could talk in the garden, and the girls could play.

And Naz had been insistent when he'd rung that morning, almost distraught, in fact. Why would his friend, who was punctual to the point of obsession, say he had to see Tim, then not show up?

"Let's make the cheese toast," Tim suggested. "I'm sure Charlotte would like some when she gets here." Restless, he added, "I'll

tell you what. We'll make a proper Welsh rarebit, like Mummy does."
Opening the fridge, he dug out some cheddar, mustard, and milk.
Then he foraged in the cupboard for Worcestershire sauce, and cut
thick slices of some slightly stale bakery bread.

"It won't be as good," Holly intoned with certainty.

"I know." Tim repressed another sigh as he poured milk into the
saucepan. "But we'll do it anyway."

By the time he had spread his cheese sauce on the toast and
popped it under the grill until it bubbled, he was beginning to feel
seriously worried about Naz. He rang his mobile again, with no result. He took a bite of the toast, which was better than he'd expected, and watched Holly make gratifying inroads on her slice, but
he couldn't stop himself from glancing at the clock. It was an old-
fashioned clock with a big face, and its second hand seemed to tick
at glacial speed as the light in the garden grew softer.

"Can we go to the park now, Daddy?" Holly scrubbed her greasy
hands against her jeans, and Tim absently got up and dampened a
cloth to wipe her fingers.

"Not quite yet, pumpkin." He rang Naz's mobile once more,
then pulled up his home number and redialed.

It was picked up on the first ring. "Mr. Naz?" The voice was
young, female, and rising with distress.

"No. Alia? It's Dr. Cavendish here."

Alia was Naz's part-time nanny, a Bangladeshi girl who minded
Charlotte during the day and took college classes at night. She
wanted, Naz had told Tim, to be a lawyer.

"Is Mr. Naz with you, then?" asked Alia. "He was supposed to be
home two hours ago and he's not answering his phone. My parents are
expecting me and I can't leave Charlotte. I don't know what to do."

"He didn't say where he was going?"

"No. And he's never late. You know how he is. If I take Char out
for an ice cream or something and we're even five minutes late, he's,
like, ballistic."

With good reason, thought Tim. "Is there anyone else you can call?"

"I tried the office, but no one answered. I don't have numbers for Charlotte's mum's family. Mr. Naz won't have nothing to do with them." She said "nuffink" in the strong Estuary accent adopted by many young second-generation immigrants to the East End. "And I don't know how to reach Ms. Phillips at home.

"He always answers his phone if he sees it's me," Alia went on. "Unless he's in court, and then he tells me ahead of time. He knows I don't call unless it's important."

Louise Phillips was Naz's partner in his law firm, and Tim didn't have her home number, either.

"I could take Char home with me," said Alia, "but I don't like to without his permission. I can't think why he wouldn't ring me if he was going to be late." She sounded near tears.

Nor could Tim imagine a circumstance in which Naz Malik would miss an appointment without notice or fail to respond to his daughter's nanny, and his anxiety spiked into fear. "Okay, Alia, let me think."

He could leave Holly with his neighbors and be in Fournier Street within half an hour. "You stay there," he told her, "and I'll come straight over."

But once there, he thought as he rang off, what could he do other than send Alia home?

He was going to have to find Naz Malik, and he was going to need help.

CHAPTER THREE

We carried on down Fournier Street. The back of Hawksmoor's Christ Church loomed large over the Georgian town houses built by the Huguenots at a time when Spitalfields was known as Weaver Town.

—Tarquin Hall,
Salaam Brick Lane

Hazel drove the secondhand Volkswagen Golf she had brought down from Scotland.

"I see you've joined the Sloane Rangers," teased Gemma, the Golf having become the car of choice among the trendy in Chelsea. Having appointed herself navigator, she pulled her pocket-size A to Zed from her bag.

"They're only Sloanie if they're new and a gift from indulgent parents who don't want their children to appear elitist," said Hazel. "And this one has certainly seen better days." She patted the dash as if consoling the car. "I was going to leave it behind, but then I considered the logistics of getting Holly from Battersea to Islington and vice versa with no tube stop on the Battersea end."

They had crossed the Battersea Bridge and were driving east

along the Embankment. Gemma glanced at Cheney Walk, then away. Her London seemed to be ever more populated by ghosts, and there were some she was more willing to allow real estate than others.

"Tell me what you know about this friend of Tim's," she said. Tim had rung just as Hazel announced it was time to open a bottle of wine, which seemed rather fortuitous timing on his part.

Hazel had listened, then put the bottle back in the fridge as she rang off, her brow creased. "Tim wants us both to meet him at a house near Brick Lane," she'd explained. "If you can, that is. A friend who's a single father hasn't come home, and Tim's worried about him and the child."

Gemma had agreed willingly enough, but now she added, "Do you think Tim's overreacting? Surely it's a miscommunication of some sort."

"I used to tell Tim his pulse wouldn't go up in an earthquake. I *wanted* him to be more emotional." Hazel's emphasis made clear what she thought of that folly. "So, no, I'd say that if Tim's worried, he has reason." She coaxed the Golf's sluggish gears through a down change, then tapped her fingers on the wheel as they idled at a light. "All I know about his friend is that they knew each other at university and recently got in touch again. He's a solicitor called Naz Malik. Pakistani. I've never met him. There was some sort of scandal with Malik's wife and I take it Tim felt sympathetic."

Gemma glanced at Hazel, taken aback by the bitter tone, but Hazel went on, "I'm really not sure why he rang, except that he knew you were visiting and he wanted your advice."

Afraid any comment would open a conversational minefield, Gemma went back to her map. "When you reach Whitechapel, you'd better take Commercial Street. I think Brick Lane is one way in the other direction."

The Saturday traffic was light and they made good time, turning away from the river at Tower Hill. Soon the stark spire of Christ

Church Spitalfields rose before them, and opposite, the dark brick facade of the old Spitalfields Market, surmounted by its new glass arcade.

Gemma had come to Spitalfields and to Petticoat Lane Market with her parents a few times as a child, and she had once been to Brick Lane on a Sunday with Rob, her ex-husband. She'd been a newly minted detective constable then, and Rob had bought cheap cigarettes and liquor that she'd been sure were smuggled or stolen. The street had smelled of rotting garbage, the buildings had struck her as dirty and squalid, and even by the standards of her Leyton upbringing the crowd had seemed raucous and unfriendly. She and Rob had ended up having a row and he'd called her—not for the first time—a self-righteous cow and she'd called him, well, she didn't like to think about it. All in all, it had not been an experience she had wanted to repeat.

"Turn right just after the church," she told Hazel.

"Hawksmoor, isn't it?" Hazel glanced up through the windscreen. "Impressive, but not exactly your warm and fuzzy neighborhood sanctuary."

Gemma had to admit that the angular silhouette of the church seemed a bit forbidding, and the proportions a bit odd, as if the spire carried too much weight.

As they turned right, she saw the short stretch of Fournier Street, its darkly severe houses anchored by the church and the crumbling facade of a pub at the top end, while the bottom end provided a perfect frame for the Bangla City supermarket on the opposite side of Brick Lane.

"There's Tim's car," Hazel said tightly, as if her ill feelings extended to the battered Volvo. She found a small space nearby for the Golf, and when she had maneuvered into it, she and Gemma got out, checking the house numbers against the scribbled address.

"It's this one." Gemma looked up at a house set in the terrace on the north side of the street. Although adjoining, each house was set off from its neighbors by slight differences in the architectural detailing and the state of repair. This house looked well tended, its brown brick contrasting with trim work and wrought-iron railings painted a soft green.

The front door was offset, so that the ground floor had only two windows to one side, while the first and second floors had three windows across. The top floor was recessed, so that Gemma just glimpsed light glinting from what looked like loft or studio windows. The front door sported a hooded canopy supported by ornate brackets, also painted pale green, and the arched shape of the canopy was echoed in the slightly arched brickwork above the windows.

Before they could ring the bell, the door opened and Tim bounded down the steps, taking Gemma's hand and giving her a peck on the cheek. "Thanks for coming." He was tall, with unruly hair and a beard that had always seemed to Gemma to add to his air of rather puppyish awkwardness. But he had an endearing earnestness about him as well, and Gemma wondered if it was this that generated confidence in his patients.

"Hazel—" He turned to his wife, belatedly, for she had already mounted the steps. "Thanks. I—"

"Any word from your friend?" Hazel asked.

"No. I've kept Alia until you arrived. I thought Gemma would want to talk to her. Alia is Charlotte's nanny," he hastened to explain, ushering them into the entrance hall.

The space was dominated by a polished oak staircase, spiraling dizzyingly upwards in symmetrical right-angle turns. But the grandeur of the staircase was offset by the iron boot rack near the door, festooned with pairs of polka dot wellies in varying sizes, and a jumble of hats. A bicycle stood beside it, a helmet hanging by its chin strap on the handlebars.

The walls were painted the same warm green as the exterior trim, and through an open doorway Gemma glimpsed a comfortable-looking sitting room.

"Charlotte is your friend's little girl?" Gemma asked.

"Yes. She's not quite three. Naz was supposed to come for a visit, and we were going to let the girls play. But that was hours ago, and he never showed up at our house, or came home, and he's not answering his phone. Look, let's go down to the kitchen. You should talk to Alia."

He led them to the back of the staircase, where a much less ornate flight led down into an open plan dining/kitchen area that stretched the length of the house.

Light from the well at the front fell on a sofa slipcovered in a cheerful dahlia print, and at the back, French doors opened onto a small garden. Cupboards and a large dresser lined the walls, and a trestle table stood in front of an enormous fireplace.

The air smelled of Indian spices, and a young Asian woman sat at the table, trying to coax a child to eat. The young woman was slightly plump, with straight black hair pulled back into a haphazard ponytail. When she looked up at them, her eyes were red-rimmed behind the lenses of her dark-framed glasses.

But the child . . . Gemma stared at the little girl, transfixed. Her light brown hair formed a mass of corkscrew curls almost as tight as dreadlocks. Her skin was the palest café au lait, and when she glanced up, Gemma saw that her eyes were an unexpected blue-green. She wore little Velcro-fastened trainers, and a dirt-smudged overall over a pink T-shirt. The ordinary clothes seemed only to emphasize her unusual beauty.

At the moment, however, she was turning her head away from the offered fork, and the young woman looked at Tim in appeal. "I made samosas," she said. "A treat for Mr. Naz and Charlotte. My mum is always telling me I need to learn how to cook so that I can get a man, which is really stupid." She shrugged. "It's a Bangladeshi thing. But I don't mind cooking for *them*." Her nod included Charlotte and,

Gemma assumed, the absent Mr. Naz. "Come on, Char," she whee-
dled, pulling the child into her lap. "Just a bite."

The child shook her head, lips clamped firmly shut, but leaned
back against the young woman's chest.

"Your daddy will be home soon, and he'll be cross if you haven't
had your tea." The young woman's attempted sternness ended on an
uncertain quaver, and Tim stepped in.

"Alia, this is my wi—" Tim regrouped in midword. "This is Dr.
Cavendish." He gestured towards Hazel, then Gemma. "And this is
Gemma James. Gemma's with the police, and I thought she might—"

"Police?" Alia's eyes widened in alarm. "I don't want—I didn't
mean to get Mr. Naz into any sort of trouble."

"I'm just here as a friend, Alia," Gemma said quickly. "To see if I
can help." She slipped into the chair beside Alia's at the table. "Why
don't you tell me about your day."

"My day?" From Alia's expression Gemma might have asked her
the square root of pi.

"Yes." Gemma smiled, trying to put the girl at ease. She gave Hazel and Tim a glance that they interpreted correctly, taking seats at
either end of the sofa. Turning back to Alia, Gemma asked, "Do you
usually look after Charlotte on a Saturday?"

"No. Mr. Naz likes to spend as much time with her as he can on the
weekend. But he rang this morning and asked if I could come in for
a couple of hours. I thought he had to go to the office, but when he
left he didn't have any papers or nothing. Mr. Naz is a solicitor. But
then Dr. Cavendish will have told you," she added uncertainly.

"And Mr. Naz didn't say where he was going?"

"No. Just that he'd be back in time to take Charlotte with him to
visit Dr. Cavendish." She looked from Tim to Hazel, obviously confused by the two Dr. Cavendishes, but this wasn't the moment to
enlighten her.

"Was there anything else different in what he said, or how he
looked?" Gemma asked.

Alia's broad brow creased as she thought. "He only gave Charlotte a kiss. Usually he picks her up and swings her round." At the sound of her name, Charlotte put her thumb in her mouth.

Perhaps he had been distracted, Gemma thought, but she went on matter-of-factly. "Then what did you and Charlotte do? Did you go out?" She smiled at the child but got no response.

"Just in the garden." Alia glanced at the back doors. "Charlotte has a sandbox, and it was nice outside. Then Mr. Naz had got mangoes, so we made a lassi in the blender. Mr. Naz had said he'd be back by three, so I had everything tidied up by then. But he didn't come home."

Gemma took in the neat kitchen. One of the work tops held the baking sheet Alia had used to heat the samosas, and a Tupperware container. The fridge, a retro Smeg, was adorned with magnets and bright crayon drawings, an ordinary scene in a household with a child. But something here was not ordinary at all. Thinking that Toby, now almost six, had not stopped talking since he'd learned how to form words, she smiled again at Charlotte and said, "Hi, Charlotte. I'm Gemma. Did you make those nice pictures?"

Charlotte merely gazed back at her, expressionless.

Wondering if the child was developmentally delayed, she said softly to Alia, "Is she very shy?"

"Shy?" Alia sounded startled. "Oh, no, I wouldn't say that. It's just that . . . since her mum . . . she doesn't talk much, especially round strangers."

"She doesn't see her mum?"

Alia stared at her, the finger she had been twining in Charlotte's curls suddenly still. "You don't know about Sandra?" she whispered.

Gemma shot an accusing glance at Tim, who shrugged, mouthing "No time."

"No. I'm afraid I don't."

Tim sat forward, hands on his knees as if holding himself down. "It was in May," he said. "I saw an appeal Naz put in the papers afterwards. That's why I got in touch." He glanced at Charlotte, then seemed to choose his words even more carefully. "She— Sandra—left the baby with a friend at Columbia Road. It was a Sunday, just as the market was winding down. She said she had an errand and she'd only be gone a few minutes. She never returned."

CHAPTER FOUR

*A domestic dream, with a low crooked ceiling and large
dresser stacked to its full height; a table of scrubbed pine
covered with wooden bowls and baskets, all spilling over
with green vegetables, white turnips, brown onions and
bright orange carrots. This is undoubtedly the house's
kitchen . . .*

—Dennis Severs,
*18 Folgate Street:
The Tale of a
House in Spitalfields*

Gemma and Hazel both gaped at Tim, but it was Hazel who got in
the first word. "She disappeared? This man's wife disappeared, and
you didn't tell me?"

"When would I have had the chance?" protested Tim.

Standing, Hazel balled her small hands into fists. "You rang up
this man you hadn't seen in years because his wife disappeared? And
you offered him counseling? That's—that's unethical. And just sick."

Tim looked up at her. "It wasn't like that. I just thought Naz
needed to talk. I never charged him. And since when are you the

queen of ethics?" The bitterness on both sides was out in the open now, blistering as acid, the air in the room charged with animosity. Charlotte started to cry.

"I don't understand." Alia looked from Tim to Hazel. Hugging Charlotte tighter, she whispered, "Hush, Char, it's all right."

"What either of you think, or did, isn't the point right now," Gemma said sharply. The simple fact of a man missing an appointment and failing to ring his child's nanny had suddenly become infinitely more complicated, and Hazel and Tim's bickering was not going to help. Rapidly, Gemma considered options.

"Tim, I think you should take Charlotte home with you for the moment, if there's no immediate family to call in. It's too much responsibility for Alia, and—"

"I can take her," put in Hazel. "I can take both the girls."

Gemma shook her head. "Charlotte knows Tim and has been to the house with her father; it will be a familiar environment. And Tim has a relationship with her father, whether personal or professional. You don't."

She turned to Alia, who was still gently rocking Charlotte. "Alia, would you mind taking Charlotte upstairs and getting some overnight things together for her?"

"Okay." Alia looked from her to Tim uncertainly. "But—but what if Mr. Naz comes home and we're not here—"

"You and Dr. Cavendish can both leave notes for him, and Dr. Cavendish will leave messages on his phones. Tim, do you have his mobile and his office?" When Tim nodded, Gemma turned back to Alia. "And Dr. Cavendish and I will both get your phone number. We'll let you know just as soon as we learn anything. And you've done a great job looking after Charlotte today." Gemma smiled, wanting to reassure the girl, but her copper's instinct was sending up fizzing red flares.

"But what should I—"

"Change of clothes, pajamas, toothbrush, hairbrush." Gemma thought a moment. "Does she have a special blanket or stuffed toy?"

"A green elephant. She calls him Bob." Alia's face relaxed into a half smile. "I don't know why."

"Okay. Bob, then. Make a game of it, if you can," Gemma added quietly as Alia got up, hefting Charlotte onto her hip.

When Alia left the room, Hazel moved to clear the dishes from the table, her movements sharp with disapproval.

Gemma could deal with soothing her friend's ruffled feathers later. She turned to Tim, who said, "Gemma, do you think—could something really have happened to Naz?"

"I don't know. But I think it would help if I knew exactly what happened to your friend's wife."

"No one knows. That's what I was telling you. She just vanished into thin air. There was a missing-person appeal, telly and newspapers. The police investigated. They even—well, they even treated Naz as a suspect." Tim's tone was defensive, and below his beard his exposed neck turned a telltale red. Hazel, her back to them as she dried the baking sheet, had gone still.

Dangerous territory, this, and Gemma thought she would have to traverse it carefully if she didn't want an explosion of hostility between the two whose cooperation she needed. She sat beside Tim on the sofa, near enough to touch. "Let's back up a bit. You said your friend's wife is called Sandra. Is she not Pakistani?" Although the name, combined with the daughter's light-colored hair and eyes and frizzy curls, made it a likely conclusion, she had to ask.

"No. Her name was Sandra Gilles." Tim used the past tense, Gemma noticed. "She grew up in a council flat in Bethnal Green, still has family there. A mother, half brothers and half sister. The family disapproved of the marriage, and Naz and Sandra disapproved of them. 'Layabouts,' Naz said Sandra called them. Or worse. Sandra wouldn't let them have any contact with Charlotte. It infuriated her that they criticized Naz, who had worked his way through school and studied law, when none of them had ever held down a decent job. They weren't pleased with Sandra's success as an artist either—said she 'gave herself airs.' "

"She was an artist?" Hazel had left her tidying up and slipped into one of the dining-table chairs, looking intrigued in spite of herself.

"Textile collage. Naz helped her through art college—Goldsmiths—when they were first married. She'd become quite successful—gallery showings, some big commissions. Naz said she loved her work."

"Any marital difficulties?" Gemma asked.

"No." Tim was vehement. "They had everything. They'd been married almost ten years when Charlotte came along. They'd almost given up on having a child. They were devoted to each other, and Sandra was a fiercely good mum." The tension in the air had risen again, palpably, with the recitation of uncomfortable parallels. Tim and Hazel had also waited a long time to have a child, and Hazel had been a model mum.

"He told you a lot," Hazel said now, with an edge of sarcasm.

Tim bristled. "Why do you have a problem with that? He had no one else to talk to."

"How do you know he didn't just tell you what you wanted to hear?" Hazel retorted.

"Stop it, the both of you," said Gemma, exasperated, even though she knew Hazel was right. What Naz Malik had told Tim might have nothing to do with the truth. Whether one was grieving or guilty, a sympathetic audience gave one the liberty to paint life as one wished it to have been. And although that in itself might be useful, they needed to move on. "Tim, you said the police investigated Naz. They didn't find anything?"

"No. Not a bloody thing." He stared at them, as if daring contradiction.

"Okay." Gemma touched Tim's knee, giving credence to his

statement. "So tell me about the day Sandra disappeared. You said it was in May, in Columbia Road?"

"She and Charlotte were supposed to meet Naz for a late lunch in Brick Lane. Naz had gone into the office—"

"On a Sunday?"

"He was preparing an important case. But they always went out for Sunday lunch together. Naz waited at the restaurant for an hour. Sandra didn't answer her phone. Then Sandra's friend Roy rang Naz and said Sandra had left Charlotte with him at the market, saying she'd be gone just a few minutes, but she hadn't come back. He'd finished breaking down the stall and didn't know what to do."

"Breaking down the stall? This friend has a flower stall?"

Tim nodded. "Roy Blakely. Sandra worked for him on Sundays all through school and art college. She'd known him since she was a child—he was like a dad to her."

"And she didn't tell him where she was going?"

"No. Several people who knew her from the market reported seeing her in Columbia Road, but there was nothing after that. Just nothing. Naz was frantic, but at first not even the police would take him seriously. Then when they did, they searched the house for signs of . . . of foul play." He swallowed, looking round uneasily, and Gemma imagined the SOCO drill: luminol, prints, any evidence of violence, alien DNA, fiber transfer. What if Sandra had gone back home unexpectedly that day, found her husband there with a lover?

"They questioned everyone Naz knew," Tim went on. "His partner, his clients, his neighbors. Naz said no one ever looked at him the same way afterwards."

"They were doing their job," Gemma said.

"I know. But it didn't help, did it? They didn't find her, and now Naz is gone, too."

Gemma paused, listening. She heard movement and a soft murmur from upstairs, not just Alia's voice but a child's counterpoint. Charlotte was talking. Quietly, she said, "Tim, you may know more about Naz's mental state than anyone else. When he rang wanting to see you today, was he upset or anxious? Do you think he might have been contemplating suicide?"

Tim's face blanched. "No. I mean, I know he was grieving, and angry, but he'd never have done that to Charlotte. And if anything, he sounded . . ." Looking puzzled, he groped for a word. "Excited."

"That doesn't rule out suicide," said Hazel, pragmatic, but it seemed to put Tim on the defensive again.

"I'm telling you, Naz wouldn't do that. There has to be some other explanation." He looked at Gemma. "Can we report him missing?"

"Not officially, no. Not until tomorrow. But considering the circumstances, the local nick should be put on alert. I'll see if there's anything in the system yet that might be connected, check out hospital admissions, have a word with the neighbors. And if you'll give me Naz's partner's name, I'll see if I can get a home number or address." There was the thump of footsteps on the stairs, the sound of a childish protest.

"Tim," Gemma said hurriedly, "I'd like your permission to have a look round the house, see if there's a note or a phone number, anything that might be helpful. Unofficially, of course."

"But I—"

"There's no one else to ask."

"Right. Okay." He straightened his shoulders, taking on the weight of this responsibility.

"And, Tim," Gemma added, "I'll need a description."

CHAPTER FIVE

While working in the eerie darkness of those deserted
Spitalfields nights—and with the room and myself working
towards the same goal—I have never felt so close to the past.

—Dennis Severs,
18 Folgate Street:
The Tale of a
House in Spitalfields

Alia had set down Charlotte's little pink bag and got as far as the front door when Charlotte realized she meant to leave without her. "Lia!" she screamed, latching onto Alia's leg with the tenacity of a limpet.

Loosening the child's grip, Alia knelt and hugged her. "You go with Dr. Tim, Char. I'll see you soon." She looked up at Gemma, helplessly, her eyes filling.

Gemma reached down and gathered Charlotte into her arms, automatically settling her on her hip as she opened the door. Afternoon was fading into evening, the shadow from the great spire of the church seeming to loom over the narrow street. There were more cars now, and the sounds of voices and television drifted from a few town house windows, left open in the August warmth.

The child's body was tense, unyielding. Strands of her hair tickled Gemma's nose, smelling of baby shampoo and, faintly, curry.

"Lia," Charlotte wailed again, "want to go with you." She wriggled, then lunged towards Alia, almost causing Gemma to lose her balance. Gemma gripped Charlotte more tightly, feeling her small, firm body and the heat radiating through her thin T-shirt.

"Go," Gemma mouthed at Alia.

Alia gave them an uncertain smile, then turned and walked swiftly towards Brick Lane, head down, her heavy leather handbag on her shoulder.

"You'd better go, too," Gemma said to Tim. Charlotte was crying, but silently now, fat tears running down her cheeks as she watched Alia disappear around the corner. "You'd like to play with Holly, wouldn't you, love?" Gemma coaxed, but Charlotte wept unchecked. Reluctantly, Gemma handed her to Tim, then fetched her things.

She looked so small, nestled in Tim's arms, but she must have found his familiarity comforting, because when Gemma offered her green plush elephant, she took it and hugged it against her chest. "Will you let Bob play with Holly, too?" asked Gemma, and got a solemn nod in response. "Good girl."

"We'll see you later?" asked Tim, not looking reassured.

"I'll ring beforehand if there's any news." Alia had left her keys, so Gemma and Tim had agreed that Gemma would take them to Islington once she'd had a look round the house.

Tim nodded, then carried Charlotte to the Volvo, carefully strapping her into Holly's oversize safety seat in the rear. He got in and drove away without looking back.

"I can stay," said Hazel. "I could help you. Then I can run you to Islington to drop off the keys."

Gemma heard the note of entreaty in her friend's voice, and was tempted. But the tension between Hazel and Tim was distracting her, and she felt suddenly that she needed to be alone in the house, to concentrate, to get a feel for who these people were and what might have happened.

"I need to make phone calls, and I don't know how long that will take." She checked her watch. The first call was personal and urgent—she needed to tell Duncan where she was and what she was doing. "You go on," she added to Hazel. "I'll get the tube from Liverpool Street when I've finished. I'm trespassing, really, without Tim or Alia here, and I'd rather you not be guilty by association." She didn't say that the house might be a potential crime scene, and the less disturbed, the better.

"But I—" Hazel left the sentence unfinished, but the silence spoke clearly—she didn't want to go home.

Impulsively, Gemma hugged her and kissed her cheek. "I'll ring you in just a bit. I promise."

When Hazel reached the Golf, she turned back. "I've been a bitch, haven't I? It's just—" She shrugged. "It doesn't matter. I hope Tim's friend is all right."

"So do I," said Gemma.

Duncan Kincaid was stretched out on the sitting room sofa, the Saturday *Times* scattered across the coffee table and the floor, a dog across his chest, a cat on his feet. The garden doors stood open to let in the slightest breath of early evening, but the air was muggy and Geordie, the cocker spaniel, was making him sweat.

"You're taking up too much real estate, buddy," he said, but he felt too lazy to make the dog move and merely stroked his dark gray ears. Geordie gave a huge doggy sigh of contentment and settled himself more firmly against Kincaid's rib cage.

That afternoon, Kincaid had paid a call on the tenant in his flat in Carlingford Road, and had taken advantage of the visit to Hampstead to take both boys and both dogs to Hampstead Heath.

There had been method in his madness—a couple of hours of

Frisbee throwing, ball chasing, and hunting for imaginary buried treasure had worn everyone out sufficiently to give him a rare bit of Saturday-afternoon peace. The boys were upstairs in their rooms, and the faint thump of bass from Kit's iPod speakers provided an oddly comforting counterpoint to doggy snores.

When his mobile rang, he stretched towards the coffee table, fumbling for the phone, and dislodged Geordie in the process. "Sorry, mates," he said as Sid, their black cat, raised his head and gave a hiss of displeasure at the disturbance.

Expecting Gemma, he was surprised by the name on the caller ID. Why ring him and not Gemma? A little jolt of dread made him sit up as he answered.

He listened, made the appropriate responses, and by the time he'd hung up, the dread had settled in the center of his chest like a fist.

When the mobile rang again, he was still sitting with the phone in his hand, staring blankly at the oil painting of a hunting spaniel over the fireplace, a gift to Gemma from his cousin Jack.

This time it was Gemma, and he took a moment to compose himself before he clicked on, saying brightly, "Hullo, love."

Before he could go any further, she launched into a complicated story involving a missing friend of Tim Cavendish's, and when he could get a word in edgewise, he said, "Wait. Where did you say you are?"

"Spitalfields," she answered. "I don't know how long I'll be. I need to talk to someone on the local force. Do you know anyone at Tower Hamlets?"

"Um, not below senior command. I'd try CID at Bethnal Green. Gemma—" It was on the tip of his tongue to ask her if this was something that really merited her involvement, but he knew as soon as the thought crossed his mind that he would be wasting his breath. She would do what she thought was right, and it was not his place to caution her.

"I'm sorry about dinner," she said, misinterpreting his silence.

"The boys want pizza. We'll save you some."

"I'll ring you as soon as I'm on my way home. Duncan—" She hesitated, then said, "This will probably come to nothing, but—"

"But you don't think so."

"Even if the husband strolls in claiming he had a bit of temporary amnesia, what happened to the wife? She's been missing for three months."

He recognized the tone—Gemma with the investigative bit between her teeth—and hoped that either there was a simple explanation or that the Tower Hamlets CID were not territorially prickly. On the other hand, a distraction might prove helpful at the moment. He was still debating whether or not to mention the phone call when Toby came in. He was carrying an umbrella from the stand in the hall, swinging it in arcs across the floor the way he had seen a man using a metal detector on Hampstead Heath, and adding buzzing and clicking noises as sound effects.

That definitely flipped the disclosure needle over to negative. "You'd better go now," he told her, "or you'll be treated to a dissertation on buried treasure, Cap'n Jack and talking parrots included."

"Oh, dear." Gemma laughed. "I won't ask. Okay, then. I'll ring you soon." The connection went dead.

Toby stopped buzzing. "Was that Mummy?"

"Yes, sport."

"Why didn't I get to talk to her?"

"Because she was busy. She'll be home later."

"Why was she busy?"

Kincaid took a breath. "Because she's out with Auntie Hazel."

"What is she doing with Auntie Hazel?" Toby swung the umbrella tip dangerously near a vase of lilies on the coffee table, and Sid vanished beneath the sofa.

"Girl stuff."

"What's girl stuff?"

"I don't know. Do I look like a girl?" Kincaid made a monster face that prompted a giggle. "Promise me you won't say 'why' or 'what' for one minute."

"Why?" Toby asked, still giggling.

"Because——" Kincaid lunged and caught him deftly, removing the umbrella. "Because I want to know if there's room in here for pizza." He squeezed Toby round the middle, then tickled him until he shrieked.

"I want pizza, I do," Toby gasped between wriggles.

"Pirate pizza?"

"No. Buggy pizza."

"He means the place on Pembridge Road," said Kit, coming into the sitting room. Kincaid realized the music had stopped upstairs. "The one with the car in the window," Kit went on. "He's convinced it's a Volkswagen bug, even though I've told him it's not." This comment delivered with all the world weariness of a fourteen-year-old contemplating a five-year-old's silliness.

Looking up at his son, Kincaid thought he'd got taller and thinner overnight. Kit's iPod earbuds dangled from his jeans pocket, and his blond hair was going darker. It needed cutting. No spots yet, Kincaid thought gratefully. Maybe Kit would be spared that teenage trauma.

"Bugs it is, then," Kincaid said, standing. "We're not waiting for Gemma."

"Who was that on the phone?" asked Kit.

"Gemma. She's still tied up with Hazel."

"No. Before that."

Kincaid cocked an eyebrow at his son. "What? Are you spying on me?"

"No." Kit's fair skin still showed color too easily. "It's just—I was sitting on the stairs. I like doing that, sometimes."

Keeping order in the universe, Kincaid thought with an inward sigh. Although this summer had been easier, Kit still tended to take personal responsibility for the well-being of everyone in his orbit. "It was Aunt Cyn," he answered, all trace of teasing gone.

Kit frowned. "Why was she calling *you*?"

Glancing at Toby, who was once more preoccupied with his umbrella, Kincaid gave a small, negative shake of his head. The news would be no more welcome to Kit than to Gemma, but he would have to tell Gemma first.

Her sister, Cyn, hadn't wanted to do it, had instead asked him to be the bearer of bad tidings. Perhaps, to give Cyn credit, she just hadn't felt able to talk about it.

The bone marrow tests had come back, Cyn had said. Neither she nor Gemma nor any of their children were a match. And their mum, Vi, had taken a turn for the worse.

Gemma stood in the hall, the silence of the house settling round her like an exhaled breath. She felt suddenly alien, an interloper in a life interrupted.

But having cleared the decks with Duncan and the boys, she meant to follow through on her promises to Tim and Alia, and she had better have a look round the house before she started making phone calls.

She touched the handlebar of the bike parked so neatly between the door and the stairs. A man's racing bike, but not, to her relatively inexperienced eye, terribly new or terribly expensive. It, like the house, looked well used and well cared for. A flower decal was stuck on one side of the businesslike safety helmet. Charlotte's handiwork, Gemma guessed, and thought it said something about Naz Malik that he had left it on. And if Naz rode the bike regularly, she wondered why he had not taken it that day.

Trailing her fingers across the newel post, she hesitated, then decided to start with the sitting room. She stepped through the doorway and stopped, taking in impressions. The wide-plank flooring continued from the hall. It looked as though it might be original to the house, as did the solid wooden shutters covering the lower half of the casements.

Paneling, shutters, fireplace surround, all simple, all in the same soft green. Sofa and squashy armchairs were slipcovered in a paler shade. A large petit point wool rug anchored the furniture, its colors so faded she could barely make out the floral design. But there the neutral palette ended.

Floral still lifes, many unframed, were propped on the chair rail around the circumference of the room. It was an odd but appealing effect, bringing the high-ceilinged proportions of the Georgian de-sign down to a more human scale.

Large baskets scattered about the room corralled toys, but from one a tattered sock monkey seemed to have made a failed attempt at escape. One foot had caught on the basket's edge, and he hung up-side down, his stitched features frozen in a grimace of surprise.

The lamps and tables were simple, but a brass chandelier filled with candles hung from the ceiling, and several sconces mounted on the walls held candles as well.

At one end of the sofa, another basket held piles of newspapers beginning to yellow. Gemma touched a finger to the top sheet—it came away covered in dust. The banner identified the paper as the *Guardian,* dated mid-May.

On the other side of the fireplace a chaise and floor lamp formed a reading area. Both chaise and lampshade were covered in an unex-pected patchwork of floral chintz, so whimsically bright it made Gemma smile. Books had been stacked on the floor beside the chaise in tottering piles. Gemma knelt beside them, reading titles. Some were coffee-table size—Georgian architecture and decoration, tex-tile design, histories of painting and furniture. But there were also books on the East End, novels with page corners carelessly dog-eared, and children's picture books, including many of Toby's favor-ite Shirley Hugheses.

On top of the largest stack, which seemed to serve as an end table, sat a blue stoneware mug. It looked as if its owner had been interrupted in the midst of a cup of tea, but when Gemma examined the mug, she found it empty and spotless.

She stood again, catching her own reflection in a great, gilded mirror over the fireplace. She tucked a strand of her hair, now growing long again, behind her ear, and saw that she'd transferred the smear of dust from the newspapers to her nose. Lacking a tissue, she rubbed at the mark with the back of her hand while examining the display on the mantel. A cracked creamware jug. A child's drawing of red stick figures under yellow clouds, framed. A porcelain border collie, its expression so lifelike she reached out to stroke it.

There were no photos.

The dining room displayed the same mixture of simplicity with a dash of eccentricity—the chairs round the imposing round dining table were mismatched, the seat cushions covered in different fabrics. Here the chair rail held yellowing oil portraits, both bewigged men and beribboned women with the effeminate, unisex faces Gemma associated with eighteenth-century portraiture. Again, both chandelier and sconces held candles. But the room looked little used, and Gemma could imagine the difficulty of bringing dishes up from the kitchen.

She took a breath. Upstairs, then. At the first landing, she looked out. Dusk was falling, and threads of neon from the curry palaces on Brick Lane had begun to dart like lances at the dark shadow of Christ Church. When Gemma reached the first floor, she fumbled until she found a light switch.

The master bedroom faced the street. It felt almost monastic—simple white linen roller shades on the windows, white quilt on the dark, carved bed. But again the chair rail held the eye; hooks held strings of necklaces and beads, tiny bud vases in jewel colors arranged above. There was a woman's vanity, its old mirror fogged, its surface littered with antique perfume bottles, a jumble of dangly earrings, an ornate but tarnished silver-plate hand mirror, a lipstick. A sari-silk dressing gown tumbled across the dressing table chair.

The cupboards built into the end of the room, a modern addition, held men's clothing on one side, mostly suits, with a few casual shirts and trousers.

Scent wafted out when she opened the other side, something spicy yet floral that Gemma didn't quite recognize.

There were no business suits here. Dresses, blouses, skirts, many of which appeared to be vintage. A ruffled petticoat, canary yellow. Folded jumpers. T-shirts. Jeans. Boots and flip-flops, and a few pairs of very high heels.

The sense of presence was so strong that Gemma snapped the doors closed. She realized she'd been holding her breath.

Next, Charlotte's room. A white, iron bedstead. A pony lamp. A pink, painted chest that Gemma suspected had been rapidly ransacked by Alia, as the contents of its open drawers cascaded out like the tiers in a fountain, bits of a little girl's clothing flowing over the edges. And on the bedside table, a photo.

Sandra. Charlotte's mum. The same corkscrew curls, but blond. An alert, intelligent face, pretty but not overly so. She looked directly into the camera, her lips curved in a slight smile. This, Gemma thought, was the face of a woman engaged with the world, not the face of a woman who had walked away from it.

Gemma went out, started up to the next level. Now the banister was plain, the steps narrower. She was moving into the old servants' territory. This time she tried the back room first, a spare bedroom with a simple double bed.

The front room had been turned into a home office, immediately masculine, legal. A heavy desk. Glass-fronted bookcases with leather-bound volumes. A green-shaded desk lamp. Papers were scattered over the blotter, but a quick perusal revealed nothing but legal documents and what looked like case notes scribbled on a yellow pad.

There was no Rolodex or diary. There was a laptop, but it was closed, and Gemma decided it was beyond her remit to open it.

She went back to the stairs and continued to climb. Enough light filtered up to the top of the stairs for her to see that she had entered a large space rather than a hall. She felt for a switch, found it. Light blossomed, and Gemma breathed an involuntary, "Oh."

The top floor *was* a loft. The windows were uncurtained, the myriad panes bouncing color back into the room. And color there was, captured in the pools of warmth cast by the simple cone-shaped lights that hung from the ceiling.

It took a moment for Gemma to organize what she was seeing. A large worktable filled the room's center. One side of the table held scraps of fabric, loose sheets of paper covered with pencil sketches. On the other, muslin had been stretched over a wood frame about four feet square. Parts of the muslin were covered with fabrics; others were bare or held only faint penciled lines.

A collage, then. Unfinished, abstract, yet suggesting the bright flare of women's dresses against dark brick. Gilded cording made Gemma think of bell-shaped birdcages. It was not birds that peeped through the bars, but women's faces, eerily featureless.

Disturbed, Gemma turned away, examining the rest of the room. Everywhere, baskets held fabrics, multicolored, multitextured, some spilling out onto the floor.

One end wall held wooden cubbies filled with smaller, folded pieces. At the other end of the room, a simple white desk, and above it, a painting of a red horse. The desk surface held more sketches, notebooks, a jumble of Post-its, and the usual assortment of pens, pencils, and elastic bands. Gemma reached out, pulled back. She'd been careful, except for the light switches, not to disturb, not to leave prints, and again, this was beyond her remit.

She turned once more, to the back wall. It was covered in corkboard and festooned with drawings, both Sandra's and Charlotte's, and—eureka for Gemma—photos. This was why there were no posed, tidily framed family portraits in the rest of the house. The photos were here, pushpinned, overlapping, candid—a family captured in the day-to-day act of living.

There were more shots of Naz and Charlotte than of Sandra, an indication that Sandra was the primary photographer. Gemma studied a photo of Naz with Charlotte in his lap, recognizing the setting as the kitchen sofa.

Tim had given her a description: Nasir Malik, forty years old (Tim assumed, as they were at uni together), medium height, medium build (a bit thin these days, since Sandra's disappearance, Tim had added), dark hair and eyes, deep olive complexion, glasses.

What Tim had not conveyed was the slight professorial air, the seriousness of the gaze through the wire-framed specs, the unexpected charm and warmth of the smile.

Gemma rubbed at the hair that had risen on her arms. She had ruled out obvious evidence of foul play or a visible suicide note.

What she had found was the certainty that Naz Malik had not given up hope of his wife's return.

CHAPTER SIX

*Breakfast after a morning at the market would be a salt-beef
sandwich with mustard on rye from the Beigel Bake at the
top of the street.*

—Rachel
Lichtenstein,
On Brick Lane

The kitchen had grown dark while Gemma was upstairs. She flicked
on the lights, then, feeling exposed, closed the heavy inside shutters
over the street windows. The French doors at the back still stood open
to the garden, and when some capricious current moved the heavy air,
she smelled garlic and spices and the hot, prickly aroma of frying oil.

Her stomach rumbled, and she realized she'd only nibbled for
lunch, having expected to have tea with Hazel, and that had been
hours ago. Hazel had left Alia's samosas on the work top, the baking
pan covered with aluminium foil. Gemma lifted the foil and took
one, feeling she was trespassing, but she certainly didn't want to go
digging round in the fridge.

It was good, she thought as she tasted the potato mixture, but
would be better warm. She looked round for a microwave and realized

there wasn't one. The cooker and the fridge seemed the kitchen's only concessions to mod cons. Studying the room more carefully, she saw that the great Welsh dresser just fit beneath the low ceiling, and she wondered if it had been part of the original kitchen furnishings. The hearth, too, was enormous, and she guessed it had been the working fireplace when the kitchen had been the dark, subterranean heart of the house.

The kitchen was still the heart of the house. She gazed at one of Charlotte's drawings, stuck haphazardly on the fridge door. Now she could see their faces, Naz and Sandra, here in this room with their child.

She finished the samosa and wiped her fingers on an embroidered tea towel. It was enough to keep her hunger from distracting her, and she had things to do. Sitting at the table, she searched in her handbag for a notepad and pen and took out her phone.

First, she called Mile End Hospital, then the Royal London, identifying herself. Neither reported a casualty fitting Naz Malik's description. Gemma wasn't sure if she was relieved or disappointed.

Next, she rang Bethnal Green Police Station, working her way through the phone-tree options until she got a real live person, a duty officer who identified herself as Sergeant Singh. From her voice, Gemma imagined her as young, slight, and pretty, but she spoke with a competent briskness.

"I'd like to speak to the detective investigating the disappearance of Sandra Gilles," said Gemma, having offered her credentials. "It would have been in May."

"Oh, right. Weird one, that." The sergeant's tone was conversational. Gemma wondered if Bethnal Green was quiet at dinnertime on a Saturday night. "Inspector Weller handled that, but he's not available this weekend."

"Surely you've got a mobile number, or some other contact where he can be reached."

"Um, no, actually. He's gone to his son's wedding in Shropshire.

Said he'd throw his mobile in the toilet if anyone rang." The hint of humor was replaced by alertness. "That case is months old. Why is it so urgent?"

"Because Sandra Gilles's husband seems to have disappeared this afternoon." Gemma gave her the details. "I know it's early for an official alert, but under the circumstances I think you can make an exception."

"I'll pass it along." All levity had disappeared from Singh's voice. "What about the little girl? Do we need to contact social services?"

"She's with a family friend for tonight." Gemma passed on Tim's address and phone number, added her own contact information, then said, "Listen, could you leave a message with your Inspector Weller, just in case he checks in? Ask him to ring me at his earliest convenience."

She hung up, knowing she'd taken all reasonable steps, but feeling restless and dissatisfied. Checking the notes she'd made while talking to Tim, she rang directory inquiries, trying to track down a personal number for Louise Phillips, Naz Malik's partner. But although it was a common name, she got no matches. Louise Phillips might be ex-directory, or might have only a mobile, as was so often the case nowadays.

A computer search might yield better results, however, and Gemma knew no one more able to follow threads on the Internet than her colleague at Notting Hill, DC Melody Talbot.

But when she rang Melody's mobile, it went to voice mail. Gemma left a brief message, apologizing for disturbing her on a Saturday night. As she hung up, she chided herself for having assumed Melody would be available. Melody was, after all, young and attractive, and the fact that she didn't share details of her personal life with Gemma didn't mean she didn't have one.

Still, Gemma was curious. Most of her colleagues were only too willing to share their off-duty exploits in excruciating detail. Why not Melody?

"She'll have the sautéed foie gras."

"No, *she* won't." Melody Talbot gave her father a tight smile. "You know I can't stand foie gras."

"The foie gras is one of the Ivy's specialities," Ivan Talbot announced, although Melody wasn't sure if the comment was directed towards the attentive waiter, who certainly bloody well knew, or their dinner guest. "Let's make that four," her father added, steamrolling over her protest, as usual. "I should think Quentin is game for a little adventure."

The Quentin in question was the latest victim of Melody's father's campaign to find her a suitable husband. A junior employee of her father's, Quentin Frobisher was tall, sandy haired, freckled, and not actually bad looking in the very English way that Melody didn't particularly fancy. Not that she would for a moment admit she found him even passable.

She had met her parents and their guest just outside the Ivy, and on the short trip through the restaurant's foyer, she had hissed at her father, "You said he was an 'ordinary chap.' No one named *Quentin* is an ordinary chap."

Now, she huddled back against the banquette, wishing she were anywhere else on earth. Why had she let her father bully her into this? And what if someone from work saw her?

Not that any common or garden-variety coppers were likely to be found in one of London's most famous and exclusive restaurants on a Saturday night. But although the Ivy reserved a good two-thirds of its bookings for "regulars," it was not particularly expensive, and anyone with a bit of time and determination could theoretically get a table.

She herself had been seduced by it tonight. Her parents had brought her here for special occasions since her teens, and she loved it—the distinctive diamonds of multicolored stained glass over the door, the streetlamp shining through the blue crescent moon, the paintings, the grand mural in the dining room, the crisp-starched white tablecloths. And most of all, the sense of the well-oiled machine ticking away above the unseen chaos of the kitchen below, creating a perfection she seldom experienced in her workaday life.

That reminder was enough to snap her back to reality. She tugged at the décolleté of her dress and gave another nervous glance around the room. Work—at least her work—and this sort of play didn't mix. God forbid she should run across some emaciated celeb wannabe snorting coke in the ladies' loo and have to choose between duty and exposure. She shuddered. At least no one would have the nerve to use a camera in the sacred precincts of the Ivy—she was very careful not to be caught in photos with her father.

He had picked the intermediate sitting, between the pre-theatre and post-theatre crush. Unusual for him, as he liked to see and be seen, but perhaps he'd thought it was the only way he would get her to accept the invitation. He was looking quite pleased with himself, in fact. Although it was against the Ivy's policy to give favored clients special tables, tonight they had got a four top at the back of the room, perfectly positioned to observe the other diners.

"Do sit still, darling, and stop picking at your dress," her mother whispered. Her mum had bought the dress from a new designer she was patronizing in Knightsbridge, and her eye had been, as usual, sharp enough to guarantee a perfect fit. The dress was black, snug as a glove, with an off-the-shoulder plunging neckline that made Melody acutely uncomfortable. She'd always been self-conscious about her broad shoulders and rather generous bust.

"Nonsense," her mother had told her that afternoon when she'd dropped by Melody's flat, bearing her gift in a scented, tissue-stuffed, beribboned bag. "You really must learn to maximize your assets, darling." She zipped Melody into the dress, then stepped back to admire her handiwork. "Very fetching. And you *do* have legs. One would never know it with those dreadful off-the-rack trouser suits you wear."

Melody had a runner's calves, a legacy of her public-school days and the jogs she still managed round Hyde Park when work allowed, but she thought the muscles just made her look chunkier and did her best to cover them up.

"And for heaven's sake, do something with your hair," her mother had added, kissing her on the cheek. "I'm sure Bobby can squeeze you in."

And so Melody had slunk into one of the toniest salons in Kensington on a Saturday afternoon, emerging an hour later freshly shorn, but feeling she'd won a small victory by having refused even the most discreet of highlights. Her thick, glossy brown hair, kept in a chin-length bob, was one of her few vanities.

Now she gave another defiant tug at the neckline of her dress and scowled at her mother. But her mum merely twinkled back at her, and Melody felt her mouth relax into an unwilling smile. It was almost impossible to stay irritated with the Lady Athena Talbot, née Hobbs. Since childhood she had been known simply as Attie, and Melody doubted she'd ever encountered anyone, male or female, who had not been instantly smitten.

Willow slender, Attie Talbot moved like a girl, and could still turn the heads of men half her age. The unfortunate Quentin was, in fact, ogling her, and Melody was tempted to kick him under the table.

Her father, however, was as adept at reading signals as Melody. He reached over and patted her mother's hand, in the process flashing Quentin a smile with just a hint of shark beneath its avuncular surface.

Quentin flushed and looked away. Point for the old man, Melody thought—territory duly marked, peon put in his place. Her father did subtlety very well.

As a teenager, she'd enjoyed the fantasy that her father had married her mother for her money, but even then she'd known it for a lie, concocted to salve her own jealousy. You had only to see the way they looked at each other still—stomach turning, really. Her mother's money and title had simply been a bonus. Her father, a grammar school boy from a Newcastle council estate, had possessed the intelligence, the drive, and, above all, the ambition to succeed on his own merits.

And succeed he had, the single thorn in his life his uncooperative only daughter.

"Melody's in police work," he said now, having chosen the wine.

"File clerk," Melody countered hurriedly, manufacturing what she was sure was a ghastly smirk. "Toiling in the basement and all that."

"Notting Hill," her mother put in helpfully. "And of course you don't toil in the basement, darling. Don't be silly. She has quite a nice flat there," she added for Quentin's benefit.

"Really?" Quentin eyed her with a bit more interest. "Some nice clubs round there. I— Um—" He seemed to realize that admitting to clubbing might not be the most appropriate way to impress the boss. "Pubs," he amended. "I had drinks at the Prince Albert the other day. With some mates."

Melody wasn't about to tell him that she lived just down the road, but she had to say something to forestall her mother. "Bit nauseatingly yuppie, don't you think, the Prince Albert?"

"I— Um. Yes, a bit, I suppose. But didn't like to refuse an invitation, you know." The more Quentin floundered, the more he sounded like something out of a Wodehouse novel, and his eyes were taking on a deer-in-the-headlamps glaze.

Melody actually found herself feeling a bit sorry for him. He might not be all that bad, but then, knowing her father's methods, she put aside any kind thoughts and probed a bit. "Frobisher. Would that be the Derbyshire Frobishers?" she asked, having no idea if there were any Derbyshire Frobishers.

"No. Hampshire," said Quentin.

"Quentin's father publishes several county magazines," explained her father. "Quentin is getting a bit of work experience in London."

Ah, Melody thought. That explained it. Two birds with one stone.

Solve problem of daughter while buttering up heir to possible future acquisition. And if Quentin was indeed sharper than he seemed, she would have to be very, very careful.

Her phone rang, making her jump. Cursing herself for having forgotten to turn it off, she fumbled in her handbag, all eyes on her. When she'd fished the offending instrument from the bottom of her bag, she glanced at the caller ID and froze. Gemma. She felt a moment of unreasoning panic. She couldn't answer. Not here. Not now. She could not gracefully explain to her boss where she was and who she was with, nor could she lie with an audience.

Swallowing, she pushed Ignore, then switched the phone off. "I think I'd like a glass of champagne for starters, Daddy," she said, smiling brightly.

Gemma went back through the house once more, checking that the lights were off, shutting doors. As she returned to the hall, the emptiness of the house seemed to close in behind her. Hurriedly, she let herself out and locked the dead bolt with the key. The thought of home, warm and light and cluttered from the boys' Saturday activities, was suddenly almost irresistible, but first she had to return Naz Malik's keys.

She stood on the pavement, feeling the thick, damp evening air, slick as butter, slip round her bare arms and legs. If she got the tube from Old Street, it was only one stop on the Northern Line to the Angel in Islington, and from there a ten-minute walk to Tim's.

She turned left, then left again, deciding to walk up Brick Lane rather than Commercial Street. At the corner, the smell of curry was enticingly strong, but even if she'd had the time, the Brick Lane curry houses didn't seem places a woman would comfortably go in for a meal on her own.

But as she walked northwards, the curry palaces quickly gave way to small shops and businesses—textiles, barbers, hairdressers, travel agents, moneylenders—all catering to the Bangladeshi community, and all closed except for the newsagents or grocers. From the open door of a newsagent's came the wailing chant of Asian music, monotonous but oddly appealing to her unaccustomed ear. The street signs were in English and Bengali, and the streetlamps, their delicate tracery in red and green metal inspired by Indian design, festively framed the narrow street.

Gemma stopped, puzzling for a moment, then realized she'd seen that same design in some of Sandra Gilles's work.

By the time she reached Hanbury Street, notorious in Whitechapel lore as the site of the grisly death of Jack the Ripper's second victim, Annie Chapman, the Banglatown part of Brick Lane had begun to recede. Here, the walls of the old Truman Brewery made a canyon of the narrow street, the smokestack a darker shadow against the night sky. But at street level, music boomed from the Vibe bar, and the pedestrians who jostled past her were young and for the most part white, clubbers dressed for a Saturday night on the town. This once-disreputable part of the East End had become a destination spot, a mecca for the hip and affluent. There was still enough of an edge, she thought as she passed a DJ setting up turntables in a makeshift stall on the pavement, for the West End patrons to feel they were living a bit dangerously.

More shops were open here, now offering vintage clothing, records, books, coffee and Wi-Fi, and as she neared the old Bishopsgate railway line, the graffiti became more visible.

Then she caught the scent of freshly baked bread and her steps quickened. She saw two bagel bakeries ahead on the left, both with lights on and doors open. As she drew closer, her mouth watered and she felt a bit light-headed. Warmed-over pizza at home seemed light-years away. She would need something to get by on.

Gemma chose the second bakery, Beigel Bake, simply because the queue was longer—usually a good sign that the food was worth the wait. But the service was friendly and efficient and the queue moved quickly, just giving Gemma time to take in the no-nonsense interior, the huge steel ovens in the back, and the two Royalty Protection Command officers in full gear ahead of her. They were enormous, like nightclub bouncers on steroids. She'd have expected some of the pierced and tattooed clubbers, or the obviously homeless man on the pavement, to give them a wide berth, but Beigel Bake's cheerful atmosphere seemed to erase boundaries.

With a cup of stewed tea in one hand, and a salt-beef bagel with mustard in the other, she came out again into the street, munching as she walked. She thought she had never tasted anything quite so good.

The sandwich lasted her almost to Old Street Station, and as she neared the tube stop, she tossed her empty polystyrene cup in a rubbish bin. She stopped for a moment to look at the Banksy painting high on the side of a commercial building on the far side of the Old Street roundabout. It was called *Ozone Angel,* she knew, and was a tribute by the anonymous street artist to a friend who had been killed by a train. But she'd never before quite realized how haunting the androgynous child was, with its angel wings and safety armor, a death's-head, a memento mori, held in its outstretched hand.

She thought suddenly of Charlotte Malik, with both her parents missing, and shivered.

Hazel sat curled in a corner of her rose-printed sofa, arms wrapped tight round her chest even though the bungalow windows were still open to the warm evening air. She hadn't bothered turning on the lights, or eating, although she knew she should do both.

Her irritation with Gemma for having so patently wanted rid of her at Naz Malik's house had lasted her the first half of the way home. Her smoldering resentment towards Tim for having searched out an old friend because it was thought his wife *might* have betrayed him had fueled the remainder of her drive.

But by the time she'd reached the bungalow—she still couldn't think of it as home, in spite of the enthusiasm she had manufactured for Gemma—even that had flickered out. Hazel was self-analytical enough by training and by nature to see her anger for what it was—a transference of her own guilt. How could she blame Tim for seeking out someone with whom he could sympathize?

Now she felt shocked and more than a little sickened by her behavior that afternoon. A family in the midst of trauma, a child in distress, and rather than doing what she could to help, as Gemma and Tim had done, she had sniped at them both.

What sort of person had she become? She seemed to have lost her compass, and with it, any confidence in her ability to make the right decisions. She'd convinced herself that coming back to London was the best thing, convinced herself that she and Tim could work together to do what was best for Holly, but now she doubted her resolve.

Hazel thought of the house in Islington, of Tim tucking in Holly and the little girl, Charlotte, as she used to tuck in Holly and Toby, and she trembled with longing. It was her place, and she had forfeited it. She could see no way back. Despair rose in her, black, bitter as bile.

A woman's voice came clearly from beyond the wall of the darkened garden. The words were unfathomable, the intonation so familiar it struck to the bone. She was calling her child in for the night.

He heard the sound of water falling. It came and went in rhythmic susurrations, like the curtains of rain that had swished across the rice fields of his childhood. His mind wove in and out of memory—smells of cooking combined with the warm, ripe scent of farmyards; the light, green filtered, always; the air thick as syrup. Air so thick it pressed on his chest . . . He opened his mouth in a gasp, trying to expand his lungs, and the movement brought him close to consciousness once more.

The faint recollection of pain made him keep his eyes shut tight, and he began to drift again.

Then there was movement. Hands pulling at him, the grunt of someone else's effort. Space spun and he flailed out as arms gripped him, lifting. He forced his eyes open but the movement made him queasy, and he saw only shifting, tilting shadows he couldn't grasp. His glasses—what had happened to his glasses?

He groped at his face, but a vaguely familiar voice was urging him forwards. He stumbled—his feet seemed disconnected from his brain—but the hands and voice kept him moving.

There was a click, and the feel of the air changed—fresher, damper—and he suddenly knew he was outside, although he hadn't realized before that he'd been inside.

The sharp scent of petrol exhaust tickled his nose. He heard the muted sound of traffic, saw moving flashes of light. Then the hand shoved him down, his forehead cracked against something hard, and blackness descended.

When he woke once more, he was moving, propelled by an arm round his shoulder, his unwilling feet tangling with each other. It was dark, truly dark. Rough things caught and scraped at his face, and when he lifted a hand to his cheek it was wet. Then he was falling, falling, and the scent of warm earth rose up to meet him.

CHAPTER SEVEN

At certain times, it was so quiet that I could hear the call to prayer from the East End mosque on Whitechapel Road, and the clatter of trains as they passed along the underground line from Shoreditch station. Sunday mornings brought the distant sounds of pealing church bells and music-box tunes played by roaming ice-cream vans. From the backs of the curry houses came the smell of Indian cooking and, when the wind was in the right direction, the sweet aroma of fresh bagels from the bakeries.

—Tarquin Hall,
Salaam Brick Lane

Gemma woke on Sunday morning tired and headachy from having tossed and turned during the night. She'd gone to bed cross with Duncan, something she hated even when the cause was a mere domestic argument. But this, this had been much worse than a squabble over chores or work. When he'd told her about Cyn's call, she'd lashed out at him in a burst of fury that left her shaking.

He'd said, with irritating reasonableness, that there would have been nothing she could do if he had told her earlier. She'd been in

Spitalfields with no car, and even if she'd taken the tube from Liverpool Street to Leyton, then what? Her mum would have been in bed, her dad exhausted, and neither glad to see her.

The fact that she knew he was right made her no less peeved. When he asked her what had happened in Brick Lane, she'd merely snapped, "Long story," and gone off to check on the children—Toby asleep, Kit texting on the phone that had been his birthday present, which she now swore was biologically attached to his thumbs.

But upstairs on her own, the anger started to drain away. Feeling sweaty and dusty, she'd shed her clothes in a heap on the mat and slipped into a hot bath. The bathroom window was open, and night sounds from the garden drifted in with the occasional breeze. It amazed her that London could be so quiet off the main thoroughfares—but when she listened very carefully she could hear an underlying faint hum of the city, and occasionally the distant squeal of brakes or slamming of car doors.

By the time the water had cooled, she'd realized that she'd merely focused on Duncan as the nearest target for her own worry and her irritation with her sister. As she patted herself dry and slipped into pajamas, she resolved to apologize, but when she went out into the bedroom, he was asleep. All she could do was curl up against his back and listen to his quiet breathing.

She was up and dressed early, before Duncan and the children were awake. As soon as she deemed it even remotely civilized, she rang her sister from the quiet confines of the kitchen.

"Cyn, why the hell didn't you ring *me*?" she hissed when her sister answered, trying to keep her voice down.

"Gemma!" Cyn sounded cheerfully surprised, artificially so, and Gemma's heart plummeted into her stomach. "I was just going to call you," her sister added. There was a murmur of voices in the background, but not, Gemma thought, Cyn's husband, Gerry, and her children, Tiffani and Brendan.

"Where are you?"

"Hospital. The London." Gemma heard rustling and the background noise faded, replaced by her sister whispering, "I can't talk. You know it's against regulations to use phones on the ward."

"Ward? Why are you on a ward? What's happened?"

"Mum's weak. Her white cell count is down. They're going to do a transfusion."

"A transfusion? But—"

"Look, you'd better just get here, all right?" Cyn's phone went dead.

Having left a note for Duncan, Gemma thought furiously as she drove across the city. The Royal London Hospital was in Whitechapel, near where she had been last night. Why was her mum there, and not at Barts in the City, where she'd been treated before? The two hospitals were part of the same system, administratively linked; perhaps it had been a matter of the availability of beds on the wards, rather than the need for a more advanced treatment.

Her route took her past Marylebone and Euston, St. Pancras and Kings Cross, then into City Road and down Commercial Street. Hawksmoor's church seemed more forbidding in the harsh morning light, offering no comfort.

Her quick glimpse of Fournier Street, however, had been reassuring. It looked as quiet and ordinary as any street should on a Sunday morning. She thought of ringing Tim, but decided it was still too early. Nor could she cope with speaking to anyone until she had learned what was going on with her mum.

The congestion increased as she traveled east down Whitechapel Road, which was clogged by the Sunday market. Any other time the array of Asian foods and spices would have tempted her, but by the time she reached the ugly warren of buildings that formed the London, she was fidgeting with impatience. The parking gods were with her, however, and she managed to slip into a metered space on a side street.

An inquiry at the main desk sent her to a ward in one of the out-buildings. God, she hated hospitals—hated feeling helpless and inadequate—hated not being able to do something, anything, that would help her mother.

A nurse buzzed her into the ward and directed her to her mother's curtained cubicle. The energy that had driven Gemma since waking that morning suddenly evaporated, and her hand shook as she pulled aside the drape.

"You're a sight for sore eyes, love," said her mum. Vi Walters was propped up in a hospital bed, IV lines taped to her arm. She looked pale but alert, and there was no one else in the cubicle.

With an inward sigh of relief, Gemma kissed her mum's cheek. It felt warm to the touch. "How are you?" Gemma asked, pulling up a chair. "Why are you here? And where are Dad and Cyn?"

"You sound just like your son." Her mother shook an admonishing finger at her.

"I know, I know," Gemma admitted, smiling in spite of her worry. "One question at a time," she and her mother repeated in unison. Gemma laughed, then sobered. "Seriously, Mum, how are you?" She couldn't help glancing at the IV. "Cyn said a transfusion . . ."

"I'm just a bit run down," said Vi. "They say it's the effects of the chemo on my immune system, so I need a little boost. And my veins have gone a bit wonky, so they're going to put in a port to make the chemo easier."

Gemma put together the bright spots of color in her mother's cheeks with the warmth of her skin. "You've got a temperature."

"Well, just a bit." Vi didn't meet her eyes. "They say it's not unusual. Low white cell count."

"Where are Cyn and Dad, then?" Gemma asked, not wanting to address what she suspected was evasion quite yet.

"You sister has taken your father home, thank goodness, so that he can get some rest and I can have a little peace." Vi closed her eyes.

"That's the worst thing, you know, his worrying. I try so hard not to . . . but yesterday I just couldn't go on with things . . ."

"Mum." Gemma took her mother's hand as she thought about the complexities of her parents' relationship. Her view had changed since her mother's diagnosis. She'd always thought her father the dominant partner, and her mother's mission in life as catering to his needs at the cost of her own.

But that had only been the surface, she'd realized, something she would have seen much more easily if her perceptions hadn't been clouded by her own place in the family dynamic.

The truth was that her mother was the stronger of the two, and that her determination to reassure him was pushing her far beyond her limits.

"Mum," Gemma said again. "Maybe . . . Maybe you should let Dad take care of you. I know you keep trying to take care of him, the way you've always done—the way you've looked after all of us—but it's not . . . I don't think it's helping him. If you put him in charge, let *him* care for *you*, then maybe he wouldn't feel quite so . . . so helpless."

"So who died and made you a psychologist?" Vi asked, with a hint of her usual asperity, but then she squeezed Gemma's hand and smiled.

"Hazel would probably report me," Gemma admitted ruefully. "Mum, I didn't mean to—"

"No, no, I suspect you're right." Vi sighed. "It's just that he's so frightened, and I can't imagine how he would manage if I, well"—she lowered her voice, as if admitting to a dark secret—"if I was gone. But I suppose learning to look after me would be a start." Frowning, she added, "Did Cyn tell you that neither of you were donor matches?"

"Yes." Gemma didn't mention that it was Duncan her sister had told. "But surely—there's an international database for donors, isn't there?"

"They've put me on the list. But they said the chance of a match was only one in ten thousand . . ."

Ten thousand? Gemma struggled to conceal her shock, then said with as much conviction as she could muster, "You're not going to need a donor match. You just need to rest, and to let the treatments do their job."

"Right." Vi sat up a bit straighter, as if Gemma's pep talk had encouraged her. "I'd better be fit in time for your wedding. And you had better choose the venue so you can set a date. You said you were going to find something this week."

"Well, I—" Gemma felt the telltale color rise in her face—she'd never been able to get away with anything as a child.

"You haven't looked, have you?" Her mother's teasing tone did not quite disguise her disappointment.

Scrambling, Gemma told an outright lie. "I have, honestly, Mum. I've narrowed it down."

"Tell me about them, then." Vi settled herself a little more comfortably, her expression expectant.

"Oh—" Gemma tried to remember some of the places she had rejected out of hand as either too big, too expensive, too pretentiously posh, or just plain silly. "Well, there's the London Eye, but I'm not very good with heights. Or the HMS *Belfast*. Or the London aquarium. Or, um, Fulham Palace."

Vi's eyes had widened. "You can get married on the London Eye? Sounds very impractical to me."

"You can get married at Westminster Abbey if you want—a civil wedding, that is. You can even get married in the changing rooms at Tottenham Hotspur. Or at the London Dungeon."

"Why on earth would anyone want to be married there?" Vi gave a shudder.

"Thrills and chills." Gemma couldn't help grinning. "The boys would love it."

"But you wouldn't. Nor Duncan, I daresay."

"No." Gemma looked away. She had left out the stultifyingly boring reception rooms in generic hotels and restaurants. All the prospects had depressed her. She just couldn't get her mind round the thought of being married in a place that meant nothing to either of them and by a person neither of them knew.

"You won't consider a church wedding?" Vi asked softly. "Even, you know, Church of England. I'm sure Duncan's family would like that."

"Yes, I suppose they would. It would have to be St. John's, though, our parish church, and we don't know the rector. Winnie—" She didn't want to voice her fears about Winnie. "And I don't feel quite right about using our parish church for hatch, match, and dispatch," she amended. "It just seems a bit callous, somehow."

"And it seems to me you have far too many scruples," said Vi, a little tartly. "Gemma, you're not—you're not getting cold feet?"

"No, of course not, Mum." She wasn't about to admit it was the second time she'd been asked that in as many days. "I just want—I just want everything to be right."

Vi seemed to shrink a little, as if suddenly tired. "Well, I hope it doesn't take you as long to make up your mind about this as it took you to decide you wanted to marry Duncan." She took Gemma's hand again. "You couldn't do better, love. And I do want to see you married."

"Mum! Don't talk like that—it's not like you at all—" Her phone chirped, making her jump. She'd forgotten to turn it off. Grabbing it from her bag, she glanced at the caller ID as she pressed Ignore. It was a London number, unfamiliar. "Sorry, Mum. I—"

"I hope I'm not interrupting?"

Gemma started at the sound of the man's voice. She hadn't heard the cubicle curtain move. Guiltily, she slipped her phone into her bag as she turned. A coat and tie—a consultant, then, and a bit sleek and overfed looking.

He gave her a perfunctory smile, letting her know that the apology was strictly rote, then turned to Vi. "Mrs. Walters? I'm Dr. Alexander, your anesthetist. We like to have a little chat before procedures."

"An anesthetist?" said Gemma, alarmed. "But—"

"It's routine. For the port," Vi told Gemma, but she looked at the consultant a little anxiously.

"Absolutely routine, Mrs. Walters. It's just to make you comfortable. You'll never know you've been under. Now," he added, his tone making it clear it was time to get down to business, "are there any allergies we need to know about?"

Vi nodded at Gemma. "You go, love. Return your call. I'll be fine." But as Gemma gathered her bag and leaned over to kiss her, Vi whispered, "But don't forget what I said."

Gemma waited until she was outside the hospital annex to check her message. The voice was male, impatient, and recognizably Cockney. "DI Weller here. Ring me at your earliest convenience." He left the same number she'd seen on the caller ID.

This was the man, she remembered, who was supposed to be in Shropshire at a wedding and not to be disturbed. Had Sergeant Singh passed along her message, after all, and now he was ringing to give Gemma a bollocking for wasting his time? In no mood to be trifled with, she found a quiet spot between buildings and punched the Return Call key.

He picked up on the first ring. "Weller."

"This is Inspector James. You rang me?"

There was a murmur of voices, quickly fading, as if Weller had moved out of range. "Look," he said abruptly, "I don't know what you have to do with this, but we need to have a word. I'm at Haggerston Park. You know it?"

Gemma searched her memory. Haggerston Park had a farm—

she'd been there once, with Toby's infant school class. And it was not far from the London, just to the north in Bethnal Green. "Yes, but—"

"North side. Come in at Audrey Street."

"But can't you tell me what's going on?" asked Gemma. "Has something—" The sudden roar of the air ambulance powering up drowned out her words. She looked up, searching for the helipad, shouting, "Sorry," into the phone. The sound grew louder, then the distinctive dark orange helicopter rose above a nearby building. The sight gave her a little chill of excitement—odd, she thought, for a person who didn't like heights.

As the helicopter moved away, she saw that she'd lost her call. It looked as though Weller had hung up on her.

So DI Weller was not in Shropshire, but in London. Gemma glanced at her watch. Not yet eleven o'clock. Whatever had brought Weller back from Shropshire at that speed could not be good.

Gemma put her mobile back in her bag and hurried towards her car. No point in ringing him back, she was only minutes from the park. And if the news was bad, she preferred to hear it in person.

Once in the car, a quick glance at her A to Zed proved that she was even closer to the park than she'd thought. She drove, trying not to anticipate, trying not to make assumptions, but when she had passed the east side of the park and reached the short dead end that was Audrey Street, the cluster of police vehicles confirmed her fears. This was a major incident, most likely a death.

She went on along Goldsmith until she could make a U-turn, then found a spot for the car. Walking back to Audrey Street, she held her identification up to the uniformed constable manning the first temporary barrier. "Inspector Weller?" she asked.

The constable nodded towards an iron gate at the entrance to a footpath that looked as if it led up into the park. Blue-and-white crime scene tape stretched across the opening. Behind the tape stood a man Gemma would have picked out without the constable's direction.

Heavyset, rumpled gray suit, gray hair buzzed short. She thought of the Royalty Protection officers she'd seen in Beigel Bake the evening before—he might have been cut from the same cloth. When she reached him, holding out her ID as she ducked under the tape, she saw that his eyes were gray as well, the color of flint and about as friendly.

"Not my team," he said. "You must be James, then."

She nodded. "Inspector Weller. What's going on here?"

Weller stepped aside to allow a white-suited crime scene tech to pass, and Gemma saw that there was a crime scene van among the marked cars in the street. He gave her an assessing stare and she wished she'd worn something more professional than jeans, tank top, and sandals. "How about you tell me what you knew about Naz Malik?"

Knew. Past tense. Her heart sank, but she said evenly, "It was in my message. Mutual friend rang me, worried that Mr. Malik hadn't turned up for a visit. Have you found him?"

"Did you meet Naz Malik at any time?"

"No," Gemma said sharply, not liking the feeling of being interrogated. "I'd never heard of him until yesterday. Why—"

"Seen a photo?"

Gemma thought about the house on Fournier Street, empty, and the family photos pinned to Sandra Gilles's corkboard. "Yes. Yesterday, when I went to the house."

Weller frowned at the cars in the street, seeming barely to hear her. She saw the glint of pale stubble on his jaw, the crinkled pouches of skin beneath his eyes. "Still waiting on the damned pathologist," he muttered, then looked back at her, including her in the scowl. "Suppose you'd better have a look, then. I could use a second ID."

He turned and started along the path. It was a gentle incline, lined by blooming shrubs and a brick wall to the right. After a few yards it forked, and Weller followed the left-hand branch.

The paved walkway narrowed slightly. The vegetation thickened, trees arched overhead, and along the left-hand side primitive-looking waist-high wooden slats provided a barrier. Gemma could see nothing but green ahead and behind. The spot felt as isolated as if it had been plucked out of the heart of the city and set down in alien countryside. An apt metaphor, she thought as the path twisted and she saw the cluster of white-suited SOCOs, looking like space invaders bent over a prize.

But it was a broken section of fencing they were examining, she saw as she drew closer, and the ground beyond. A white-suited photographer moved in an awkward squat, increasing the surreal quality of the scene.

And then she was near enough to see the object of their activity—in the undergrowth beyond the broken fence lay a man's body, face-down, his limbs splayed, like the extrusions on a jigsaw piece.

The techs moved back when they saw Weller. Eyeing Gemma again, critically, he pulled paper boots and gloves from one of his jacket pockets. While she put them on he said, a little more conversationally, "Early morning jogger. Noticed the broken section of fence, then the shoe." He pointed. "When she realized the shoe was attached to a leg, she waded in to investigate. Ballsy of her, but likely buggered up my crime scene."

Recognizing the proprietary tone—she had used it often enough herself—Gemma glanced at him as she finished snapping on the gloves. "You said second ID. You were the first?"

Weller nodded. "Interviewed him a dozen times over his wife's disappearance."

"What happened? How did he—"

"Why don't you tell *me*."

Gemma wasn't sure if this was a challenge or if Weller genuinely wanted her opinion. Looking back at the body, she felt her own reluctance. This seemed uncomfortably personal, but putting it off wasn't going to make it any better. The day was warming fast and the flies were gathering—would have been gathering since daybreak— and the smell would ripen quickly in the heat. Her hands had already begun to sweat in the gloves.

She eased through the gap in the fence and crouched, trying to resist brushing at the flies as she cataloged the details. "Clean, well-groomed, male," she observed. "A little thin, but not obviously malnourished. The clothes match the description given by Naz Malik's nanny—tan trousers and a casual polo shirt." Only his right hand and arm were visible. The left was tucked beneath his body. "There are a few minor scratches on the backs of his hand, consistent with contact with the undergrowth." She bent closer, this time giving in to the impulse to swat at a fly, looking carefully at the back of the victim's dark hair, and at the leaf litter round the edges of the body. "No obvious signs of trauma, or of blood seeping from a wound we can't see. No smell of alcohol." She looked up at Weller. "ID?"

"Wallet was accessible, in his back pocket," he answered.

Carefully, Gemma moved round to the other side. From what she could see, the victim's profile certainly matched the photos she'd seen of Naz Malik. But something was missing— She looked at the crime scene techs. "Anyone turn up his glasses?"

"No, not a trace," said a plump woman who wore oversize glasses herself.

"And was the body positioned exactly like this? Nose down in the soil?"

"Said we were waiting for the bloody pathologist, didn't I?" Weller sounded tired as well as irritated. "Of course we didn't move him. And fortunately the jogger had more sense than most."

"Was he already dead when he fell, then?" Gemma was asking herself as much as Weller.

"Either that or too incapacitated to move. Drugs, maybe," Weller speculated.

"He didn't do drugs," Gemma protested. "Not according to my friend. Maybe he was ill—"

"And just managed to break the fence while having a heart attack?" Weller didn't bother to moderate his sarcasm.

"You can't know—"

"I suspect you are both theorizing in the absence of fact." The voice that interrupted Gemma was clipped, precise, and made Weller jump.

Glancing up, Gemma saw that a man had come up behind Weller. He was Asian, thirtyish, with skin slightly darker than Naz Malik's. His short jet-black hair was gelled into spikes, and he wore frayed jeans and a black T-shirt that said THE ROTTEN HILL GANG on its front. He also carried a pathologist's kit.

"Good God, man," said Weller. "You want to give me a heart attack?"

"Maybe you should get your hearing aid checked, Inspector." The man opened his kit and pulled on gloves.

"And you, Rashid—you decide to have a lie-in this morning, or what? We've been waiting more than an hour."

"I had another case, in Poplar, and unfortunately, levitating across London is not on my list of accomplishments." The pathologist gave Gemma a speculative look, and she realized that his eyes were not the expected brown but a dark gray-green. "You have a new colleague, Inspector?"

Gemma stood, lurching awkwardly on the uneven ground, and spoke before Weller could reply. "Gemma James. Detective inspector, Notting Hill."

"Bit off your patch," said the pathologist, looking interested.

Weller didn't offer an explanation. "Inspector James, this is Dr. Rashid Kaleem, esteemed Home Office pathologist and local wiseass."

There were a dozen or so accredited Home Office pathologists practicing in Greater London and the southeast, many of whom Gemma had met in the course of her work both at the Yard and at

Notting Hill. But if Kaleem were new to the service, he and Weller appeared to have an established relationship, and in spite of the banter it seemed friendly enough.

Gemma made way for Kaleem, trying to retrace exactly her steps back to the path.

Kaleem worked efficiently, snapping photos with his own digital camera, murmuring observations into a pocket recorder as he conducted his external examination. He then eased up the tail of Naz Malik's polo shirt to insert his temperature probe, and Gemma looked away from the sight of Malik's exposed back. It was somehow worse than blood or a wound, that expanse of smooth, bare skin.

A shaft of sunlight penetrated the trees, burning Gemma's bare shoulder, and she realized she had forgotten to put on sunscreen. Shifting position slightly, she watched as Kaleem took more close-ups of Malik's head. Then, without asking for help, he gently turned the body over.

"Lividity is fixed," he said. "I don't think he was moved. What time was he last seen yesterday?"

When Weller looked at Gemma, she answered, "He left his house around two yesterday afternoon. That's the last confirmed report."

Kaleem shook his head. "Rigor mortis is still fully developed. There are other factors, of course, but in this heat, if he'd been dead almost twenty-fours hours, I'd expect it to be passing off."

"If he died before sunset, it's likely someone would have seen the body last night," Weller said, frowning. "Although the park stays open till half past nine this time of year, so it would have been fully dark by closing—"

"He might have been here for some time before he died—perhaps between the park closing and the early hours of the morning." Kaleem put the last of his things into his kit and stood up. "I'll know more when I get him on the table."

Weller didn't seem ready to end the discussion. "If he took drugs, then came here to die, or if he took the drugs here—"

"You're assuming this was a suicide, Inspector?" Kaleem's voice was sharp.

"The man's wife went missing three months ago," Weller explained. "He had reason enough, especially if he was involved in her disappearance—"

"Regardless of the victim's personal circumstances," broke in Kaleem, "if this was suicide I'd say this man had an odd sort of assistance."

Weller stared at him. "What are you talking about, Rashid?"

"I've been doing this job for ten years, Inspector, and I've never seen a person fall with their head in that position. Even if this man was dead when he fell, the impact would have turned his head to one side or the other. I'd guess this man died of suffocation, regardless of any other incapacitating factors."

Weller looked at him blankly. "Suffocation?"

"His breathing would have been severely restricted by the position of his head." Dr. Kaleem glanced at Gemma, as if expecting an ally. "And I'd wager you that someone made quite sure it stayed that way."

CHAPTER EIGHT

*There was a strong sense of an artists' community at that
time in Brick Lane. The rich and famous were yet to move in,
the streets still felt like unexplored territory and it was
possible to survive financially in the area on very little.*

—Rachel
Lichtenstein,
On Brick Lane

Dr. Kaleem had released the body and ordered it to be sent to the
mortuary at the London. "I'll see how soon I can get him into my
schedule," he told Weller as they walked back towards the street.

"You can put any old ladies eaten by cats in the cooler for a bit,"
Weller told him, clapping him on the shoulder.

"I do have my priorities, Inspector, thanks very much," Kaleem
retorted. "I'll ring you as soon as I have a prelim." Then he flashed
Gemma a brilliant smile and jogged across Audrey Street. He slipped
through the police cordon, bag swinging, and disappeared from view.

"You two know each other well?" Gemma asked Weller, wondering at the barbed familiarity of the exchange.

"Snotty-nosed little Bangladeshi from a council estate," said

Weller, gazing after him. "I used to sort out the kids who bullied him when I was on area patrol. Gave him ideas above his station." This was uttered fondly, and with the closest thing to a smile Gemma had seen. "Who'd have thought he'd end up a bloody forensic pathologist? His father beat the crap out of him if he caught him with a book, and his mum never learned to speak English. Rashid practically lived in the Whitechapel Library—the Idea Store, they call it now," he added with a snort of disapproval, "and put himself through medical school driving a minicab. Bet his old man's turning in his grave."

"Why didn't his father want him to read?"

"Strict Muslim. Thought anything other than the Koran would corrupt the boy. Right bastard, old Mr. Kaleem. I suspect the missus gave thanks to Allah when he died. Heart attack. Keeled over right in the middle of his dinner." Weller stuffed his hands in his already baggy pockets and shrugged. "Rashid was surprisingly cut up."

Gemma wondered if it had been Weller who'd informed Kaleem that his father had died. Then the enormity of what *she* had to do struck her. "Oh, lord. I've got to tell Tim. And we'll have to ring social services. There's no one for Naz Malik's little girl to go home to."

Weller had said he'd follow Gemma in his own car, leaving Gemma grateful for a few minutes alone. Her Escort had been parked in the sun, and she swore as the driver's seat scorched the backs of her thighs through her jeans. She rolled down the windows and started the car. Hot air blasted from the vents into her already-burning face as she carefully reversed and turned the car round.

She debated ringing Kincaid, but didn't want to talk without pulling over, and DI Weller, in an old white BMW that looked as rumpled as Weller himself, stayed right on her tail.

All too soon she'd reached Islington, and still she had no idea how to break the news to Tim. Death notification was always difficult, but telling a friend was so much worse . . . She realized that the last time she'd had to break such news to someone she knew well, it had been Hazel.

It felt odd now, pulling up in front of the detached house in the leafy square, rather than turning into the side road and parking in front of the garage that had been her flat. Last night, in a hurry to get home, she had handed Tim the keys at the door. She hadn't actually been in the house since Hazel had moved out. Although they had kept up with Tim, he had come to them, or they had occasionally met him out for a drink or a meal.

Then, to her surprise, she saw Hazel's car parked in front as well, and after yesterday's tensions she wasn't sure if her friend's presence would be a help or a hindrance.

Weller found a spot nearby and got out of the BMW, closing the door as carefully as if it had been the newest model. He looked tired, and she realized he must have driven back from Shropshire that morning. Perhaps his rumpled look was more circumstantial than habitual.

When he reached her, he nodded back at his car, and she felt embarrassed that he'd seen her studying it. "Putting two kids through uni doesn't leave much for upgrading the old wheels," he said, as if in apology. "And besides, they don't make the Beamers the way they used to. I've got quite fond of the old girl." He looked up at the house. "This your friend's? Not bad digs."

"He's a therapist," said Gemma. "Well, they both are, Tim and his wife, Hazel, but they're separated and Tim's kept the house. They share custody of their daughter, and it looks as if Hazel's here, too." The explanation seemed awkward, but she didn't want to have to make it in front of Hazel and Tim.

"He kept the house?" Weller gave her a curious look, but followed her up the walk without further comment. Gemma rang the bell, aware of his large presence beside her, aware of the sweat trickling down her neck, and the sound of her own breathing. No one answered, and there was no sound from within the house. Gemma rang again, and waited. After a moment, she said, "Let's try the garden. They must be here unless they've gone to the park."

As she led Weller back into the street, an older-model Ford drew up and pulled into the curb. The driver seemed to check the house number against a note, then spotted Gemma and Weller. "CID?" she called out briskly as she opened the door and got out.

Weller introduced himself, then Gemma.

"I'm Janice Silverman." She pumped their hands with the same cheerful energy. "Social services." She was, Gemma guessed, in her forties, with short, wavy, graying hair, and even in the August midday heat she wore a serviceable but lint-specked black sweater and skirt.

"Didn't expect you so quickly," said Weller, sounding genuinely impressed.

"I'm super-social-worker. Changed in a phone booth." She gave them an unexpectedly impish smile. "Seriously, I was in the neighborhood, just leaving a council estate in Holloway, so thought I wouldn't keep you waiting. What's the situation here?"

"Father found this morning. Suspicious death. Mother missing for the last several months." Weller pulled at his collar, the sun glinting off the stubble on his chin. He nodded at the house. "Friend of the father. Kept the child last night when the dad didn't come home."

"And the child"—Silverman glanced down at her notebook—"a little girl? She's two? Has anyone spoken to her yet?"

"She's almost three," said Gemma. "And no, she's not been told anything."

"Best let me handle it." Silverman sighed, and some of her vitality seemed to dissipate. "Mother disappeared, you say?" She shook her head. "That seems particularly hard under the circumstances. Still"—the briskness came back in force—"best get it over with."

"No one's answering the door," Gemma explained, and as she led them round the side of the house they heard children's voices coming from the garden.

Her flat looked just the same, except that the black garage door was shiny with new paint. Tim must have been busy with DIY, she thought. But when she glanced in the windows by the garden gate, she saw the familiar furnishings, the black half-moon table next to the tiny kitchen, the modern steel-and-leather chaise she and Duncan used to call the torture lounger, the neatly made bed with its bookcase headboard. It seemed only the fresh flowers Hazel had always left for her were missing, and the untidy flotsam of Toby's books and toys. She felt eerily out of sync, as if her life had zigzagged back on itself.

And today, she saw as she looked over the wall, it was not Toby and Holly playing in the garden, but Holly and little Charlotte Malik. Tim sat on the patio, a beer on the flagstones beside his chair. Hazel, wearing the same cotton shorts and sleeveless blouse as the previous day, pushed the little girls on the swings.

When Gemma opened the wrought-iron garden gate, Holly flew out of the swing and ran to her, shrieking, "Auntie Gemma! Auntie Gemma! Come and push me!"

Gemma picked her up and hugged her. "I've missed you, too, poppet. But I can't push you just now. I've got to talk to your dad." She let Holly slide to the ground and sent her on her way with a pat.

Tim stood slowly, taking in Gemma's face and the presence of the man and woman beside her. Hazel let Charlotte's swing come to a rest. Then, looking down at the child, she called to Holly, "Come push Charlotte's swing for a bit, sweetie. It's your turn."

"But I don't want—"

"Now," said Hazel, in a tone that brooked no argument. Holly went, her expression sulky, but she glanced back at her mother as if sensing something amiss. Hazel crossed to the patio and stood a few feet from Tim.

Gemma made the introductions. "Tim. Hazel. This is Detective Inspector Weller, from Bethnal Green. And Janice Silverman, from social services."

"It's bad news, isn't it?" said Tim, starting towards them.

"I'm sorry, Tim." Gemma touched his arm. "Naz Malik was found dead in Haggerston Park this morning."

"What— How—" Even though Tim had seemed prepared, he swayed a little. "I don't—"

"Why don't we sit down, Mr. Cavendish." Weller steered him back to his chair. Tim sank into it, grasping the arms as if they were anchors, and Weller pulled up another. "We don't yet know exactly what happened to your friend," continued Weller. "If you could go over what you told DI James, here—"

"But I—" He looked across the garden and lowered his voice to just above a whisper. "Charlotte. Oh, Christ. What about Charlotte?"

"She'll have to go into foster care," Janice Silverman explained, "until we've contacted any relatives."

"But Naz had none. He was orphaned, and the aunt and uncle who brought him up here died a few years ago."

"There's the wife's family."

Tim shook his head. "They didn't see Sandra's family. Didn't want Charlotte to have anything to do with them. Why can't she stay here?"

"Do you or Mrs. Cavendish have any legal status regarding the child?"

"Well, no, but she's comfortable here. She knows me, and Holly—"

"We're separated," broke in Hazel. "Tim and I are separated. We share custody of Holly, so she's only here during the school week."

"Then it would certainly be unsuitable for the child to stay with you, Mr. Cavendish. Now, I'll need to talk to her, and then I'll get the placement machinery rolling." She glanced at the children, her expression softening. The girls had stopped swinging and were watching the adults. "Charlotte is the younger of the two?"

"Yes," said Tim.

"Perhaps you could call your little girl, Mr. Cavendish?" suggested Silverman.

Hazel reacted first. She called Holly to her, then, taking her hand, said, "Mummy needs some help in the kitchen, sweetheart. It's hot—we'll make some cool drinks, shall we?"

Holly went with her willingly enough, glancing back only once at her playmate as she entered the house.

"Do you have to tell her? About her dad?" Gemma said quietly to Silverman.

"Yes, I'm afraid so." Silverman went to Charlotte and knelt beside her swing, Gemma following. "Charlotte, I'm Miss Janice. I'm going to be looking after you for a bit."

Sliding from her swing with her thumb in her mouth, Charlotte looked from Silverman to Gemma, her eyes wide.

"Your daddy's had an accident, Charlotte," Silverman went on gently. "He was hurt, and he died. That means someone else will take care of you now. I have a nice friend you can stay with, where you'll be very safe."

Slowly, Charlotte removed her thumb from her mouth. "Don't want to," she whispered, shaking her head. "I want my daddy."

"Your daddy is not coming home, Charlotte. I'm sorry."

"My mummy is coming home," Charlotte stated with conviction.

Silverman glanced at Gemma, then said, "Well, that may be. But your mummy isn't home now, so you'll have to stay with someone else. Why don't we—"

"I want my daddy!" Charlotte's wail ended on a hiccupping sob, and when Janice Silverman reached for her, she threw herself at Gemma.

Gemma gathered Charlotte into her arms, cradling her head and feeling the dampness of the child's tears against her shoulder. The girl smelled of the newly mown garden grass, and faintly, of chocolate. Tightening her grip, Gemma murmured, "You are a little love, aren't you?" and suddenly found she couldn't bear the thought of this precious child being turned over to a stranger.

"Look, Mrs. Silverman," she said, "can't I take her? I'm a police officer. I've got two boys, and my—partner"—she'd been about to say *husband* and realized she couldn't, not yet—"my partner and I could look after her until things are sorted."

"She's obviously formed an attachment to you. Have you done any foster care?"

"No, but—"

Silverman shook her head. "Then you're not in the system. I'm sorry, but you'd have to be evaluated, and we need someone who can take her right away. I'll just—"

"Wait," said Gemma as inspiration struck. "I know someone. Just let me make one phone call."

"I've a friend," Gemma explained when the still-tearful Charlotte had been coaxed into Tim's arms. "She's fostered children before. If she's willing, would that be acceptable?"

"If she's in good standing," Silverman said cautiously. "I'd have to speak to her myself, and do a check."

"I'm sure she'd be fine. She's the mother of the friend who helps look after our kids. She's great with them." Gemma knew she was over-explaining, and that it was as much to reassure herself as Janice Silverman. Excusing herself, she walked to the back of the garden and looked out over the garage flat as she made the call, fingers crossed.

When she heard Betty Howard's cheerful voice, West Indian accent still intact after more than forty years in Notting Hill, she breathed a sigh of relief. "Betty, it's Gemma. I've a favor to ask." She explained the situation as succinctly as she could.

"Oh, the poor child," said Betty. "I'd be glad to take her, Gemma. Only thing is, I've got the costumes for carnival—"

"We could help out," Gemma offered. Betty had sewn elaborate costumes for the Notting Hill carnival since the seventies, and Gemma knew what a time-consuming job it was. "If that would make a difference."

"Wesley should be able to pitch in a bit," said Betty, in a considering tone. "Though it would mean less time with your two. But if you could take the child the odd hour or two in the evening, I think we could just manage."

"You're a dear, Betty. I'll let you speak to Mrs. Silverman, then."

When Betty had given her information to Janice Silverman, and the caseworker was calling her own office to confirm them, Gemma went into the house to put together Charlotte's things. She found Hazel in the kitchen, pouring orange squash into glasses that held a few meager ice cubes.

"This is all there is," Hazel said. "Tim's run out of anything decent to drink. Not to mention he's forgotten to fill the ice trays. And I can't," she added, her voice rising, "bloody find anything." She opened the fridge door, then slammed it shut again.

Gemma stared at her in surprise, but Hazel didn't meet her eyes. "Even water would be fine," Gemma said after a moment, treading carefully, not sure what had triggered the outburst. "It doesn't matter, really. Hazel, I just need to get Charlotte's things together. Do you—"

"No. I don't know where Tim's put her things. I've just said I don't know where anything is." Hazel pushed the most recently filled glass into the others on a tray, causing them all to slosh, then went into the sitting room, wiping her hands on a tea towel. Gemma heard her say more calmly, "Holly, can you put Charlotte's things in her little bag? Is it in your room? Good girl. Just bring it down when you're done, and don't miss anything."

Then Holly clattered up the stairs, and Hazel came back into the kitchen, muttering, ". . . herd of elephants." Her eyes were red. "I'm sorry," she said to Gemma. "I didn't mean to snap, and at you, of all people. It's just that—last night, I thought Tim was manufacturing a drama. I never thought—poor little Charlotte—her father's really dead?"

"Yes. I saw the body."

"Oh, God." With the tea towel, Hazel swiped at the spilled drink on the work top. "Now I feel a complete bitch. Did he—was it suicide?"

"We don't know. *They* don't know," Gemma corrected as she glimpsed Weller through the kitchen window, reminding herself that it wasn't her case. "There were no obvious signs of foul play. We'll have to wait for the postmortem."

"Surely he wouldn't have deliberately left that adorable child—" Hazel gestured towards the garden. "Will she be all right?"

"For the moment. I've fixed it so that she can stay with Betty Howard." Gemma went to stand beside her friend. Lowering her voice, she said, "Mrs. Silverman told Charlotte her father was dead. I know, when we—the police—give a death notice, we get it over with as simply and quickly as we can, but for a child that young it seems awfully harsh—"

"No, Mrs. Silverman was right." Hazel nodded in agreement. She had often worked with children in her therapy practice. "Allowing her to think her dad was coming home would be worse for her in the long run. She would have to be told eventually, and the deception would damage her ability to trust. Not that I would know anything about that." Hazel folded the tea towel, then shook it out again, staring at it. It had a pattern of little red roosters on a beige background. "This is hideous," she said. "Where *did* he find it?" She glanced at Gemma, then away. "And he's painted the kitchen."

"I noticed." Gemma searched for the right thing to say. "It looks nice. But it's . . . different."

"Everything's different," said Hazel. "And I know it's all trivial in comparison to what's happened to Tim's friend, but I didn't think it would be so hard."

"Dr. Cavendish, from what DI James has told me, you'll be best placed to help us with inquiries into your friend's death," Weller was saying to Tim as Gemma came back out onto the patio.

She'd just given Charlotte a last hug, and a promise that she'd come to visit her later that afternoon. She didn't know how much the little girl understood. She had clung to Gemma, and after a final fit of sobbing, she'd gone mute in Janice Silverman's arms.

"I've already told Gemma everything I know." Tim had emptied his glass of squash, apparently having no objection to its safety-glow orange color. Now he sipped at the melting ice cubes, then rubbed the back of his hand across his mouth. "Naz loved Sandra and Charlotte. He'd never have done anything to hurt either of them. They were the perfect family."

Hazel, having got Holly started playing in her sandbox on the far side of the garden, had come to stand at the edge of the patio. At Tim's words, she winced.

"Perfect, except for the fact that Sandra Gilles disappeared," said Weller.

Tim stared at him with dawning recognition. "You investigated the case. I remember Naz talking about you. You made him feel he'd done something wrong."

"And had he done something wrong, Dr. Cavendish? You'd be the one he confided in, the one he felt safe with—"

"No." Tim thrust his head forward. "Naz thought you'd not taken Sandra's disappearance seriously, that you'd overlooked things. He said you'd never investigated her brothers thoroughly."

"Sandra Gilles's brothers had alibis for the day of her disappearance."

"Given by their mates down the pub—"

"Naz Malik did not," said Weller, ignoring the dig. "He said he was in his office, on a Sunday, but there was no corroboration."

"You're saying Naz had something to do with Sandra's disappearance?" Tim was half out of his chair, his fists balled.

Weller raised a hand. "No, Dr. Cavendish. I'm merely saying that you can't take anything for granted. Even from the mouths of friends.

Now, you tell me if your mate Naz Malik really thought his wife was coming back."

Tim sank back in his chair, his anger seeming to drain away. "No. Yes. Look at it from Naz's viewpoint, will you? Either something terrible had happened to his wife and the mother of his child, whom he adored. Or everything he believed about his life was a lie, and his wife, his beloved wife, had voluntarily left him. How could he choose between those alternatives? So one day he believed one thing, the next, the other. But I think in his heart he thought something dreadful had happened to her . . . except . . ."

"Except what, Dr. Cavendish?" All Weller's weariness seemed to vanish in an instant. Gemma found herself tempted to caution Tim, but she couldn't—it was not her interview, she couldn't interfere. And she wanted to know what he had been about to say as much as Weller.

"I—it was nothing. A rumor. I'd never repeat it if Naz were . . . here."

"Go on. What sort of rumor?" asked Weller.

Tim, fidgeting, with obvious reluctance, glanced at Hazel, then back at Weller. "It isn't anything—" He shook his head. "Some of the last commissions Sandra did were for a club in Spitalfields. A private club. The owner's name is Lucas Ritchie. Naz heard—"

"Naz heard what, Dr. Cavendish?" prompted Weller.

"There was . . . talk . . . that Sandra was having an affair with Ritchie."

CHAPTER NINE

From hence I only infer that an Englishman, of all men,
ought not to despise foreigners as such, and I think the
inference is just, since what they are to-day, we were
yesterday, and to-morrow they will be like us.

—Daniel Defoe,
The True-Born
Englishman

"Why didn't you tell us this?" demanded Weller.

"It didn't occur to me—Naz only told me the last time we talked." Tim glared back at Weller.

"And Mr. Malik didn't think this was germane to our investigation of his wife's disappearance?" DI Weller shot back. His large hands twitched, and Gemma felt sure his annoyance was not feigned.

"He only heard it a couple of weeks ago," said Tim. "And he didn't take it seriously. Sandra didn't run off with Lucas Ritchie—Ritchie's never left London. Naz went to see him."

"Oh, he did, did he? And this Ritchie assured him he had nothing to do with his wife's disappearance, and that was that? Was your friend really that naive, Dr. Cavendish? That's not the only scenario.

If Sandra Gilles was having an affair with this man, maybe she wanted more. Maybe she threatened to expose him and he shut her up—"

"No! It wasn't like that—at least not from what Naz told me. Look, according to Naz, Lucas Ritchie is single and well off, with no shortage of available women in his life. Who would Sandra have threatened to expose him to? She would have been the one with something to lose."

"So maybe Ritchie wanted her to leave Malik. Maybe she refused and they fought."

"No. Naz didn't believe she was having an affair, and I don't believe it, either. She wasn't—she wasn't that kind of person."

"And what kind of person is that?" Hazel said, her voice shrill with fury. She'd been standing at the edge of the patio, listening, half forgotten by the others. "Did she come with some sort of guarantee? A *no-fault wife*?"

Tim looked horrified as he realized the import of what he'd said, but he defended himself. "Hazel, will you just not take everything so bloody personally? All I meant was that Sandra Gilles had no use for Lucas Ritchie's lifestyle. She told Naz it was all gloss and window dressing, hype, and she valued real things, like her husband and her child and her work." He faced his wife, not backing down. "You were not so different, once."

By the time Gemma got away from Islington, she couldn't face another visit to hospital. A phone call had reassured her that her mother was resting comfortably. She drove across London, feeling barely able to breathe in the car. The late-afternoon heat was stifling, and she was still tense from the atmosphere at the Cavendishes'.

Weller had left after telling Tim he'd want to speak to him again. "I'm not about to skip the country," Tim had muttered, earning another dirty look from Hazel.

Hazel had followed close on Weller's heels, refusing to speak to either Tim or Gemma. "I don't understand," Tim said to Gemma as they watched her drive away. "Everything she's done has been her choice. Why is she so angry with me?"

"I'm sorry, Tim." Gemma gave him a quick hug, not wanting to confess that Hazel's behavior had shocked her as well. Tim had suffered the loss of a friend, and now he had to face the task of telling Alia, Naz Malik's nanny, that Naz was dead. Gemma couldn't imagine the Hazel she had known failing to express sympathy or being unable to put aside her own concerns in a crisis.

When she reached Notting Hill, the square brown brick house with its cherry red door seemed comfortingly, reassuringly familiar. She found the boys watching a video in the sitting room, the dogs sprawled lazily by the garden door.

She hugged Toby until he yelped, squirming, and Kit ducked away from her, grinning. "No squishing for me, ta very much."

"Why aren't you outside?" asked Gemma.

"Too hot. Dad said we had to watch something Toby liked, so it's *Pirates* again." Johnny Depp swaggered across the screen, gold tooth glinting, and Toby folded himself cross-legged on the floor once more, transfixed.

"So I see." The dogs were panting gently. "Where is your dad?"

"Doug called him into the office, something about reports that had to be finished by Monday morning. He said for you to ring him."

Gemma hoped that meant she was forgiven for her bad temper of the night before, and she realized she'd been mentally criticizing Hazel when she'd been guilty of behaving unreasonably herself.

"Would you two like to pay Erika a visit?" she said on impulse. "We could walk."

"Too hot," said Kit.

"We could get an ice cream afterwards."

Toby dragged his attention from the screen. "Yay, Mummy! What kind?"

"Yeah, okay, so I'm susceptible to bribery," agreed Kit.

"Let me give Erika a ring, then get cleaned up a bit."

It wasn't until they were walking down Ladbroke Road a few minutes later, Gemma having taken a quick shower and changed, that she confessed to an ulterior motive.

"I want to see Erika, too," she said, "but while you're visiting I need to stop by Betty Howard's for a few minutes."

"You're going to see Wesley's mum without us?" Kit stared at her suspiciously. "Why can't we go? Betty always wants to see us."

"Of course she does, but this time it's a bit complicated." She explained that Betty was taking care of a little girl named Charlotte who needed a place to stay for a while, and that Charlotte wasn't ready to meet anyone else new quite yet.

She knew she would have to tell them about Charlotte's parents, but she wasn't eager to broach the subject with Kit. Kit merely said, however, "You won't be gone long, will you?"

Gemma had become friends with Erika Rosenthal in the course of investigating a case when she had first been posted back to Notting Hill. In the past few months they had become even closer, when the unexpected appearance of an antique brooch at auction had opened a window into the older woman's troubled past.

A retired academic with no children of her own, Erika had taken a special interest in Toby and Kit, and the boys considered her family—a courtesy grandmother. They saw Erika, in fact, much more often than they saw Gemma's or Duncan's parents. Toby's dad, Rob, had walked out on Gemma when Toby was an infant, and Rob's parents had cut off all contact, thereby helping their son avoid paying maintenance for Toby. Good riddance, as far as Gemma was concerned.

And as for Kit, his maternal grandparents had proved even more difficult. After a failed attempt to gain custody, they were allowed only supervised visits with Kit, and so had stopped making any effort to see their grandson. Kit's relationship with his grandmother had been unpleasant at best, abusive at worst, and if he missed his grandfather, he never said. He had quickly become attached to Duncan's parents, and was fond of Gemma's, but his relationship with Erika was special. They were in many ways kindred spirits, despite the differences in age and background.

When they reached the house in Arundel Gardens and rang the bell, Erika answered immediately, beaming at them and brushing back the snow white hair escaping from its usual twist. She wore a flowered pinny and had a smudge of something on her cheek. "Ah, kitchen help," she said. "What good timing."

"Are you making something for us?" Toby asked as they followed her into the hall.

"No. I'm having a guest for dinner, and the entrée must be something very French. It's too hot to use the cooker, so I'm making a seafood salad, and I thought Kit could help me with the calamari."

"What's calamari?" said Toby.

Kit wiggled his fingers at him. "Squid."

"Ooh, yuck," Toby pronounced, but the smell of garlic, lemon, and fresh herbs coming from the kitchen made Gemma's mouth water.

"I can do squid," Kit added with relish. "You disembowel them."

Laughing, Erika said, "Well, before you start your operation, I have a little treat for you both, just some things I picked up at the market yesterday." From a shelf, she fished an antique double-decker bus for Toby, and for Kit, a book, its cover stained and musty. Looking over Kit's shoulder as he opened it, Gemma saw that it was filled with beautifully detailed, colored zoological drawings. Kit exclaimed in delight and leaned down to kiss Erika's cheek.

"It's brilliant," he said. "Where did you find it?"

"One of the stalls on Portobello Road itself. Lucky this one didn't fall into the hands of the print dealers," Erika added, touching a finger to the book. Many old, and sometimes rare, editions containing botanical or zoological drawings were bought in job lots by the print dealers, who cut them from the books and matted them to sell individually.

"These are lovely, Erika," said Gemma, "but you're spoiling the boys." For a moment she regretted leaving them, even for the few minutes it would take her to visit Charlotte at Betty Howard's—she had little enough time with Kit and Toby as it was. But she couldn't get little Charlotte Malik's face out of her mind, and she had made Charlotte a promise that she had to keep.

"And who better to do that?" Erika countered with a twinkle. "When I get fish gutting in return?"

"You're very cheerful today." Gemma eyed her affectionately. "You said your menu had to be French—would your guest by chance be French, as well?"

"A little something for my friend Henri, yes," Erika admitted, smiling. "Now, if you will run your errand, I'll make tea in the garden when you come back. And I think you promised ice cream? Perhaps you could pick some up."

Leaving the boys in the kitchen, she walked Gemma to the door. "This is very sad, about the little girl," she said quietly. Gemma had told her a bit of Charlotte's story over the phone. "But children are very resilient, and she is in good hands."

"Erika . . ." Gemma paused on the threshold. "Do you think a child that young understands what death means? If she should ask me . . ."

"Yes, that might be difficult. You don't know her references. Were her parents religious?"

"I don't know." Gemma considered what she'd been told about Naz and Sandra, and what she'd seen in their house. "I'm inclined to think not."

"Then I think I would wait and see how she makes sense of it. She might surprise you."

. . .

Gemma turned into Portobello Road at Elgin Crescent, stopping a moment to look up the hill. The street, baking in the late-afternoon heat, seemed alien in its Sunday-afternoon emptiness. The arcades were shuttered, the stalls down, and the pubs seemed to be doing only desultory business. Even her friend Otto's venerable café in Elgin Crescent was closed, it being his rule that Sunday afternoons were reserved for time with his daughters.

There was something about the deserted landscape that appealed to Gemma; for a moment she felt as if she owned the street, in all its cheerful and slightly Mediterranean tattiness.

She turned and walked north, down the hill, and turned into Westbourne Park Road. Betty Howard and her son, Wesley, lived in the same flat Betty's parents had first occupied in 1959, fresh off the boat from Trinidad. Betty and her husband, Colin, had bought it from the slum landlords who had once owned it, and had brought up their six children in it. But Colin had passed away a few years ago from an early heart attack, and Wesley's five older sisters were grown and gone.

Wesley liked to tease his mother, saying he only stayed because he couldn't afford the rent on his own place. But while that was as true for Wes as it was for any young person in London, Gemma knew that he worried about his mum and didn't like the idea of leaving her on her own.

Reaching Betty's building, she pressed the buzzer for the top-floor flat, and when the door released, climbed the stairs. Betty opened the door just as Gemma reached it, holding her finger to her lips.

"She's asleep, poor love," Betty said quietly, giving Gemma a quick hug. She wore her usual bright headscarf, today in turquoise, with just a little graying hair showing against her dark skin. "It was the oddest thing," she went on as she led Gemma into the sitting room. "When Mrs. Silverman left, the little thing, she cried and cried. Not even Wesley could comfort her. Maybe she's not used to our dark faces.

"Then she spied those fabrics in the corner. She went right to them, burrowed in like a mole, and was out like a light. I took her little trainers off without waking her. Will you look at that?"

At first glance, Betty's sitting room seemed a chaos of color and texture. But a closer inspection revealed that the first impression was deceptive, a product of many things occupying a small space. A multitude of clear plastic boxes held collections of buttons, feathers, braiding, sequins, and spools of thread. The sewing machine, a new and expensive model, sat on a table at the front window, where Betty could overlook the street as she sewed. As well as her work on costumes for carnival, she made slipcovers, drapes, Roman blinds—"Anything that can be stitched together"—as she liked to say. Her father had been an upholsterer and had taught Betty to sew as a tot. She'd left school at sixteen to work for a milliner and had been proudly following the family tradition ever since.

Looking where Betty pointed, Gemma saw the bolts of cloth stored between the sofa and the window. There were silks and taffetas in rainbow hues, heavy brocades and satins, gauzy nets, and one roll of gold lamé.

Charlotte had indeed burrowed in between the bolts, pulling a fold of the shimmering gold cloth over herself like a blanket. Only her curls showed at one end and her stockinged feet at the other.

"A little princess," said Betty. "Going right for the gold."

"Oh, I should have realized," whispered Gemma, her chest tightening. "It looks like home to her. Her mother's an artist who works with textiles. She had her studio in the house."

"An artist? Mrs. Silverman said the mother went missing?"

"Yes. In May. And now this. Her dad . . ." Gemma pushed away the image of Naz Malik's body, with the flies buzzing round it in the heat. It would be cold now, on a trolley in the mortuary.

"She's an odd mix, this little one," said Betty. "Striking. Her mother white, her father Pakistani, Mrs. Silverman told me, but with that hair, I'd swear she's got more than a drop of West Indian in her.

Wesley will have his camera out, soon as her tears have dried, mark my words."

"Where is Wes?" asked Gemma.

"Bread-and-butter shoot. Molly Janes, the fishmonger's daughter, it was her birthday party this afternoon. I don't envy Wesley having to deal with a pack of sweets-fueled children in this heat."

Although Wesley was taking evening classes at university towards a business degree, he earned his keep working at Otto's café and helping out with Toby and Kit. But his true love was photography, and he was getting more and more of what he called bread-and-butter jobs—weddings, birthdays, family portraits—through word of mouth in the neighborhood. He had a particular gift for capturing children, and had given Gemma a beautiful candid portrait of Toby for her birthday.

Charlotte stirred, disturbed perhaps by the sound of their voices, although they had kept them close to a whisper. Pushing the cloth from her face, she blinked and rubbed her eyes, starting to whimper. Then she caught sight of Gemma and held out her arms.

Gemma knelt, gathering Charlotte's small, warm body into her arms, and it felt to her as if she had always held this child. "Hello, pet," she whispered. "Did you have a good sleep?"

Charlotte rubbed her nose against Gemma's shoulder, an indeterminate answer, but at least a response. Gemma eased herself into a sitting position with her back against the sofa, cradling Charlotte in her lap. "I'll bet you're hungry." Tim had told her that Charlotte had barely touched her food last night or that morning. Looking up at Betty, Gemma said, "Something smells fabulous. What are you cooking?"

"Pork roast with achiote rub, black beans and rice. Not anything special."

"It would be at my house." Gemma chuckled and ran a soothing hand through Charlotte's curls, saying meditatively, "I wonder if Charlotte likes beans and rice?" Again the nose rub, but this time more of a nod than a shake. "I'll take that as a yes. Betty's the best cook in the whole world," she stage-whispered in Charlotte's ear, "but don't tell her I said so."

Charlotte turned her head just enough to peek at Betty.

"The roast is about done," Betty said. "And I might just have some mango rice pudding. Why don't I go and see?"

Gemma nodded and Betty left the room. After a moment there came the comforting sound of Betty moving about in the kitchen, and her soft voice singing. Shifting her position a bit, so that Charlotte could see more of the room, she said, "Betty has some pretty things, don't you think?" She pulled a box of thread spools closer with her free hand.

Lifting the top, she began to rummage through them, pulling spools out for inspection. "There's blue, and red, and lime green, and a very pretty yellow. What about this one?" She held up a deep pink spool. "What color is this?"

"Magenta," whispered Charlotte, reaching for it with fingers that were still toddler chubby.

"Magenta? What a clever girl you are."

Charlotte slid from Gemma's lap and knelt by the box. "My mummy has threads." She began to take spools out and stack them, sorting by color. "Reds together, blues together, greens together."

"Where does the pink go, then?"

"Between the reds and the blues." Charlotte looked up at her, frowning, as if the answer were obvious. "They're families. Reds are mummies, blues are daddies, and the pinks can be the little children." She had the slightest lisp, but her diction was remarkably clear for not quite three. This was a child who had spent much time in the company of adults.

"Yes, that sounds a good idea." Impeccable color-wheel logic, thought Gemma. "Does your mummy let you play with her thread?" she asked, having noted Charlotte's usage of the present tense.

"I help. I'm her best helper." The red spools toppled, and Charlotte gathered them up with studied patience. "They shouldn't run away. That's naughty. My daddy says families belong together."

Present tense for Daddy, too. Treading very carefully, but wanting to get an idea of just how much Charlotte understood, Gemma said, "But your daddy's not here now, is he?"

Charlotte pushed her stacks of spools a bit closer together and shook her head. "No," she said, as matter-of-factly as if Gemma had asked about the weather. "Daddy's gone to look for Mummy."

Weller always felt there was a persistent hum to a hospital. Even in nether regions like the basement, you could sense the unseen activity, a working hive.

Unfair to compare Rashid to a bee, however—there was no mindless industry here, in this room of tile and steel and precision instruments. And there was definitely no smell of honey.

"You getting soft, old man?" said Rashid, glancing up from the table. "You're looking a bit green." He'd finished the postmortem on Naz Malik and had sent his assistant off, preferring to do the close himself. He liked, as he had told Weller often enough, the sense of closure. And then he'd flashed his wicked pathologist's grin at the bad pun.

"Still suffering from the ravages of too much wedding champagne," Weller said, rubbing his temples. "Cheap stuff, too, although I can't say I blame the bride's family, considering everything else they had to shell out."

"Sorry I couldn't make it. One of the pathologists on the rota, Dr. Ling, had a family emergency. So duty called and all that. Give Sean my regrets."

Weller's son and Rashid were the same age, and had become friends over the years. "You were well out of it, although you might have had a good laugh," Weller told him. Rashid didn't drink, and Weller imagined that a hotel ballroom full of thoroughly pissed guests would get a bit wearing after a while if you didn't share their rather skewed perspective.

His tie felt too tight, even in the cold room. Pulling at the knot, Weller repositioned himself against the tile wall so that Kaleem's body half blocked his view of the table. "Look, Rashid, I appreciate you moving this one up." Weller didn't like to call in favors, but he was feeling less and less comfortable about this case. He'd gone back to Bethnal Green, gone over the notes on the Sandra Gilles case, wondering what he might have missed besides this man Ritchie. Tim Cavendish had had no further information on Ritchie or his club, so Weller had put Sergeant Singh on to a search.

Nothing had come in on Naz Malik. It was too soon to expect any results from the techies, and so far no good citizen had reported seeing Malik in the park last night or yesterday afternoon. Where had Malik been in those hours between the time he left his house in Fournier Street and the time Rashid estimated he had died in the park?

"Interesting, the DI from Notting Hill getting herself involved," commented Rashid, as if guilty of mind reading.

"Interesting, or interested?" teased Weller. "She's a looker."

"She looks *attached*. I can spot it from a mile away. I've got radar about these things. And you're prevaricating."

"Ooh, they teach you big words in medical school," Weller retorted, but he knew Rashid was right. "So, you still convinced this guy didn't top himself?"

Rashid shot him a look. "We'll see what comes back on the tox. But I still think he was heavily sedated when he died. And if he was that trashed, how did he get himself to the park and onto the trail? He didn't take anything when he got there—not unless he had a handful of loose pills in his pocket and swallowed them without liquid. I went through his clothes. No pill bottles, no syringes, and the techs didn't find a drink or a water bottle near the body."

"I had the SOCOS bag the rubbish in the bin at the park entrance," said Weller. "We'll check it for his prints."

"Well, I suppose he might have got that far," Kaleem said, going on with his stitching, "but I think you're reaching for it. If it was a suicide, why dispose of the evidence?"

"Because he didn't want his daughter to grow up knowing he'd killed himself?"

"He'd have known the drugs would show up on a tox screen, so what would be the point?" asked Kaleem.

"Maybe he thought we'd assume he dropped dead of a heart attack."

"You said this guy was a lawyer. Give him a bit of credit."

Weller tried one more time. "You're sure he didn't croak from natural causes?"

"No. He was still breathing when he fell. I found bits of dirt and leaf mold in his nostrils. No sign of stroke or aneurysm. A bit thin, as I said earlier, but not enough to cause him any problems. Other than that, your Mr. Malik was healthy as a horse. Except, of course, for the unfortunate fact that he's dead." Rashid finished closing the Y incision with a neat knot. He unfolded a sheet over the body, then stripped off his gloves. "I'll send you the transcribed copy of my report. And you can have the techs pick up the personal effects. I've already sent the hair and fiber I gathered off to the lab."

He glanced at the evidence bag on the cart by the door and frowned. "Could have sworn I put the phone in first." There was a slim mobile phone near the top of the bag. Rashid shrugged. "Double shift. Too much coffee, not enough sleep." He fixed Weller with the penetrating stare he usually reserved for the nonresponsive. "So what's up with you, old man? It's more than champagne hangover. Why are you so determined to prove this wasn't murder?"

Weller straightened up, sighed. "Because if Naz Malik was murdered, I suspect it means I screwed up. Big-time. And that means this case is out of my hands."

CHAPTER TEN

. . . the land which is now Bangladesh was part of India until the partition in 1947, then it was East Pakistan from 1947 until the 1971 war of liberation, which saw the birth of Bangladesh as an independent nation.

—Geoff Dench, Kate Gavron, Michael Young, *The New East End: Kinship, Race and Conflict*

Another weekend spent finding excuses to come in to work. Worse still, Doug Cullen had even managed to get his guv'nor in on a Sunday afternoon, which hadn't earned him any scout points. Sitting at his desk in his office at the Yard, Kincaid had pushed the printouts aside, steepled his fingers, given him a look worthy of the chief super, and said, "Just how bored are you, Doug?"

"Don't know what you mean, guv," Cullen had said, but he'd colored, knowing full well.

"This report could have waited until tomorrow morning."

"But I thought if the chief had it first thing . . ." He'd sounded lame even to himself.

"Get a hobby, Doug. Check out the joys of Facebook or something." Kincaid stood and stretched. He'd come to the office in T-shirt and jeans, hair rumpled. "I'm going home. And the next time you call me in on a Sunday, it had better be life or death."

Cullen had stayed for a bit in the empty office, but not even the Yard's air-conditioning had kept up with the heat of the afternoon. The room was stuffy, and the building had that stale, dregs-of-the-week feel that came with Sunday afternoons. When the janitors came through, he'd switched off the computer and left them to it.

The guv was right, he thought as he rode the stifling tube back to Euston Road. Since his break-up with his ex-girlfriend, she of the hyphenate, Stella Fairchild-Priestly, he'd become a mole. Cullen had always been focused on work—one of the reasons behind the failure of the relationship—but lately he'd become obsessive, and he'd read enough pop psychology to know such single-mindedness wasn't healthy. Not to mention the fact that he wanted above all to succeed at his job, and pissing off the boss was not the way forward.

But nothing else seemed to motivate him. Social networking was not his cup of tea, although he'd lurked on Internet sites. It was an easy habit to acquire when part of your job was finding out things about other people, but that made him even less likely to want to put information about himself in the public domain.

As the train lurched into Euston Square station, he waited, sweating, as he listened to the carriage creak and groan. He hated the tube, even when it wasn't sweltering. It occurred to him that he could buy a car and avoid public transport altogether—that would be something new to occupy him for a bit. But then parking near his flat would be a nightmare, and as he often had access to transport pool cars during an investigation, it seemed a pointless expenditure.

He climbed the stairs to the street and walked east, his steps slowing as he neared his building. He hated his flat, a boring gray cube in a boring gray building near Euston Station. Stella had liked to say that he lived on the edge of Bloomsbury, but that was stretching it, in terms of style as well as geography. She'd always wanted to make him sound cooler than he was. Hell, that was an understatement—she'd always wanted to *make* him cooler than he was.

As part of her "fix Dougie" mission, she'd done the flat up for him in a trendy minimalist style that he'd hated from the first minute. But he'd not wanted to hurt her feelings, and since they'd split, he'd never found the energy or the imagination to change it. He'd bought some nice audio equipment, but Stella had made fun of his music collection so often that he was reluctant to share it with anyone else, and in truth he listened to his iPod most of the time.

And then, after Stella, there had been Maura Bell, the prickly detective from Southwark, and that little interlude had put paid to any remaining self-confidence. He tried not to think about that disaster.

Entering his building, he took the elevator to his floor and unlocked the door. The place was tidy, at least, but roasting. He pulled open the sitting room window as far as it would go, letting in a faint current of exhaust-scented air, then looked round the flat in increasing dismay.

Why *did* he stay? His lease was coming up for renewal next month, he realized, and he hadn't yet signed the papers. The flat had been the best he could afford before he'd been promoted to sergeant, but he'd had several pay rises since then. He even had some money in the bank—aside from splashing out on electronics and decent clothes for work, he didn't spend much, and he'd paid off all his university debt.

An exhilarating sense of freedom swept through him. He could go . . . anywhere. Someplace nearer work. Someplace near the river, maybe. Kincaid was right, he needed a hobby. He'd rowed at school, and it had been the only athletic thing he'd ever been halfway decent at. Maybe he could find a flat in Fulham or Putney, near the rowing club.

He booted up his computer, then checked the fridge. One beer, but that would do for now. He sat down again and typed in "Flats to Let."

The next morning Cullen went in to work early, excusing his further zealousness on the grounds that he wanted to take some time off at lunch. He'd not slept much, lying awake with visions of flats dancing in his head, knowing it was unlikely any would live up to their adverts, but unable to resist the siren lure of fitted kitchens, power showers, and hardwood floors. One flat even claimed to have a view of the river, and although he knew that probably meant standing on a box in a room the size of a postage stamp, he'd put it first on his list.

Schooling himself to take care of business before calling estate agents, he shut himself in Kincaid's office with the assistance requests that had come in overnight for the murder investigation teams. He'd make a start on assignments, then Kincaid could check them when he came in.

He was happily humming something by Abba when he stopped dead, staring at the monitor with wide eyes.

"Gemma's name on an incoming-case file?" Kincaid asked, frowning. He loosened his tie, which he never managed to keep properly knotted once he got in his office, and took the printout from Cullen, scanning for essentials.

He recognized the name of the victim, Nasir Malik, found dead in Haggerston Park, and tried to remember what Gemma had told him about yesterday's events. She and the boys had come in after he'd got home from the Yard, and the evening had passed quickly with the Sunday family routine: dinner, discussing the boys' plans for the week, finishing up the laundry, weekend chores.

In a lull during the washing-up after the meal, when the boys were out of earshot, they had talked about Gemma's mum. And then Gemma had told him a little about her day. Tim Cavendish's friend had been found dead, and she'd been called to the scene by the investigating officer. Afterwards, she said, she'd managed to have the victim's little girl placed in foster care with Betty Howard. She'd talked about the child with such concern that Kincaid had wondered if she was displacing her worry over her mother.

But before he'd had a chance to ask her more about the case, Toby had come in wanting a story, and by the time the boys were tucked up, they had fallen into bed themselves, exhausted, and he had given it no more thought.

Now, pulling out his mobile, he rang her. "Didn't you say the pathologist thought Tim's friend's death was suspicious?" he asked.

"Yes, that was my impression," she said. "But there was no sign of trauma, and they won't have the tox results yet. Why?"

"Tox results or not, the DI in charge"—he peered at the page, wondering if he was going to have to give in to reading glasses— "Neal Weller, his name is, has sent us the case. You said you met the pathologist. Any good?"

"He seemed very thorough. But Weller, he's a bit of a bulldog. I'd not have thought he'd hand it off so easily. He argued with Dr. Kaleem."

"Well, it looks like something's spooked Weller. What's your gut feeling on this?"

He waited, listening to the hum of activity on Gemma's end of the line.

"I'm in the CID room. Give me a sec." Then he heard a door shut and the background sound vanished as if a switch had been flipped. "Um, I think I'm inclined to agree with the pathologist," Gemma said from the sanctity of her office. "Something didn't feel right."

"But on Saturday, you said Tim was worried about his friend. I gathered he thought he might be suicidal."

"Tim was worried, but he's adamant that Naz didn't kill himself." She paused, and Kincaid heard the tap of a pencil on her desk, her habit when she was thinking. After a moment, she said, "It's a dodgy case, any way you look at it. And Weller was the one who investigated the wife's disappearance."

Kincaid picked up a pencil himself and doodled interlocking circles. "Then Weller's treading on eggshells now, I would guess. Afraid he missed something. Could be a right balls-up, and he's getting out while the getting's good."

"I'd guess he's close to retirement," said Gemma. "He wouldn't want to finish his career on a black mark. So . . ." She hesitated, and Kincaid grinned at her restraint. "So, if you think the case merits reassignment, will you take it yourself?"

"Would you kill me if I didn't?"

"Oh, worse than that. Much worse," Gemma answered, and he heard the smile in her voice.

"And where would you start?" he asked. "If it were your case."

"You'll want to see Weller, of course. And Tim. And the pathologist. But if it were me, I think I'd start with Naz Malik's law partner. She's bound to know more about Naz and his wife than anyone else."

Kincaid flipped through the case notes, saw the name and address of Naz Malik's firm.

"You'll keep me in the loop?" added Gemma.

"Have you ever known me to overlook a valuable resource?" he asked, and smiled as he clicked off. Cullen was staring at him, his lips pursed as if he'd just eaten a lemon.

"We're going to take this one?" Cullen repeated Gemma's question, but with much less anticipation.

Kincaid's sergeant tended to be territorial, and wouldn't care for Gemma's involvement in the case. That alone was enough to make Kincaid want to stir the pot. "You have any objection?"

"I—I was going to look at flats at lunchtime," Cullen said, and

Kincaid had the distinct impression he'd been about to say something else.

"Good for you," Kincaid told him with cheerful bonhomie. "About time you made a change, Doug. But I think you'll have to do it another day."

After a more thorough look through the case file, Kincaid had rung DI Neal Weller. A brusque message on Weller's voice mail informed him that Weller was in court and would return calls as soon as possible.

"Court," Kincaid said to Cullen, who grimaced.

"That might take him out all day. Or longer."

"Might not be a bad thing." Kincaid didn't mind gathering his own impressions of the case before he discussed it with Weller, starting with the crime scene. Not that he expected to find evidence that the SOCOs had missed, but he always liked to see where a death had taken place, even if he was coming into a case after the fact. It helped him organize his mental landscape.

"We'll start with Haggerston Park," he told Cullen. "Call down for a car, and I'll clear things with the guv'nor."

"Will your personal connection cause any conflict of interest?" his chief superintendent, Denis Childs, had asked when Kincaid was shown into his office.

"Not unless our friend Tim Cavendish starts to look like a suspect," Kincaid had answered. In fact, the personal connection might give Kincaid an advantage denied another detective. "I'll let you know if I think there's a problem," he'd assured Childs.

Once he'd finished his meeting with Childs and found the car ready, he had Cullen drive them east, skirting round the top of the City, through Shoreditch and into Bethnal Green.

Haggerston Park looked benign, if a little faded by the August heat. Young Asian parents strolled with babies in push chairs; a passing jogger swigged from a water bottle; an elderly white couple walked arm in arm, soaking up the sun.

As they drove past Hackney City Farm, Kincaid caught the unmistakable whiff of manure. The smell, etched into the sensory circuits of his childhood, triggered a spasm of longing for the dairy fields of Cheshire. And then the thought of home led him to wonder what he would tell his mother the next time she asked about plans for the wedding.

Gemma had been more and more evasive on the subject, not to mention prickly in general, and now there was the business with her mother . . . Not that he wasn't concerned about Vi, but it worried him deeply that family stresses seemed to make Gemma pull away from him, rather than drawing her closer. At least she'd been voluble enough in talking to him about this case. Perhaps the investigation would give him an opportunity to get her to open up about whatever was bothering her. If formalizing their relationship was going to change things between them, he'd rather go on as they were.

Checking the map against the case report, he directed Cullen into Audrey Street, where they parked and got out. The scene had been cleared. A strip of crime scene tape hung limply from the iron gate at the park entrance, and a placard to one side held the previous day's date and asked that anyone having seen suspicious activity at that location report it to the police help line.

Kincaid followed the path, taking in the details, until he reached the section of broken fence still marked off-limits by tape—not that a strip of tape would keep kids and curiosity seekers at bay.

"A good spot for a rape or a mugging, at least after dark," said Cullen, studying the terrain. "Or a drug deal gone wrong, a gang knifing. But odd for a suicide."

"Or a murder." Kincaid walked farther along, until the trees thinned and he could see the land curving away towards Hackney City Farm. He then went back and examined the taped area, thinking about the scene photos included in the file. "What was this guy doing here?" he mused. "Meeting someone?"

"And then he just dropped dead?" Cullen tested the fence a few feet outside the taped area. "I don't think the weight of a body falling would have broken the fence."

"Unless it was already damaged. We'll have to check with the groundskeepers. And I want to talk to the pathologist myself. But first let's have a word with Mr. Malik's partner."

"It's not far," said Cullen, having taken over navigation while Kincaid drove. "Just this side of Bethnal Green Road."

"That might make a bit more sense of Malik being found in the park." Following Cullen's directions, Kincaid pulled up in front of an undistinguished building in a side street off Warner Place. It was the second house in a rather grimy terrace. Gray-brown brick, blue door and blue trim work. Lettering over the ground-floor windows read MALIK & PHILLIPS, SOLICITORS, and to one side, a little more discreetly, there was a phone number.

Kincaid pulled into the curb and got out. Studying the shop front while waiting for Cullen to come round the car, he peered through a gap in the miniblinds, but saw nothing but shadows. He pressed the buzzer, and after a moment the door released. He pushed it open and entered a small hallway, Cullen close on his heels. To their left, an open door led into the reception area he'd glimpsed through the blinds.

The room was empty, but it looked more inviting from the inside than it had from the window. Comfortably worn brown leather chairs and sofa, a serviceable desk, an industrial-grade Berber carpet, but the room was clean, and the freshly painted cream walls held imaginatively hung canvas reproductions of Banksy street art. An interesting choice for a solicitor, Kincaid thought, the ultimate outlaw artist.

A female voice called from upstairs. "Naz, you forget your keys again? Why the hell didn't you ring me—" A woman peered down at them from the first-floor landing. "Sorry. I thought you were my partner. He's late, and the receptionist isn't in today. Can I help you? We usually see clients by appointment." The tone was slightly disapproving. She started down the stairs, and as she came into the light cast by the glass transom in the front door, Kincaid saw that she was dark skinned, and West Indian rather than Asian. She was a little too thin, and wore a navy business suit with a plain white blouse. Her dark hair looked as if it had been straightened, and was pulled back in an unflattering knot. As she reached the bottom of the stairs, he caught the reek of stale cigarette smoke.

"You're Louise Phillips?" He held out his warrant card. "Superintendent Kincaid. Sergeant Cullen. Scotland Yard."

"Scotland Yard?" She stared at him. "If this is about Azad, you know I can't talk to you. Unless"—she took a sharp little breath and her eyes widened—"is it Sandra? Are you here about Sandra?"

So she didn't yet know what had happened. Naz Malik's death had made a paragraph that morning in one of the tabloids, but it was probably not the sort of paper Louise Phillips read, and Naz's death hadn't been violent enough to get more mention. "Mrs. Phillips, is there somewhere we could talk?" he asked.

"It's *Ms.*," she corrected. "I'm not married. Not that my marital status should be anyone's business." The little speech seemed rote, tossed off while she gathered her thoughts. She glanced into the reception area, then shook her head, rejecting it although it looked the obvious spot. "Come upstairs, then. I suppose we can talk in my office."

Turning, she led them up the stairs. The cigarette smell intensified as they climbed, and as they entered the first-floor office, Kincaid saw why. A plastic pub ashtray held place of honor on the cluttered desk. It was filled with cigarette ends, and one lipstick-smeared specimen had burned to ash in the slotted edge. The room was not much more attractive. Scuffed and untidy, it lacked any of the reception area's charm, and in spite of the heat, its two windows were shut.

Louise Phillips waved an ineffective hand at the fug in the air. "Naz is always getting on at me, but it's *my* office and I don't know why I should have to be politically correct."

Kincaid managed a smile, wondering how much exposure to secondhand smoke it took to contract lung cancer, and sat in one of the metal and faux-leather chairs that fought to occupy space between boxes stuffed with files. Cullen freed another chair, and Phillips sank down behind her desk with the apparent relief of one returning to charted territory, or at least escaping from a smoke-free zone.

"Are you sure you don't want to wait and talk to Naz?" she said. "Whatever it is—I can't imagine why he's late. He's never late—"

"Ms. Phillips," Kincaid broke in. It was always better to get it over with quickly. "We can't talk to your partner. I'm sorry, but Naz Malik is dead."

"What?" Phillips stared at him, and her dark skin seemed to go slightly gray. "You're joking." She swallowed, pressing her fingers to her lips as she shook her head. "No. You said 'police.' You don't joke. But I don't understand. When? How? Was it an accident?"

"We think not."

"But—" Reaching for a packet of Silk Cut on her desk, Phillips fumbled a cigarette free and lit it with a cheap plastic lighter. Through an exhaled stream of smoke, she squinted at him. "No, it wouldn't be, not if you're Scotland Yard. And you said you were a superintendent. Major crimes unit, I should think."

Kincaid fought the impulse to cough as the smoke reached him. Out of the corner of his eye he saw Cullen, who had got out his notebook, glance at the window. Giving Cullen an infinitesimal shake of the head, he said, "Ms. Phillips, when did you last talk to your partner?"

"Friday. Friday afternoon. We've been working on a case that goes to trial next week. We had a meeting with the barrister in his chambers. Naz was—" Her voice wavered. "I can't believe it." She ground out the barely smoked cigarette, then lit another. "I'd been trying to ring him since yesterday. Couldn't figure out why his phone was turned off—it went straight to voice mail. I left him a message this morning. I couldn't believe he was late." She looked at them in appeal. "What's happened to him?"

"We're not sure, Ms. Phillips," Kincaid answered. "Do you know of any reason why your partner would have been in Haggerston Park?"

"Haggerston? No. Except Naz and Sandra used to take Charlotte to the farm sometimes, or for walks . . ."

"Did the park have any special significance for them?"

"No, not that I know of. They often had family outings to places in the area. But Naz isn't really the nature type on his own . . ." Louise Phillips stood and began to pace in the small space behind her desk. "Look, you're absolutely sure it's Naz? There could be a mistake—"

"Detective Inspector Weller, who investigated Sandra Gilles's disappearance, identified the body."

"Weller." Phillips grimaced. "Yes, he would know Naz. But why are you asking about Haggerston? Is that where he was . . . found? What happened to him? You still haven't told me."

Patiently, Kincaid said, "Mr. Malik left his daughter with her nanny on Saturday afternoon, saying he would be back shortly. His friend Tim Cavendish reported him missing when both he and the daughter's nanny began to worry. Mr. Malik's body was found by a passerby in Haggerston Park yesterday morning. The pathologist has not made a ruling on the cause of death."

"Yesterday?" Louise Phillips whispered. "Why didn't anyone tell me?"

"I believe you're ex-directory, Ms. Phillips? Unless DI Weller had your home number?" Kincaid remembered Gemma telling him she'd tried without success to find Phillips's home number.

"Oh, no. Weller never asked. It never occurred to me that he'd need it. And I—I never imagined . . . I never imagined anything happening to Naz . . ."

"Did your partner seem particularly upset about anything the last time you spoke?"

She hesitated. "I wouldn't say *upset*. We'd been . . . . It's this case." Phillips sat down again and lit another Silk Cut. With an apologetic glance at Kincaid, Cullen set his notebook on a file case and went to the window.

"Do you mind?" he asked Phillips.

"Stuck shut," she answered. "Naz was . . . Naz nagged at me to get it fixed, but I—I didn't want—I don't know why I was so bloody-minded about it." She stubbed out the cigarette, and Cullen retreated to his chair, having scored at least a minor victory.

"The case?" Kincaid prompted.

"We're representing a Bangladeshi restaurant owner named Ahmed Azad. He owns a curry house just off Brick Lane. He's accused of importing young people and forcing them to work without pay in his home and restaurant."

"House slaves?" Cullen looked surprised.

"Well, the home charge will be harder for the prosecution to prove. He's sponsored these young men and women—they would have to testify that he's forcing them to work without pay, and not allowing them to seek employment elsewhere."

"But they won't?" guessed Kincaid.

Phillips rolled her eyes. "It's *alleged* that he threatened to rescind his sponsorship, which would result in their deportation. And it's *alleged* that if they seek other employment, he threatens to harm their relatives back in Sylhet. Of course, they're not going to talk."

"But somebody did."

"A couple of ex-employees from the restaurant. They seem to have a grudge against him over some back wages. And there was a young man, a second cousin, I think, who was working as a dishwasher. He agreed to testify that Azad refused to pay him, and had threatened them. But he seems to have, um, disappeared, so the prosecution's case is looking a bit weak."

"The man sounds an obvious crook," said Cullen.

"He's our *client*," corrected Phillips wearily. "If we only repre-sented model citizens, we'd soon be out of business."

"A witness disappeared, Ms. Phillips?" Kincaid asked sharply. "When?"

"Two weeks ago. We only learned about it when Customs and Im-migration questioned Azad. They'd been keeping this boy, the cousin or nephew or whatever he was, under wraps."

"Apparently with good reason."

Phillips shrugged. "He probably just decided that getting his own back against Azad wasn't worth deportation."

"And you don't think that Customs and Immigration will have offered him a deal?"

"We're not privy to that information," Phillips said rather primly. "But . . . Naz wasn't happy. It was too close to home, the disappear-ance. We'd had— Things had been a bit tense in the office lately. Friday . . ."

Leaning forwards, Kincaid schooled his face into a sympathetic expression, concealing his interest. "You had a row?"

"I wouldn't exactly call it a row." She reached for the cigarettes, then stopped, as if making an effort to control the urge. Kincaid wondered how much of her smoking was due to nicotine addiction and how much was nervous habit, merely something to do with her hands. Without the easy prop, she resorted to twisting the ring she wore on her right hand. Her nails were short, the cuticles ragged, as if she bit them. "A disagreement, if that. It was just—Naz wasn't sure he wanted to go on representing Azad. I told him that was bol-locks. We were committed, and we needed the money. We couldn't afford his scruples. He—" She clamped her lips tight, hands sud-denly still.

"He what, Ms. Phillips?" Kincaid tone was firm.

"It's just that, since Sandra disappeared, Naz has been . . . different. Well, naturally you'd expect that, but . . . We've known each other since law school. We've been partners for ten years. We were good together. But lately . . . Naz had been something of a liability. He couldn't concentrate. Anything would send him off on a tangent, get his hopes up about Sandra. Or make him unreasonable, like this business with Azad. But I thought he'd adjust, somehow . . ."

"You thought he'd adjust to the loss of his wife? You didn't think she'd come back?"

"No." Phillips's answer was flat. "Sandra Gilles wasn't the type to walk away from everything she'd worked for. We had *that* in common, Sandra and I."

"Not even if she'd had an affair?" Kincaid asked.

"An affair? No." Phillips shook her head. "There was speculation, of course, when she disappeared, that she'd run off with a man, but I never believed it. Sandra was no saint, and I'm sure she and Naz had their differences over the years, but she'd never have left— Oh, God." She stared at Kincaid, wide-eyed. "Charlotte. What's happened to Charlotte?"

Gemma popped a CD of Handel anthems in the little player she kept in her office, hoping the music would propel her through the Monday-morning deluge of reports on her screen. But as the voices soared, she closed her eyes, mouse in hand, and let the music wash over her.

It made her think of Winnie, and of the small and perfect wedding she'd imagined, with Winnie officiating, and for a moment she indulged in the daydream. Then she opened her eyes and turned down the volume, chastising herself for her selfishness in putting her wishes over concern for Winnie's health. She would ring Glastonbury this evening and check up on her, and that, she realized reluctantly, meant she'd have to tell Winnie and Jack about her mum as well.

She'd rung her mum at the hospital last night and first thing that morning, getting the chipper *I'm just fine, dearie* speech both times. She'd just made up her mind that as soon as she could decently duck out of the office, she was going to see for herself, when there was a tap on her door and Melody Talbot came in. They'd spoken only in passing at the department briefing that morning, a busy one, as intense heat always seemed to increase their caseload, and the buzz of excitement over the approaching carnival had added to the ferment.

"Boss," said Melody, closing the door, "got a minute?"

Gemma glanced down at the report she'd been reading. A boy had been knifed near the Ladbroke Grove tube station on Saturday night, and although he'd survived, he was refusing to name his attackers. She sighed, sympathizing with the investigating officers' frustration, and with a click reassigned the case to a team who were working two similar incidents. They might very well be connected.

Then she smiled at Melody, blanked the computer screen, and switched off the CD. "I'm all yours. What's up?"

"Um." Melody hesitated, unusual for an officer who was usually the model of efficiency. Curious, Gemma nodded towards a chair. Melody sat, looking deceptively demure in her navy skirt and white blouse. She'd already shed her suit jacket. Not even Melody could keep up her standards of crispness in this heat. "It's about Saturday night," she said, still not meeting Gemma's eyes.

"Melody, what on earth are you talking about?" asked Gemma, baffled.

"I missed your call, and I never rang you back. It was a family dinner. I had my phone turned off, and then didn't think to check messages."

"Oh, that. I'd completely forgotten." Gemma realized she was sweating and shrugged out of her light cotton cardigan. "You weren't on duty, Melody. There's no need to apologize. You have a right to personal time."

"But if you'd needed me . . ."

"As it turned out, I don't think there was anything you could have done." She told Melody about Tim's call and what had followed, but even as she reassured Melody, she felt a flicker of doubt. If Naz Malik had still been alive when she'd rung Melody, was there some way they might have found him in time? She shook her head, telling herself that was useless speculation, and finished her story.

"You got the little girl placed with Wesley's mum?" said Melody. She was sitting forward, on the edge of her chair now, interest apparently having banished her momentary awkwardness. "Brilliant. How's she doing?"

"As well as you could expect, I think. Although I'm not sure what you *would* expect." Gemma thought of Charlotte as she'd left her yesterday afternoon, sobbing in Betty's arms, and remembered how she had hated to let the child go. "She'll be all right," Betty had reassured her. "It's just she's had a long day, and she feels safe with you."

"I'll come see you tomorrow," Gemma had promised Charlotte, kissing her damp, sticky cheek.

"I've promised to visit her again today," she told Melody. "And I've got to check on my mum. She's in hospital since yesterday."

"I'm sorry, boss," Melody said quickly. "Anything I can do?"

The flash of concern in Melody's eyes made her feel a surge of panic. "No. No, it's nothing major," she said. "She has a little low-grade infection. Her immune system's depressed from the chemo. And they're putting in a port for the treatments—" She stopped, aware that she was rattling on to reassure herself rather than Melody. "I'm sure she'll be fi—"

Her mobile rang, rescuing her. But when she saw Betty Howard's name on the caller ID, she excused herself, feeling the same instant prickle of worry she got when one of boys' schools rang. "Betty, hi," she answered quickly. "Is everything all right?"

She listened for a moment, frowning, tapping a pen on her desk, then said, "Let me check into it. I'll ring you back."

"Is something wrong?" asked Melody when Gemma ended the call.

"I don't know." Gemma frowned. "Betty says she got a call from the social worker, Janice Silverman. Silverman said she contacted Charlotte's grandmother, who told her she wanted nothing to do with Charlotte. But later this morning, Sandra's sister, a woman named Donna Woods, rang her up. She says she wants to take Charlotte."

"But surely that's a good thing," said Melody. "The child should be with family."

"Yes, well, maybe," Gemma said slowly. "But it depends on the family." It occurred to her that the idea of Toby and Kit in her own sister's care horrified her—although they wouldn't be mistreated, they wouldn't be cared for the way she would look after them. And a blood relationship was certainly no guarantee of love, as Kit's experience with his grandmother had taught them all too painfully. "According to Tim, Naz and Sandra were adamant about not wanting Charlotte to have any contact with Sandra's family," she continued. "And we don't know anything about this sister."

"We?" Melody looked at her quizzically.

"The police. Social services. You know what I mean," she added, a little exasperated.

Melody scrutinized her a bit longer, as if debating, then said, "Well, what it sounds like to me is that *you* don't want to let Charlotte Malik out of your sight."

CHAPTER ELEVEN

*The British Bangladeshi population has therefore described
itself in several different ways during the last sixty years:
Indian, Pakistani, Bengali, Bangladeshi. Nowadays the last
two terms are used interchangeably. In addition, many use
the term "sylheti" to describe themselves, this being the part
of Bangladesh from which most British Bangladeshi families
originate.*

—Geoff Dench,
Kate Gavron,
Michael Young,
The New East End

Kincaid didn't like not having his own team on the ground from the
beginning of an investigation, but as Bethnal Green had got in first,
it made sense to run the incident room from Bethnal Green Police
Station. And he wanted Weller whether Weller wanted him or not,
so once the DI was out of court he'd have to put up with a new SIO
on his patch.

He'd set up in a conference room with a computer terminal and
a whiteboard, assigning an officer to man the public phone line and

another to correlate the statements taken from witnesses in the park. Then he'd had the very attractive DS Singh bring him every bit of information on file regarding Naz Malik and Sandra Gilles.

He handed the Malik files to Cullen and started in on the disappearance of Sandra Gilles himself, reading with interest. People did simply vanish, of course; one only had to read the missing persons files. But in most cases, enough digging would unearth a trigger—a row, depression, financial problems—or a witness would report some small thing that gave credence to a theory of violence. But Sandra Gilles, successful artist, devoted wife, and adoring mother, just seemed to have been swallowed by the earth on that bright Sunday afternoon in May. There must have been something more.

He read through the e-mail Gemma had sent him, describing in detail the events of the weekend. Then he compared Gemma's notes with the brief report DI Weller had filed. There was no mention in Weller's report of Tim Cavendish's comments about Sandra Gilles's alleged affair with a man named Lucas Ritchie. Why?

Tim had referred to Ritchie as a club owner, but if he had mentioned its name, Gemma hadn't caught it. Kincaid dialed Tim Cavendish on his mobile, heard the surprise in Tim's voice when he said he had questions about the case. "Yes, I've got my fingers in the pie now," he told Tim, but didn't elaborate. "Tim, about this Lucas Ritchie bloke—did Naz tell you anything else? The name of the club?"

"No. Look, I shouldn't have said—"

"Don't be daft, man," Kincaid interrupted. "You should have told Gemma on Saturday. I'll ring you back."

He called in Sergeant Singh. "Does the name Lucas Ritchie mean anything to you? Owns an exclusive private club in the area?"

She shook her head, but her brown eyes were alert, her expression interested. "No, sir. But I can run a search of local business records."

He gave her a friendly smile. "Do that, why don't you, Sergeant. And get straight back to me with the results." He was treading carefully here. It wasn't a good idea to openly criticize Weller to his staff, but he didn't want any failures of communication.

"Yes, sir," Singh answered, a slight frown creasing her smooth forehead. Pondering the implications, Kincaid thought. A bright girl. "Oh, but, sir," she added, "I was just coming in to tell you. Dr. Kaleem, the pathologist, rang. He wanted to speak to DI Weller, but since he's not available at the moment—"

"Sergeant," Kincaid interrupted her firmly. "I know it's a bit awkward for you, but I'm in charge of the Malik investigation now, so anything comes directly to me. I'm sure DI Weller will have a chance to make that clear when he comes in. Now, where would I find Dr. Kaleem?"

"At the London, sir."

"I want you to set up the team in charge of going over the Maliks' house," Kincaid told Cullen as they drove the short distance to the Royal London. "I want our lads, not Bethnal Green. And I want them to go through everything with a fine-tooth comb, including any records of Sandra Gilles's business transactions. The one thing we do know about this Ritchie is that he was one of Sandra Gilles's clients."

Glancing at his watch as the bulk of the hospital came into view, Kincaid added, "Oh, and, Doug, drop me at the front and I'll meet you at the mortuary in about ten minutes."

Cullen glanced at him for an instant, then shifted his gaze back to the road. "Right, guv."

"It will probably take you that long to park in this warren," Kincaid said, but didn't offer any further explanation. He wasn't in the mood to discuss Gemma's personal business with Doug, especially considering Cullen's pouting over Gemma's involvement in the case.

He jumped out of the car as Cullen stopped on the double yellows in front of the main building. Admittedly, the hospital's venerable original building was quite hideous, but looking at the disparate styles of the mushrooming annexes, Kincaid couldn't help but think the planners would have been better served by sticking with uniform ugliness.

A quick query at the main information desk sent him outside again, and a brisk walk took him to the building that housed Vi Walters's ward. He found her alone, and dozing, but when he came in she opened her eyes and gave him a delighted smile. "Duncan! What are you doing here? Did you come all this way to see me?"

He kissed her cheek. "I was in the neighborhood. A new case," he said. "But I couldn't pass up a chance to check on you and make sure you were behaving yourself. I can't stay long." He was waffling, he knew, covering his shock. She seemed to have shrunk since he'd last seen her, and her skin was almost translucent. Her left arm was neatly bandaged.

"Sit, then," she said. "You look wilted as an old lettuce. Is it hot?"

He stayed beside the bed, hand on the rail. "Broiling." Thank God the wards had air-conditioning.

"You'd never know it in here." Vi gave a shiver, and he realized that her bed was heaped with blankets. "Always did like a touch of the sun," she added, a little wistfully.

"Well, you should be home soon, and you can toast yourself to your heart's content."

Vi started to lift her bandaged arm, then seemed to think better of it and waggled her fingers at him instead. "Maybe tomorrow. I've got my own personal plug, as of this morning. No more sticking me black and blue with needles."

Gemma had told him about the chemo port, and he wasn't at all sure that was a good sign. "You're brilliant," he said. "A regular bionic woman. Gemma's coming in to admire the handiwork a bit later, I think."

"She shouldn't come all this way." Vi sounded a little fretful. "I've told her a dozen times."

"I'm glad she listens to you," he tossed back, grinning.

"Oh, go on with you." Vi shook her head, but her smile was back. "Give us another kiss, then, and go on about your business."

When he leaned down and touched his cheek to hers, it was cool. At least she no longer had a fever. "I'll see you soon."

"Duncan." She touched his hand as he straightened up. "About Gemma. You know she's been stubborn as a mule since she was in nappies. Don't let her balk."

Kincaid gave her a gentle squeeze in return. "And you know as well as I do that no one can *make* Gemma do anything."

If it had been cold on Vi's ward, it was arctic in the hallway leading to the mortuary. Kincaid pulled up the knot of his tie and shrugged the lapels of his jacket a little closer together, wondering if the denizens of these depths lived in thermal underwear. But a consultant wearing a coat and tie walked briskly towards him, showing no evidence of Eskimo bundling. The man gave a curt nod as they passed, shoulders almost brushing, but Kincaid stopped. "Dr. Kaleem?"

"What?" The consultant looked startled.

"Can you tell me where to find Dr. Kaleem?"

"Oh. Office just down the hall. No one could miss it." The tone was impatient, as if implying that no one sensible would have had to ask.

"Thanks," Kincaid said, shrugging as he went on. Suddenly, he caught the distinctive smell that had been masked by the cold, decay compounded with chemicals, and he heard Cullen's voice. Then, when he reached the office, he saw that the passing consultant might have been referring to the office itself rather than Kincaid's navigational abilities.

Books covered the shelves, made towers on the floor, and overflowed the surface of the desk, where a computer monitor looked as if it were fighting for its life. File boxes were interspersed with the books, and the only visible spot on the wall was covered with an intricate bit of graffiti art. There were no chairs other than the one behind the desk.

Louise Phillips's office sprang to Kincaid's mind, but while Phillips's clutter had seemed indicative of carelessness, this room somehow conveyed enthusiasm, as if its occupant's interests had overruled the limits of the physical space.

The voice he'd heard responding to Cullen's was male, with a cut-glass accent, and now seemed to be coming from beneath the desk. "Bloody printer's jammed." There was a thump, then a whir, followed by an exclamation of satisfaction. "Kicking it sometimes helps. I love technology."

A man emerged, holding a sheaf of papers victoriously aloft. Kincaid grinned. No wonder Coat-and-Tie had radiated disapproval. For if this was Dr. Kaleem, the pathologist was at the very least a sartorial nonconformist. He wore a faded, rock band T-shirt and tattered jeans, and his blue-black hair was gelled into spikes. He was also, as Gemma had curiously failed to mention, extraordinarily good-looking.

"Rashid Kaleem," he confirmed, transferring the papers to his left hand and reaching across the desk to shake Kincaid's right. "You must be Superintendent Kincaid. Sergeant Cullen here has been telling me you're taking over from DI Weller." He glanced round, as if thinking of asking them to sit, then propped himself on a corner of his desk, pushing a stack of books precariously aside as he did so.

"I was telling Sergeant Cullen," Kaleem continued, "that I managed to rush the tox scans. I was curious about this case." He tapped a page. "Your victim was loaded with Valium, which was not too surprising."

"Then he did commit suicide," said Cullen, sounding almost disappointed.

"No, wait." Kaleem waved the papers at them. "That's not all. I found ketamine as well, and while the high concentration of the two drugs could certainly prove fatal, it's an unlikely suicide cocktail."

Kincaid stared at him. "What the hell was Naz Malik doing with ketamine in his system?" The veterinary tranquilizer was cheap and popular as a street drug, and made veterinary clinics obvious targets for robbery.

"It's possible he might have taken the Valium, valid prescription or not, and bought the ketamine off a street dealer to boost the high. In which case, he might have died from an accidental overdose," said Kaleem.

"But you don't think so."

"No. This guy would have been out of it. It's like I told the old— It's like I told DI Weller. I don't believe the victim could have got himself into the park in his condition, and there was no evidence indicating that he took pills or used a needle on the site. Nor did I find any puncture marks on the body. So my guess is that somebody walked him, or half carried him, to the spot where he was found. And then there's the head."

Kincaid frowned. "What about it? There was no evidence of trauma."

"I explained to the DI from Notting Hill—" Kaleem paused, a little smile turning up the corners of his mouth, as if he was remembering something pleasant. "People don't just fall with their noses in the dirt." All trace of amusement vanished, and Kaleem's handsome face hardened. "I think he was helpless. I think someone held his head in that position, with his breathing compromised, and waited for him to suffocate. And that is very, very nasty indeed."

"Why haven't I met you before?" Kincaid asked when they had gone over the rest of the report with Kaleem.

"I worked the Midlands for almost eight years. I've only been back in London about ten months, although I grew up here, in Bethnal Green. The prodigal returns, and all that."

The pathologist must be older than he looked, Kincaid surmised.

But he was, as Gemma had been, impressed with Rashid Kaleem. Glancing up at the spray-painted wall, he asked, "That yours?"

"Have to keep my skills up," Kaleem said with a grin.

"Nobody minds?"

"Nobody comes down here voluntarily. Look." He stopped them as they turned to leave. "About Weller. He did the right thing turning this over to you. He's a good copper, but this—I think this is something that's out of his league. Just watch yourselves."

Gemma sat through what seemed another interminable staff meeting, fighting post-lunch dullness as she listened to Sergeant Talley trying to micromanage everyone else's cases. She'd had trouble with the career sergeant repeatedly, and she supposed it was time to have another little talk. But it was better done privately, in her office.

She wondered, not for the first time, why Melody Talbot, who was much more competent than most of the department's sergeants, was content to stay a detective constable. Gemma had broached the subject of promotion a few times, telling Melody she'd be glad to make a recommendation, but Melody had merely smiled, said she'd think about it, and never raised the subject again. It seemed odd, as everything else about Melody's performance and character marked her as a highflier.

Gemma had decided she was going to have to interrupt the long-winded sergeant when her phone clattered and scooted across the conference table like a crab, then beeped stridently. So much for the inconspicuous Vibrate option. Aware of all eyes on her, Gemma grabbed the mobile and read the text message from Kincaid, a succinct *Ring me.*

"I'll have to take this," she said, escaping gladly into the corridor.

"You've just rescued me from staffing hell," she said when he answered. "What's up?"

"And I've just had a meeting with your pathologist," Kincaid said.

"*My* pathologist?" Gemma decided to ignore the teasing note. "Dr. Kaleem? What did he say?"

"Naz Malik was pumped full of Valium and ketamine."

"Ketamine? You think it was suicide, then," said Gemma, "or accidental overdose." She felt an odd stab of regret. Not of course that she wanted Naz Malik to have been murdered—that was unthinkable—but she hated the idea that he could have willingly abandoned Charlotte to an unknown fate.

Kincaid interrupted her thoughts. "No, actually, Kaleem doesn't believe the drugs were self-administered." He went on to detail the pathologist's reasoning. "Kaleem's adamant. And if he's right, it means that we not only have a murder that was premeditated, we have a murderer who was willing to bide his time and watch Naz Malik die."

Gemma digested this, feeling ice down her spine. "He?"

"Grammatically speaking."

"A man is more likely, if Kaleem believes Naz was walked or carried into the park."

"Malik wasn't a particularly large man. A strong woman might have managed. Or two people."

"But how would you get the drugs into an unwilling victim?" she asked.

"I'd assume the Valium could have been administered in drink or food, at least enough to make the victim compliant," Kincaid said. "I don't know about the ketamine. We'll have to talk to Kaleem again."

"We?" said Gemma with a little jolt of excitement.

Kincaid responded with a question of his own. "You're planning to visit your mum this afternoon, right? So you'll be in the East End. And you've met the nanny—" She heard a rustle of paper, as if he were checking notes. "Alia Hakim. I'll need to interview her, and I thought it would be helpful if you came along."

Kincaid had given Gemma the address of the council estate in Bethnal Green where Alia lived with her parents. It was not a high-rise, Gemma saw with relief, and the brown brick blocks were interspersed with panels of turquoise plaster. If the council had intended to add a note of cheer, it seemed the residents had responded in kind. There was an unusually well-kept common lawn. Flags of laundry hung bleaching in the sun on balconies and the ground-floor patios, amid hanging baskets and the inevitable chained bikes.

The Hakims lived in a ground-floor flat at one end of a unit, with access through a gated front patio fenced with eight-foot-high chicken wire. Shrubs had been planted outside the fence, and beside the gate, a half whisky barrel planter held a large palm. A framework of wooden slats had been built over the garden to hold a canvas canopy, now rolled back, and the garden itself held flowering plants, clotheslines, and a motley collection of children's toys. The Hakims had extended their living space quite efficiently, Gemma thought as she waited for Kincaid to join her.

Watching him cross the lawn, she saw that he'd discarded his tie altogether and had rolled up the sleeves of his pale pink dress shirt. He wore sunglasses, and the sun sparked gold from his chestnut hair.

"It's blistering," he said when he reached her, tucking the sunglasses into his shirt pocket.

"You look like you should be in Miami," she said, repressing the sudden desire to touch his face. "I like the glasses."

"If it were Miami, there would be ocean. And we would be in it." He studied her. "Not looking forward to this, are you? I spoke to Mrs. Hakim on the phone. She said Alia's very upset. Her father's taken off work."

Gemma frowned, thinking of the offhand comments Alia had

made about her parents. "Not necessarily a good thing, I suspect," she murmured. "But best to get on with it. Where's Doug?"

"Gone back to the Yard to do some research on one of Naz Malik's pending cases. I'll fill you in later."

Both the gate and the flat's front door were open, the doorway protected by a swinging curtain of beads. Gemma and Kincaid entered the garden, but before they could ring the bell, the beads parted and Alia came out. Today, although dressed in jeans and a long-sleeved yellow blouse, she wore the hijab. Her face looked pale and puffy against the head scarf, and the heavy frames of her glasses didn't quite disguise the fact that her eyes were red from weeping.

"Alia," said Gemma, "this is Superintendent Kincaid. We just need to talk to you for a bit."

The girl glanced at Kincaid, then ducked her head and whispered to Gemma, "Is Charlotte okay? I've been so worried."

"She's fine," Gemma assured her. "She's with a good friend of mine." She didn't mention Sandra's sister's petition. "How are you doing?"

Alia touched Gemma's sleeve and dropped her voice further. "I didn't tell my parents I was keeping Charlotte on Saturday. They don't like—my *abba*—"

"Alia," called a man's firm voice. "Bring your visitors inside."

"Coming, Abba." To Gemma, she whispered, "Do I have to—"

"Yes, I'm afraid you do," Gemma said.

With a resigned nod, Alia held the curtain aside, and Gemma and Kincaid entered the flat.

Except for a box of toys, the sitting room reflected none of the jumble of the front garden. There was a three-piece suite in a floral print and a coffee table made from a brass tray on a stand, and center stage against the far wall an enormous flat-screen TV played a Bollywood channel with the sound off. Gemma wondered if the flat had been tidied especially for their visit.

Shelves held colorful Eastern knickknacks, but there were no visible books or magazines. On a side table, a rotating fan pulled in warm, sluggish air and feebly distributed it round the room. Gemma saw that Alia's upper lip was beaded with sweat, but didn't know if the girl was suffering from nerves or the heat.

The woman sitting on the sofa was an older, rounder version of Alia. She, like her daughter, concealed her hair with a scarf, but she wore a matching orange *salwar kameez* rather than Western dress. As she gave them a shy smile, a man Gemma assumed must be Alia's father came into the room from the kitchen, wiping his hands on a tea towel.

"Mr. Hakim?" Kincaid held out his hand. "I'm Superintendent Kincaid. This is Inspector James. Thank you for seeing us."

"It is our duty." Having draped the towel over a chair in the small dining area, Mr. Hakim grasped Kincaid's hand, but appeared not to see Gemma's. Short and stocky like his wife and daughter, he had thick, dark hair going gray, and a severe mustache. His white shirt was neatly tucked into dark trousers. "Will you sit, please? My wife will bring tea." Like Alia, he wore thick glasses.

Alia's mother nodded and slipped soundlessly from the room. As Gemma and Kincaid sat side by side on the sofa, Mr. Hakim remained standing, his hands clasped behind his back. He continued, "This is a very bad thing. It is bad for our daughter to be associated with this, and I am hoping your questions can be answered quickly."

Perching on the edge of one of the overstuffed armchairs, Alia tapped a sandaled toe against the carpet. Her toenails were painted a bright coral with pink polka dots, a surprisingly feminine contrast to her plain, un-made-up face. "Abba—"

"Mr. Malik was a man of good character, although we did not think it right for our daughter to be in his house with his wife away. I cannot think how this thing can have happened." *When his wife was away?* Gemma wondered if this was a euphemism, or if Mr. Hakim didn't know that Sandra Gilles had gone missing months earlier.

"Abba," Alia said more forcefully, and this time her father looked at her. "I'm trying to tell you. I was there on Saturday, taking care of Charlotte. I know you don't like me to be there on the weekends, but Naz—Mr. Malik—asked me to come for just a few minutes while he went out." Her accent, in contrast to her father's singsong lilt, seemed even more nasally Estuary than Gemma had noticed before. "I might have—maybe I was the last person to see him alive."

Mr. Hakim's mustache turned down at the corners as he tightened his lips. "You, Alia. If this is true, you have been very disobedient. I think you will have to pay a visit to your auntie in Sylhet if you cannot show respect for your parents' wishes. We have had enough of this nonsense about lawyer school, this going and doing without any sense of what is proper. Your sisters—"

"My sisters have married totally boring men and lead totally boring lives," Alia said vehemently as her mother came back into the room with a tea tray. "All they think about is babies and sweets and the latest Indian pop song—"

"Alia." The sharpness of Kincaid's tone stopped her midword. "You may not have been the last person to see Mr. Malik alive. We think Mr. Malik may have been murdered, and I need you to tell me anything you can remember about that day."

The shock was mirrored on the faces of parents and child, but it was Alia who spoke. "Murdered? Naz murdered? But how— Why—"

"The police pathologist thinks someone gave him drugs and he suff—" Kincaid hesitated, and Gemma guessed he was searching for a more palatable description. "He stopped breathing."

"Drugs?" said Mr. Hakim. "Alia, for you to be involved—"

"I am *not* involved," Alia snapped at him. "And neither was Naz. Naz wouldn't have anything to do with drugs." She turned back to Kincaid and Gemma. "Why would someone do this to him?"

Out of courtesy, Gemma accepted a cup of the tea Mrs. Hakim had poured, sipping gingerly. It was lukewarm, tasted of cardamom, and was teeth-achingly sweet. "Did Naz say or do anything that was different on Saturday?" she asked, glad for an excuse to set down her cup.

"No." Alia shook her head slowly. "But he was . . . distracted. I told him I'd made samosas, and he—he didn't thank me." She carefully avoided meeting either parent's gaze. "He was usually very polite."

Gemma suddenly wondered if there were more to Mr. Hakim's disapproval than fatherly overprotectiveness. Perhaps not on Naz Malik's part, but it was only natural that this rather awkward girl might have developed a crush on her employer, especially if she had romanticized Sandra's disappearance in some way.

"Did he mention anything about a case he was working on?" asked Kincaid. "He was defending a Mr. Azad, a restaurant owner."

"No. Naz—Mr. Malik—never talked about work. Well, only a little, when I'd have questions about my law texts, but then it was only, you know, general. It would have been unethical for him to discuss his clients."

Definitely an echo of hero worship in the slightly prim reply, thought Gemma, but she said, "Alia, did Mr. Malik ever mention a man called Ritchie? Lucas Ritchie?"

"No." Alia frowned. "Who is he?"

"Someone Sandra might have known. Did Mr. Malik ever talk to you about what he thought had happened to Sandra?"

"No. No—well, only at first. The same sort of things you're asking me. 'Did she say anything?' or 'Was there anything different?'"

"Do you know why Naz and Sandra didn't get along with Sandra's family?"

"I— No, not really," said Alia, but her covert glance at her parents was unmistakable. "It wasn't my business," she added, making Gemma even more certain that she had absorbed every detail of Naz Malik's and Sandra Gilles's lives.

"And it is no longer her concern," Mr. Hakim broke in, addressing Kincaid. "I think my daughter has nothing more to tell you, and I must get back to my work."

"Mr. Hakim, we can interview your daughter here, or we can talk to her at the police station. A murder investigation does not revolve around your convenience. And Alia is of age—your presence is not required."

"But I don't know what else I can tell you," said Alia, with another anxious glance at her father, and Gemma thought they'd get no more out of her in these circumstances.

"We appreciate your time, Alia." Having apparently come to the same conclusion, Kincaid stood and pulled a card from his pocket. "If you think of anything else or need to get in touch—"

Alia plucked the card from his hand before her father could reach for it. "I'll walk you out. I'll only be a moment, Abba." She obviously intended to forestall her father with speed, and Gemma just had time to say a quick good-bye to Mrs. Hakim, earning another shy smile. As she followed Kincaid and Alia from the flat, she wondered how much of the conversation Alia's mother had understood.

Alia led them out through the patio garden and onto the lawn, then, when she was out of earshot, turned back so that she could survey the flat. "You have to understand about my father," she said quietly, vehemently. "I don't want you to think badly of him. He is not an uneducated man. In Bangladesh, he had a university degree. And he's a good businessman—he owns a call center in Whitechapel Road. But he works all day with immigrants. He sees himself as an immigrant. His dream is to make enough money to retire in Bangladesh, and he wants . . ." She frowned, as if struggling to work out the words. "He doesn't want anything in *this* life to—to stain *that* one." Alia took a breath and went on, more hurriedly, "But me—I'm British first and Bangladeshi second. It doesn't mean I disrespect my parents or my culture, but it's different for me."

Mrs. Hakim came out of the flat and began hanging laundry on the patio, glancing over at them as she lifted a sheet from her basket.

"Alia," Gemma said urgently, afraid they would be interrupted, or that Alia would lose the nerve to make the confession she was obviously trying so hard to justify. "What is it that you don't want your father to know?"

"My father—he disapproved of Naz and Sandra's marriage, even though Naz was not Muslim. In Abba's eyes it's not right for an Asian to be with a white person. And Sandra—if he knew about her family—he would think I'd disgraced him, just by my connection with them. Even though I don't know them personally." Alia cast a wary eye towards her mother and ran a finger between her chin and the hijab. "It's—what do you call it? Guilt by association."

"What? How?" asked Gemma. "What could be that bad?"

"Drugs," Alia whispered. "Sandra's brothers do drugs."

Kincaid raised an eyebrow. "Alia, half the city does drugs. Surely that's not so unusual—"

"No." Alia shook her head. "You don't understand. I don't mean they smoke a bit of weed or pop X at a party. I heard Naz and Sandra arguing, before Sandra disappeared. Sandra's brothers deal heroin."

CHAPTER TWELVE

> In its heyday, the pub [the Bethnal Green Arms] had been
> the haunt of the Kray twins and various other East End
> underworld figures and thugs. But since then, its popularity
> had dwindled, possibly because the décor and ambience
> dated back to the same period.
>
> —Tarquin Hall,
> *Salaam Brick Lane*

"I have to ring the social worker." Standing in the street with Kincaid, beside their respective cars, Gemma fumbled in her bag for her mobile.

"Slow down, love," Kincaid said. "We have no idea if it's true, to begin with. Could be just a rumor, or could be the girl misheard or misunderstood, or she might even be making things up for a bit of drama. It sounds as if her life is going to be pretty grim without Naz Malik in it."

"Yes, well, maybe so. But I don't think she's making it up. Tim said Sandra didn't get on with her brothers at all."

"That's hearsay, and even if the brothers are involved with drugs,

that doesn't mean Sandra's sister is as well. I'm sure the little girl will
be fine."

"Charlotte. Her name is Charlotte," said Gemma, and was surprised by her own vehemence. "And you can't know that she'll be all
right. She's already lost both parents, at least as far as we know."

He sighed. "Okay, you're right. Call the social worker. But those
decisions are hers to make, not yours. And—" He held up his hand
like a traffic cop to stop her interrupting. "And I'll see what I can dig
up on Sandra Gilles's brothers. According to the reports, they did
have alibis for the time Sandra Gilles disappeared. But we don't know
yet about the day Naz was killed. Now"—he glanced at his watch,
which suddenly seemed to Gemma an infuriating habit—"I've got to
get back to Bethnal Green. I'll ring you if we come up with anything
concrete." He kissed her cheek. "Go see your mum."

Gemma watched as he got in his car, waving to her as he pulled
away. She suddenly felt ridiculous, standing in the sun in the middle
of a street whose name she didn't remember, feeling angry with Kincaid for no reason other than that he had been bossy and slightly
patronizing. If she were going to get her knickers in a twist any time
a man behaved like that, she'd long ago have given up her job. It must
be the worry over her mum getting to her.

She would go to the hospital, of course. But first she was going to
ring Janice Silverman. And then, after she'd seen her mum, she was
going to pay another visit to Tim Cavendish. Tim had been reluctant
to tell them about Sandra's rumored relationship with the mysterious club owner because he was protecting Naz. And if he'd held
back one thing, were there others? Had Naz told him about Sandra's
brothers?

"Okay, what have we got?" Kincaid looked round at the occupants
of the incident room at Bethnal Green station, who looked as bedraggled as the room itself. Polystyrene cups and plastic sandwich

boxes littered the tabletops; papers had drifted out of folders and onto the floor; articles of clothing had been draped over chair backs—all signs of what Kincaid hoped had been a productive afternoon. While he'd been out someone had got the whiteboard organized and tacked up a set of the crime scene photos.

He cleared space to sit on one of the tables as the female constable who'd been taking the public calls said, "Nothing on the phones, sir. A couple of nutters—we'll check them out just in case—but nobody who sounds reliable has reported seeing anything in the park. I've pulled a photo of Naz Malik from the Gilles file and had it copied. We'll get it posted round the park, and will have someone take it door-to-door in the nearby streets as well."

"Nice initiative," Kincaid said, trying not to notice that the constable had stripped down to the barest of tank tops and didn't appear to be wearing a bra. "And you're—"

"Ashley, sir." She pushed a damp wisp of hair into her glossy brown ponytail and smiled. "Detective Constable Ashley Kynaston."

"Newly promoted to CID," put in Sergeant Singh, with the emphasis on *newly,* apparently not disposed to tolerate grandstanding by another attractive female officer.

"I'm beginning to think this is better than working at the Yard," Kincaid murmured to Cullen, who had just come in, but Cullen looked at him blankly. Kincaid sighed. No wonder the poor bugger couldn't get a date.

He addressed the group again. "Okay, no joy there. Anything from forensics?"

"Nothing immediately useful from the park," said Singh, briskly taking charge. "But they've filed samples for comparison in case they're needed later—a few unidentified shreds of cloth as well as the soil and leaf mold. It was too dry for prints. Nor was there anything of note in Mr. Malik's personal effects. The techies have turned the mobile over to us, and I've got someone going through the numbers. All the most recent calls were from his friend Dr. Cavendish, his nanny, and his partner." She spoke without notes, and Kincaid guessed he had her organizational skills to thank for the whiteboard and photos.

"And the house?" he asked.

"Still working on it. We'll need prints for comparison, but there's nothing obvious. They've taken two computers in for analysis."

"All right. They can carry on, but I'll want to have a look myself at anything interesting in the house—papers, diaries, photos." These were the items he always preferred to see himself, as it was often the things you weren't looking for that turned out to be the most helpful. And in this case, particularly, when they might be dealing with not one crime but two, he wanted to get a sense of this couple, this household.

Gemma had seemed to feel a connection with them, and with their child—perhaps too much of a connection, he thought, remembering their last conversation. "Sergeant Singh, when you investigated Sandra Gilles's brothers after she disappeared, was there any suggestion that they were involved with serious drugs? As in dealing?"

"I can tell you that."

Turning, Kincaid saw a man leaning against the doorway, hands in the baggy pockets of his trousers. He still wore the jacket of his gray suit, which stretched across his broad shoulders, but the tail end of his tie hung from the jacket pocket. His graying hair was buzzed short, accentuating the pouches under his eyes.

"DI Weller," said Kincaid.

"Got it in one." Weller came into the room, propping himself on the edge of Singh's table, and Kincaid sensed a subtle shift in the room's alliances, a withdrawal. None of the Bethnal Green crew would want to be seen sucking up to Scotland Yard in front of their boss.

"Kevin and Terry Gilles are not the brightest clams in the pail," Weller went on. "I can't see them doing more than threatening kids for their lunch money. One of them, Kevin, I think it is, has been taken in a few times for disorderly conduct, had his driving license suspended. Apparently has a bit of a problem with his drink, but that's a long way from drug kingpin."

"Duncan Kincaid, by the way. Scotland Yard," Kincaid said, ignoring Weller's slightly mocking tone. The DI was doing a fairly good job of playground bully himself, but they were all going to have to get along nicely if they were to get anything accomplished. "And this is Sergeant Cullen," he added, and Cullen gave Weller a wary nod. Kincaid glanced at his watch, smiled at the rest of the room. "Long day, everyone, and good job. Let's reconvene first thing in the morning, shall we?" He turned back to Weller. "Inspector Weller, can we buy you a drink?"

They sat at one of the few tables squeezed onto the pavement outside a pub in Commercial Street. Kincaid had chosen the establishment because it was within spitting distance of Naz Malik's Fournier Street house and he wanted to check on the forensics team afterwards. Weller had chosen the table on the pavement because he wanted to smoke.

"I quit for six months," Weller admitted when Cullen had gone for their pints. "But my son got married this weekend, and then this case . . ." He shrugged and lit a Benson & Hedges. Squinting past a stream of exhaled smoke, he held out a hand to Kincaid. "It's Neal, by the way. Sorry if we got off on the wrong foot. Bad day."

Cullen returned with three carefully balanced pint glasses and managed to set them down with only a slight slosh. Weller nodded his thanks and held out a hand to him as well. "Neal."

"Doug."

Proper introductions settled, Weller drank, then wiped the foam from his lip. "I was saying. Didn't get a conviction today on a bastard we're certain is a serial rapist. Jury considered the evidence circumstantial and the judge couldn't convince them otherwise. Eighteen-year-old kid looks like a choirboy, and then there was me. Who're they gonna believe?"

"Tough luck," Kincaid agreed.

"For the next woman he lures into an alley." Weller crushed out his cigarette with unnecessary force, then sighed. "But that's neither here nor there, is it? You want to talk about Naz Malik."

"First, I want to talk about Sandra Gilles," Kincaid said. "What do you think happened to her?"

Weller shrugged. "What are the options? One—the most likely— domestic row turned ugly, husband got rid of the evidence. But within an hour of her leaving the kid at Columbia Road, Naz Malik was seen very publicly waiting for his family in a bus-turned-restaurant in Brick Lane. What could he have done with her in that hour? His office wasn't far, but we went over every inch of the place and found nothing. And if she were meeting her husband, why leave the kid? And why not tell the friend at Columbia Road that she was meeting her husband?" Weller drank more of his pint and Cullen shifted in his chair, as if anticipating being sent to fetch the next round.

"So maybe she went home for something, caught her husband unexpectedly in the house with someone else," Cullen suggested.

Weller shook his head. "Again, not enough time. Malik went straight from the restaurant to Columbia Road, took the kid home, and when his wife hadn't turned up by dark, he called the police. When would he have disposed of a body? And there was no evidence in the house. Same as the office, it was clean as a whistle. So, option two." He shook another cigarette from the pack and lit it.

"Sandra Gilles decided she was tired of being a wife and mum and simply disappeared from her life, either on her own or with someone else. It happens. Maybe she hitched a ride and is working as a fry cook at a Little Chef halfway to Scotland. I'd like to think so."

"But you don't," Kincaid said, knowing the answer. "And option three?"

Weller's eyes hardened. "Somebody snatched her off the street in broad daylight. Somebody like that psycho who got off today. Maybe he pulled over in a car, asked for directions, and dragged her in. Maybe everyone just happened to have their lace curtains closed at that very moment. And if that's what happened, God help her. I hope it was quick." He finished his drink in one long draft and Cullen stood up obligingly.

"Guv?" Cullen nodded at Kincaid's glass, but Kincaid shook his head.

When Cullen had gone inside, Kincaid said. "What about her brothers? Apparently Naz thought their alibi was dodgy."

"They were drinking in a pub near the Bethnal Green tube station. Not a nice place, to put it politely. Clientele mostly drunks and punters, and yes, some of them were mates of Kev and Terry. But the landlord didn't care for the brothers, and he vouched for them regardless. And even if their alibi hadn't checked out, what would they have done with her? Kev's car, a clapped-out Ford, was up on blocks on the council estate, and they live with their mum, so it's not likely they took her home."

Cullen came back with a new pint for Weller and a glass of what looked suspiciously like tonic water for himself. "A scrum in there," he said, edging his way past two standing drinkers to slip back into his chair.

The after-work crowd had now spilled out of the pub's open doors. Most of the men and women wore suits, but Kincaid spied a patron or two in jeans and T-shirts, and one girl in full Goth regalia, black fingernails included.

"The City is moving in." Weller eyed the suits with obvious distaste. "I suppose that's a good thing—lowers the crime rate anyway, less work for us. But most of them are bloody wankers. They get jobs at some City bank, buy some overpriced tarted-up flat that's barely been cleared of rats, and they think they belong here."

"So who does belong here?" Kincaid asked, thinking about their earlier conversation with Alia Hakim. "The Bangladeshis? The Somalis? The artists?"

"There is that," Weller agreed. "Not very many true Cockneys left—but what were Cockneys but poor immigrants who shoved out the immigrants who came before them?"

"Must have been a bit glamorous in its day, though, the old East End," said Cullen. "The Kray twins—"

"Vicious bastards. I worked with blokes who'd seen the Krays' handiwork up close—they had stories would make your hair stand on end. No"—Weller glanced round at the crowd—"good riddance to the Krays and their ilk, but just because the villains are less visible doesn't mean they aren't there."

"What about this Ahmed Azad that Naz Malik and his partner were defending?" Kincaid asked.

"Ah, he's a villain, all right, although certainly more civilized than the old-style gangsters. A first-generation immigrant as a teenager, he worked his way up in a relative's restaurant while taking night classes in English and accountancy. Now he owns the restaurant and runs it well. He's a wily old sod, with a foot in both communities."

"Sounds like you know him well."

"He's been the complainant more often than not, when the white gangs have wreaked havoc in Brick Lane. And while it's rumored he has a finger in a number of questionable operations, I haven't heard him linked to murder."

"Louise Phillips told us that the prosecution's star witness in a trafficking charge against him has vanished. If Azad was responsible, and Naz Malik found out—"

Weller shrugged. "If Naz thought Azad had removed a witness, he might have declined the case, but I can't imagine Azad taking out his own lawyer. Might damage his prospects for future representation just a bit."

"What if Naz thought Azad was involved in Sandra's disappearance?"

"Sandra Gilles had no connection with Azad."

"That you know of." Kincaid locked eyes with Weller. "You didn't know about Lucas Ritchie either."

"We questioned everyone who had an immediate connection with Sandra Gilles. But we had no evidence that a crime had actually been committed. We had no reason to go through the woman's client list."

"If you didn't think you had missed something, or that there was a connection between the wife's disappearance and the husband's murder, you wouldn't have called us in."

For a long moment, Weller stared back belligerently, then his shoulders relaxed and he drained his pint. "Point taken," he said, carefully aligning his glass on the beer mat. "Rashid sent me the tox report. If he's right—and he usually is, the smug bastard—it would be a very odd coincidence if Sandra Gilles disappeared and three months later someone just happened to kill her husband. But I'll be damned if I know who to move to the top of the list."

"How about we start with Azad," Kincaid suggested.

Weller frowned. "Butter wouldn't melt in his mouth, Mr. Ahmed Azad. I don't think you'll get very far." He pushed his empty glass aside. "But I can introduce you to him, if you like. He lives right round the corner."

Gemma wasn't sure if her call to Janice Silverman had reassured her or made her more anxious about Charlotte.

"Oh, not to worry about the sister," Silverman had said. "We ran a check on her. She's had half a dozen reports filed against her— neglect, too many boyfriends coming and going, her three little boys showing up at school with the unexplained bruise."

"She still has her kids?"

"For the time being, although they've had a couple of short-term stays in foster care." She sighed. "We can't put half of London permanently in foster care, so we do the best we can. Her caseworker is making regular visits."

Gemma passed on what Alia had told them about Sandra's and Donna's brothers.

"I'll send a note to Donna's caseworker. Her boys may not have regular contact with their uncles, but the information should go in the file. Thanks. And thanks for recommending Mrs. Howard, by the way," Silverman added. "A nice woman, and she seems to be doing a good job with Charlotte. Nice of you to visit, as well. The more interested parties, the better, in our business."

Gemma had said she'd look in on Charlotte again as soon as she could, and hung up feeling a warm rush of pleasure at the idea that she might have made a positive difference.

That soon faded, however, as she chewed over scenarios involving Sandra Gilles's brothers and drugs. If the brothers dealt in heroin, it made it more likely that they would have access to the Valium and ketamine that had been used to drug Naz.

But why would they have killed Naz? And how could they have got the drugs into him if he refused to have any contact with them?

She did her best to put the questions aside while spending an hour with her mother at the hospital. But when she could see Vi beginning to tire, she kissed her good-bye and drove to Islington.

When she pulled up, she found Tim sitting on the front steps of the house, drinking a mug of tea and watching Holly play in the front garden of the house next door. The treetops in the communal garden had begun to filter the late-afternoon sun, and Gemma sat down beside Tim gratefully, watching the slightest ripple of breeze through the foliage.

"Too hot to stay in the house," Tim said. "Too hot to drink tea, really," he added, inspecting his mug. It had been one of Hazel's favorites, Gemma remembered, with a pattern of leaves and cherries on a cream background and lettering that spelled out TIME FOR TEA. It looked awkwardly feminine in Tim's hand. "But it's that time of day, and too early for beer," he continued. "Would you like some?"

"Beer, or tea?" Gemma asked, teasing. She thought he looked exhausted. "No, thanks, really. I've just had a liter or two of industrial-strength brew at the hospital."

"How's your mum?"

"Better. They're sending her home tomorrow. She's rather proud of her chemo port—calling herself a bionic woman and showing it off to all and sundry." She didn't say that Vi had looked frighteningly frail. Settling more comfortably on the step, she watched the children. Holly's playmate was a dark-skinned little boy, perhaps a year or two younger, and Holly was giving him intricate instructions that Gemma couldn't quite hear. "She's quite the little martinet, isn't she?"

"Dictator in the making," Tim agreed with a chuckle, then sobered. "She does have a soft spot beneath all the bossiness, though. Hearing that Charlotte's dad died upset her, and she's taking being separated from Hazel very hard."

Gemma hated to let go of the few minutes of peaceful reprieve, but now that Tim had brought it up, there was no putting it off. "Tim. About Naz. We've had the toxicology report. They found very high levels of Valium and a veterinary tranquilizer called ketamine. He—"

"But that's not possible." Tim smacked the mug down with a scrape of porcelain against concrete that made Gemma wince. "I've told you—Naz wouldn't touch—"

"They're not saying he did." Gemma touched Tim's knee in reassurance. "The pathologist thinks someone else dosed him."

"But how—"

"We don't know. Tim, did Naz ever talk about Sandra's brothers being involved with drugs?"

"Sandra's brothers? Could they have done this?" At the sound of her father's raised voice, Holly looked over from next door, her small face creased in a frown.

"Daddy?" she called, dropping the plastic spade she'd been using as a stick horse and coming towards them.

"It's all right, love." Tim took a deep breath and waved her away. "You play with Sami while I talk to Auntie Gemma for a bit longer."

Holly went back to her playmate obediently, but cast worried glances their way. With the muting of the children's voices, Gemma noticed how quiet it was in the street. A car swished by in the next road; somewhere a small dog yipped, but even those sounds seemed faded. No birds sang. The evening itself seemed drugged with heat haze, and it was hard to imagine the things that had happened to Naz Malik on an equally tranquil Saturday night.

"Do you think Naz would have gone somewhere with them?" she asked Tim.

"No. Not unless—not unless it had to do with Sandra. But they were cleared of having anything to do with Sandra's disappearance."

"So they were," Gemma mused. "But that doesn't necessarily mean they didn't know anything about it. Tim, are you sure that Naz didn't tell you anything else? I know he was your friend, and I know you don't want anyone to think badly of him, or of Sandra, but—"

"No." Tim's whisper had the force of a shout. "I've been racking my brain. We just talked about, I don't know, ordinary things. Our childhoods. University. Kids. Naz said"—Tim looked away—"Naz said he didn't know what he would do if he were separated from Charlotte."

Suddenly, Gemma saw what Hazel had seen so clearly. Tim had needed a confidant as badly as Naz. Someone to sympathize, someone who understood what it was like to have the foundations of your life snatched away.

She asked, knowing she had no right, "Tim, did you tell Naz about Hazel?"

"Of course not," he said, too quickly. "Well, just that we were separated, obviously, but nothing more." He picked up his cup again, staring at the dregs of tea as he swirled them, then looked up at her. "Gemma, I'm worried about Hazel. I've been ringing since she left here yesterday. She won't pick up and she won't return my calls. She only has a mobile, so she should have it with her." He wrapped his arms round his knees, dangling the mug by its handle. It made him look like a gangly, overgrown boy. "I know if I showed up at her place, she'd be furious—she hasn't even invited me inside when I've dropped Holly off."

A cooling feather of air touched Gemma's cheek. The wind was shifting, a milky scum of cloud creeping over the sun. She glanced at her watch—it had gone six, and she was suddenly anxious to be home, although she had spoken to Kit and Toby on her way to Islington. She felt an irrational need to have everyone she loved corralled, like errant ducklings, and she wanted to talk to Duncan. He hadn't rung her since they'd parted at Alia's.

"I wouldn't worry," she told Tim. "But I'll ring her, and I'll tell her to ring you." Although their friendship had never been physically demonstrative, she leaned over and kissed Tim's bearded cheek, then stood. "Or else."

She'd meant to wait to ring Hazel until she reached the house, but the image of Hazel as she'd been on Sunday, gaunt, unwashed, brittle with rage, unnerved her and she couldn't focus on her driving. Pulling off the Caledonian Road, she stopped the car in a quiet street near the canal.

Although she'd told Tim not to worry, she hadn't reassured herself. Why hadn't she called to make sure Hazel was all right? What sort of friend was she?

The thought of Sandra Gilles and Naz Malik leapt unbidden into her mind—the specter of meetings not kept and phones not answered, of things gone terribly wrong.

Switching off the Escort's engine, she took her phone from her bag and punched in Hazel's number. A gull cried out over the canal, and as the signal connected, she felt the rumble of trains from nearby Kings Cross, a bone-deep counterpoint to the shrill and persistent ringing of Hazel's phone.

CHAPTER THIRTEEN

By the early eighteenth century the City's ancient walls had burst and the last of the fields had been built over to form London's first suburbs. Another natural human desire—for more light, cleaner and fresher air—attracted the City merchants out in the direction of a rural life suggested by other street names around us now, Blossom, Elder and Primrose.

—Dennis Severs,
18 Folgate Street:
The Tale of a
House in Spitalfields

It was an anomaly among the terraced Georgian houses—a high wall, covered with creeping vines and flowers, secured by a heavy wooden gate. Beyond the terrace, the spire of Christ Church seemed to brood over the street, as if reminding its mortal inhabitants not to take life too lightly. A man in skullcap and *salwar kameez* hurried past, not raising his eyes to theirs.

Weller pushed the ornate brass bell set into the wall, and from within the compound they heard an answering chime. "Welcome to the seraglio," Kincaid murmured.

"Closer than you might think," Weller replied.

The gate opened a crack and a young Asian woman peered out. She took in their suits with a frightened glance, then started to close the gate again, whispering, "Not home. Not home," but Weller wedged his shoulder in the gap.

"Oh, I think he is home. Tell Mr. Azad that Inspector Weller is here to see him."

She flinched away from him, giving Weller the advantage, but didn't loosen her grip on the gate. "No, Mr. Azad not home," she insisted, but she looked more terrified than stubborn.

Kincaid saw that the gate opened onto a courtyard filled with tubs of plants anchored by an ornate three-tiered fountain. Water burbled over the lips of the fountain bowls, and he caught the scent of hot cooking oil and spices. It seemed Ahmed Azad had his bit of paradise, indeed.

Before the tableau at the gate turned into a shoving match, a man's voice said, "Leave it, Maha." The gate swung wide, revealing a short, plump man with a wide face and thinning dark hair, the long strands of which were carefully combed over his bald spot.

The young woman pulled her head scarf a little tighter and hurried back towards the house, but her steps were hampered by her sari.

"To what do we owe the honor, Inspector Weller," said their host. Azad's English was formal and only faintly accented, and he wore Western dress, a crisp white short-sleeved shirt loose over tan trousers.

"We'd just like a word, Mr. Azad, if we could come in. It's about Naz Malik."

"Ah. I have heard the sad news about Nasir Malik. Tragic." Azad's eyes narrowed, as if he were considering. "Come into the courtyard, then, where we will not disturb my family."

As they passed through the gate, Kincaid saw that wooden benches were set among the potted plants. Beyond the garden stood the house, a square, stucco structure painted a soft pink and sporting several arched doorways. Kincaid caught a glimpse of movement inside, a flash of color, and heard the murmur of voices not quite masked by the splash of the fountain.

Near the fountain, a pair of benches faced each other. Azad took one, Weller and Kincaid the other, leaving Cullen in the awkward position of having to choose between sitting next to Azad, or standing. He chose the latter, stepping back a little way and looking usefully idle.

Azad studied Kincaid with dark, intelligent eyes. "And your friends, Inspector Weller?"

"Superintendent Kincaid. Sergeant Cullen." Weller made no mention of Scotland Yard, but Kincaid thought he saw a flicker of calculation in Azad's gaze at the mention of his rank.

"A superintendent," said Azad with evident approval. "It is very fitting that Nasir Malik should have a superintendent to investigate this crime, you know. This is a lawless country, Mr. Kincaid. Such a thing would never have happened in Bangladesh."

"What exactly do you think happened to Naz Malik, Mr. Azad?" Kincaid asked, knowing that the cause of death was still speculative even within the investigating team.

But Azad said smoothly, "He was found dead in the park. I assumed he was set on by youths. These young people have no respect, and some of them, I am sorry to say, are Bangladeshi." He shook his head with the regretful exasperation suited to a fond uncle. "Nasir was a good man, in spite of the questionable wisdom of some of his choices."

Weller cocked his head like a large, rumpled bird. "Choices?"

Azad shrugged. "I mean no offense, Inspector, but Nasir married a white woman. Marriage is difficult enough without racial and cultural differences."

"Malik spent most of his life here," said Weller. "He seemed very English to me."

"Did you know Sandra Gilles, Mr. Azad?" asked Kincaid.

"Of course I knew Sandra. Everyone in and around Brick Lane knew Sandra. She often stopped into my restaurant."

"You didn't like her?"

Azad looked irritated. "I said nothing about liking, Mr. Kincaid. It was simply a matter of what is appropriate. And she brought shame on Nasir."

"Shame? How?"

"A man must be able to keep a wife, Mr. Kincaid."

"So you think Sandra Gilles left Naz voluntarily, Mr. Azad?"

Azad shrugged again, less patiently. "It seems that is the most likely thing to have happened."

"Why is that, when you immediately assumed that Naz had been killed by a gang?"

"Because you have found poor Nasir, but not Sandra," Azad said, as if his logic were irrefutable.

"Perhaps she went to the same place as your nephew—or was it great-nephew?" suggested Weller, lazily.

The pouches of flesh under Azad's eyes tightened, and although he didn't move, there was a sudden tension in his posture. "This has been very pleasant, Mr. Weller, but if you are going to discuss my personal business, I'd think I'd prefer that my lawyer be present."

"That would be Miss Phillips, then?" said Weller. "It must be rather inconvenient for you, losing one of your lawyers just as your case is coming to trial. And I can't help but wonder," he added, "how comfortable you feel with a woman as your sole representative."

Smiling, Azad stood. "Thank you, gentlemen, for your condolences on the loss of my friend. If you will ring Ms. Phillips in the morning, I'm sure we can agree on a mutually convenient time to continue our discussion. Now, let me show you out."

Having decided that she would go home and check on the boys before deciding what to do next about Hazel, Gemma walked into a quiet house redolent of the smell of baking.

Neither boys nor dogs came to greet her. There was no blare of the telly, no murmur of voices. There was, however, she realized as she stood and listened, a soft clanking of dishes coming from the kitchen.

"Anybody home?" she called, setting her bag on the hall bench.

"In here," replied a familiar voice. Wesley Howard came out of the kitchen, holding a blue pottery bowl in the crook of one arm and a spatula in his other hand. He had a streak of something white across his nose, and a broad smile on his face.

Wesley, Betty Howard's youngest child and only son, acted as part-time nanny to the boys, and Gemma had felt a special connection with the young man since the day she'd met him.

"Wes," said Gemma, delighted. "What are you doing here? I thought you had to work tonight. And where is everyone?"

"The boys are walking the dogs. Toby and the mutts were bouncing off the walls—it was like Arsenal versus Man United in here. And I'm borrowing your oven." Wesley put the spatula in the bowl and wiped his fingers on the tea towel tucked into the waist of his jeans. He wore an orange T-shirt emblazoned with the words PEACE, LOVE, AND REGGAE, and had tied his dreadlocks back with a royal blue bandanna. Like his mother, he embraced color. "Tuesday is our slow night at the café," he added. "I don't have to be in for a while yet."

"What are you making? It smells heavenly." Gemma sniffed again, following him as he headed back into the kitchen. She had a sudden worried thought about Charlotte. "Tell me the cooker in your flat hasn't gone out."

"No, just didn't want to heat the place up any more. You know how small the kitchen is, and it was already stifling."

Gemma took in the empty layer pans scattered across the work top. On the kitchen table, a large plate held a beautiful cake, half iced.

"And I thought Kit and Toby might like to help with the cake," Wes continued. "It be verra good strawberry," he added for emphasis, making Gemma laugh. She'd learned early on that Wes was a chameleon—he turned the West Indian accent on to suit, and usually as camouflage when he didn't feel comfortable with someone. "You've missed your calling, Wes. You should be an actor."

"I think we'll save the stage for Toby." Wes danced a little fencing step, using the spatula as a rapier.

Gemma raised her hands in mock horror. "Oh, no, please don't encourage him. He's bad enough already."

Wesley returned the spatula to the bowl, scooping out more icing and smoothing it carefully onto the top layer of the cake. "I'll tell him pirates didn't have cake. Especially not cake with cream cheese icing and pureed fresh strawberries in the batter."

Sid, their black cat, jumped up on the table and eyed the cake, his whiskers quivering. "No, you don't, you bad cat. You know you're not supposed to be on the table," scolded Gemma. She scooped him up gently, however, and set him on the floor, pausing to rub his head. "So what's this all about?" she asked Wes, teasing. "Is there a new girlfriend?"

"You might say that." Wesley dolloped more icing on the top of the cake. "Her name is Charlotte," he added, grinning. "I brought home a slice of Otto's best chocolate gâteau from the café last night, but she wouldn't eat it. So I thought I'd try something different."

"Oh, Wes." Gemma sank down in one of the kitchen chairs, feeling a rush of gratitude. "I knew you'd spoil her."

"You mean you were hoping I'd spoil her."

"I was counting on it." She smiled. "How's she doing today? Will she talk to you?"

"Not much, yet, but I'll keep trying. Maybe strawberry cake will do the trick. Mum got out some of the girls' old toys this morning, but she doesn't seem much interested in anything but Mum's sewing. She's a natural for the camera, though—not the least bit self-conscious."

"I think her mother took a lot of photographs."

"That would explain it, then." Wesley finished smoothing on the last of the icing. Reaching for a bowl of carefully sliced strawberries, he began to make a border round the top of the cake.

"I'll check on her," said Gemma. "But first I have to go to Battersea to see Hazel."

Wesley gave her a puzzled glance. "But isn't Hazel coming for tea? I've got out the best teapot and mugs." He gestured towards a tray on the work top, where he had placed Gemma's treasured Clarice Cliff teapot and cups. "I thought I'd have the cake iced by the time she got here. The two of you can have some with the boys, then I can take the rest home for Mum and Charlotte."

Gemma stared at him, equally perplexed. "Wes, why would you think Hazel was coming for tea? I've been ringing her for an hour with no answer, and Tim hasn't been able to get her for two days. I'm worried about her."

Frowning, Wesley said, "But she was at my mum's when I left. I just assumed she was coming here afterwards."

"Your mum's?" Gemma felt even more confused. "Why was Hazel at your mum's?"

Wesley looked at her as if she'd missed the nose on her face. "She came to see Charlotte, of course."

"Well, that's put the wind up him," Cullen said as Azad's gate clicked shut behind them. He cast a disapproving glance at Neal Weller.

"That's simply marked your position on the board," Weller shot back. "Don't think you could have put anything over on Azad. The question is whether he knows more than he's told us."

"And do you think he does?" Kincaid asked as they moved away, heading back towards Commercial Street.

"Azad prefers to be cooperative as long as it doesn't interfere with his interests, and he didn't get prickly until I mentioned the missing nephew." Weller stopped at the corner. "And that surprised me, to tell the truth. I wasn't expecting a reaction to the dig—he's usually too cool for that. Maybe Malik's death has him worried about his prospects in court."

"Will he stay with Louise Phillips?" Kincaid asked.

They had stopped by the ancient horse trough in front of Christ Church. The pedestrian traffic flowed around them as if they were three suited boulders in a stream, while Weller scratched at the stubble on his chin, considering his response. "He's not the sort to appreciate women in their professional capacity," he said after a moment. "But at this point, I don't think he has much choice, and I suspect that's making him unhappy."

"According to Louise Phillips, Naz was getting cold feet about Azad's case," Kincaid said. "Maybe Azad was afraid Naz would complicate things. He was certainly ready to lay blame for Naz's death."

"Laying blame and being responsible are two entirely different things."

"You almost sound as if you like him," said Cullen.

"No law against it." Weller shrugged and looked at his watch. "I'm off. I'll see you two hearties bright and early at the station. Thanks for the drinks." He raised a hand in salute and turned into the crowd.

"Cheeky bastard," muttered Cullen. "Who the hell does he think he is?"

"We're on his patch, Doug," Kincaid said. "He knows the currents and undertows—he can read things we'd miss altogether. We need him." He gave a shrug as expressive as Weller's. "At least for the moment. I suspect that Ahmed Azad isn't the only one who knows more than he's telling."

"You think Weller's involved in this somehow?"

"No. Why would he have called us in if he was?" Kincaid shook his head. "But there's something . . . I just haven't quite put my finger on it yet." He looked round. Shops were closing, passersby carried bags of shopping, and the front of the church had begun to take on a faint gold glow in the western sun. "I've got to go, as well. I'm going to stop in at Naz Malik's house."

"I'll come with you," offered Doug.

"No, you go on, Doug. I won't stay long. And you should have a look at some more flat adverts." He clapped his sergeant on the shoulder. "I don't want you to lose your momentum."

Fournier Street was a canyon of shadow. The chimney pots looked starkly uniform in the flat light, marching across the tops of the terraces like rigid orange soldiers. Kincaid found the house easily in the short row. There was no crime scene van in the street, and when he tried the door, it was locked. He took out the copied key Sergeant Singh had given him before he left Bethnal Green, unlocked the door, and stepped in.

The house was shuttered and dim. He fumbled a bit for the switch—in these old houses, the wiring was often exposed, and terminated in odd places. In this one, the switch for the entry hall was coupled with the switch for the sitting room, and was just outside the sitting room door. His fingers came away smudged with black—the fingerprint demons had made their appointed rounds.

The illumination revealed more black dust: the doorknobs and stair rail, the handlebars and crossbars of the bike that stood propped against the wall, the jauntily flower-decaled helmet hanging from one rubber grip.

He looked into the sitting room, then went downstairs to the kitchen, where he checked to make sure no rubbish had been left in the kitchen bin. As far as he knew, the house had no caretaker, and the odor of rotting garbage could permeate the place quickly. Someone had tidied, however, either Naz Malik's nanny or the SOCOs—or Gemma.

Returning to the ground floor, he stood for a moment, wishing he had seen the house the way Gemma had seen it on Saturday. It would still have had human presence then, a pulse of life and energy. Now it had taken on the too-quiet pall of the uninhabited. The air felt stale, unused, and the fingerprint dust gave the rooms an atmosphere of shabby neglect.

And as he stood in the stillness, Kincaid realized something else. In spite of the differences in age and architectural style, this house felt very much like their own. There was the same comfortable feel to the mix of contemporary and antique furniture, the splashes of rugs and artwork, the clutter of books and children's toys.

Gemma would have felt very much at home here. Perhaps that had contributed to her attachment to the child.

He climbed the stairs, looking briefly into the rooms on each landing, finding he liked the little eccentric touches. Sandra's influence, he guessed, remembering the conservative tidiness of the reception room in Naz Malik's office, echoed here in the office he kept at home. He didn't spend time looking through Naz's papers. The computer was gone, in the hands of the boffins, and he would have Doug, whose father was a solicitor, look through anything that remained.

Reaching the top floor, he felt again for the light switch, then stood there, dazzled. Gemma had described Sandra's collages, but he supposed he had visualized something dated, slightly fussy, if he had bothered to think about it at all. Nothing had prepared him for the blaze of color and shape that leapt out to meet him. He moved closer, drawn to study the work in progress on the table, others propped against the walls.

The images were not as abstract as he'd first thought. They teased mind and eye, as the hauntingly familiar merged into the unexpected. In one, the glass towers of the City dwarfed small shop fronts in crumbling buildings. Bright-colored bolts of fabric spilled, like fallen bodies, from the shop doorways.

Kincaid dragged himself away and went to the white trestle table that apparently had served Sandra as a desk. Over it hung a large painting of a red horse on a white ground, and he realized that nowhere in the house had Sandra displayed her own collages.

The desktop was a jumble of notebooks and loose papers, and he saw at once that it would take more time than he had that evening to go through the clutter. But he picked a few things up idly—a sketchbook filled with drawings and jottings, a folder of press cuttings from gallery shows, a bound album filled with photos and handwritten captions. When he looked more closely, he saw that the photos were all of Sandra's installations, with the captions noting the place.

A school, a library, several in what appeared to be corporate offices, a local clinic, some private homes and businesses—Kincaid had flipped through to the end of the album, now he went back more carefully, looking for the notation that had caught his eye.

There. The collage was more representational than most, and depicted a narrow, canyonlike street, its wall of buildings broken by the flower-draped facade of a pub, and by recesses that held small sculptures of various traditional tradesmen, and incongruously, a tilting cannon.

The caption read: *Lucas's good-luck piece. Not sure he appreciated the joke.*

Lucas. Lucas Ritchie. In the photo, the collage hung in an elegant, high-ceilinged lounge.

Kincaid recognized the pub, the Kings Stores, in Widegate Street, near Artillery Lane. He vaguely recalled the sculpted tradesmen set into the recessed alcove on the front of the building next door, but he was sure there was no cannon. Had that been a private joke between Sandra and Ritchie—some play on *Artillery Lane* and perhaps *loose cannon?*

In any case, that gave him enough to go on. If the collage was a representation of the club, he would start in Widegate Street.

Only then did Kincaid examine the photos tacked to the corkboard on the far wall, and he stood there for a long moment. Sandra Gilles—for it was obvious that Sandra had been the primary photographer—had not posed her subjects, but had captured the family in a testament to the ordinary: eating, talking, cooking, playing, reading. His throat tightened and he swallowed, blinking as he gazed at a snap of a little curly-haired girl, her faced pinched tight with concentration as she drew with a crayon.

Charlotte. Charlotte Malik. He would never again think of her as "the child."

A thought struck him and he looked round the studio, examining Sandra's worktable and desk, shelves and baskets. It was obvious that Sandra had been an avid and talented photographer. Where was her camera?

Gemma pulled up in front of Betty Howard's house just as Hazel walked out of the door and started down the steps. She'd tried ringing Hazel once more and, getting no answer, had asked Wes to wait for the boys, then bolted out of the house.

Now, she pulled the Escort awkwardly into the curb and jumped out. "Hazel!"

Hazel looked up. "Gemma. I was coming—"

"What are you doing here?" Gemma found she was trembling with a surge of anger mixed with relief. "Why didn't you answer your phone? Tim's been worried sick about you. I've been worried sick about you—"

"I didn't mean . . . I forgot I'd turned it off." Hazel dug in her bag for the phone and switched it on. Then her eyes widened in horror. "Oh, god, is Holly all right? I didn't think—"

"No, no, she's fine," Gemma assured her, regretting her outburst.

"I just saw her an hour ago. But you'll have fifty million voice messages from Tim and me." Gemma noticed that although her friend still looked gaunt, her hair had been washed and her clothes were clean. "Are *you* all right?" she asked, her anger evaporating.

"I'm not sure, to tell you the truth," Hazel said haltingly. "I think I might be."

Gemma stared at her, baffled. "We need to talk." Looking up and down the street, she saw rows of cars baking in the still-brittle evening light, but nowhere to sit. "Let's go back to the house. Or we can get something to drink at Otto's."

"No, I— Not yet." Hazel swayed a bit. "My knees feel a bit like jelly, all of a sudden."

Gemma thought for a moment, then linked her arm through Hazel's. "Let's just walk for a bit. I have an idea." She guided them round the corner into Portobello Road and turned north. Their steps fell into a rhythm, and after a few minutes she felt some strength return to Hazel's stride. At Tavistock Road, the trees provided welcome shade, but Gemma led them on, under the cavernous shadow of the Westway.

"We'll get some juice," she said, leading Hazel into a natural foods store, one of the small shops built under the motorway.

Gemma bought them both plastic bottles of mango-orange juice and thanked the proprietor. Then she led Hazel out the far side of the underpass and into the rectangular green of Cambridge Gardens.

The small garden looked deserted without the jumble of its Saturday market stalls, but farther down the parallel arcade, kids were taking advantage of the empty pavement to skateboard. The hum of the overhead traffic meshed with the whoosh of the boards' wheels in a comforting symphony of white noise. Gemma picked the bench that seemed to have the least accumulation of pigeon droppings and sat, pulling Hazel down beside her.

She popped the top off the juice bottle and sipped, then turned to face her friend and said, "Tell me."

Hazel drank, then closed her eyes and wiped the back of her hand across her mouth. "It's good. So mango-y. I never realized that mangoes don't taste like anything else."

"Hazel—"

"I know— It's— It's just that I don't know how to explain— talking about how I felt—how I feel—seems horribly self-indulgent now. I've done enough damage thinking about me as it is."

"Don't go all therapist on me. Just tell me what happened," said Gemma patiently. "Start with the phone. Why did you turn it off?"

Hazel shook her head. "I— You're going to think—" She saw Gemma's fierce expression and went on hurriedly. "All right, all right. It was Sunday. After I got ho—back to the bungalow, from Islington. I was so angry. At you, at Tim, at myself."

"At me?" said Gemma, surprised.

Hazel gave a small smile. "You didn't want me there on Saturday night, at the house in Fournier Street."

She hadn't, Gemma remembered with a flush of guilt. "But, Hazel, I didn't know what had happened. I had to—"

"Oh, I know you had good reasons, professional reasons. But the truth was that you could have worked round them if you'd had the mind. I was being a bitch and you didn't want me there. And I knew it." When Gemma started to protest again, Hazel touched her arm. "No, let me finish. I knew it, but I couldn't seem to stop myself. I was jealous of that family, those poor people. And Sunday, even when I knew he was dead—Tim's friend—it just got worse. I felt like—oh, I don't know—like I was sinking under a weight of black oil, suffocating in it.

"And then, when I got home, and I realized I had done nothing to comfort that little girl . . . and that I had been so mired in my own nasty, seeping bitterness that I hadn't even cared for my own child's feelings . . . I—" Hazel stopped, drinking a little more juice and watching the skateboarders, and Gemma waited.

After a few minutes, Hazel went on. "That was when I turned off the phone. I couldn't bear the thought of talking to anyone. I couldn't explain myself. I sat for a long time, in the dark. And it began to seem as if it might be better for everyone if I just . . . disappeared. Like Sandra Gilles. I wanted to just step into the street and vanish. I wanted to find some way—"

Gemma felt cold. "Hazel, I—I should have realized. I should never have let you—"

"It's all right." Hazel took Gemma's hand and squeezed it. "I don't think you could have helped me. You're too close to me, to everything that's happened."

Gemma shook her head. "No, I should have called you—I should have checked—"

"No. Listen. It wouldn't have helped. What I needed was the kindness of strangers."

"What?" said Gemma, not making sense of that at all.

Seeing Gemma's look of bewilderment, Hazel gave a shaky laugh. "My neighbor ministered to me, with vegetable rice and dahl. You remember two of the boys you met? They're brothers. Tariq and Jamil. They live in the council flats at the end of the road. I told you they look out for me. They saw me come home, for the second night, and sit in the dark—they can see the bungalow from their bedroom windows. They told their mother they were worried. She worried, too, and after a bit she came with the food she had made, and knocked on my gate. She's very shy and she doesn't speak much English, but she kept knocking until I answered.

"When she saw me, she put her arm round me and led me inside. She turned on the lights, and fed me, and ran me a bath. Then she sat up all night in the chair in my sitting room while I slept." Now tears ran down Hazel's cheeks, unchecked. "And when I woke up yesterday morning, I knew I couldn't betray her care. So I have been trying to put myself back together, to think things through, to begin to make amends for the person I've let myself become. And I wanted to start with Charlotte . . . Somehow my . . . callousness . . . seemed the ultimate failure. Do you see?"

Gemma fumbled in her bag for a packet of tissues, remembering her own shock at Hazel's behavior, trying to work out what to say. "I think I do understand. But, Hazel, nothing you've done is irredeemable. You're just human, and humans make mistakes. The important thing is to remember that Tim and Holly love you—we all love you. Don't shut us out. Don't shut *me* out." She handed Hazel a tissue and waited while Hazel blew her nose. "I'm your best friend, and if I haven't made a very good job of it, I'm going to do better.

"Now," she said with decision as she zipped her bag, "you're going to ring Tim, and then you're coming back to the house with me. Wesley's made cake for Charlotte, but he promised to leave us a bit."

"Oh, Gemma," Hazel said, accepting the hand Gemma held out for a boost up. "You should have seen Wes with Charlotte. She followed him around like a little duckling. Do you think he'll be allowed to visit once she goes to her grandmother?"

"What?" Gemma stared at her, frowning. "What are you talking about? What do you mean 'once she goes to her grandmother'?"

"Didn't the social worker call you?"

Gemma fought a rising flood of panic. "There must be a mistake. I talked to her earlier this afternoon. Sandra's sister had petitioned for custody, but Mrs. Silverman said she has a record of neglecting her own kids, so that's out. There was nothing about the grandmother. When they contacted her on Sunday, she said she didn't want Charlotte."

"Um." Hazel looked at Gemma a little warily. "Mrs. Silverman rang Betty while I was there. It seems as though Sandra's mother has changed her mind."

CHAPTER FOURTEEN

Spitalfields had been London's main Huguenot district and later a Jewish neighborhood. Close to the port, it and neighboring Whitechapel were first stops for many aspiring immigrants. In the sixteenth and seventeenth centuries Bethnal Green was a haven and staging-post for Huguenot refugees escaping from persecution in France, who made an enormous contribution to the architectural, economic and demographic history of East London . . .

—Geoff Dench,
Kate Gavron,
Michael Young,
The New East End

"You can't possibly consider letting Sandra Gilles's mother have Charlotte."

"Inspector James." Janice Silverman's voice, usually cheerfully friendly, had taken on a frosty note. "I appreciate your concerns. But you, of all people, should understand that you have to let us do our job."

Gemma took a breath and loosened her grip on the phone.

Yesterday evening, she'd talked to Betty, confirming what Hazel had told her about Charlotte. Then this morning she'd snatched the first free moment in her office to ring Janice Silverman. "Of course," she said, trying to sound conciliatory. "But from what we've heard, Gail Gilles is not at all suitable—"

"Gail Gilles is Charlotte Malik's grandmother, her nearest living relative. As such, we have to give her due consideration. That doesn't mean"—she went on before Gemma could interrupt again—"that we will ignore the issues you've raised. Charlotte will stay with Mrs. Howard for the time being. I've explained to Ms. Gilles that her sons need to move out of the flat, and that we'll be checking to ensure that they have done so. We'll be initiating a home study, and I'll present the results of our findings to the family court judge at the next hearing."

"And when will that be?" asked Gemma.

There was a rustle of pages, as if Silverman were checking a paper diary. "Two weeks from yesterday, unless there's a delay. Of course, you should attend if you have any information that would be helpful to the judge—although I'd suggest it be concrete."

The phrases "home study" and "family court hearing" were all too rawly familiar to Gemma. She'd assumed that when Silverman said, "But you, of all people," she'd been referring to Gemma's work as a police officer. But now she wondered if Silverman had checked the records and found that Gemma and Kincaid had themselves fought Kit's maternal grandmother for custody.

And won, with good reason, she reminded herself, but a cursory review by someone who hadn't known the parties involved might make her seem a bit of a nutter.

And was she? she thought, feeling suddenly shaken.

Was the fact that she and Duncan knew firsthand how much damage a supposedly benign grandparent could inflict on a vulnerable child, making her overly sensitive?

Maybe, she had to admit, although no amount of rationalizing could dispel her gut feeling that this child was at risk. And if there was no one else to champion her, Gemma couldn't afford to alienate the social worker.

To Mrs. Silverman, she said with as much composure as she could muster, "I'll keep that in mind. Thank you."

"You could benefit Charlotte most by helping her adjust to her foster home." The nip in Silverman's voice had thawed, but now Gemma just wanted to get off the phone and think.

"I'll do whatever I can to help Charlotte, and Betty," she said, adding, "Thanks for your time, Mrs. Silverman."

Melody came in as Gemma ended the call. "Coffee run," she said, handing Gemma a Starbucks cup with a plastic top. "How did it go?"

"She thinks I have a grudge against grannies." Gemma sipped, wincing as the still-scalding latte burned the roof of her mouth.

"And do you?" Melody perched on the edge of a chair and sipped her own coffee as if she were Asbestos Woman.

"You think I'm overreacting because of Eugenia?" Gemma worked the lid off the coffee and watched the stream rise in a little cloud. Kit's grandmother seemed to have become more mentally unstable, and these days it was only his grandfather Bob who came for the scheduled monthly visits. On the last occasion he'd confided that he didn't know how much longer he could care for Eugenia on his own.

"No, there's no doubt that she was seriously off her rocker," answered Melody. "But what about your family? Do you get on with your grandparents?"

"I only vaguely remember my mum's folks. They died within months of each other when Cyn and I were little. My mum always said they never really recovered from the war. And my dad . . . my dad never even talks about his family. He left home when he was thirteen and never went back."

"Can't have been a good situation, then. But Duncan's parents are all right?"

"They're lovely. And you're beginning to sound like a caseworker," Gemma added with a touch of asperity. And that was unusual, she realized, as Melody tended to avoid discussing personal matters. "What about you?" she asked, giving tit for tat.

"Oh, I was hatched from aliens," Melody said with a grin, then quickly sobered. "So what are you going to do about little Charlotte?"

If Gemma knew about self-serving grandmothers because of their experience with Kit, she also knew that the social services' home studies were undertaken thoroughly and responsibly. But she realized that in the last few minutes her worry had hardened into resolve. She was not willing to trust Charlotte Malik's fate to the bureaucratic machine.

"I think," she said, "that I want to have a nice, long talk with Gail Gilles."

Kincaid stepped out of the buzz of the Bethnal Green incident room to take Gemma's call. He listened, nodding at passersby in the corridor whose faces were already becoming familiar.

"No, I don't want to talk to Gail Gilles yet," he said when he could get a word in edgewise. "And I don't want you to talk to her either. Not until I've interviewed Kevin and Terry Gilles. We're having a hard time tracking them down, and the last thing I need is their mum putting the wind up them."

He'd sent an officer to both brothers' purported places of work that morning, one a betting shop on Bethnal Green Road, and the other a minicab business nearby. Neither business seemed to be too sure what the brothers did for them, or to know where they were at the moment. Kincaid had staked plainclothes constables on both places, as well as a third on Gail Gilles's flat.

"If social services has told them to move out of the mother's flat, they'll have to go somewhere," said Gemma. "I'd try the sister."

"Good idea. I'll hunt up the address." He'd heard the disappointment in her voice when he'd said he didn't want her talking to Gail. "I understand how you feel, Gem. Really. But the caseworker's right. You have to let social services do their job. If there's anything dodgy, I'm sure they'll find it."

"Are you?" said Gemma, her tone decidedly distant.

He was cursing himself for saying the wrong thing when Sergeant Singh came out of the incident room and beckoned. "Sir, they've rung from downstairs," she mouthed. "Mr. Azad is here with his solicitor."

"Look, I've got to go," he said to Gemma. "I'll ring you just as soon as I've run the Gilles brothers to ground."

Ahmed Azad had been as good as his word. Louise Phillips had rung first thing that morning, making an appointment to come in with her client as soon as possible.

Sergeant Singh showed them into the office Kincaid had purloined as an interview room and equipped with a table, chairs, and a pot of coffee. He meant to at least begin their discussion under the semblance of a friendly chat. Cullen was still at the Yard, and Neal Weller was involved with his own division's business. Kincaid was curious to see what Azad would say without Weller's interference.

He wasn't quite sure what to make of Weller, who had defended Azad on the one hand and felt obliged to play the bully on the other.

Sergeant Singh showed Azad and Louise Phillips into the office and, at Kincaid's nod, unobtrusively took a chair in the corner. Kincaid poured the coffee himself.

This morning Ahmed Azad was dressed in a deep blue suit, perfectly tailored for his slightly plump frame. The fine fabric had the sheen of silk, as did his pink-and-blue-striped tie. He was freshly shaved and smelled strongly of bay rum.

Louise Phillips, on the other hand, looked haggard and hollow-eyed, as if she hadn't slept, and her rumpled black suit was liberally speckled with what looked to Kincaid like dog hair.

"Thank you for coming," he said when they were all settled with their cups. Singh had made the coffee, and it was strong but good.

"Very considerate of you." Azad sipped his coffee and nodded his approval. "One appreciates that, Mr. Kincaid. There is no reason why we cannot talk in a civilized manner."

"Oh, I agree, Mr. Azad. Completely. And I appreciate your taking the time from your busy schedule to clear up some things for us."

Singh's eyes had widened. Kincaid flashed her a smile. She was obviously more accustomed to Weller's interrogation methods. Not that Kincaid was averse to playing bad cop when it suited him, but he'd read Azad as the type to respond more willingly to flattery than force.

"And you, Ms. Phillips?" he asked, turning his attention to her. "How are you coping?"

"I'm here representing my client, Superintendent." Her voice was sharp, and she sat stiffly in her chair, her coffee untouched. Clearly, she was not going to consider this interview a social occasion.

Kincaid carefully replaced his cup on the low table. "Now, Mr. Azad. Since you've come in, perhaps you wouldn't mind telling us when you last spoke to Naz Malik."

"Let me see. That would have been on Wednesday last week. Or was it Thursday? Yes, I believe it was Thursday."

"All right, Thursday then. Was this at Mr. Malik's office?"

"No, no, Nasir came by the restaurant. We spoke in my office there for just a few moments. Not long enough, it seems now," he added, his voice heavy with regret.

"And why did Mr. Malik want to see you?" Kincaid asked easily, but he saw Louise Phillips tense.

"Mr. Azad does not have to—"

Azad cut her off with a wave of his hand. "There's no reason I should not be frank with the superintendent, Louise. Yes, Nasir and

I talked about my nephew, if that is what you are wanting to know. Actually, the young man is my great-nephew, the son of my favorite niece in Sylhet. I told Nasir that I did not know where my nephew had gone. Nor did I believe this nonsense story that Mohammed meant to testify against me. He is a foolish young man, yes, but he is not that foolish. All he would gain by such a thing is deportation, and the bringing of shame on his family." Azad's tone implied that the latter was by far the worst consequence.

"But if Naz believed your nephew meant to testify against you, he might have thought you had good reason to—let's say, *help* your nephew disappear."

"Nasir would never have suggested such a thing," said Azad, his chin quivering with his disapproval. "He understood the importance of family. He was merely . . . concerned for the well-being of my relative."

"So you didn't argue with Naz about your nephew that day?" Kincaid asked.

"No. You can ask my staff if you feel it necessary."

"Did you argue with Naz on the day he disappeared?"

Louise Phillips moved abruptly. "That's enough, Superintendent. I can't allow—"

"I did not see Nasir again," Azad said, interrupting her once more. Kincaid wondered why he had insisted on her accompanying him. "Saturday is our busiest day at the restaurant. I was there from before lunch until well after closing on Saturday night. And I had no reason to argue with him. He was my friend as well as my attorney." Azad's round face seemed to sag with melancholy. He finished his coffee, tipping back the small cup to catch the last drop. When he'd placed the empty cup on the table, he brushed his hands against the knees of his trousers. The "game over" signal was as clear as a banner. "Now, Mr. Kincaid, is there anything else?"

"I think he's lying," said Sergeant Singh when Azad and Louise Phillips had left the room. She'd followed the conversation carefully, watching alertly even as she took notes.

"Oh, I think our very urbane Mr. Azad is certainly lying," Kincaid agreed. "But the question is, what is he lying about? Does he know what happened to his nephew? Did Naz accuse him of getting rid of the inconvenient nephew? Did he see Naz again? Or is it something else altogether? And why did he drag Louise Phillips along for that dog-and-pony show—unless it was for her benefit rather than ours?" He thought for a moment. "See if you can catch Ms. Phillips, why don't you, Sergeant? I think I'd like a word with her on her own."

"You know I can't discuss my client's affairs with you," Louise Phillips said when Singh brought her back into the small office. She smelled strongly of smoke, and Kincaid guessed Singh had caught up with her in the street as she'd stopped to light a cigarette.

"Thank you, Sergeant." Kincaid dismissed Singh with a smile, then turned to Phillips. "I realize that. But you *can* discuss Naz Malik's." He motioned her back into the chair she had so recently vacated. "Would you like that coffee now? I think the pot is still hot."

She glared at him, but after a moment, she sank back into the chair and sighed, as if she were too tired to keep up the bristling posture. "Yes, all right," she said, accepting a fresh cup. "I've been trying to give it up. My doctor says my blood pressure is sky high. But with Naz gone, it seems a bit stupid to be worrying about things like caffeine and blood pressure." Shrugging, she added, "What difference does it make, if you can walk out of your house and end up dead in a park? Or get blown up on a bus? Or get shot in the tube?" She shook her head, then drank half the cup as if she was fiercely thirsty.

"In that case, why don't you tell me whether or not Naz believed

Azad did away with his nephew—excuse me, great-nephew. That would explain why Naz suddenly decided he wanted to drop Azad's case. And then you can tell me if you think Azad is capable of having got rid of Naz, if Naz had learned he was responsible for getting rid of said nephew. A bit convoluted, but you follow. And you notice I'm not asking if Azad is guilty as charged."

"I thought you said we weren't going to talk about Azad," Phillips countered, but with the faintest suggestion of a smile. "Although I do appreciate the thread of your argument."

"Merely following your lead. And we are talking about Naz."

"Quite. But I'm afraid, Superintendent, that I can't tell you what Naz thought, because I don't know." She drank more of her coffee. Already the caffeine seemed to have given her more energy. "If you want my opinion, however—completely off the record—I don't believe Azad harmed his nephew. I *do* think the old sod's quite capable of slipping the boy out of the country in the back of a truck and sending him back to his mum in Sylhet for a good bollocking." She reached for her bag, an automatic gesture, then drew her hand back. "I do *not* think that Azad would have had any part in harming Naz. Azad has his own code of loyalty. I don't know if I fit into it, but I think Naz did. And I think Sandra did, too."

"So who does benefit from Naz's death, then, if not Azad? Did Naz have a will?"

Phillips rolled her eyes. "Naz was a lawyer. Of course he had a will. I'm the executor. Naz and Sandra both left everything in trust for Charlotte."

"But they didn't name a guardian?"

"No. That was the thing, you see." She rubbed at one of her ragged cuticles. "It was . . . awkward. They couldn't make a decision. There was no one they trusted."

"With Charlotte, or with their money?" Kincaid asked.

"Charlotte. I don't think either of them cared that much about the money, except as it provided for their child."

"Will there be much?" Kincaid thought of the house in Fournier Street, and of prices he'd seen in the area estate agents' windows.

"Yes, a good bit, I think. The value of the house may have dropped a bit in this economy, but it will still be worth a small fortune. They didn't owe much on it. And Naz was always careful. They didn't spend much on themselves, other than what they put into fixing up the house, and he invested the rest."

Kincaid thought for a moment. "All this is assuming, of course, that Sandra Gilles doesn't walk back into the picture tomorrow."

"Unfortunately, yes," said Lou Phillips. "And as long as Sandra is missing, things are going to be very complicated, indeed."

"I'm going out for a bit. I've got to run an errand." It was the mid-afternoon lull, and Gemma had caught Melody in the corridor outside the CID room. "All the case assignments are up-to-date. Ring me if anything urgent comes up."

"What are you up to?" Melody said quietly. "You're not going to see Charlotte's grandmother, are you?"

Gemma wasn't in the mood to confide in anyone. "I just need a bit of fresh air." It was true enough, Gemma told herself. Although the weekend's brutal heat had relented, it was still warm, and her office was miserably stuffy. Her head was splitting from staring at the computer screen, and she was beginning to wonder why she had ever wanted a promotion to a desk job.

"I won't be long," she added, and with that, she ran down the stairs and out the front door of the station. On the steps, she bumped into a uniformed male constable, who grinned and said, "Where's the fire, guv?"

"Corner shop," she said, smiling back.

"Coffee and ciggies for me, then," he called after her, and she waved back.

She turned into Ladbroke Grove. Having decided not to take the car, as she didn't want to get caught in rush-hour traffic coming back, she walked up to Holland Park and took the District and Circle to Kings Cross. There, she changed for Old Street, and as she stood on the platform, closing her eyes against the warm wind from a train going in the opposite direction, she mulled over what she was doing. It might be rash, but she felt compelled by the bond she had formed with Charlotte. Who would act if she did not?

What she hadn't told Melody was that she'd rung Doug Cullen and asked him to look up an address in Sandra Gilles's file.

"Roy Blakely?" Cullen had asked. "Who's he?"

"According to Tim, Blakely was the last person to see Sandra Gilles the day she disappeared. I just want to talk to him about Sandra. I don't know that he has any direct connection with Naz Malik, so don't worry, I'm not trespassing on your investigation."

"That means you've told Duncan?" Cullen had said suspiciously.

"No, but I will." Gemma had begun to feel irritated. "Just give me the address, Doug. I'll sort it out with him later."

But by the time she climbed the stairs at the Old Street tube station and emerged, hot and sweaty, into the street, she was beginning to wonder if this had been such a good idea after all. Then she looked up and saw the *Ozone Angel,* and felt again the odd sense of connection with Sandra she had experienced that first night. Yes, she needed to do this, and if it stepped on toes she would just have to deal with the consequences.

She walked on down Old Street, her stride relaxing into a long, easy swing. As she neared Columbia Road, she turned off into a side street and consulted the address she'd scribbled on a scrap of paper, then her A to Zed. A few more minutes brought her to a cul-de-sac filled with relatively new flats. They seemed more like town houses, Gemma thought as she looked at them more closely, houses with two stories and sloping red tile roofs, set in blocks surrounded by pleasant landscaping.

Roy Blakely's flat was on a corner of one such block. It had a neatly tiled front entrance, and the front door stood open. Gemma peered in as she pushed the bell, but the interior was in shadow and her eyes hadn't adjusted from the glare of the sun. She heard the faint sound of a television, then footsteps, and a man entered the hall.

"You from the gas board, darlin'?" he asked, looking at her approvingly. "Damn sight better than the last geezer they sent." His accent was decidedly Cockney, and he was solidly built, perhaps in his fifties, with muscular shoulders shown off by his white T-shirt. His thick silver hair was cut short, and fine silver down glinted on his bare forearms.

"Mr. Blakely?" said Gemma.

"In the flesh. What can I do for you?"

"My name's Gemma James, and I'd like to talk to you about Sandra Gilles."

Roy Blakely's friendly face was instantly shuttered. "Can't help you, darlin', and I've got work in me garden. So——"

"Mr. Blakely, wait. I'm a police officer, but I'm not here officially. I'm here because I'm concerned about Charlotte Malik, Sandra's daughter. Did you know that Naz Malik was dead?"

"I heard from some mates who saw it in the paper, yeah. I'm sorry about that. But what's it to do with me? Or Sandra? Look, I've told the police everything I know about that day a hundred times." He started to swing the door shut.

Gemma made a last-ditch attempt at persuasion. "You knew Sandra well, didn't you, Mr. Blakely? What would you say if I told you that Sandra's mother was petitioning for custody of Charlotte?"

"Gail?" He paused, his hand still resting on the door, and scowled at her. "You said you weren't here 'officially.' What the hell does that mean?"

"It's a long story, Mr. Blakely, and it's a hot day. If we could just talk somewhere cool . . ." She pushed the damp hair away from her face.

"You criticizing my Cockney hospitality, darlin'? That's a right insult, that is," he said, but the scowl was less fierce. "All right, then. Come and sit in the garden, and I'll make you something to drink."

He pushed the door open wide, and Gemma followed him into a sitting room that was dimmed by the light pouring in from the double glass doors in the back. The doors stood open to an oasis of green, splashed with bright colors. The voices she'd heard were louder, and she realized it was the radio rather than the telly, playing somewhere else in the house. She recognized a BBC 4 presenter, and caught something about gardening.

Then she stepped out onto a flagged patio shaded by the house, surrounded by raised beds so thick with plants that there was not an inch of bare soil. She recognized brilliant orange and yellow roses shaped into trees, a profusion of bee-swarmed lavender in one border, a drift of plumbago in another, and a lemon tree. As for the rest, she was hard-pressed to come up with names. The spicy scent of the lavender tickled her nose.

Two carved wooden chairs stood to one side, and a long worktable against the rear of the house held pots and tools and seed trays.

Roy Blakely shifted a chair for her, then came back a moment later with a plastic tumbler of water, cold from the fridge.

"Thanks." Gemma took it gratefully. "I walked from Old Street. Your garden is lovely. Did you design it yourself?"

As Blakely sat on the edge of the other chair, Gemma noticed the mud stains on the knees of his jeans.

"I'm a one-man *Ground Force*, darlin'," he said. "Now, what's this all about? Are you telling me that little Charlotte is with Gail?"

Gemma set her glass down on the flagstones and leaned forward. "Not yet. Charlotte's in foster care for the moment. But Gail is her nearest living relative, so unless the court has good reason to decide against her petition, Charlotte will go to her."

He grimaced, then said, "And what do you have to do with any of this?"

She explained about Tim and Naz, and how she had come to be involved in the investigation into Naz's death, and how she had helped arrange a temporary placement for Charlotte.

"But my friend told me that Naz and Sandra didn't want Charlotte to have anything to do with her grandmother," she continued, "and I've since heard some other things that make me think . . . I'm afraid of what will happen to Charlotte."

Blakely shook his head. "I never thought—when Sandra disappeared . . . I know it was tough for Naz, caring for a child on his own, but I thought he was the coping sort. I never imagined—what the hell happened to him? The rumors floating round could sink a ship."

"We"—she caught herself—"*they* don't know exactly, but it looks like he was murdered."

"Murdered?" Blakely stared at her. "Why would somebody want to kill Naz Malik? Nice bloke. Good father, good husband. Helped people out when they needed it." He shrugged his powerful shoulders. "Although, since Sandra's been gone, he's been a bit of a walking ghost. Not quite all there. I have to admit I was beginning to wonder if he could go on without her, if you want the truth." He hesitated, then said, "You're sure he didn't—"

"The pathologist and the local police believe it was murder. Scotland Yard's been called in."

Blakely's hands twitched and flexed, as if he were uncomfortable in not having something to do with them. She thought he'd paled a little beneath his tan. "And Sandra?" he asked. "Have they found out something about Sandra?"

"No, though they can't help but wonder if Naz's murder and Sandra's disappearance are somehow connected. Are you certain there's noth—"

"Do you think I haven't gone over every single word said that day a million times, trying to find something, make some sense of it?" He turned towards her, his knuckles now white where he gripped the chair arms. "I've memorized every word she said. I dream them. And there's nothing, absolutely nothing, that explains where she can have gone."

"I'd like to hear, if you could manage to tell it one more time," Gemma said softly.

He leaned back again, closed his eyes. When he spoke, it was carefully, as if every word mattered. "She came late, just as we were beginning to shut down the stall. I looked up, and she was standing there with Charlotte on her hip, watching me. I said something like, 'Come for the best of the lot, have you?' because we always joked about me saving the knockdowns for her at the end of the day. Charlotte piped up, wanting a cupcake, but Sandra told her to wait. And then she said, 'Roy, can I ask a favor? I've an errand, but I won't be long. We have to meet Naz at two.'

"Charlotte wanted to help with the flowers. Sandra set her down. Then she looked at her watch. And now, when I look back at it, I think she hesitated for a minute, a fraction of a minute. But then she kissed Charlotte, and waved at me, and walked away. The next time I looked up, she was gone. That's it," he finished roughly.

"Did she have anything with her?" asked Gemma, trying to imagine the scene.

"Just her handbag. But I used to tell her she could get the bloody London Eye in that thing."

"Did she look different, or sound different—"

"No!" Blakely rubbed a hand over his mouth, as if he were making an effort to maintain his patience. "No. She had on jeans and a T-shirt. I don't remember what color the shirt was. I've tried. Some days she tied her hair back, but that day it was loose. I don't think she had on any makeup. There was only—there was only that bit of hesitation, like she almost changed her mind about what she was going to do. Or maybe I'm just making that up." He shook his head. "But it wasn't like Sandra to hesitate. Once she made up her mind to do something, God forbid you got in her way."

"She worked for you a long time?" Gemma asked.

"All through high school and art college. Even after she and Naz married she liked to do her bit. But I'd known Sandra since she was a tot. Truth is, I'd known Gail since *I* was a kid. Grew up on the same council estate."

"So why didn't Sandra and Gail get on?"

Roy shrugged. "The wife always said Sandra must have been one of those babies substituted at birth—a changeling."

"Your wife?"

"Billie. She's on holiday in Spain. A girl's jaunt—hen party for our niece."

Gemma shied away from the mention of hen parties. "You have kids?" she asked.

"No. I suppose that's one reason we were always so fond of Sandra, not that she wasn't a mouthy little thing sometimes. Took after her mother there, but in a good way."

"You haven't told me why Naz and Sandra didn't want Charlotte to have anything to do with Gail."

Blakely was silent for a moment, then he said, "You know that Sandra never knew her dad, and that her sister, Donna, and the boys are her half siblings? And Donna and the boys have different fathers as well."

"But the boys have the same father?"

"Yeah, he stayed around for a bit, that one, although I think he was gone by the time Terry was born. It was Donna's dad stayed the longest, but he was a right tosser. Lived off Gail's benefits."

"Gail never married any of them?"

"No. Gail's mum helped out with the kids, but she's gone now. That was the old Bethnal Green, extended families, everyone helping each other out. Not that it did much for Gail, but it at least kept Sandra from going the same way as her mum. She's got no judgment, Gail. She could never keep her knickers on, from the time she were twelve. Blokes have been taking advantage of her ever since, including those useless sons of hers. And she never cared a fig for either of the girls."

"But Sandra managed to make something of herself in spite of her family," said Gemma.

"And they didn't thank her for it, believe me. Called her 'hoity-toity' and 'jumped-up cow.'"

"Her brothers, too? I heard they didn't get on. And that Naz thought they might have had something to do with her disappearance."

Roy's face wrinkled in disgust. "Kev and Terry are a couple of shiftless louts who've been nothing but trouble for Sandra since she was a kid. And yeah, Naz came to see me, wanted me to say I'd seen them that day, but I hadn't. And why would they hurt her? She was the one person they could count on to bail them out of trouble, worst case.

"Not to mention that if they had done something to her, at least a hint of it would have leaked. Those two couldn't keep their mouths shut if their lives depended on it, and word still travels in these parts."

"Was there anyone else that Sandra didn't get on with, besides her family?"

Blakely reached for Gemma's empty water glass and rubbed his thumb round the rim. "Sandra was . . . connected. Interested in people. And she crossed the border into the Bangladeshi community, something not very many old East End families are willing to do. Only person I can think of that she had a falling-out with was Pippa, and then she didn't talk about it."

"Pippa?" asked Gemma, her interest piqued by the unfamiliar name.

"Pippa Nightingale. Owns a gallery on Rivington Street. She'd been Sandra's mentor since art college, and she represented Sandra's work for years."

"She doesn't anymore?"

"I don't think so. Like I said, Sandra didn't really talk about it. You could ask Pippa yourself. Her place is called the Nightingale Gallery."

"Mr. Blakely—Roy." Gemma hesitated, not wanting to break the rapport she felt she'd established with Sandra's friend, but she knew she had to ask. "There were rumors when Sandra disappeared that she might have been—that there was another man—"

"Bollocks!" He stood. "I don't know who started it, but I heard those whispers when Sandra disappeared. It was crap then, and it's crap now. No one who really knew Sandra would have believed it for a minute, and it made life a misery for Naz."

"I'm sorry." Gemma stood up as well. It was obvious she'd worn out her welcome. "Thank you, Mr. Blakely. But tell me one more thing. Would you be willing to see Charlotte raised by Gail Gilles?"

Blakely took a breath, then let it out slowly. "No. Not if I can bloody help it."

CHAPTER FIFTEEN

Being outside and extreme is what Spitalfields is all about.
In medieval times the area was occupied by two classic
categories of outcasts: the lepers and the insane, and
Spitalfields derives its name from the leper hospice, St Mary's
Spital and the fields on which it stood. The insane were taken
out to the gates of St Mary's of Bethlehem or "Bedlam", which
occupied the site of what is today Liverpool Street Station.

—Dennis Severs,
18 Folgate Street:
The Tale of a
House in Spitalfields

Kincaid and Cullen found the club in Widegate Street through the process of elimination. The short and very narrow street was anchored at one end by the Kings Stores pub, loomed over at the other by the glass-and-brick hulk of Broadgate. In between, there were offices and a few discreet shops.

When they hadn't turned up either of the Gilles brothers by lunchtime, Kincaid had decided it was time to hunt down Lucas Ritchie and his mysterious club. He'd grabbed a quick sandwich, then asked Cullen to meet him at the Liverpool Street station. It was only one stop on the tube from Bethnal Green, and he hadn't fancied trying to park in the narrow streets of old Spitalfields.

Now, it was the entrance without insignia that interested Kincaid. It was an elegant frontage, with brass detailing, a bell, and a pass-card slot. When Kincaid examined the building more closely, he saw that the brick was new, but fitted seamlessly into the facades of the older buildings on either side.

"Hmm," he said to Cullen. "A bit Diagon Alley. Let's see what happens if we ring the bell."

A moment later, a pleasant female voice issued from the tiny speaker beside the bell. "Can I help you, sir?"

Looking up, Kincaid saw the discreet camera mounted below the sill of the first-floor window. "Duncan Kincaid to see Mr. Ritchie," he ventured.

The response was a buzz, followed by a click as the door latch released. Kincaid grinned at Cullen, said, "Open, sesame," and pushed. Cullen followed, looking as though he might be entering a dragon's den.

They stepped into a reception area that hovered somewhere between warehouse and posh hotel. Brick walls, wooden floors, unornamented windows, industrial-style pendant lighting—but the leather upholstery on the contemporary furniture grouped before the plain fireplace looked butter soft, the curved reception desk was an exotic-looking wood polished to a mirror shine, and the floral arrangements on the desk and in the sitting area were exquisite—as was the young woman standing behind the curved desk.

Asian—perhaps Anglo-Chinese—flawlessly groomed and made up, she wore a crisp white blouse under a perfectly tailored charcoal pinstripe suit. She was breathtaking, but behind the desk hung the collage that Kincaid had seen in the photo in Sandra Gilles's studio, and it was this that held him riveted.

The photo hadn't prepared him for the size of the piece, or for the depth of the colors and the intricacy of the design. He thought if he stared long enough, he could fall into it, peeling back the beckoning layers of life and history.

"Sir," said the girl at the desk, bringing him back with a jolt, "can I help you? You said you wanted to see Mr. Ritchie?"

Kincaid smiled and showed his warrant card. "Just a quick chat, if you don't mind."

Although the girl's eyes widened, her smile stayed in place. "If you'll give me a moment, I'll see if he's available. Please make yourselves comfortable." She gestured at the sitting area. "Can I get you water, or a pot of tea?"

When Kincaid declined, she ducked through an unobtrusive door to one side of the desk.

"What *is* this place?" Cullen said when she'd gone.

"Not your old-fashioned St. James's gentlemen's club, I don't think." Kincaid looked round, now noticing other artwork: two wood sculptures, a contemporary and unidentifiable metal piece, a beautiful pottery vase on a lit display stand. Nothing, however, compared to Sandra Gilles's collage. "The question is, what's on offer?"

"Sir." The girl was back. She pushed a button on the other side of the desk and a door slid open, revealing a mirrored lift. "Mr. Ritchie will meet you on the first floor. My name's Melanie, if there's anything else I can do to assist you."

Kincaid and Cullen stepped into the lift. When the door closed, Cullen whispered, "Does she mean—"

"I doubt it." Kincaid grinned. "And if she did, you couldn't afford it."

The doors opened again, soundlessly, and they faced an expansive space. The front of the room was another sitting area with a bar; the back, a dining room furnished with long oak refectory tables set with crisp white linen, silver, and crystal.

It was getting late for lunch, but the tables were still well filled, as was the bar. The clientele was mostly male, Kincaid saw, but there were a few women in business attire. Another of Sandra Gilles's collages hung over the fireplace in the lounge area, this one depicting what Kincaid thought was Petticoat Lane Market.

Kincaid noticed several young women dressed in suits identical to Melanie's, moving among the tables, so gathered that the charcoal pinstripe must be a uniform of sorts for the club staff. Very classy indeed.

A man came towards them from the direction of the dining room, hand outstretched. "Melanie said you wanted to see me? I'm Lucas Ritchie." He was tall and fair, with the faintest hint of designer stubble, and was considerably younger than Kincaid had expected. When Kincaid shook the offered hand, he found it surprisingly hard and calloused. It was an interesting contrast to the man's impeccable tailoring and carefully classless London accent. Kincaid thought he recognized Ritchie's cologne as the spicy Jo Malone fragrance Gemma had given him the previous Christmas.

While Cullen shook Ritchie's hand, Kincaid produced his warrant card. "I'd like to talk to you about Naz Malik and Sandra Gilles, Mr. Ritchie. Is there somewhere—"

"In my office." As polished as his receptionist, Ritchie hadn't blinked. Had he been expecting a visit from the police?

He led them back into the lift. "These are our public rooms," he explained as the lift doors closed. "My office is on the next floor, where we have our private meeting and conference rooms."

They stepped out into a lounge area much like the one below, but smaller and cozier. Ritchie led them down a corridor behind the lounge, passing a number of rooms with conference tables and wall-mounted flat-screen televisions, and several small sitting rooms and private dining rooms. His office was at the very end of the corridor, a small room flooded with light from the single window. It was furnished with a sofa, comfortable chairs, and a desk, its surface bare except for an open laptop. Behind the desk hung a painting of a red horse, and although slightly different in composition, it was obviously by the same artist as the painting in Sandra's studio. Looking more closely, Kincaid thought the signature was a scrawled "LR."

"I heard about Naz Malik," said Ritchie as he sat down at the desk. "One of the girls who knew Sandra saw it in the paper. But the story said he was found dead in Haggerston Park. Why is Scotland Yard making inquiries? Does this have something to do with Sandra?"

Lucas Ritchie was obviously accustomed to being in charge. Kincaid wondered what would shake him. "Our evidence suggests that Naz Malik was murdered. We don't know whether his death is connected with his wife's disappearance. We were hoping you might be able to tell us."

"Me?" Ritchie raised his sandy eyebrows, but his tone seemed more exasperated than surprised. "Don't tell me someone's dug up that old chestnut about Sandra and me again. I thought that was well put to rest."

"Apparently not," Kincaid answered, "since Naz mentioned it to a close friend not long before he died."

Ritchie rocked back in his chair, but kept his hands folded in his lap. So far the shift in position was his only display of ruffled composure, as his desk provided none of the usual outlets for fiddling. "Naz knew there was nothing to that rumor. Sandra and I had known each other for years. We were at art college together, and I'd supported her career whenever possible. We were good friends."

"Do you have any idea what happened to her?" Kincaid asked.

"God, no." Ritchie rocked the chair forward again with such force it squeaked. "Do you think I wouldn't have said at the time if I had? I'd given her lunch here the week before. We'd talked about an idea for another collage for the club, and just, you know, the ordinary things, gossip about people we both knew. We planned to talk again soon—she was going to bring me some preliminary sketches.

There was nothing—absolutely nothing—to indicate that she would walk into Columbia Market and bloody disappear."

"You went to art college?" said Cullen. "Seems a far cry from all this." His gesture took in the club.

Ritchie seemed unoffended. "I acted for a bit, and I was a passable painter. But I was always better at putting things together, managing things. I had an idea, and I met some people in the City who were on the lookout for an investment." He shrugged. "I must say it's been quite successful."

"So you're the manager rather than the owner?" Kincaid said.

"A mere employee of the board of directors. A minion. And it suits me perfectly well. No strings."

"Why is there no name or public listing for the club?"

"A gimmick. There's not even an Internet listing. Strictly word of mouth. It's the ultimate exclusivity for the businessman—or woman—who has everything. And believe me, even in a recession, there are still people with money to spend."

"The anonymity has nothing to do with the kind of services you provide?"

"Services?" Ritchie laughed. "Very tactful of you, Superintendent. We provide the same services as any other reputable private club. And if you are referring to our delightful female members of staff, they are very good at selling very expensive bottles of wine to the clientele, but that's all they do. And they would be quite insulted if you suggested otherwise."

"I wouldn't dream of it," said Kincaid with an answering smile. "You said you gave Sandra lunch. That implies that she was not a member?"

"You didn't know Sandra." Ritchie chuckled again. "No, she was not member. This was not her cup of tea, to put it mildly. In her fonder moments, she would tell me I was a shallow, capitalist pig." His smile faded. "I miss her. Everyone needs a friend who tells them what they *don't* want to hear." He looked thoughtful for a moment.

"Although for all her philosophically elevated position, she was very practical, and not above poaching my clients."

"Poaching?"

"It was a joke between us. She called me her 'one-man PR band.' If I hung her work in the club, the members would want their own. She got quite a few commissions out of it."

"Are you saying you didn't pay for the collages?" asked Kincaid.

"Of course I paid for them. Or I should say, the board of directors paid very nicely for them, as they have for the other artworks I've suggested. All lovely, aboveboard, and tax deductible."

"I can't help but notice that you refer to Sandra in the past tense, Mr. Ritchie," Kincaid said levelly, holding Ritchie's gaze.

Ritchie looked irritated for the first time. "I'm not an idiot, Superintendent. Sandra was happily married, at least as far as she confided in me. She loved her child. Her career was successful. She didn't drink, other than the occasional glass of wine, and she didn't do drugs. In all the time I knew her, she never showed the least sign of mental instability."

"You think she's dead?"

"I hope not. But I think it's the most logical explanation. What I don't understand is why the police haven't come up with a single clue as to what happened to her. And now Naz—" Ritchie shook his head. "What the hell happened to Naz? Why would someone kill him? He was a nice bloke who'd been through hell."

"Do you know of anyone who had a grudge against him?"

"I didn't know him well enough to be privy to something like that. And Sandra never mentioned anything to me."

"Did Sandra ever talk to you about her family?"

"No. Closed subject." Ritchie thought for a moment. "I suppose I got the impression that her family didn't approve of her work, but we just didn't go there. Neither of us was comfortable with it." He glanced at his watch. "Look, the dining room is still busy, and I need to keep an eye on things. If there's nothing else—"

"Mr. Ritchie, have you any idea who started the rumor about you and Sandra?" Kincaid asked as he stood.

Ritchie sighed. "It could have been one of the staff here. I don't go out with the girls, Superintendent. The complications are bad for business. But occasionally one of them gets a bit too attached and it gets . . . difficult. There was one I had to let go—Kylie. I don't know where she is now."

"Another missing woman?" Cullen asked.

"She's not *missing*, Sergeant," Ritchie said with exaggerated patience. "She just doesn't work here anymore. Ask Melanie about her if you like. They were flatmates for a bit. Now—" He stood and ushered them back into the corridor. As they passed the private bar, a man came out of the lift, glanced at Kincaid, then frowned and came towards them.

"Don't I know you?" he said, holding out a hand. "Miles Alexander."

The man's face looked familiar, and there was something sleek and a little padded about him that made Kincaid think of a seal. The comparison triggered recollection. "I saw you at the London," Kincaid said. This was the man who had passed them in the corridor as they were going to Dr. Kaleem's office, and had responded rather irritably to Kincaid's request for directions.

"Ah, that was it. I'm a consultant there." Alexander seemed sociable enough now.

"Miles is also one of Sandra's patrons," said Ritchie. "Miles, these gentlemen are from Scotland Yard."

"Is there news about Sandra?" Alexander asked. He looked more interested than distressed.

"No. We're here about her husband, Naz Malik," Kincaid said. When Alexander looked at him blankly, he added, "Mr. Malik was killed this past weekend."

"I hadn't heard." Alexander frowned. "That's too bad. You'd

think Sandra going missing was enough tragedy for one family." He shook his head. "Not only do I miss her work, but she was a great benefactor of the clinic."

"The clinic?"

"Miles is one of the directors of a sexual-health clinic in Shoreditch," explained Ritchie. "It provides free screening and services for local women. Sandra felt really strongly about it, and contributed her time as well as her artwork. Many of the Asian women don't want their husbands or families to know they're seeing a doctor, so the clinic allows them confidentiality."

"It's a small return to the community." Alexander glanced at his watch, then gave them a perfunctory smile. "Sorry. A business appointment. If you'll excuse me." He nodded, then left them to join a cluster of men at the bar.

Ritchie turned towards the lift and handed Kincaid a business card. "If there's anything else I can do, Superintendent, you know where to find me."

"There is one more thing, Mr. Ritchie," Kincaid said. "We'll need to know your whereabouts last Saturday."

"A bit full of himself, don't you think?" said Cullen as they stepped out into Widegate Street. "Conceited git. Just assumes that every woman is gaga over him."

"Maybe they are." Kincaid grinned. "Seems like a good-looking bloke, but we might want to get a female opinion. What I think is more interesting is his address." He touched the card in his breast pocket. With some reluctance, Ritchie had scribbled an address and phone number on the back.

"I was at my parents Saturday afternoon and evening. It's a slow day for the club, and there was a birthday party for my niece," he'd told them.

"St. John's Wood," Kincaid said thoughtfully as they walked back towards Liverpool Street. "If he comes from that sort of background, why the neutral accent?"

"Maybe he doesn't want to scare off working-class boys who made good. But you can still tell he's public school."

"How?" Kincaid asked, looking curiously at Cullen.

Cullen shrugged. "I don't really know. You just can."

"Makes you wonder about his 'contacts in the City' who were so willing to funnel money into the club, doesn't it?" Kincaid mused. "Old schoolmates? Friends of his parents?"

"He will be connected," agreed Cullen. "Whether he likes it or not. And he has a bloody suntan," he added darkly, as if that were the worst imaginable offense.

"Maybe he jogs, or rows, or plays tennis. It is August, after all," Kincaid said with a grin. "*You* might even have a suntan if you ever got out of your flat. How's the flat hunting going, by the way?"

"Not." Cullen sounded discouraged.

"Well, if nothing major breaks, maybe you could take off a bit early this afternoon. But first, check out Ritchie's alibi, and see if you can track down the not-missing girl. Kylie Watters."

Melanie's pretty mouth had turned down in distaste when they'd asked her about her former flatmate. "I don't know where she is," she'd told them. "And her mobile's disconnected. I tried to ring her last week because she still owes me money on the rent. She was always late and coming up with excuses for it."

"You don't have another address or number for her?" Kincaid had asked.

"No. We weren't really friends. It was just a convenient arrangement. And then she made a fool of herself with Lucas and made us all look bad. Silly cow."

With a little more coaxing, she'd given them the defunct mobile number, said that she thought Kylie came from Essex, and had offered a description. "Mousy. And a bit chubby. I can't imagine why Lucas hired her" had been her final, damning pronouncement.

They crossed Bishopsgate and Kincaid paused as they reached the escalators that led down into Liverpool Street Station, turning to Cullen. "Oh, and any luck with Azad's missing nephew, by the way? We seem to be accumulating missing persons at an alarming rate."

Gemma walked back towards Old Street, more slowly this time. She was beginning to wish she'd worn more sensible shoes. Given the continuing hot spell, strappy sandals had seemed the right choice that morning, but now she had a blister starting.

She slowed a little more, favoring her foot and thinking about her conversation with Roy Blakely as she walked. She'd given him Janice Silverman's number and he'd said he would ring her. But when she'd asked if he would appear in family court, he'd hesitated, saying, "Of course I want what's best for Charlotte . . . but I've known the family most of my life. And I've nothing specific to say, other than that Gail hasn't done that great a job with her own kids, and that's just my opinion."

"Well, have a word with Janice. That's a start," Gemma had said, sensing she couldn't push him further at the moment, and with that she'd had to be content.

But she had a clearer picture of what had happened the day Sandra disappeared, and she was more convinced than ever that Sandra had not gone voluntarily. And she was curious about this woman called Pippa Nightingale who Roy had mentioned.

She stopped and checked her A to Zed. Rivington Street ran parallel to Old Street, and she was almost within a stone's throw. She would check in with work, and then she could just pop in Pippa Nightingale's gallery for a quick word.

Not knowing the exact address, she started at the bottom end of

the street and walked up, searching for the name. Rivington Street
had that air of slightly shabby trendiness she was coming to associ-
ate with the East End. There were clubs and clothing boutiques, a
health clinic, offices, and galleries. Too many galleries—she reached
the top end of the street, anchored by the friendly looking Rivington
Grill, without finding the gallery she wanted. Starting back the
other way, she looked more closely. Halfway down the street, she
was rewarded by the sight of very discreet lettering announcing the
NIGHTINGALE GALLERY, beside a plain facade and an anonymous-
looking door.

Gemma studied the building, then pushed the buzzer. When the
door latch clicked, she went in. She found herself in a small vestibule
with a staircase. There was nowhere to go but up.

As she climbed, she saw that tiny jewel-like paintings hung on
the stairwell walls. The works were abstract, with layers of line and
color that created such depth she had an odd sensation of vertigo.
But it was the handwritten prices on the cards mounted beside the
paintings that made her gasp. Lovely, but certainly beyond her reach.

When she reached the first floor, the space opened out into a
long, narrow gallery. The walls were painted a stark white, the floor
was unvarnished planks, and light poured in from a large window
at the front. Only half a dozen works hung on the walls. Gemma
wasn't sure if she should call them paintings, for they were monochrome, except each picture had one splash of brilliant scarlet pigment.

She moved closer, fascinated. The meticulously rendered drawings made her think of the Hans Christian Andersen tales she'd been
reading Toby. There was a magical, foreboding feeling to them, a
sense of deep woods and snow. Female figures morphed into wolves,
male figures into stags, and half-formed creatures peered from crags
and branches. The red was visceral, shocking. As were the prices,
again.

Gemma stepped back and looked round. The space seemed cavernously empty, but there was a door at the back of the room. She walked towards it, calling out, "Anyone here?"

A woman stepped out, and Gemma had the impression that one of the drawings on the wall had come to life. Waif slender, the woman was dressed in black, but her skin and hair were ice pale. "I'm sorry," she said. "I was on the phone. Can I help you?" Her voice was polished and surprisingly husky.

"Are you Pippa Nightingale?" asked Gemma. As she moved closer, she saw that the woman's eyes were red, as if she'd been crying.

"Yes." Now she sounded slightly wary. "Did someone send you?"

"Not exactly." Gemma gave her a condensed version of her explanation to Roy Blakely, finishing with "Roy said you and Sandra had known each other for a long time, and that you represented Sandra's work. So I wondered if you could tell me anything more about Sandra's relationship with her family."

Pippa Nightingale's eyes filled, and she clutched at the skirt of her black jersey dress. "I can't believe Naz is dead," she whispered.

There were no chairs in the gallery area. Spying two chrome-and-black-plastic models in the office, Gemma guided Pippa inside, saying, "Here, sit down, why don't you?" Pippa sank into one of the chairs, the backs of her fingers pressed against her upper lip. "Can I get you some tea or something?" Gemma asked.

Pippa took a shaky breath. "There's a kettle on the worktable, and some teabags." She nodded towards the back of the room. Unlike the gallery space, the office was cluttered—it looked as if every bit of detritus that might have sullied the pristine display space had been sucked into this room. Paper spilled from desk and worktable; file folders lay open, disgorging their contents in cascades; stacks of stapled exhibition brochures teetered precariously near edges.

Gemma found the sleek stainless-steel kettle, some obviously hand-thrown pottery mugs, and a box of PG tips. The kettle had water in it, so she flipped the switch and it boiled quickly. She didn't see milk or sugar, so poured water over the teabags, then stirred the cups for a moment with a used and bent spoon she'd found beside the kettle. She fished out the teabags, tossed them into an overflowing rubbish bin, then carried them round the desk. She cleared a spot for Pippa's cup, then sat in the other chair, holding her own.

"Thanks." Pippa's voice had recovered some of its huskiness. She lowered her hand, taking the pottery cup gingerly by the rim and handle. "Sorry the place is a tip. I haven't been keeping up with things very well lately. And this . . ." Her eyes started to tear again and she shook her head.

"You knew Naz, then?" Gemma asked.

"Of course I knew Naz. Sandra and I were friends before they married. It's not that Naz and I were ever all that close—I think Naz resented my influence on Sandra, and vice versa, I'm sorry to say—but I—" She stopped to sip at the still-steaming tea. "It's just that—I can't believe he's dead. Now I don't think Sandra will ever come back." This time the tears ran unchecked down her cheeks.

"You thought Sandra would come home?" asked Gemma, surprised. She realized it was the first time anyone she'd talked to had genuinely seemed to believe it.

"I know it's stupid, but yes. Somehow I thought she would just walk back into her life one day. But with Naz gone, I can't imagine Sandra coming back."

"What about Charlotte?" Gemma felt immediately incensed on Charlotte's behalf.

"Oh, I don't mean she didn't love Charlotte. She adored her. But long before Charlotte was born, Naz and the house were her lodestones, the things that mattered most to her—even more than her work." This was said with the faintest of frowns on her unlined, almost translucent face.

"Should her work have mattered more?"

"That's not what I meant." Some of Pippa's initial wariness seemed to have returned. "I'm still not quite sure why you wanted to talk to me. I never met any of Sandra's family."

"Roy Blakely said you and Sandra hadn't been as close lately, and that you weren't representing her work any longer."

"Sandra told him that?" Pippa stared at her, and Gemma found her pale eyes disconcerting. "It wasn't that simple. Sandra and I had . . . a difference of opinion . . . over the direction her career was taking. I thought she was accepting too many commissions. She should have sold only through exhibitions and galleries—that's how you build a reputation." She gestured towards the gallery space. "I have two artists here now who may win major prizes. You won't find them selling paintings to any Tom, Dick, or Harry who wants something pretty for his sitting room."

"That's a bad thing?"

"It is if you want to be taken seriously. And it is a business, make no mistake. Sandra thought art was meant to be seen, and that it was up to the viewer to decide the meaning of a piece." From Pippa's tone, Sandra might as well have insisted that the world was flat. "That silliness I could have dealt with by careful marketing, building a mystique," Pippa went on, "but I could only do that by representing her exclusively." She drank more of her tea, although Gemma still found it too hot to touch.

"But Sandra wouldn't agree to that?" she said, as neutrally as she could manage.

"No. Sandra could be infuriatingly stubborn. So I told her in that case I couldn't represent her at all, thinking it would change her mind. But it didn't. And there we were." Pippa hunched over her mug, pushing back the curtain of her long, flaxen hair as it fell over her face. The color, Gemma saw, went all the way to the roots, and at the parting her scalp was pink. "I never meant it to go on," Pippa said. "It wasn't worth losing a friendship. And now I can't take it back."

"I'm sorry," Gemma said. "That must be hard. But we don't know for certain what happened to Sandra."

"No. But I can't imagine . . . and I can't bear to think of her learning Naz was dead. Do you—I know you said you weren't officially with the police—but do you know what happened? How—how Naz was killed?"

Knowing that no information about the drugs in Naz's system had been released, Gemma couldn't enlighten her, although she wondered what Pippa Nightingale's reaction would be. Instead, she said, "Pippa, when I came in, you already knew about Naz's death. Who told you?"

Pippa Nightingale looked up, her delicate eyebrows raised, and Gemma had to resist the urge to look away from those strange eyes.

"Why, Lucas of course," she said.

Ahmed Azad must have more relatives than most people had acquaintances, Cullen thought as he sat wearily back from the computer screen at his desk.

According to the immigration records Cullen had accessed, Azad had already sponsored nieces, nephews, great-nieces and -nephews, cousins, and a few second cousins thrown in for good measure. Mohammed Rahman, the missing great-nephew, was only the latest ripple in a years' long flood. And young Mohammed had been working at his uncle's restaurant, living in his uncle's house, reporting regularly to his contact with the prosecution—and then he was not. Mohammed Rahman's blip had simply disappeared from the radar screen.

Cullen had tried every database he could think of, including missing persons and John Does. Mohammed's friends and acquaintances had been questioned by Immigration, but Cullen would have to institute another go-round.

Nor had he had much better luck with Lucas Ritchie's former employee Kylie Watters. There had been no activity on her national insurance number, so she wasn't drawing benefits, and if she was working, it was off the record. The mobile number Melanie had given them was indeed out of service, having been canceled for non-payment a few days after she had moved out of Melanie's flat.

Kylie's national insurance number linked back to an address in Essex. He'd found a phone number through reverse look-up, but there had been no answer. That meant more legwork, as did checking out Lucas Ritchie's alibi for the day Naz Malik had been killed. The St. John's Wood address Ritchie had given them was listed as belonging to a Matthew Ritchie, and a quick search had revealed that Matthew Ritchie was not a banker, as Kincaid had speculated, but a record company executive, with two children listed as Lucas and Sarah. So perhaps Ritchie had been telling the truth about the niece's birthday party, but learning whether all his time could be accounted for would require a personal visit. And family alibis were always liable to be dodgy.

Looking at his watch, Cullen saw that there would be no flat hunting on the agenda that afternoon. As he pulled out his mobile to check in with Kincaid, he thought about the call he'd had earlier from Gemma, asking for Roy Blakely's address. Should he mention it? Had she told Kincaid, as she'd promised? Either way, Cullen would look like a telltale if he said anything about it, and that irritated him. Whatever her rationale, she was meddling in their case, and he didn't like it. He disliked even more the fact that he couldn't complain about it.

But he would just have to bide his time.

Betty Howard rang just as Gemma was walking into the house. Putting her handbag down, Gemma juggled her mobile while trying to pet the dogs jumping excitedly at her legs. There was no suit jacket tossed carelessly over the coat rack—Duncan wasn't home yet. Nor was there any immediate sign of the boys, so she guessed they were in the garden.

Betty's rich voice came distantly until she managed to get the phone to her ear. "—hate to bother you so soon, Gemma, but Wesley's working at the café tonight and I've got a carnival meeting—an emergency costume summit." Betty chuckled. "Would you mind keeping little Charlotte? It will only be for an hour or two."

Gemma suddenly found that her heart was beating a bit faster. "No, of course I don't mind. What time will you bring her? Or do you want me to pick her up?"

"I'll drop her in half an hour, if that's all right. She'll have had her tea."

"Right. See you then." Gemma was hanging up when she heard a tread on the front steps and Duncan came in, jacket already thrown over his shoulder, tie off and shirt sleeves rolled up.

"You look positively pink," he said. She felt the rasp of stubble as he kissed her cheek. She put a hand to his shoulder and held her cheek to his a moment longer. When she let go, he studied her. "Are you sunburned, or are you glad to see me?"

"No. Yes, I mean. Both." She didn't know why she felt so flustered. It wasn't as if she didn't know how to look after a toddler, although it had begun to seem a long time since Toby was that small. "What I mean is, we're having company."

CHAPTER SIXTEEN

*. . . for home to me was certainly never anything remotely
material. It consisted, I have decided, in something I sensed
as refuge: an atmosphere of safety in the love between my
parents. It came in a tone of voice, in the preparation and
eating of meals, in conversations during washing up and
being busy in the garden.*

—Dennis Severs,
*18 Folgate Street:
The Tale of a
House in Spitalfields*

It was rough going at first. Charlotte had come willingly into Gemma's arms when Betty had dropped her off, but once in the house, the dogs barking and jumping up had frightened her and she had buried her head against Gemma's shoulder.

"It's all right, lovey," Gemma had soothed. "The doggies just want to be friends with you." But Charlotte had clung even more tightly to Bob, her plush elephant, and watched the dogs with wide, frightened eyes. Naz and Sandra hadn't had a dog, Gemma thought, so perhaps she wasn't accustomed to them.

Duncan had changed into T-shirt and jeans and gone out to fetch the boys from the garden. Now, having seen Betty's little van drive past, they all came trooping in to examine their guest.

"Say hello to Charlotte, boys," said Gemma.

Toby, already wound up from playing outside and the excitement of Duncan's homecoming, stomped through the hall shrieking, "I'm Captain Hook, and I'm going to feed you to the crocodile," and holding up a clawlike hand.

In desperation, they had retired his *Pirates of the Caribbean* films and replaced them with every version they could find of *Peter Pan*. Now, Gemma wasn't sure that had been an improvement.

"Toby, if you can't behave nicely, you can go to your room," Gemma told him as Charlotte buried her head still farther.

When Duncan gave him a warning look and said, "Calm down, sport," Toby subsided a bit, but kept singing under his breath and making little flying motions.

Duncan touched Charlotte's curls and said gently, "Well, you're a pretty girl, aren't you, love?"

Kit, who had been standing back, observing, took charge. "She's afraid of the dogs," he whispered, then he turned to Charlotte and said, "Hi, Charlotte. I'm Kit. That's Tess and that's Geordie." He pointed at each dog in turn. "They can do tricks. Would you like to see?"

Charlotte peeped out from Gemma's shoulder and gave a very small nod.

Kit put the dogs in a sit, then a down. He had Geordie lift a paw to shake hands, and Tess roll over. The little terrier looked so comical with all four legs straight up in the air and her shaggy face upside down that Gemma thought she felt Charlotte begin to giggle. But when Kit asked her if she'd like to shake Geordie's paw, she shook her head and clutched Gemma more tightly.

"Oh, dear." Gemma shifted Charlotte a little more securely onto her hip. "Maybe we should put the dogs up for a bit until she gets used to us, at least. And I don't know what we'll do for dinner—I never got to the shops. I thought I was going to visit Gran at the hospital, but they sent her home this afternoon."

"Is she better, then?" asked Kit.

"Yes, she's feeling much better." Gemma didn't mention that Vi had sounded exhausted at the prospect of going home. "We'll go see her at the weekend."

"Pizza, pizza for dinner," Toby chanted, and Duncan groaned. "I'm going to turn into a pizza."

"Are not," said Toby.

"Oh, yes I am." Duncan patted his middle. "Or at least I'll be round as one."

"I can make us omelets," offered Kit. "We have eggs and cheese, and some mushrooms. And I think there's a tomato. The last time I was at Otto's, Wes taught me to flip omelets in the pan. I've been practicing with dried beans."

"That sounds dangerous," Gemma said, laughing, "but delicious. Can we watch?"

Kit grinned. "Only if you say 'Yes, Chef.'"

"Mushrooms are *disgusting*." Toby made a face and stuck out his tongue.

"Pirates eat mushrooms," Duncan told him, with great seriousness.

"Do not."

"Do, too. That's what makes their teeth black."

Toby's eyes grew big. "Really? Will they make mine black, too?"

"Only if you eat enough of them." Duncan tousled his hair. "Give the dogs biscuits and put them in the study for a bit, sport. We'll see if Miss Charlotte likes cats."

Gemma sat at the kitchen table with Charlotte in her lap while Kit, with Duncan acting as sous-chef, assembled the ingredients for omelets and salad. Toby, having put the dogs up, ran through the house looking for Sid, who had disappeared with typical feline alacrity when wanted.

After a few minutes, Gemma felt Charlotte begin to relax, then the little girl squirmed round so that she had a better view of Kit.

"You are an absolute rock star in the kitchen, Kit," Gemma said admiringly as Kit deftly chopped mushrooms and tomato. "You'd better be careful or you'll set a precedent. You're a much better cook than I am."

Kit grinned at her, coloring a little. His cheeks were already flushed from the heat. "I just watch Wes."

"You could give your dad lessons," she teased Duncan.

"Hey," Duncan protested, flicking a tea towel at her. "I've made an omelet. I can scramble eggs, and grill things, and, God forbid, order pizza."

"Lame, very lame," said Kit cheekily.

But when the first omelet was bubbling in the pan, Kit's courage failed. "We only have just enough eggs," he said, frowning. "Maybe I'll just turn them with a spatula."

"That's probably a good idea," Gemma agreed, not wanting him to dent his pride or donate someone's omelet to the dogs. "We'll buy extra eggs next time so that you can practice."

While Kit whisked eggs and swirled them in the omelet pan, Duncan laid the table, tossed the salad, and corralled and scrubbed Toby. As everyone sat down, Gemma still held Charlotte on her knee, but loosely. The child was sitting up, gazing from one boy to the other as if they were the most fascinating creatures she'd ever seen, but she still hadn't spoken.

Then, when Gemma made the first cut into her golden, cheese-oozing omelet, Charlotte reached out and said clearly, precisely, "I want 'shrooms."

Gemma fed Charlotte bites of her omelet, talking softly to her as the boys chattered. When they'd finished—Toby having eaten his mushrooms with a great show of fortitude—Duncan cleared the plates. "Let's leave the washing up for later, when it's cooler, and take Charlotte into the garden while there's still light," he suggested. "Maybe she'd like to swing."

The house had its own garden, separated from the communal garden behind it by only an iron fence and gate. The communal garden, a long park with a terrace of houses on either side and high fences at the ends, was one of the great blessings of the house, and it had afforded both children and dogs many happy hours. A weathered wooden swing, courtesy of some previous neighbor, hung from one of the large trees near their patio garden.

Toby banged out through the gate, followed by the dogs, who were riotous with freedom. While Toby climbed into the swing, the dogs chased madly round in a circle. The sun had dropped behind the houses on the far side of the garden and the light filtering through the trees was a soft, hazy gold. The air had cooled, and a breeze carried the scent of the night-blooming jasmine Gemma had planted in a pot on the patio.

Duncan came out through the dining room doors, carrying two glasses of chilled white wine. "You left your phone in the kitchen. Betty just rang. She said she'd be a bit later than she thought. I told her not to worry."

Gingerly, Gemma lowered Charlotte to the patio, and when she sat down, Charlotte didn't climb back into her lap. Bob, her green plush elephant, had been left behind in the kitchen.

Watching Toby and the dogs intently, Charlotte whispered, "Georgy. Teth."

Kit came out, tucking his phone in his jeans pocket with one hand. In the other, he held a plastic tube filled with the dogs' favorite squeaky tennis balls. Squatting by Charlotte, he took a ball out and squeaked it for her in demonstration. She giggled. "Would you like to throw the ball for the dogs?" he asked.

Charlotte looked up at Gemma, who nodded encouragement. "You go on, lovey."

When Kit held out a hand, Charlotte took it, and together they went through the gate. She was hesitant at first, but Kit helped her toss the ball, and soon she was running with the boys and the dogs, squealing with glee. Her brown legs were still toddler chubby beneath her pink shorts.

Lights began to come on in the houses across the garden as Duncan sank down in the chair beside Gemma's and picked up his wine. "My God," he said, watching the children. "She is lovely, isn't she?" There was a hint of apology in his tone. "You were right, you know," he added softly. "I'd hate to see her go to someone who didn't care for her properly."

"I went to see Roy Blakely today," said Gemma, seeing her opening.

"Blakely?"

"Sandra's friend on Columbia Road. The one she left Charlotte with that day." She glanced at him. "You didn't tell me I couldn't."

"Cheeky." He gave her knee a gentle pinch. "So what did you find out?"

"Gail Gilles was a lousy mother."

"And you're surprised?"

Gemma shrugged. "Roy Blakely has known her since they were children. He wouldn't be very comfortable testifying against her in family court, but he's not happy with the idea of her taking Charlotte, either."

"Did he give you anything specific about the brothers?"

"No," Gemma said, not disguising her disappointment. "But he told me that Sandra hadn't been getting on with her former dealer"— seeing Duncan's startled glance, she clarified—"art dealer, I mean. And so I, um, went to see her, too."

"Unofficially?" Kincaid asked, raising an eyebrow.

Gemma sipped her wine. "Unofficially."

"And?"

"Her name is Pippa Nightingale, and she's . . . interesting. She seemed genuinely distressed by Naz's death, because she seems to think it means Sandra really isn't coming back. Guilty conscience over her falling-out with Sandra, it sounds like, although she still couldn't help sounding bitter over their disagreement. She felt Sandra didn't take her art seriously enough—more or less accused her of being an interior designer rather than an artist. And she heard the news about Naz from Lucas Ritchie. It seems they were all three mates from art college days, although I think Pippa is a bit older."

"Ah, Lucas Ritchie," Duncan said meditatively. "Interesting bloke."

Gemma turned towards him. "What? You met him? What's he like?"

"Very polished. Very credible. Sandra's art prominently displayed in his very posh club that seems, on the surface, to be aboveboard. And he seems, at least on first pass, to have an alibi for the day of Naz's death. As does Ahmed Azad, by the way."

"Azad could have hired goons," Gemma suggested.

"So could Ritchie, I think. But I haven't come up with a really good reason why either of them would have done so. Lucas Ritchie says he and Sandra were longtime friends, and even if they had been having an affair, I can't see why he would have harmed her. It still looks like Sandra's brothers are topping the charts."

"You talked to them?" The children looked up from their play, and Gemma made an effort to lower her voice. "What did they say?"

Duncan swirled the dregs of his wine. "Ah, well. That's problematical. I *didn't* talk to them. And I'm not going to, at least any time soon," he added, tipping up his glass to empty it. "I had a visit this afternoon from the guv'nor, who'd had a visit from a high-up muckety-muck in Narcotics. Apparently, Narcotics have been running an undercover op in the area for a couple of years.

"Major drug smuggling from Europe, a couple of homicides

involved. And while the Gilles brothers may be very small fry, things are at a critical enough stage that they don't want anything to rock the boat."

"So they are into drugs." Gemma didn't know whether to feel vindicated or horrified.

"Minor players, but yes. And Narcotics think if we talk to them, it might put the wind up bigger fish. And that means I can't talk to Gail Gilles either."

The children had interrupted them, trailing back up to the patio and demanding drinks. Toby had taken Charlotte by the hand and was bossing her about quite insufferably, but as Charlotte seemed happy, Gemma didn't correct him.

After fetching them chilled, bottled water from the kitchen fridge, she'd gone back inside to do the washing up. Duncan had offered, but she'd needed some time to think over the events of the day, and she'd wanted to give him the opportunity to be on his own with Charlotte and the boys.

What sense could it possibly make to a child, she wondered, to have mummy gone, then daddy, then to be taken from home and nanny and all things familiar to a strange house with a new family, then left again in a different house with a different family. Although Betty had, of course, told Charlotte she would be coming back for her, Gemma wasn't sure Charlotte was old enough to understand that. Or whether she would believe it, given the capriciousness of the blows life had recently dealt her.

It was she, Gemma realized as she turned off the tap and began to dry the plates, who had been the only constant in Charlotte's life since the afternoon of her father's disappearance. The thought made her feel both frightened and possessive.

Voices drifted in through the open doors in the dining and sitting room; Duncan's low chuckle, the high-pitched tones of the little ones, and Kit's still unreliable shift between tenor and baritone, with an occasional canine yip as counterpoint.

But by the time she'd finished up in the kitchen, it had grown quiet, and when she entered the sitting room she saw that they had all migrated inside. A pool of lamplight fell on Kit, who was draped sideways over the armchair, cocooned with his iPod and earbuds.

Toby sat cross-legged on the floor a few feet from the television, the sound off, watching mesmerized as Cathy Rigby swooped and swaggered across the screen. The dogs were stretched out, panting, beside him, and Sid had taken up a safe vantage point on the bookcase.

And Duncan . . . Duncan sat on the sofa with Charlotte cradled in his arms. She was fast asleep, her curly head tucked under his chin, and on his face was an expression of surprised and wondering tenderness.

When Betty had collected the still-sleeping Charlotte—and it seemed to Gemma that Duncan had lowered her into her car seat with some reluctance—and the boys were in bed, Gemma and Duncan lay side by side, the sheet thrown back to catch a breeze from the open window.

Drowsily, she shifted towards him until their thighs touched, wondering if the warm, humid air would stick their limbs together like glue. "So, what are you going to do about Gail Gilles and her sons?" she asked. He'd told her that the plainclothes officers he'd put on watch had seen Kevin and Terry Gilles moving some of their belongings from their mother's council flat to their sister Donna's flat nearby. "Have you let Janice Silverman know Kevin and Terry are under investigation?"

"I'm not to contact her. They don't want any chance of a leak. But . . ." He trailed his fingers over her thigh, raising goose bumps. "I thought—since you've already established that you're interested in Charlotte's welfare—I thought you might have a word with Gail Gilles after all. To express your condolences, and your concern for Charlotte."

"Unofficially?" Gemma shivered and moved closer. Although she certainly wanted to meet Gail Gilles, she wasn't sure who was taking advantage of whom in this little arrangement.

He touched a finger to her lips. "You never heard it from me."

CHAPTER SEVENTEEN

Fears are entertained that the locality is being taken over,
with Bethnal Green becoming Bangla Green.

—Geoff Dench,
Kate Gavron,
Michael Young,
The New East End

Gemma went into work on Wednesday morning knowing she was going to have to have a word with her boss, Mark Lamb. She couldn't take any more time off work unless she discussed it with him. And as much as she hated using her mother's health as an excuse, she couldn't see another option. It wouldn't be politic for her to say she was helping Kincaid with an investigation, and especially not when she was looking into something that he'd been warned against.

Superintendent Lamb's expression of concern made her feel even guiltier, but the guilt did nothing to dampen the sense of urgency she felt about Charlotte. After she'd left Lamb's office she plowed through work, trying to clear as much as she could of her caseload, then she called her parents' house in Leyton to check on her mum. By late morning, she was able to leave her desk with her conscience at least a little clearer.

This time, she took her car to the East End. Although the address Kincaid had given her was not far from the Bethnal Green tube station, she was not keen on the idea of wandering round an unfamiliar—and probably not particularly safe—East London housing estate on foot. And she was still a bit sunburned from yesterday afternoon's excursion.

She found the estate easily, just south of Old Bethnal Green Road, and it was worse than she'd expected. A gray monument to late-sixties concrete-block architecture, its five stories squatted incongruously on a patch of green lawn. Every inch of concrete within human reach had been tagged with ugly, leering, giant-size faces and symbols. On the upper-level balconies, ragged laundry hung limply, as if wilting in the heat, and Indian pop music blared from an open window.

Finding a place to park, Gemma got out and gazed up at the building, shading her eyes. If Sandra had grown up here, how had she survived with the urge to make beautiful things intact? Or had the desire to create beauty grown out of desperation? Leyton had by no means been beautiful, but this . . . She thought of the Fournier Street house, with its comfortable and quirky elegance, and felt a new understanding of Sandra's need to make a welcoming home. Sandra must have wanted to give her daughter what she had never had.

Gemma didn't bother trying the lift. Even if it worked, which was unlikely, she didn't want to be trapped within its hot and undoubtedly smelly confines.

The urine-saturated stairwell was bad enough. She climbed to the fifth floor, trying to remember to breathe through her mouth, and being careful not to touch the walls or handrail. Halfway up, she saw a broken tricycle on the landing. She didn't want to think about the possibility that a child had fallen with it.

When she reached the top floor, sweating and a bit queasy, she saw from the door numbers that Gail Gilles's flat must be near the end of the long corridor. The concrete floor was awash with plastic bags, empty soda bottles and beer cans, cigarette ends, and against one wall, the shriveled husk of a used condom.

As she approached the peeling blue door at the corridor's end, she suddenly realized that she had no idea what she was going to say. Having a distant claim of friendship with Naz was not likely to cut any ice with Sandra's mother, but she'd have to do her best. There was no buzzer, so she knocked. After a moment, the strident shouting of a telly advert coming from inside the flat went quiet, and Gemma was sure she was being scanned through the peephole in the door. Resisting the temptation to knock again, she made an effort to relax her posture and paste a pleasant expression on her face. She imagined her lime green linen jacket looked as bedraggled as the washing she'd seen hanging outside, but she doubted whether a starched wardrobe, like her connection with Naz Malik, would earn her any points here. At least she probably didn't look like a bill collector.

The door swung open, and Gemma stared at the woman who must be Sandra Gilles's mother. She saw a busty figure gone to plumpness, blond hair, perhaps once the same burnished straw color as Sandra's, but now bleached to platinum and piled high on her head. On her bare feet, Gail Gilles sported gold toenails, a fitting accompaniment to the tight black Capri trousers, the clingy leopard-print top, the overabundant makeup, and the immediately apparent attitude.

Hand on hip, she said, "I told you already. They've gone. You got no call to come back like the frigging police."

"Mrs. Gilles?" Gemma hoped her baffled expression was good enough to hide her jolt of shock at the word *police*. It had taken her a second to realize she hadn't given herself away—Gail Gilles obviously thought she was a social worker, checking on her sons' removal.

"Whose business is it?" Gail asked, still sounding hostile but not quite so certain of her ground.

"Um, my name's Gemma. I thought you must be Charlotte's grandmother, but you don't look old enough . . ."

Gail's expression softened at the bald-faced flattery. "I might be. Not old enough to be anyone's grandma, but I was just a baby myself, wasn't I, when I 'ad my daughter." She looked more closely at Gemma and frowned. At least Gemma thought it was a frown—her mouth turned down but her brow didn't wrinkle. "But I don't know you, do I?"

Gemma rushed into an explanation, babbling a bit, but thinking that if nerves made her sound like a nitwit, all the better. "I'm so sorry about your son-in-law. It must be a terrible shock. I'm a friend of your son-in-law's—your late son-in-law's—friend, the one who reported him missing. I helped out with Charlotte until social services came. I don't know why they didn't call you straightaway. She's a cute kid, and I thought, well, she should be with her family, shouldn't she? And I thought, well, I happened to be in the neighborhood, and I wanted to say I was sorry for your loss, and ask if there was anything I could do, but . . ." She trailed off, as if unsure of what came next, which was certainly the case, and praying Gail didn't ask how she'd come by the address.

But Gail Gilles seemed unable to resist the temptation of a sympathetic ear, however unlikely its appearance on her doorstep. Pulling the door wide, she said, "That's the truth, innit? I always say as kids should be with family. It hain't natural otherwise. Why don't you come in and 'ave a cuppa? What did you say your name was?"

"The kettle just boiled," said Gail. "Should still be 'ot enough. Have a seat and I'll bring something in." Glancing in the kitchen, Gemma saw on the work top an open takeaway pizza box, a shiny new espresso machine, and beyond that, an old plastic electric kettle. The flat smelled faintly of bad drains, or perhaps rotting garbage.

As directed, she sat down gingerly on the edge of a new, over-

stuffed, cream-colored leather sofa, taking advantage of the opportunity to check out her surroundings. Her first impression was that
the flat was the center of an ongoing jumble sale. The sofa had both
matching chair and loveseat, all squeezed together like puffy cream
mushrooms, and every bit of space left in the room seemed to be
crammed with something. Odd bits of furniture, some of it broken.
Children's toys. Piles of clothing. Even a rug, rolled up and stood on
end in a corner.

The yellowed walls held a motley collection of cheap prints, Princess Diana portraits, and a few family photos depicting two chunky
boys and a girl who slightly resembled Sandra. Her face was prettier
than Sandra's, but less interesting and intelligent. Sandra's younger
sister, Donna? In another photo, the same young woman appeared
older, with three unnaturally stiff-looking little boys clustered round
her. There were no photos that Gemma could see of Sandra—or of
Charlotte.

"That's my Donna," said Gail, startling Gemma as she came
back into the room. She carried two mugs of what Gemma soon
discovered was tepid instant coffee. It had obviously been made with
water from the old kettle, as bits of scale floated on the top.

"Um, thanks." Gemma smiled and set the mug on the coffee
table, trying to keep up a slightly vague expression. She had been
thinking that if Gail's sons were dealing drugs, they weren't doing
too well at it, when she caught sight of the large flat-screen television
half hidden by a pile of moving boxes. Beneath the TV, a satellite
box and DVD player sat on the floor, beside a Bose sound system.
Plastic Guitar Hero guitars lay to one side, next to toppling stacks
of DVD boxes.

Put those things together with the sofas, ugly but probably expensive, and the fancy coffee machine in the kitchen. All were items
that could easily be bought with handy, untraceable cash.

"She's a good girl, my Donna. And those are Donna's kids," Gail
went on, sitting down on the bloated chair with her own cup. "She

had 'em all fixed up for that portrait studio, you know, the one where you get all the different sizes and the little ones you carry in your wallet."

Gemma noticed that she didn't refer to the children as her grand-children. "They're very good looking. Like Charlotte."

Her face clouding, Gail said, "That Charlotte. You said you seen her, so you'll know. She's a darkie. Still." Gail gave a gusty, martyred sigh. "She's my flesh and blood, and it's my duty to take her in."

"Will you be moving, then?" Gemma gestured at the boxes.

"Oh, no. Not me. It's my boys. That social worker says they've got to move out before I can have my own granddaughter. My boys pushed out of their own 'ome, if you can credit that! I don't know as what I'd do without my boys. Why just Saturday, they borrowed their mates' van and took me to pick out this furniture. Brought it home that very night, too." Gail shook her head and her blond hair wob-bled. "They look after me, don't they?" She gave Gemma a sudden fierce glare. "It hain't your friend who told that social worker lady those bad things about my Kev and my Terry?"

"Oh, no. It can't have been," said Gemma, thinking it wasn't an outright lie, as *she* had been the one who'd passed the drug rumors on to Janice Silverman. "Where will they go, your sons?"

"Well, they can stay with their sister until we get this sorted. Not that she 'as room, mind you, but she wouldn't turn 'em away. She's a good sister, our Donna, not like some who think they're too good for their own." Gail kicked her gold sandals off under the coffee table, wiggling her toes, and as Gemma glanced down at one toppled shoe she saw that the label read Jimmy Choo.

She had to stop herself whistling through her teeth and put on a baffled look instead. "I'm sorry. I don't understand . . . Who—"

"Sandra." Gail's tone was venomous. "Always thought she was too good for us, from the time she was no bigger than that daughter of hers. And then she married that Paki, and he turned her. Bad enough we have to live here with 'em. God knows what 'e's done to that little girl, but we'll soon see about that. It won't take me long to sort 'er out."

The scummy instant coffee Gemma had been forced to taste for politeness's sake came back up in her throat. She thought the fury coursing through her veins must be visible, throbbing in her face. Swallowing hard, she said, "I didn't know your daughter, Mrs. Gilles—Gail—do you mind if I call you Gail?" Not waiting for an answer, she prattled on, "About your daughter—I never really heard—what was it happened to your daughter?"

"She run off." It was aggravation, not grief, that colored Gail's voice. "Just upped and run off. Probably to get away from that Paki husband of 'ers. How she could leave that baby, I don't know. It's unnatural, innit?"

"Oh, I—" Gemma stood up so quickly that the coffee she'd set on the table sloshed from the mug. Her anger boiled up, and she felt she might be physically sick. "Oh, I am so sorry," she managed to mumble. She fished a tissue from her handbag, grateful that for a moment her hair fell forward to hide her face. Mopping at the brown liquid, she said, "I—I'm afraid all of a sudden I'm not feeling too well."

"Not catching, is it?" Gail looked at her suspiciously.

"No, no, I'm sure it's not. It's just the heat. Listen, ta ever so much for the coffee. I hope things work out for you. And for little Charlotte." She flashed Gail a sickly smile and headed towards the door, dodging round the packing boxes.

"You," Gail called after her. "What did you say your name was? Gemma?"

She turned back, her heart thudding. "Gemma. That's right." She had blown it, and now she was going to have to bail herself out, somehow, and without blowing the narcotics op as well.

"You said you helped look after Charlotte before the social worker lady took her." To Gemma's surprise, Gail's voice had taken on a wheedling tone. "So you know that Silverman woman. Any way you could put in a good word for me?"

Gemma clattered down the stairs, barely missing the tricycle, and cannoned out onto the patch of green lawn. She was breathing as if she'd been running a sprint, and it was only when she reached her car and pushed her hair back from her face as she fished for her keys that she saw them.

Two young men, one more heavyset than the other, both with heads shaved to a dark stubble, watched her from near the bottom of the stairwell. Although they were older than they had been in the photos, she recognized them from the family portraits in Sandra Gilles's flat. Kevin and Terry Gilles, undoubtedly. Had she gone right past them? Did they know she'd come from their mother's flat? If not, they would soon enough.

She glanced away, keeping her face deliberately blank, just as her searching fingers found her keys. Casually, she inserted the key in the lock, opened the door, and climbed into the Escort. The driver's seat scorched the backs of her thighs even through her trousers, and the steering wheel felt molten, but she switched the blower on high and drove slowly, cautiously away, without lowering the windows, and without looking back.

Crossing Bethnal Green Road, she made the first right turn she saw and pulled the car over near a quiet churchyard. It seemed miles from the council estate. With the car idling, she lifted her shaking hands from the wheel and lowered the windows.

What had she been thinking, going into that flat as unprepared as a lamb? What if the sons had come in?

And what had she accomplished for the risk?

She thought it through. She now knew that although Gail Gilles seemed to have no means of support, her sons, who had menial jobs at best, kept her well supplied with high-priced merchandise, and God knew what else that was not so visible. That made it pretty certain that Kevin and Terry had undocumented—and probably illegal—income.

And they had seen her. She hadn't identified herself, hadn't given her last name, but would it be enough to make them, or their hypothetical bosses, suspicious?

And what if Gail hadn't been fooled by her dithery act? What if Gail had been playing her, having marked her as an undercover cop? And a lousy undercover cop, at that.

Bloody hell. The worst thing was that she could not—absolutely could not—repeat anything she'd learned to Janice Silverman. Gail Gilles was vain, grasping, callous, bigoted, and still seemed to hold a vicious grudge against her missing daughter. Nor did she seem to feel an iota of genuine concern for her granddaughter. The thought of Charlotte being abandoned to the woman's care—if you could call it that—made her feel ill again.

As she wiped her sweaty face with a handkerchief, trying to work out what to do next, her phone rang, and she saw with relief that it was Melody and not Kincaid. She wasn't ready to tell Kincaid that she just might have made a balls-up of things.

"Boss." Melody sound reassuringly crisp and cheerful. "You said to call if anything came in, so I am. There's been a burglary, a hairdresser's shop down the bottom of Ladbroke Grove. Last night, but they just now got round to reporting it. Manager apparently waited until the owner came in. Want me to put Talley's team on it?"

"What?" It took Gemma a moment to make sense of what Melody had said. In the last two weeks, they'd had a string of nighttime burglaries of small shops, although the culprits usually didn't manage to get much more than a little merchandise and some petty cash. "Oh, right," she said, recovering. "Yes, Talley should take it. He's been working the others." A thought occurred to her. "Look, Melody, could you get away for a bit? I'm in Bethnal Green."

Melody had suggested they meet at the Spitalfields Market. "There's a good salad place there. I haven't had lunch, and I'm watching my calories." If she was curious as to why Gemma was in Bethnal Green when she'd said she was going to Leyton to visit her mum, she kept it to herself.

Although Gemma hadn't far to drive, it took her so long to find a place to park that Melody, having come on the tube to Liverpool Street, was there before her.

On this Wednesday afternoon, the vendors' tables in the main arcade of the old market were stacked and folded, and the empty trading space seemed to echo a little wistfully under the great glass vault. She found the salad kiosk round the corner, across the arcade from some of the trendier cafés. It had a buffet line on the inside, and a few tables with umbrellas out in the arcade, as if it were a sidewalk café.

"I finally parked in the Bangla City carpark," Gemma said when she reached Melody. "I hope I don't get towed." The Asian supermarket was at the Brick Lane end of Fournier Street, and she had walked past Naz and Sandra's house on her way to the market. The house seemed to her to have taken on an indefinable air of desertion in the few days since she had seen it.

"What are you doing here?" Melody asked. "I thought your mum had been sent home."

"She has. I—It's . . . complicated."

Melody looked at her critically. "Well, I'm starved, and you look positively knackered. Have you eaten?"

"No, but—"

"We'll get something. And then you can tell me about it." When Gemma started to protest, Melody overrode her. "You have a seat and I'll choose. I know what's good here, and I know what you like."

Gemma sat down at one of the little round tables, willing enough to be managed for the moment. The shade and the drafts of air moving through the arcade were welcomingly cool, and by the time Melody came out, with plastic boxes of salad and cups of coffee, she had begun to feel a bit more collected.

The prospect of coffee made her quail, but then she thought per-

haps she should approach it as if she were getting back on a horse—
if she didn't erase the taste of Gail Gilles's horrible brew now, she
might never be able to face coffee again.

Melody had brought her a plain latte, her favorite coffee drink,
and the salad was a colorful mix of beetroot, carrot, chickpeas, and
hard-cooked egg on greens. "How did you know about this place?"
Gemma asked, finding as she tasted the salad that she was hungry
after all. And the coffee was deliciously strong and mellow.

"Oh, I like to come to the Saturday market." Melody shrugged
offhandedly, displaying her usual reluctance to discuss her personal
life. "It's mostly touristy tat now, but there are still some good stalls.
So, is this about the Malik case?" Melody asked, changing the subject before Gemma could question her further.

Gemma finished a bite of salad, considering. She badly wanted
someone to confide in—but how much could she say without betray-
ing Kincaid's confidence?

And she was Melody's boss, which made it even trickier to admit
that she'd skived off work and lied about going to visit her ill mum,
especially when the one thing she absolutely could *not* say was that
she'd done it at Kincaid's instigation. But then, Melody was so solidly dependable, and had never let her down. If there was anyone she
could talk to . . .

"I went to see Gail Gilles," she blurted out. "Sandra's mother. I
wasn't supposed to, and I can't talk about it. I can't have been there,
do you see?"

"Okay," Melody said thoughtfully. "You weren't there. I get that.
So what didn't you see when you weren't there?"

Gemma pushed her salad away, her appetite suddenly gone. "Oh,
Melody, she's horrible. She doesn't care anything about Charlotte—
in fact, I'd say she actively dislikes her, or at least the idea of her. I
don't think she actually knows her at all. And I can't imagine her
looking after a child, although her own children seem to have grown
up by hook or by crook. Crook being more like it."

"The sons?"

Gemma nodded. "And I *cannot* talk to Janice Silverman about the things I saw that will probably be tidied up before social services make their first home visit, or about the things she said to me that she would probably never say to a social worker."

"Eat," Melody ordered, scooting the salad back in Gemma's direction. "And let's think about what else you can do. If she doesn't want Charlotte out of grandmotherly concern, then why is she willing to take on a child?"

Picking obediently at the shredded beetroot, which had stained the hard-cooked egg a lovely pink, Gemma said, "It's got to be money. If the house is unencumbered, it's worth a lot. And Sandra's unsold artwork—it may be valuable, too." She thought of the prices she'd seen on the works in Pippa's gallery. "I should have thought to ask Pippa Nightingale."

"Nightingale?" Melody looked bemused, but waved her fork. "Never mind. Go on."

"Duncan said Naz's law partner is the executor of his will, but Naz and Sandra didn't name a guardian for Charlotte."

"But the estate will have to make provision for her care, so maybe Grandma thinks if she gets the kid, she'll get a piece of it, or at least a regular allowance," suggested Melody. "But I would think that the mother's disappearance would complicate matters. Can you talk to the lawyer?"

"I don't see why not," Gemma said slowly. "As long as I don't mention anything about . . . where I didn't go."

"That's one avenue, then. So who's this Pippa person? That's a posh name if I ever heard one. Could she add anything you *could* repeat about Gail Gilles?"

"Pippa is—was—Sandra's art dealer. Roy Blakely told me they'd had a falling-out, but Pippa says it was a disagreement over the way Sandra was marketing her art. She says she didn't know Sandra's family, and that Sandra never talked about them."

"I'm beginning to see why," said Melody.

Gemma grimaced. "That's an understatement. But the odd thing was, Pippa said she and Sandra and Lucas Ritchie were all three friends."

"Lucas Ritchie was the guy Naz Malik told Tim Sandra was rumored to have had an affair with—well, that's a bit garbled, but you know what I mean." Melody waved her fork dismissively. "Did you ask Pippa about the alleged affair?"

"No." Gemma drank some of her latte, savoring it. "I was there as a friend, because of Charlotte, and Pippa seemed so upset about Naz's death, and about Sandra . . . it just seemed . . . inappropriate. Duncan asked Lucas Ritchie, though, and he said he and Sandra had been friends since art college, and that Naz would never have believed such a rumor." She went on to recount Kincaid's description of the club. "It's just round the corner here, in Widegate Street. And the interesting thing is that when Duncan asked Ritchie who started the rumor, he said it might have been a former employee, who is now conveniently missing."

"So." Melody tossed both their salad containers in the nearby rubbish bin and came back wiping her fingers with the paper napkin. "Is there any reason you can't talk to Lucas Ritchie, as a friend of Naz's?"

"I'd have to have got the information about the club from the police—"

"Tell him you got it from Pippa Nightingale."

"But—"

"Or tell him you want to know if you can hire his posh club for your hen party. Ask him if he'll allow a male stripper." Melody grinned impishly.

Gemma groaned. "Don't be absurd. And I don't want to have a hen party. Why would you think I did?"

"Because some of the girls at the station have been talking about it." Melody grew serious. "They think they're being snubbed. That they're not good enough for the boss."

"Snubbed? But I haven't even made plans for the wedding," Gemma protested.

Melody hesitated, then said, "And I'm not usually one to repeat gossip or to pry, but tongues are starting to wag about that, too. Boss, are you and the super not getting along?"

Gemma gaped at her. She'd had no idea people were talking. "Of course we're getting along. We're fine. It's just—it's just that I don't want a *wedding*." There, she'd said it, and the world hadn't fallen in. At least, not yet. "It's turned out to be something for everyone except us, and I just hate the whole idea." She thought of the way things had been the previous evening, with Duncan and the boys and Charlotte, and it was that . . . that *intimacy* she'd wanted to celebrate.

"Well, post banns and go to the register office, then," Melody suggested. "I'll be your witness."

Touched, Gemma said, "Thanks, Melody." Then she shook her head. "But my mum really wants this for me, and right now—I just don't think I can disappoint her."

Melody gave her a searching look, then shrugged. "It seems to me that you can either disappoint your mother or disappoint Duncan." She stood. "So Duncan said this Ritchie guy is good looking? Come on, let's go see for ourselves. I'll be your partner in crime."

CHAPTER EIGHTEEN

*The latest arrivals in Brick Lane, the 'haircuts' (as some of
the locals like to call them), are the ones buying up old
warehouses and turning them into vintage-clothing stores or
dot.com companies . . . As the City moves further towards
territory traditionally belonging to immigrant groups
tensions are increasing.*

—Rachel
Lichtenstein,
On Brick Lane

To Gemma the street seemed like a canyon, a last bastion of the old
London, close and crowded, steeped in the bustle of centuries, while
beyond it the great towers of the modern City advanced inexorably,
like armies of jagged glass shards. "I wonder why it was called Widegate?" she said aloud.

Melody, who was scanning the frontages as she walked beside her,
answered absently. "These are eighteenth-century silk merchants'
houses, most of them. Maybe there was a gate into Spitalfields—
literally into the fields, I mean. Look, this must be the club. It's a new
building, but very cleverly done."

The building matched the description that Kincaid had given Gemma. She rang the bell, and after a moment, the door clicked open.

The girl who met them in the elegant reception area, however, was not the girl Kincaid had described. This one was a delicate blond, with a Nordic look that reminded Gemma of Pippa Nightingale, but Gemma's gaze was held by the large fabric collage over the desk. Sandra's work, undoubtedly, and as stunning as the pieces she had seen in Sandra's studio.

They had no sooner asked to see Lucas Ritchie than a tall, fair man appeared from the small office area behind the reception desk. He came towards them with a hand outstretched, but his expression was a bit wary. "I'm Lucas Ritchie. Can I help you?"

"I'm Detective Inspector Gemma James, and this is DC Talbot. But I'm not here officially, Mr. Ritchie." As Gemma shook his hand, she gave him the same explanation she had given Roy Blakely and Pippa Nightingale, and took the opportunity to study him. Good looking, yes, but—she couldn't quite put her finger on what she found disconcerting. Perhaps he was just a bit too neat and perfectly tailored, although there was a suggestion of muscle under the fine fabric of his suit jacket. Or maybe it was the faintest hint of red to his fair hair, or the freckling on his lightly tanned skin—something she had a personal bias against. "Pippa said that you and Sandra went back a long way," she went on, trying to mesh this very polished man with what she knew of Sandra. "I thought that if you'd known her family . . ."

Ritchie moved away from the desk, although the blond girl had disappeared into the office area. A pale, heatless flame flickered in the sitting-area fireplace, even on such a warm day. It was meant to invoke a cozy atmosphere, Gemma supposed, but Ritchie didn't offer them a seat.

"I told your superintendent—Kincaid, was it?" Ritchie said, and Gemma nodded vaguely, as if she hadn't a clue as to who he meant. She certainly wasn't claiming possession at this point. "I told Superintendent Kincaid yesterday that I really didn't know Sandra's family." Ritchie leaned against the back of an armchair, folding his arms. "You have to understand, when we first met, we were kids in art school. Those aren't the sort of things we talked about. We were going to change the world, and we didn't want any baggage while we were doing it." There was a faraway look in his caramel-colored eyes. After a moment, he added reflectively, "Although I think you could say Sandra tipped the balance for the better. And she had more cachet than most of us, even in the beginning, being a genuine working-class girl, although she didn't make stock of it."

"Was she ashamed of her background?" asked Melody. In her tastefully pin-striped dark suit, she looked as if she belonged on the club staff.

"Sandra?" Ritchie laughed. "You didn't know Sandra. She was proud of being an East Ender—a real East Ender, some would say now—although Sandra was never the type to exclude anyone. She was unusually touchy about prejudice against race or religion, even for the multicultural crowd we hung out with."

"Mr. Ritchie," said Gemma, trying to come up with a tactful way to say it, "were you and Sandra always . . . just friends?"

He gave her an assessing look, then shrugged. "I don't know why it should be anyone else's business. As I've said, it was a long time ago. But if you want the truth, I always fancied Sandra more than she fancied me. She thought I was all flash and no substance, and I have to admit my track record hasn't been great, relationship wise. And then, when she met Naz, everyone else was history."

"How did she meet Naz, do you know?"

"He bought flowers from her."

The blond girl came out of the little office, carrying a tray set with a teapot and cups. "Sorry, Lucas," she said. "Phone kept ringing." She set the tray down on the coffee table in the sitting area, then hurried back to the desk as the front door buzzed.

"Thanks, Karen," he called after her. Then, motioning them to sit, Ritchie joined them and poured the tea himself. Two men came in, greeting the blond girl. The doors behind the desk opened to reveal a lift, and a group of men stepped out, making way for the incomers. They nodded at Ritchie as they headed for the front door.

"Last of the lunch crowd clearing out," Ritchie murmured. "It'll be drinks soon."

"So Sandra met Naz when she was working for Roy?" said Gemma, pleased by the idea.

"A bit fairy tale, but yes. I think he came every Sunday for a month before he got up the nerve to ask her for coffee."

"You've known Naz for a long time, too, then." Gemma balanced the fine white china cup on her knee. She wasn't sure why Ritchie was being so accommodating—she had the sense that it was in some way a performance—but she wasn't going to let an opportunity go by. "What was he like? It's been harder to get a feeling for him, for what made him tick."

"We all thought she'd gone bonkers at first. It wasn't that he was Asian—if you were racially prejudiced you certainly didn't admit to it—but he was a lawyer, for God's sake. Older, sober, hardworking—none of those things was in our art student manifesto." Ritchie drank some of his tea and stared into the cold fire. "It was only later, as I got to know him a bit better, that I saw the sense of humor beneath that serious exterior. But there was also a sort of rock-solid steadiness to Naz. They balanced each other, or maybe it was that he saw something in Sandra that no one else did.

"And they were both completely committed to being a family." He frowned, as if testing his memory. "I don't think Naz had any family left, and Sandra, well, it comes back to that, doesn't it?"

He glanced at her, as if considering, then went on more slowly. "There was something that happened, I'd forgotten. In art college, when she first starting going out with Naz. She came to class one day with a black eye. She hadn't tried to cover it up, she wasn't like that—there was always a bit of defiance to Sandra—but she wouldn't talk about it either. If you asked something she didn't want to answer, she would just give you a look that would freeze your marrow.

"But I asked her, because I didn't know Naz well then, if it was this new guy, and she looked truly shocked. She said, 'Bloody hell, do you think I'm some sort of slag?' and she wouldn't speak to me for a week."

"Was she living at home still?" Gemma asked.

"Yeah. Dreadful council flat. I picked her up and dropped her off now and again, but she never let me come in."

"So do you think someone in her family did that to her?"

"Well, if it wasn't Naz—and I don't believe it was—she had those two younger brothers. I got the impression she'd never known her dad, but then I suppose her mum might have had boyfriends . . ."

"Don't discount the mum," Melody put in. "It wouldn't be the first time a mother lost her temper, even with a grown daughter."

Gemma had considered that Gail might neglect Charlotte, or verbally abuse her, or expose her to bad influences, but it hadn't occurred to her that Gail might physically harm her. But of course it was possible. She felt stupid, and more than a little horrified.

"Mr. Ritchie, would you be willing to testify in family court about the possibility that Sandra was abused by someone in her family?"

"Family court?" He stared at her as if she were the one who'd gone bonkers. "But it's completely unsubstantiated. And it was years ago. I really don't see—" He looked round and even though there was no one else in the reception area, lowered his voice. "I can't afford to be involved in some sort of squabble that would damage the club's reputation."

"Squabble?" Now it was Gemma's voice that rose. "Mr. Ritchie, a child's well-being depends on—"

Melody touched Gemma's arm, a definite back-off signal. "Boss, I think Mr. Ritchie's been very helpful."

Realizing that Melody was right, Gemma forced a smile. "Of

course. I understand your concerns, Mr. Ritchie. But if you think about Charlotte——"

"Look, I'm not much of a kid person. And Sandra didn't bring Charlotte when she came to the club, so I suppose I haven't seen her since she was in nappies—she's not still in nappies, is she?" Ritchie looked a little dismayed at the thought.

"No. She's almost three, and she's a lovely, bright little girl." Gemma leaned forward, at her most persuasive. "She is, I imagine, a lot like Sandra. And she's missing her mum, and now her dad. Mr. Ritchie, I've met Sandra's mother, and I don't think anyone who cared for Sandra would want Charlotte to go there."

"That's straight-out blackmail, and you're very well aware of it," he shot back, but the animosity had gone from his tone. "Look, I want to help Sandra's little girl. But it has to be something better than repeating a speculation about an incident that happened years ago. Are you sure Pippa can't tell you anything more? She and Sandra were closer, in some ways."

"Roy Blakely told me that Sandra and Pippa hadn't been getting on. When I asked Pippa, she said they'd disagreed over the way Sandra was marketing her work, and that Pippa was no longer representing her. But she seemed very upset over Naz."

"Put it down to a guilty conscience over being a bitch," said Ritchie, with such unexpected bite that Melody, who had been watching a newcomer get into the lift, looked round, as startled as Gemma.

Seeing their faces, Ritchie shrugged and set his empty cup down on the tray. "You have to take anything Pippa tells you with a grain of salt. She disapproved of Sandra's commissions for me, and for my clients. Those who can't do have to find some way to criticize those who can."

"Pippa was jealous of Sandra?" asked Gemma, thinking back over their conversation.

"Pippa would have killed for Sandra's talent. Oh, I don't mean that literally, of course," he amended, seeming to realize what he'd said. "And to give Pippa credit, she does have a gift for recognizing talent. But her own work was always derivative, all about following the latest trend rather than expressing any personal vision. Not that I was much better." His smile was rueful. "But Pippa . . . Pippa couldn't give up gracefully. If she couldn't create art, she wanted to control it, and Sandra wouldn't play. Sandra just wanted to do what she loved and make a decent living at it. Most of us should be so fortunate." His eyes went to the collage hanging over the reception desk, and the emotion drained from his face. He stood. "I'm sorry, but I've got a club to run."

Karen had been fielding a steady influx of members and had begun to cast harried glances Ritchie's way.

Having obviously been dismissed, Gemma and Melody followed suit, and he walked them to the front door. As he opened it, he said, "Surely there's someone looking out for Charlotte Malik's interests."

"Social services, Mr. Ritchie," said Gemma, now more certain than ever that that wasn't good enough. "And me."

"What's his game, do you think?" asked Melody as they walked back towards Spitalfields. "He never actually answered when you asked him if he and Sandra were lovers."

"No, he didn't, did he?" answered Gemma. "And I'm not quite sure why he would evade one way or the other. What does he have to lose? But I do get the sense that he and Pippa Nightingale aren't on the best of terms."

"Really?" Melody grinned at her. "So do you think this Pippa has the unrequited hots for him, and held a grudge against Sandra because he preferred her?"

Gemma considered as she walked. They passed the old nut-roasting warehouse, the lettering on the brick facade faded against the deep August blue of the sky. "Pippa's a strange one. A bit fey . . . and I think Ritchie's right about the controlling issue. She likes being the center of the drama. And maybe there was more to her falling-out with Sandra than art."

"Could she have been jealous enough to kill Sandra?" asked Melody.

"You're assuming that Sandra is dead." Gemma kept her voice even, and didn't look at Melody.

"Aren't you?"

"I don't want to think so." But Gemma recalled the short walk from Columbia Road Market to Pippa Nightingale's studio, and she couldn't shake the image of the monochrome paintings with the brilliant splashes of red pigment. What if Sandra had gone there that day to talk to Pippa, and they had argued? Gemma had sensed a ruthlessness beneath Pippa's elfin looks, and Lucas Ritchie had confirmed it—if he was telling the truth.

They had reached Brushfield Street, and the permanent canopy erected over the west end of the Spitalfields Market looked jaunty, like a sail. A busker in bright African costume played the steel drums, and families congregated in the awning's shade, talking and laughing and eating ice cream. Surely, Sandra and Naz had brought Charlotte here, Gemma thought, and she had had ice cream, too.

"I might want to have another chat with Pippa Nightingale," she said to Melody. "But just now I want to go home, check on the boys, call Betty, see how Charlotte's doing today. What about you? Can I give you a lift?"

Melody seemed to hesitate. "There was something . . . no, never mind." She shook her head. "Thanks, but I'll get the tube. I have an . . . errand . . . to do before I go back to Notting Hill."

Melody got off the train at High Street Kensington, and walked—or rather shoved—her way down Kensington High Street the short distance to the Whole Foods Market, for it had just gone six o'clock and the pavements were teeming with shoppers and commuters.

The enormous natural foods store offered a respite from the heat as well as the crowds. It was an American chain, and Americans seemed to consider air-conditioning a religion, a quirk of national character for which Melody at the moment was profoundly grateful. She doubted there was a dry spot left on the once-crisp blouse beneath her suit jacket.

Having had much practice, she made a beeline for the ready-meals case at the rear of the store. After a moment's consideration, she chose a carton of carrot and coriander soup, and a small plastic tub of pomegranate salad—and on second thought, she went on to the wine section and picked up a bottle of pinot grigio.

After her late lunch with Gemma, that should be supper enough, and her shopping was a delaying tactic as much as a necessity. As she walked back through the store, she passed the oyster bar and the champagne bar, and tried to imagine a life in which she would waltz up to either and order without guilt. Maybe the next time she came in, she would live a bit more dangerously.

The DJ at the mixing station near the front entrance looked up as she passed and smiled at her, cueing Corinne Bailey Rae's "Put Your Records On."

She smiled back, an indulgence she usually didn't allow herself, and tried not to bounce to the beat.

But her temporary buoyancy evaporated quickly when she reached the street. She walked on, her purchases heavy in one hand, still mulling over what she had seen that afternoon in Lucas Ritchie's club.

She'd thought she recognized a man who had come in, not as someone she'd met, but from a photo she'd seen in a newspaper, and fairly recently.

Well, she had an archive at her fingertips, almost literally, and this evening she couldn't resist the temptation to take advantage of it, in spite of the attendant risks.

Turning the corner, she looked up at the great Art Deco building that housed one of the country's most blatant purveyors of tabloid news, the *Chronicle*. Then she used her pass card in the door.

"Evening, Miss Melody," said the guard at the main desk as she crossed the lobby towards the lifts. "Your dad's just left."

"Just as well, George." Melody stepped into the lift and pressed the button for the top floor.

CHAPTER NINETEEN

It was in January 1978 that Margaret Thatcher had famously spoken on television about the fear of white people that they were being 'swamped by people with a different culture'. White panic had already been triggered and was not allayed. Bangladeshi tenants had been encountering increasing harassment, and violence had already started to boil over on the streets.

—Geoff Dench,
Kate Gavron,
Michael Young,
The New East End

Melody had to skirt the editorial room. She passed by quickly, nodding at a few familiar faces but not stopping to chat, and hoping that she wouldn't have the bad luck to encounter her erstwhile blind date Quentin.

She slipped into her father's glass-fronted office suite, glad to see that his über-efficient personal assistant, Maeve, had gone as well.

There must not be any major breaking news—or a juicy scandal—to keep the *Chronicle*'s owner late at his desk.

No one had questioned her right to be here—no one would dare question Ivan Talbot's only child. This had been her world through childhood, the humming heart of the great newspaper, with its adrenaline yo-yo of breaking stories and frantic deadlines, countered by the desperate tedium of filling space on dead-news days.

This could be her world still if she chose, and her father had never given up hoping that she would give up this silly policing idea and put her talents to proper use. But even if she started as a junior reporter, she would always be the boss's daughter, and she would never believe she stood on her own merits.

The skills she'd absorbed by osmosis, however, often proved extremely useful. Availing herself of Maeve's desk and computer station, she accessed the system, typed in the paper's internal password, and began to search.

A hour later, she sat back, not certain if she was more satisfied or puzzled, and rang Gemma.

Gemma was picking up bits of Lego from the sitting room floor when her mobile buzzed. Recognizing the number, she tried tucking the phone between ear and shoulder as she tossed what she thought was a dinosaur—Toby having decided that pirates would most definitely encounter dinosaurs—towards the toy basket at one end of the sofa. The basket at the other end held dog toys, and she often wondered how the dogs managed to tell which assortment was which. If anyone transgressed, it was more likely to be Toby.

"Melody?" she said. "Hang on." Transferring the phone to her hand, she threw a questionable stuffed teddy into the dog basket, then wandered into the dining room and sat down on the piano bench. "Okay, sorry about that. What's up?"

She listened, idly picking out one note, then another, on the keyboard, a frown beginning to crease her forehead. "Ahmed Azad? You're certain?"

Duncan came in, a bottled beer in hand, an eyebrow raised in query. He'd been in the study, rereading the reports on Naz Malik. His mood, touchy since the warning-off passed down from Narcotics, had improved since Gemma had told him that the Gilles brothers had borrowed a van on the afternoon and evening of Naz's death, and he'd been looking for any mention or sighting of a van.

"Yeah, I'll tell him," Gemma said, glancing at Duncan. "Thanks. I'll see you tomorrow."

As she ended the call, Duncan pulled a chair up beside the piano bench. "It's too hot for wine." He waved the beer bottle, displaying the already-forming condensation. "Want one?" When she shook her head, he asked, "Who was that? And what's this about Azad?"

The office door opened just as Melody clicked her phone closed and her father came in, his tan face split in a grin.

"Melody, darling. George said you were here. Why didn't you ring me? I'd have stayed and taken you to dinner."

"Just doing a bit of research, Dad. No fuss."

"Is it a case?" He came round to stand behind her before she had a chance to blank the computer screen. She couldn't fault his reporter's instincts. " 'Bangladeshi businessman protests vandalism by white toughs; criticizes the Met's failure to take action,' " he read. "Don't tell me you're looking into your own organizational failures."

Melody ignored the barb. "No, Dad. I was just curious about this guy. I saw him today at a club in Spitalfields. A very posh club with no name, managed by a man named Lucas Ritchie."

Ivan looked thoughtful. "I know a place like that in Notting Hill. Four-hundred-pound bottles of wine, and beautiful, but unattainable, hostesses."

Melody swiveled to look up at her dad. "So what does Mum think about you going to these places?"

He gave her the shark grin. "Oh, I've taken her with me once or twice. These sorts of clubs are the evolution of places like Annabel's and Mark's Club—at Annabel's and Mark's, only the elite can get in, but at these new places, only the elite even know about them. The anonymity is part of the pull."

"The Secret Seven factor?" Melody had loved the Enid Blyton stories as a child.

"Every grown-up's fantasy," Ivan agreed. "Their own secret society. So, do you think this club is involved in something dodgy?"

"No reason to think so." Melody had begun to wish she hadn't offered even a minimal explanation. Her father was like a ferret once he got on a scent.

She exited the online archives, wishing she'd had a chance to print the story she'd found, but unwilling to arouse her father's interest any further.

"Thanks, Dad," she said as she stood up. "I've got to go."

"Why don't you stay? I just came in to check on tomorrow's leader. I could take you to that café you like down Abingdon Street for a glass of wine."

Melody gathered up her shopping bag from Whole Foods. "Sorry, Dad. I've already bought something, and it won't keep." She kissed his cheek, still smooth even at this time of evening. She'd discovered years ago that he kept an electric razor in his desk drawer. Not for Ivan Talbot the stubbled look. Where he had grown up, in working-class Newcastle, that had meant you were poor or a drunk.

"Your mother's expecting you on Sunday," he said as she reached the door.

"I know. I'll be there." She turned back, giving him a quelling look. "But this time, Dad, no blind dates."

"That was Melody." Gemma hesitated. "I think I might like a glass of wine, if you wouldn't mind? It's been chilling since I got home." On her way back from Spitalfields, she'd stopped at Mr Christian's for cold meats and salads, and popped into Oddbins for a bottle of wine. At home, she'd shucked off her work clothes and put on shorts and a tank top.

While Kincaid went into the kitchen, Gemma picked out a few more notes, and found she was playing "Kip's Lights," from Gabriel Yared's score for *The English Patient*. It was one of her favorite pieces when she wanted to think, and good practice for her rusty fingers.

Although she'd told Kincaid about her visit to Gail Gilles, they'd got caught up in the melee—dinner and time with the kids, and she hadn't mentioned the unplanned call on Lucas Ritchie. But now that the boys were upstairs she had no excuse for not coming clean.

"I like that bit," Duncan said when he came back with her glass. He touched her bare arm with his fingertips, cold from the wine bottle. "Can you play and talk at the same time?"

No avoiding it now. Gemma took a fortifying sip of a Pouilly-Fumé she'd found in the sale bin and slid halfway round on the bench so that she could face him. "Melody met me in Spitalfields today. We had lunch at the market, and afterwards, we walked round to Lucas Ritchie's club. I thought he might know more about Sandra than he told you. And I was curious." Before he could interrupt, she added, "I identified myself, but told him it wasn't official. I more or less implied I didn't know you from Adam."

"Thanks. I think." His gaze grew a little more intent. "So how did you say you tracked him down?"

"Through Pippa Nightingale. She said it was Lucas who told her about Naz."

"Okay." He considered that for a moment while he drank some of his beer. "And were your charms any more effective than mine on Mr. Ritchie?"

"He's a bit slippery," Gemma admitted, "but he seemed to want to talk. I got the impression that he and Sandra were lovers *before* she met Naz, although he never quite came out and said so. He did say that when she first started going out with Naz, he thought Naz had beat her up. But when he confronted her, she was furious with him for suggesting it. She was still living at home."

Duncan frowned. "Kevin and Terry, then?"

"Could be. Although Melody suggested it might have been one of Gail's boyfriends, or even Gail."

"Gail? Do you think that's possible?"

Gemma thought of the undercurrent of viciousness she'd heard in Gail's voice when she talked about Sandra, and of Charlotte, defenseless, and couldn't repress a shudder. "Yes."

"But Ritchie couldn't confirm what had happened."

"No. And he wouldn't make a commitment to speak up for Charlotte either." Gemma brought her hand down on the keys, sounding a dissonant note.

"I can't say I'm surprised. And I doubt it would do much good. So where does Ahmed Azad come into this?" Duncan asked.

Suspicious-sounding thumps were coming from upstairs and Gemma cast a worried glance at the ceiling. "Melody saw him going into the club," she said a little hurriedly. "She didn't know it was him, just that he looked familiar—she thought she'd seen him in a news story. Then when she tracked it down—he'd complained publicly that he'd been vandalized by white gangs and that the Met had failed to investigate properly—she recognized his name from what I'd told her about the case. Azad didn't mention to you that he knew Lucas Ritchie?"

"No." Duncan ran a hand through his hair, pushing damp locks back from his forehead. "But then I didn't ask. And I certainly didn't think to ask Lucas Ritchie if he knew Azad. This puts rather a different slant on things. We knew that Sandra and Naz knew Azad, and that Sandra and Naz knew Ritchie, but not that those two had a connection."

"There was something else—" A loud crash from upstairs interrupted what Gemma was going to say about Ritchie and Pippa Nightingale.

"Mummy!" came Toby's wail.

"Oh, lord." Gemma handed Duncan her glass with a sigh. "He's been practicing jumping ship from the bed again."

On Thursday afternoon, not having found any mention of a van in either the statements or the witness reports relating to Naz Malik's case, Kincaid had put Sergeant Singh and her team at Bethnal Green on to tracking down any known associates of the Gilles brothers with a vehicle fitting that description.

"Just a van?" Singh had asked, a bit dubiously. "Like a transit van?"

"All I know is it had to be big enough to transport a full-size sofa, a loveseat, and an armchair," Kincaid told her.

Singh gave him a look through narrowed eyes. "And you know this how, exactly?"

"A completely reliable source." He tried his best grin on her, but she looked unconvinced.

"And how do you suggest we do this without stepping on Narcotics' toes?"

"Some discreet inquiries, to start with. Ask the officers who were watching the brothers' purported places of work, and the sister's flat, if they saw anything. You're inventive, Sergeant. I'm sure you'll come up with something."

"Maybe they really did move furniture," she said.

"I think it's likely they did," he agreed. "But if that's the case, they also had access, through the afternoon and evening, to a vehicle in which they could have held Naz Malik and then transported him to Haggerston Park. And I want it found. Now."

Singh got the message. "Sir." She had charged into the incident room, figurative guns blazing, and Kincaid had gone to look for Neal Weller, stopping off at the canteen to pick up a cup of execrable coffee.

Weller was in his office, suit jacket off, reading glasses perched on the end of his nose. He took them off, rubbing at his eyes, when Kincaid came in. "You've put a serious dent in my manpower, you know. And now what's this about a van?"

"News travels fast." Kincaid didn't sit down.

"I have my means. Just what do you intend to do with this van if you find it? You can't order a search based on unsubstantiated information from an unidentified source. And even if you could, Narcotics would have your bollocks."

"There's always a traffic stop," Kincaid said. He'd had to take Weller into his confidence, but they weren't broadcasting information about the drugs investigation to the rank and file. "Let's cross that bridge when we come to it." Now he perched on the arm of the spare chair, looking round for a place to set the undrinkable liquid in his polystyrene cup. He squeezed it into a bare spot on the edge of Weller's desk. "Did you know that Ahmed Azad knew Lucas Ritchie?"

"Ritchie of the mysterious club?" Weller looked surprised.

"Azad seems to be a member of the club, as a matter of fact. And Ritchie had an employee who's gone missing, like Azad's nephew. I've got Cullen working on tracing her."

"A woman?"

"A young woman named Kylie Watters."

Weller shrugged. "Never heard of her. But you're stretching a connection, don't you think?"

"Maybe." Kincaid straightened the crease in his trouser leg. "Or maybe Azad had the ability to help Ritchie get rid of an inconvenient employee. Or Ritchie had the means to help Azad with a more than inconvenient nephew."

"What does any of this have to do with Naz Malik or Sandra

Gilles?" asked Weller. He didn't, to Kincaid's relief, ask how Kincaid had come by the information.

"I don't know, except that they all seem to be connected. But I think I'd like to have another word with Mr. Azad."

"I'll come with you." Weller dropped the reading glasses on top of a stack of reports, looking like he was glad of an excuse to escape.

But Kincaid stood quickly, retrieving his cup. "I think I'll go on my own, if you don't mind. Just for a friendly chat, this time without the lawyer. I thought I might catch him at the restaurant. I might even have a curry."

"Good luck with that." Weller sat back in his chair, his expression making it quite clear he knew Kincaid had just pulled rank, and that he was not pleased. "And you can drop that swill in the bin on your way out."

Gemma tucked in on Thursday, determined to set things right on her own manor. Not only was she behind in her work, but she felt guilty for having taken advantage of her guv'nor's goodwill the day before. Still, she thought what she'd learned about Gail Gilles had made her dereliction worthwhile, if only she could figure out what to do with the information. And if nothing else, the tip about Gail's furniture-shopping expedition might move Kincaid's investigation forward.

By late afternoon, she had made a dent in things. She was opening up the last case report in her inbox when Betty Howard rang her mobile.

Picking up the phone, she said, "Hi, Betty. Is everything okay?" Her instant fear was that Betty had had another call from the case-worker.

"Oh, everything is all right, Gemma," Betty said softly. Gemma could hear the music from an afternoon children's program on the telly in the background. "It's just that little Charlotte keeps asking me for her ducky pencils, and I'm not rightly sure I know what she means. I've given her every pencil in the house, and none of them will do. I can't console the poor thing, and I'm that worried."

Casting her mind back over the things she'd seen in Sandra's studio, Gemma thought she remembered a cup of colored art pencils in a mug on Sandra's worktable. "I might know the ones she means. They were her mum's. Maybe Charlotte was allowed to play with them."

"Is there any way you could get them for her? And she's needing some more clothes, too. I'd be glad to buy some things for her, and I've got the allowance from the social, but it might be better for her to have her own things. Something familiar, you know."

"Let me see what I can do. I'll ring you back."

The Fournier Street house was no longer officially a crime scene—had the investigating team turned the keys over to Naz's executor, Naz's partner, Louise Phillips? And if so, would Phillips give Gemma permission to go in the house and get some things for Charlotte?

She pulled out the little notebook she kept in her handbag and flipped back through the pages until she found the number she had written down for Naz and Louise Phillips's office that first night. Glancing at the clock, she saw that it was not yet five—hopefully Phillips would not have left for the day.

She punched in the number. A woman answered on the first ring with a brusque, "Malik and Phillips."

"Could I speak to Louise Phillips, please?" asked Gemma.

"Speaking." The voice was no less brisk. "Receptionist's gone home for the day. What can I do for you?"

Gemma explained who she was and what she wanted. "I wondered if you could meet me at the house? Of course, I'd need your approval for anything I took for Charlotte."

There was such a long pause that Gemma thought Phillips meant to refuse her request altogether.

Then Louise Phillips said, so slowly that Gemma thought the brusqueness had been a cover for exhaustion or grief, "I haven't been in the house. I just—I couldn't— Why don't you meet me at my flat, in an hour or so. I'll give you the keys. You can pop them back through my letterbox when you're done. And you can make a list of anything you remove, for protocol's sake, but I'll assume you're trustworthy. You'd better be"—she gave a hoarse laugh—"because at this point I'd be none the wiser if you walked off with the entire contents."

Phillips gave Gemma an address, then added, "You'll find the place easily enough. It's just off Columbia Road."

CHAPTER TWENTY

So the house has a mission, and it believes that the natural state of human intelligence is not—like a painting—flat or square, but like this room it extends out and all around us. The house plots to work its magic to ensure that each visitor goes away with that perception. It may already have begun to happen to you.

—Dennis Severs,
18 Folgate Street:
The Tale of a
House in Spitalfields

Although the sun was far from setting, the neon signs burned over the curry palaces of Brick Lane. Many of the restaurants advertised air-conditioning, but the doors stood open, and the pervasive smell of Indian spices mingled with the dust and petrol fumes of the street.

Some of the less prosperous places had touts outside to lure tourists in with practiced patter, although Kincaid seriously doubted whether the restaurants ever gave the refunds so persuasively offered.

Ahmed Azad's place, however, was easily picked out by its sleekly modern frontage. The closed front door hinted at real air-conditioning, and the interior Kincaid glimpsed through the window was minimalist, with brick walls, gleaming wooden tables, and sculpted leather chairs. There was the barest hint of an Indian theme in the deep orange-red patterned place mats and coordinating linens. The prices posted on the menu in the window were a little high, but not stratospheric, and there were quite a few diners, even at the early hour.

Sergeant Singh had told him that there would be queues later in the evening, even on a weeknight, and that the food wasn't "half bad." He guessed that coming from her that counted as a compliment. "Angla-Bangla, of course," she'd added, "but they do it well, and they manage to sneak in a few more authentic dishes."

Most of the diners, Kincaid saw, were in Western dress, but there were very few women. When he stepped inside, he was met by a blast of cool air, and then by a barrage of aromas that made his mouth water.

The waiters looked as sophisticated as the interior, all young men dressed in black shirts and trousers. Kincaid wondered if there had been anything about Azad's great-nephew that made him stand out of the mix.

It was not one of the waiters who came forward to greet him, however, but Azad himself, wearing another expensive-looking suit cut for his rotund frame.

"Mr. Kincaid," Azad said, shaking his hand. "To what do we owe the pleasure? Have you come to sample our cuisine?" Although his tone was friendly, his dark eyes were sharply alert.

"I've heard it's very good, Mr. Azad, but I've just come for a chat, if you have a minute." Kincaid's stomach was telling him that it was a long time since he'd had lunch. But as tempted as he was by the aromas, he didn't want to put himself at a disadvantage with Azad by becoming a customer.

"I take it this chat will not require my solicitor's presence?" The question seemed to be rhetorical, as Azad smiled and motioned him forwards. "Come into my office. Perhaps you would like to try a chai tea?" Without waiting for Kincaid's response, he signaled one of the waiters and barked an order in rapid Bengali.

He led Kincaid through the restaurant and into a small room to one side of the partially open kitchen. The office was clean and utilitarian, but the walls were adorned with fine photographic prints of a lush, green landscape that Kincaid assumed must be Bangladesh.

By the time Kincaid had taken the chair Azad offered, one of the black-clad waiters appeared with a glass mug of a milky, fragrantly spicy tea.

"You serve alcohol?" Kincaid asked, having noticed wineglasses on some of the tables.

"I don't drink it, Mr. Kincaid, but this is a business." Azad shrugged his padded shoulders. "If you want to be successful, you must please the customers."

"It seems you have quite the City clientele." Kincaid sipped his tea and found, rather to his surprise, that it wasn't as sweet as he'd expected, and that he liked it.

"They have money to spend, and a little more refined taste than the average tourists, who just want their chicken tikka masala. But why should this be of interest to you, Mr. Kincaid?"

"Because I was wondering what you could tell me about Lucas Ritchie and his club."

Lou Phillips lived in what Gemma guessed was a newer terrace, near the bottom end of Columbia Road, but the buildings were unusually constructed. While the ground-floor flats had little open patios, each pair of first-floor flats seemed to open onto a shared balcony, served by its own staircase.

Gemma checked her address again—yes, Louise Phillips's flat was one of the first-floor pair at the end of the building, the one with the jungle of plants and flowers filling the balcony.

The one with the German shepherd dogs. There was an iron gate at the top of the stairs, and the two big dogs sat just inside it, watching her with what seemed a friendly interest.

A young man came out of the left-hand flat. He had spiky, bleached-blond hair and stud earrings, and wore a black T-shirt emblazoned with the enigmatic slogan GOT SLIDE? Giving the dogs a casual pat as he went by, he clanged out the gate and clattered down the stairs. As he passed Gemma, he said, " 'ullo, love," and gave her a cheeky grin.

Had he come from Louise Phillips's flat, wondered Gemma? But no, according to the number, Phillips's flat was the right-hand one. At least the dogs seemed friendly enough.

But when Gemma started up the stairs, both dogs stood, and the larger one gave a sharp bark. Gemma stopped, unsure of what to do. The doors to both flats stood open, and she was about to call out when a man wearing shorts and a Hawaiian shirt came out of the left-hand flat. He had brown hair drawn back in a ponytail, impressively muscled legs, and a pleasant face, and he carried a large old-fashioned watering can.

"You here to see Lou?" he called down to her. "Don't mind the dogs. They're a good combination of doorbell and burglar deterrent, but they won't hurt you."

The dogs' tails had started to wag at the sound of the man's voice, and they looked pleased with themselves, as if they knew they were being talked about. Gemma kept climbing, still with a bit of trepidation, but as she neared the top the man called the dogs to him. "Jagger, Ginger. Sit," he commanded. The dogs sat, but their tails were wagging furiously. Their black and reddish-tan coats were glossy, and the expressions on their alert, intelligent faces seemed almost human.

"Jagger and Ginger?" said Gemma, stopping at the gate.

"As in Mick Jagger and Ginger Baker. My partner manages rock bands. The names are his little homage to the greats—although I doubt any of his current crop are likely to fill their boots. Except maybe Andy there," he added, nodding in the direction the young man had disappeared in. "I'm Michael, by the way." He came forward and opened the gate.

Gemma stepped through, and the dogs seemed to consider the gate shutting behind her as their release signal. She stood still as they came charging towards her, then let them sniff her thoroughly with their long, damp noses. She was glad she was wearing trousers and not a skirt.

"Here, I'll call them off—," began Michael, but Gemma stopped him.

"No. They're lovely. They're just getting acquainted with my dogs."

"Ah, no wonder they like you. I take it you're not here for Tam?" When Gemma shook her head, he glanced into the open door of the right-hand flat, calling out, "Lou, you've got a visitor."

"I'm coming, I'm coming," said the same slightly irritable female voice Gemma had heard over the phone.

A moment later, a woman appeared in the doorway. "Sorry, sorry," she said. "Had to get out of the business suit and the bloody tights before I died. It should be against the law to wear things like that in this weather. You're Gemma?"

The shorts and halter top Lou Phillips had changed into should have shown off her coloring, but Gemma thought her dark skin had a grayish tinge to it, and her bared shoulders were unflatteringly bony. Her dark hair was scraped up into a ponytail that lacked the élan of the one worn by her neighbor Michael.

"I've got the keys," Phillips went on, without waiting for an answer. "If you'll just make me a list of the items you take and return it with the—"

"Actually," Gemma broke in, "I was hoping we could have a chat."

Louise Phillips stared at her for a moment, then sighed. "All right. I suppose we can talk. But only if you like gin and tonic. And we'll have to sit on the balcony. I can't smoke in the flat, or Michael and Tam won't let the dogs come in. Don't want them exposed to secondhand smoke." She rolled her eyes at this, but Gemma saw that there were two chairs on her side of the balcony, and an ashtray between them. "And they make me wash out the ashtray every day," Louise grumbled as she led Gemma into the flat. Sotto voce, she added, "I cheat when it's cold. I open the back window."

"You're not fooling anyone, Lou," Michael called from the balcony, but his tone was affectionate. "We can smell it on the dogs' coats."

"Nazis," Louise called back, but she smiled. "How Tam survives taking the bands to rock clubs, I don't know. But now even those have been taken over by the no-smoking brigade."

The flat was cluttered, apparently furnished with cast-off odds and ends, and most surfaces were covered with books and papers. The small kitchen at the back, however, was relatively neat, and Gemma suspected it was because Lou Phillips didn't cook.

There was a lime on the cutting board, beside a tall glass and a bottle of Bombay gin and another of tonic. "Easy on the G for me," said Gemma. "And heavy on the T. Have to drive." She watched as Louise got another glass and filled both with ice, gin, and tonic, adding only a splash of gin to Gemma's.

"Have you been here long?" Gemma asked. "It's an interesting flat." She accepted the drink Louise handed her. Tasting it, she found it delicious, the tartness of the lime and the bitterness of the tonic the perfect antidote to the heat.

"Ten—no, eleven years." Louise was already pulling the cigarette packet from her shorts as they walked back through the flat. "I found it just a few months after Naz and I bought the practice."

When they reached the patio, Louise sank into one chair, her cigarette already lit, while Gemma took the other. She saw that the ashtray was indeed clean.

Michael had gone inside the other flat, but the dogs remained, stretched out on the cool concrete, panting gently.

"Are you the green thumb?" Gemma asked, admiring the profusion of flowers and plants, only a few of which she recognized.

"Lord, no. That's all Michael's doing. He's a floral designer, and living so close to Columbia Road is mecca for him. I kill everything I touch, and Tam's not much better."

"Did Michael know Sandra, then? From when she used to work the market with Roy Blakely?"

"Oh, Michael knew Sandra. But then it seems that everyone knew Sandra." Louise exhaled a long stream of smoke and ground out her half-finished cigarette. "Sandra had a way of insinuating herself into people's lives."

"Insinuating?" Gemma asked, a bit puzzled by the word choice.

"I don't mean that in a negative way. It was just that Sandra was interested in everything and everyone, and she made connections, and the connections made connections . . ."

Gemma thought about the unlikely-seeming thread between Sandra, and Azad, and Lucas Ritchie, and Pippa . . . and imagined those tendrils multiplied, exponentially. "How could someone who knew so much about everyone else reveal so little about herself?" she asked, as much to herself as to Louise. "No one I've talked to seems to know anything about Sandra's background, or her relationship with her family—except maybe Roy Blakely, and that's only because he's known her family for years."

"Naz knew enough," Louise said flatly. Lighting another cigarette, she dropped the cheap plastic lighter. It rolled off the table to clatter onto the concrete, but Louise didn't reach for it.

"What do you mean?" Gemma tried to keep the quickening of interest from her voice.

"And why does it matter to you?" The gaze Louise Phillips fixed on Gemma was sharp, a reminder that Phillips was, after all, a lawyer, and that, regardless of the gin and tonic, not much slipped past her.

"Because I care what happens to Charlotte," Gemma said simply. "And I don't believe that Sandra's mother will provide a good—or safe—environment for her," she added, thinking that such an understatement only touched the tip of the iceberg.

"Naz would have agreed with you." Draining her gin and tonic, Louise placed her glass on the table with great deliberation. "And I let him down."

Ahmed Azad didn't blink. "Why should I be able to tell you anything about this Mr. Ritchie?"

"Because you belong to his club," Kincaid answered.

"Ah." Azad drew out the word, and his small smile conveyed no humor. "I see someone has been indiscreet. But no matter. It is no great secret, although some of my more—should we say, observant— brothers might be less than approving."

"Was it Sandra Gilles who introduced you to Lucas Ritchie?"

"As a matter of fact, it was, yes. They were old friends, I believe, and Sandra thought our association might further my business interests."

"And did it?" Kincaid asked, drinking more of his tea.

Azad glanced out at the restaurant and lifted his hand in an encompassing gesture. "It is always good to have connections. I could not run this restaurant strictly on the custom of Bangladeshis, and some of my . . . connections . . . have provided the occasional cash infusion. With a good return, I must say."

"And yet you've had trouble with the white community, I understand, Mr. Azad. Vandalism, was it?"

"Do you call throwing rocks and gasoline bombs through the window 'vandalism,' Mr. Kincaid? Perhaps you do not take it any more seriously than did your colleagues?" Although Azad's voice remained level, Kincaid sensed a deep-coursing anger.

He wondered what it took for this man to keep it buried when he

socialized with the white, City types at the club in Widegate Street—
men who had never known prejudice, never experienced the violence
of a Molotov cocktail, never trembled in fear of a mob.

"I'm sorry the police weren't more helpful, Mr. Azad," he said
genuinely. "Do you have any idea who might have been responsible?"

Azad looked at him for a long moment, then stood and walked
over to one of the lush, green photographs on his office wall. Studying it, he said, "It is always our dream, Mr. Kincaid. To make our
fortune here, then to go home to Sylhet as rich and respected elders,
the envy of all our neighbors and relatives. But for most of us, it
does not happen. Our lives are here. Our children's lives are here. We
do not want to make difficulties with those who become our friends,
our associates." He fell silent.

"You knew them," Kincaid said quietly. "And you didn't tell the
police. Who were they, Mr. Azad?"

Azad didn't turn. "I saw their faces. They had their hoods up,
like the thugs they are. But still, I recognized them. Sandra Gilles's
brothers."

Standing abruptly, Lou Phillips picked up her glass again and rattled
the ice in it. "I'm going for a refill. Do you want another?"

Gemma shook her head. "No, thanks. I'm fine," she said, but she
stood as well and followed Louise back inside the flat. In the kitchen,
as Louise broke a few more ice cubes from the tray and plunked
them in her glass, Gemma asked, "What did you do, Louise? How
did you let Naz down?"

Louise half filled the glass with gin, then topped it off with tonic.
"After Sandra disappeared, Naz rewrote his will. He asked me if I
would be Charlotte's guardian." She turned, leaning against the work
top, but didn't meet Gemma's eyes. "I said no."

Gemma stared at her in disbelief. "Why?"

"Because . . . because I didn't think anything would happen to

Naz. Because I thought Sandra would come back. And then, when she didn't, I thought—I began to wonder—I know most of these things are . . . domestic." She looked at Gemma now, appealing. "It's my job. Yours, too. We see the worst."

"As in *it's usually the spouse*? You thought *Naz* was responsible for Sandra's disappearance?"

"God help me." Louise reached for her glass and wrapped visibly unsteady hands round it. "I suspected him. I didn't see how he could have done it. But he was so different afterwards, so distant—I thought . . . And I was so angry with him because he shut me out. If he talked at all, it was about this friend, this Dr. Cavendish, when Naz and I had been friends for years. I was jealous. It was petty of me, and stupid. And now . . . now I can't put it right."

"Can't you? Louise, couldn't you change things now, as executor? Isn't there some way you could take legal responsibility for Charlotte?"

Louise shook her head. "No. The will was witnessed. It will stand." She hesitated, then said, "I'm sorry I didn't do what Naz wanted, I really am. But even if it were legally possible, I couldn't take care of Charlotte."

"I don't understand."

"I—I'm not cut out for it. I don't—I'm fond of Charlotte, but she never really . . . warmed to me. This"—she looked towards the balcony—"this place, and Tam and Michael, this is all I'm likely to have in the way of family. I'm just not suited to looking after a child."

"And you think Gail Gilles would do better?"

Although it was a struggle to keep her temper in check, Gemma had gone back out to the balcony and sat for a while longer with Louise. She had tried to imagine Charlotte with Louise, and found to her dismay that she couldn't.

There was something about Louise, something more than her

obvious grief, that wasn't quite right. She seemed damaged, crippled in some indefinable way, and there was a solicitousness in the way Michael and his partner, Tam, looked after her.

In the end, she had got Louise to agree that she would do what she could, if Gail should gain custody of Charlotte, to restrict Gail's access to the estate's funds.

And then, as she drove the short distance to Fournier Street in the fading light, Gemma wondered if that had been a wise request. Would putting a damper on the money only make Gail more likely to mistreat the child?

She parked across from Sandra and Naz's house, struck once again by the contrast between the severity of the church at one end of the street and the play of neon from Brick Lane at the other. How hard had it been for Sandra and Naz to balance between the two worlds? And the two cultures?

Once inside the house, she switched on lights and opened the garden door in an effort to bring in light and fresh air. In just a few days, the house had begun to smell musty, and ordinary dust had gathered on the furniture, joining the black powder left by forensics.

She walked through the rooms, feeling oddly divided between a sense of trespass and a sense of aching familiarity. In the sitting room, she picked up a stray picture book and a stuffed toy, stowing them in their respective containers, just as she would have in her own house.

Then she climbed the stairs to Charlotte's room. She found a flowered holdall in the wardrobe and began to fill it with things from the chest of drawers. She held up a pink-printed sundress with a matching white cardigan, remembering the little girls' clothes she had looked at in the shop windows when she was pregnant, daydreaming of the daughter she would dress.

Carefully, she folded the sundress and cardigan, then reached for a jacket in the same corally pink, a pink-and-white-striped T-shirt, and white cuffed dungarees. Then a yellow eyelet top with a pink-and-yellow-flowered skirt and a pair of pink-and-white ballet flats. Had Sandra loved picking out these things, just as Gemma had imagined doing?

She added a few more clothes and more worn stuffed toys—company for Bob the elephant—and the most well-thumbed of the picture books on the table by the bed. The photo of Sandra still stood beside the books. Gemma hesitated, but in the end she left it. Not yet, she thought. It was too soon for such a vivid reminder.

She made notes for Louise of the things she'd taken, then, leaving the bag on the landing, she climbed up to the studio.

The cup of colored pencils stood on the worktable, just where she had remembered. Looking round for a box or a bag, or even an elastic band to contain them, she was struck once more by the beauty of the collage Sandra had left unfinished.

The Caged Girls, as she had come to think of it. The shrouded, unfinished faces of the girls and women were haunting, and she wondered what story had motivated Sandra to design this piece—and who had been the intended recipient.

Still searching for an elastic band, she moved to the desk and rifled through the drawers. The shallow one held the flotsam and jetsam that accumulated in desks as if drawn by magnets—broken pencils, defunct pens, paper clips, and pennies. There were a half-dozen colored elastic bands, but they were too small for the bundled pencils. Pulling the drawer all the way open, Gemma saw a bit of paper crumpled at the back. She fished it out and smoothed the crinkles. It was a receipt, written out to Sandra Gilles for one pound, in payment for an unspecified work of art, and stamped with the name and address of the Rivington Street Health Clinic.

Gemma remembered seeing a clinic on Rivington Street when she'd gone to Pippa Nightingale's gallery—was it the same place?

On an impulse, she took out her notebook once more and found the page on which she'd written Pippa's number. As she looked in her bag, she found one of her own elastic hair bands, which she thought would do quite nicely for the pencils.

Bundling up the pencils, she put them in her bag, then took out her mobile and rang the number for the Nightingale Gallery. It was late, and Gemma had begun to think it a wasted call, but after a few rings, Pippa answered the phone.

Gemma identified herself, then asked about the Rivington Street clinic.

"That was one of Sandra's good-works projects," Pippa said with asperity. "I told her she couldn't just give things away, but she wouldn't listen."

"They paid her a pound. I found the receipt in her desk. What sort of clinic is it?"

"That sounds about par for Sandra's record keeping. At least she left a proper paper trail for the Internal Revenue." She gave a derisive sniff, then went on. "The place is a free sexual-health clinic that caters mostly to local Bangladeshi women."

Gemma had been gazing at the piece on the worktable. She described the piece in progress to Pippa, then asked, "Do you suppose she was thinking of the women who go to this clinic? Or that she was making it for the clinic?"

"It's possible," Pippa said thoughtfully. "But it sounds as if the piece has a very strong Huguenot theme, which was something Sandra came back to again and again. She was fascinated by the lives and history of the French immigrant weavers, and she felt a personal connection—she *wanted* there to be a personal connection. Gilles is a French Huguenot name, and because Sandra never knew her father, I think it was important to her to try to find something meaningful in her mother's lineage. Not that her mother knew or cared." Pippa sighed. "You might look at her journals."

"Journals?"

"Sandra kept scads of them. Black, artists' sketchbooks, filled with notes and drawings. That was where she worked out her ideas. They may be worth a good bit of money if she—" There was a pause, then Pippa said, "Look. I've got to go. But if you find those books, you'd better make a note of it for the estate. And have whoever's in charge contact me."

Clicking off the phone, Gemma looked round the room, thinking that Pippa Nightingale might be grieving for Naz and Sandra, but she was not about to let it interfere with business.

Gemma moved away from the desk and worktable. Hadn't she seen black notebooks somewhere, when she was here before? Yes, there, on the shelf with the boxes of buttons and ribbons and the other objects Sandra used in the collages—at least a dozen identical black books.

Lifting the top one from the stack, she opened it and thumbed carefully through it. Notes, in many colors, the tiny script crammed into margins and any vertical and horizontal space not filled with drawings. And the drawings . . . Gemma looked more closely, fascinated. There were designs; some looked like bits of fabric, others seemed to be architectural details—Gemma thought she recognized the ornate curved lintel from a house opposite, and the Arabian curves of the decorative arches in Brick Lane. There were even tiny reproductions of some of the street art Gemma had seen sprayed along Brick Lane. And there were portraits. Asian women, young and old. A grizzled, shabby man under a striped market awning. A drawing that suggested, in just a few deft lines, the sweet face of a young Asian girl.

Gemma closed the book and held it, thinking. This was Sandra Gilles—here, in these pages—or at least all that Gemma, or Sandra's daughter, might ever know of her. Pippa had suggested that the notebooks would be valuable, objects of desire for collectors, but what about their value to Charlotte? Surely, that was more important.

Setting aside the notebook, Gemma rummaged in her bag until she found her own little spiral notebook, and the list she had been making for Louise. She stared at the page for a long moment, then put the notebook back.

Carefully, she gathered all the black sketchbooks from the shelf, added the bundle of pencils from her bag, and left the studio.

On the way down the stairs, she retrieved Charlotte's flowered holdall and tucked her acquisitions inside.

Reaching the ground floor, she turned out the lights and locked the garden door, then let herself out of the house and locked the front door as well.

She glanced up and down, as was her habit, but the street was empty. Walking quickly to her car, she opened the rear door and leaned in, meaning to place the bag securely on the floorboard.

Then, a hard shove slammed her forwards, cracking her head against the Escort's roof.

Staggering, shaking her head, she instinctively dropped the bag, clenched her keys in her fist, and spun round.

There were two of them, crowding her, so close she could smell the mingled odors of sweat and beer.

They must have been waiting round the corner in Wilkes Street, to have come on her so fast. One man was bigger, heavier, with pouches under his hard blue eyes; the other was thinner, acne scarred, jittery.

And she knew them.

CHAPTER TWENTY-ONE

The streets of the East End were awash with heroin, or
smack, which was no longer the exclusive junk of emaciated
squatters with puncture marks running the length of their
arms. Although as addictive as ever, the new improved
heroin came in an easy-to-smoke brown resin at a vastly
reduced price . . . In the East End, smack was now easier to
obtain than marijuana.

—Tarquin Hall,
Salaam Brick Lane

Sandra Gilles's brothers. Kevin and Terry.

"Get the hell away from me," Gemma spat, but they were too close—her back was against the car. She clutched her keys tighter, thinking she could hit only one, and that she'd have no time to react against the other.

"We saw you," said the bigger one. "Didn't we, Ter?"

Acne scar nodded.

"Snooping at our mum's," continued the big one. Kevin. "And now you're at our sister's 'ouse. You some sort of spy for them social workers?" He jabbed a finger at her collarbone and Gemma smacked it away, her reaction automatic.

"Keep your hands off me. Back off," she said, cold with fury. "Who the hell are you?"

"Just told you," said Kevin, but he moved back a few inches. "This 'ouse"—this time he jabbed the sausagelike finger towards the house across the street—"belongs to *our* sister"—jab—"and *our* niece"—jab—"and you got no business 'ere."

"Neither"—Gemma jabbed a finger back at him—"do"—she jabbed again—"you. Now bugger off before I call the police." It was pure bravado—her mobile was in her bag, on the floor of the car.

Kevin ignored the threat. "Who gave you our mum's address?" Gemma glanced at Terry, wondering if he could talk. Kevin pulled her attention back. "You after our sister's money or what?"

"I don't know what you're talking about." She glared at him. "And I'm leaving now. Bugger off." She tensed, wondering what she was going to do next.

Then a voice, male, vaguely familiar, came from behind her. "You heard her. Move it." She turned her head a fraction, saw a man in a T-shirt and jeans. Dark, spiky hair, olive skin, green eyes. Rashid Kaleem, the pathologist. He had his mobile in his hand. "I've called the cops," he said. "They'll be here any second."

Kevin's eyes darted one way, then the other. A couple turned the corner from Brick Lane into Fournier Street, walking towards them. Somewhere in the distance a siren sounded. He stepped back, grabbing Terry by the shoulder. "Come on," he said to his brother. Then he fixed Gemma with a hard stare. "You remember what we said." He glanced at Rashid and spat. "Paki scum."

With his brother in tow, he turned and moved quickly away. The two men passed the shadow of Christ Church and disappeared into the bustle of Commercial Street.

Gemma turned to Rashid. She realized her legs were shaking. "Did you really call the police? Where did you come from?"

"I was coming from the mosque, and I saw you. I live near here. What are you doing here? Who were those guys?"

"The police?" she said again, urgently. "Did you call the police?"

"No. No, I didn't take the time. I was afraid they were going to hurt you." He lifted the phone. "I'll ring now. We've got a good description—"

"No. Wait." Gemma leaned against the car, pushing her hair back from her face. She was suddenly aware that she was drenched with sweat, and her head was pounding.

With a look of concern, Rashid Kaleem reached out with gentle fingers and moved her hair just enough to examine the bump at her hairline. "You're going to have a goose egg. Did they do that to you?" At her nod, he dropped his hand and began to key the phone.

"No, wait," said Gemma. "It's complicated."

Rashid looked up, his fingers still, his face closing.

"I'm not protecting them," Gemma hastened to explain. "It's something else. It has to do with Naz Malik, the man you examined in the park."

"Malik?" Slowly, Rashid's distant expression relaxed into curiosity. He studied her more closely. "You need to sit down. Let me take you for a coffee."

He led her round the corner into Brick Lane and up to the Old Truman Brewery. There was a coffeehouse in the back, behind the trendy shops and artists' studios. Rashid ushered her inside and sat her down on one of the hard wooden benches, saying, "Wait here." He disappeared towards the back.

It was only then, as she sank onto the bench, that Gemma realized just how shaken up she was.

Good God, what might those two have done to her if Rashid Kaleem hadn't come along? She told herself that it had still been daylight, that it had been a residential street, that the Gilles brothers were bullies and had only meant to frighten her, but none of those logical reassurances helped.

She'd seen too many knife crimes and muggings; she knew how quickly things could flare out of control and how badly people could be hurt.

And now she knew how it felt to be a victim.

The rage that shot through her was so intense it made her feel sick. The pain in her head grew worse. She forced herself to breathe, to focus on something besides the nausea. She gazed out, watching the patterns of sunlight made by the leaves of a tree in a planter, and after a moment she realized she was looking out into the old brewery yard.

On the expanse of concrete stood a double-decker bus, an old Routemaster, with tables and umbrellas in front of it, and the name ROOTMASTER painted cheerfully across its side.

The pun made her smile, in spite of her anger and her headache, and then she remembered where she had heard the name before.

This was where Naz was supposed to have met Sandra and Charlotte that Sunday afternoon, the afternoon Sandra had disappeared. This was where Naz had waited for the wife who had never come.

Rashid returned, and she tore her gaze from the bus, glancing at the mug he'd set down on the table before her. She groaned. "That's not coffee. Don't tell me—it's hot, sweet tea. I hate sweet tea."

"I didn't think coffee was a good idea with that bump on your head. You've got enough bruising without a big jolt of caffeine increasing your blood flow. So, tea"—he held out his other hand—"and ice." He'd cadged a plastic bag filled with ice cubes and wrapped it in a somewhat bedraggled tea towel. "Put this on your head, and drink up. Believe me, they didn't like parting with the ice, but I know the owner."

Gemma obeyed, finding that the searing heat of the tea was comforting, and the ice felt good on her pounding head.

"Now," said Rashid as a waitress in shorts and a midriff-baring

T-shirt brought him a cup of espresso, "tell me about those unsavory characters."

"Unsavory?" Gemma suppressed a slightly hysterical laugh because it hurt her head. And suddenly she realized what a fright she must look, damp and shaky, with a lump on her forehead and water dripping down her face.

The thought of Kevin and Terry sobered her quickly enough, however, and as she drank a little more of her tea and held the ice pack to her head, she told Rashid as much as she dared about Charlotte and about her visit to Gail Gilles. She left out any mention of Kincaid and the Narcotics investigation, finishing with, "So, you see, I can't report them, because if I do I'll have to identify myself, and I'll be admitting that I visited the grandmother under false pretenses."

"But you didn't actually lie."

"No, but I'm afraid my interference will bugger up the custody issue."

"And you don't think the caseworker needs to know that those louts threatened you?" Rashid's dark eyebrows were drawn together in a scowl. "This little girl is mixed race, then? The father was Pakistani, the mother white?"

Gemma nodded, not adding the speculation that Sandra's father had been at least partly Afro-Caribbean.

"You know those two will use her as a punching bag, if they get their hands on her." Rashid's face was hard. "And from what you're telling me about the family, no amount of oversight is going to keep them from having contact with their mother."

"I *have* been trying to convey that," Gemma said, attempting to keep her frustration in check.

"And the scrawny one is a user," Rashid added. "You see it on every Bangladeshi estate. After a while you can't miss the signs, whether the kids are white, black, or brown. Acne. Twitching. That charming, vacant stare."

"Dealers aren't usually users, though," said Gemma, thinking about the Narcotics investigation.

"Not if they're any good at it. But I wouldn't discount the other brother. The talker."

"Kevin." The thought of Kevin's face made Gemma press the ice pack to her head again.

"You okay? Any dizziness?" Rashid was half out of his seat, looming over her.

Gemma inched back on her bench. "You should work with live people. Great bedside manner."

Rashid subsided onto his own bench, looking sheepish. "Sorry. Too many years of looking after neighbors and aunties and cousins who don't take me seriously."

"But you're a doctor," Gemma said, surprised.

"I'm a snotty-nosed kid from a housing estate." For just an instant, Gemma could see the boy Neal Weller had described.

"Not anymore." Gemma smiled at him, and he returned it. Then she asked, "Do they come to you for advice, these neighbors and aunties and cousins?"

"Only in a very roundabout way. Medical degree or not, I'm still a male, and they're not comfortable talking to me."

She thought about the clinic in Rivington Street. "Would they talk to other women?"

"Maybe. If they felt safe." Rashid finished his coffee, then cast a disapproving glance at her half-drunk tea. "You should finish that. And it might not be a good idea for you to drive. I should see you home."

There was something so charmingly old-fashioned in the way he phrased it that Gemma found herself beginning to blush. "No, really, I'm fine. My head just hurts a little."

"They don't know where you live, those two? You shouldn't be on your own."

"No. I've got kids—and my partner—waiting at home for me."

She felt stupidly awkward, wondering why she'd felt the need to explain her situation, and the flush intensified. "I really should go. Thanks for your help."

Tentatively, she felt the tender spot on her forehead. It had just occurred to her to wonder how on earth she was going to explain what had happened to Duncan. He would want Kevin and Terry Gilles's heads on platters, and that would not be good at all.

CHAPTER TWENTY-TWO

One of the few sentiments which unites all generations of the Bangladeshi community is the feeling that white families fail to protect the interests of needy members. . . . Even though their successful children may now want to live separately from their parents when they marry, and even leave home when single in a few cases, most still believe in the moral solidarity of the family and the importance of putting family interests before those of the individual. Indeed, in most situations individual interests are seen as best served by the family.

—Geoff Dench,
Kate Gavron,
Michael Young,
The New East End

It was Toby who noticed it first. "Mummy, what happened to your head?"

She was putting away the groceries she had picked up at the supermarket on her way home, having taken advantage of the fact that she had the car, but now she felt a little queasy at the thought of eating.

Kit looked up from the fantasy novel he was reading at the kitchen table. "Ow. You do have a lump."

"I went to get some things for Charlotte, and I bumped my head in the loft."

"What did you get for her?" asked Toby, who was picking through her shopping bags like a puppy looking for treats.

"Some art pencils."

"We went to visit Charlotte today," Toby informed her. "Wes took us." He abandoned the bags as unrewarding. "Can I draw with the pencils?"

"No, they're Charlotte's. You'll have to ask her first."

"When? When are you going to give them to her?"

"I don't know," Gemma snapped, her patience fraying. Her head was splitting, and there were times she thought her son was a terrier disguised as a little boy.

She had meant to stop at Betty's on the way home, but at the last minute she had put it off. She didn't think she could face seeing Charlotte, not with the image of the girl's uncles still so freshly imprinted in her mind.

"Kit, will you light the grill? I've got some chicken for dinner, and a salad." Gemma had discovered that the oil-fired cooker she had so fancied was a monster to cook on in the summer heat, so most evenings they resorted to cold salads or pasta, or used the charcoal grill on the patio.

Fortunately, Kit was a nascent pyromaniac, and having applied himself to the project with scientific intensity, had become an expert at lighting and tending charcoal.

"Roger that," he said, and got up, but instead of heading for the patio, he came over to her and looked at her head more closely. "You should have that looked at."

"I'm fine, really." She summoned a smile. "Go on. Everyone's starving, and I'm sure your dad will be home soon."

She was thinking that the "bumping her head in the loft"

explanation would have to do for Duncan as well until the children went to bed, when her mobile rang.

"I'm going to be late," Kincaid said without preamble when she answered. "It turns out that Kevin's boss owns a white transit van. I'm trying to get Narcotics to let me pull it over on a traffic stop, or at least to tell me if they think this guy, Roby, is involved in the drugs thing. If they've been watching him, too, they may know where the van was last Saturday."

Gemma spilled a bagged salad into a bowl and fetched dressing from the fridge. "I don't fancy your chances."

"No. But nothing else is panning out. Lucas Ritchie has as much of an alibi for Saturday as we're likely to get, by the way. He *was* at his niece's birthday party in St. John's Wood. His mum showed Cullen photos. And he didn't drive there, so it's not likely he ducked out of the party long enough to have met Naz and dumped him in the park. Cullen got the names of some other guests to follow up, but . . ."

"Not likely," Gemma agreed. "What about the missing girl from the club? What was her name? Kylie?"

"Nothing definite, but her parents think she's living in a squat in Plumstead. Or was it Wanstead? Undoubtedly the dodgy end. Cullen's checking on it." He sounded tired.

"Drugs involved?" Gemma thought about Rashid's speculation that Terry Gilles was a user, and the implications of that for the Narcotics investigation.

And for Charlotte.

But she couldn't pass those suspicions on to Janice Silverman without an explanation of how she had come by them. And she couldn't talk to Kincaid about it now, not with Toby and Kit coming in and out of the kitchen.

"Maybe," Kincaid said, then he added, "You okay? You sound a bit wobbly."

"Oh, fine. I'm fine. It's just been—a long day. I'll fill you in when I see you."

But when Kincaid got home a few hours later, having finally had a very unrewarding conversation with his opposite number in Narcotics, he found Gemma in bed, fast asleep.

And when he woke the next morning, a bit late, he came downstairs to find Kit and Toby finishing breakfast, and Gemma already gone.

"She got a call," Kit told him. "Another burglary in the middle of the night. Golborne Road, this time." He sounded pleased with himself for passing on the information. "Here. I've made you toast."

"Thanks, sport." Kincaid glanced at the kitchen clock. "But I'd better eat it on the run if I'm going to get Toby to child care on time."

He'd sent Toby to get his backpack, and had washed a mouthful of toast and jam down with coffee, when his mobile rang. When he saw that it was Cullen, he took another bite of toast as he answered. "I'm on my way," he said. "Just as soon as—"

Cullen broke in, his voice a register higher than normal. "Guv, you're not going to believe what made the bloody tabloids this morning."

"Boss." Melody ducked her head in the door of Gemma's office. "The super's here to see you."

Gemma looked up from the report she was scrolling through on her computer. It hadn't been burglary this time, but a robbery. The owner of a small grocery had been assaulted as he unlocked the shop at daybreak. "Mark?" she said, assuming Melody meant Superintendent Lamb, her guv'nor, and wondering why Melody felt the need to announce him.

"No." Melody's voice dropped to an emphatic whisper. "*Your super. Duncan.*"

She disappeared from view and Kincaid walked into Gemma's office, his face set in a thunderous scowl. He closed the door behind him as he tossed a newspaper on Gemma's desk. "Have you seen this?"

Gemma turned the paper round. It was that morning's *Chronicle,* and the headline read: *Slave Trade Linked to Rumored Whitechapel Sex Club.*

"What?" She pulled the paper closer and skimmed the lead. In the *Chronicle*'s usual lurid style, the article said it had learned that police were conducting an ongoing investigation into an exclusive private club in Whitechapel, which a well-known Bangladeshi businessman, soon to stand trial for modern-day slavery, was known to frequent. It gave Azad's name, the details of the prosecution's human-trafficking charges against him, and a summary of the various businesses in which he was allegedly involved.

It then, without actually giving an address, described in fulsome terms the club near historic Artillery Lane in Whitechapel, including the beautiful young hostesses whom it suggested were little better than high-class prostitutes. It ended by insinuating that the club harbored members whose ill-gotten wealth allowed them to scoff at British law and human rights.

"What the—" Gemma stared blankly at the page, then looked up at Kincaid. "That's Ritchie's club. They're talking about Ritchie's club. Where the hell did they get this?"

"I've no clue." He sat down on the other side of her desk. "But I've already had the chief superintendent on the phone, who's had the assistant commissioner on the phone, who's had God knows who on the phone, all wanting to know *what* ongoing police investigation. I've said I merely made some routine inquiries in the course of a homicide investigation, and that there is no direct involvement on the part of the club. The question is, did anyone see *you?*"

"No. No, I don't think so. I only spoke to Ritchie." Gemma lowered her voice. "And my visit had nothing to do with Narcotics."

"Neither of us wants to explain that you were there pursuing a personal line of inquiry. Interfering in a murder investigation would not go down well with your boss or mine. And we'll not be getting any further cooperation from Lucas Ritchie, or from Azad, on this case."

With a sinking feeling, Gemma realized it was not likely she would get any help from Lucas Ritchie in Charlotte's custody case either, nor would she be able to talk to him again.

"It's not surprising that some of Ritchie's club members have friends in high places," Kincaid went on. "But as long as you're not pulled into it, the funny-handshake brigade can complain all they like."

"But the club wasn't named," Gemma protested.

"Didn't need to be, for those who move on that level. I don't know who's going to be the most pissed off, Ritchie and his board of directors, or Azad." He tapped the paper. "And the club may be perfectly respectable, but I guarantee there will be members who won't want any association with the least rumor of high-class prostitution. Not to mention the fact that Azad will be a bit of an embarrassment."

"Will he be blackballed, do you think?"

"I doubt he's broadcast his legal troubles, so the charges may come as a shock to the other members, if not to Ritchie. It might make Azad the odd boy out at school for a while. But he's a wily sod; I expect he'll recover. If he doesn't go to prison."

Gemma was studying the paper again. "That's not looking very likely, is it, with the prosecution's star witness still missing?" She looked up at him, rubbing her aching head. "Bloody hell. I should never have gone to the club. What if Lucas Ritchie mentions me? It's all going to come back on you. I—"

Kincaid didn't give her a chance to finish. "I think Ritchie will be keeping his head down. And there's no reason why Ritchie, or anyone else, should connect your visit with this story. I doubt Ritchie or Azad will complain to the Met, although Azad may raise hell with the newspaper." He studied her more closely, really focusing on her face for the first time. "Is that a bruise?" His brow creased. "What on earth happened to your head?"

Now Gemma wished she had waited up to explain the night before, but she hadn't felt well and had had trouble staying awake. "I had a little run-in with Kevin and Terry Gilles yesterday," she said reluctantly, then went on to explain what had happened, including Rashid Kaleem's part in her rescue.

Kincaid had come in glowering. Now he looked volcanic. "Those bastards!" He stood up, pacing in her small office. "Fucking lowlife slime." He didn't swear often—not as much, Gemma hated to admit, as she did—and when he did, it was usually for effect in interviews. "I'll have them in, whether Narcotics likes it or not, and I'll have their balls in a vise. They're not going to get away with making threats and laying hands on you, for God's sake." He clenched his fist. "Those little shits—"

"They didn't actually hit me," broke in Gemma, trying to calm him down. She had known he'd be upset, but she hadn't expected him to be quite so angry. "They just pushed me into the car. And you absolutely cannot jeopardize the drugs investigation. You can't let Kevin and Terry Gilles know that I'm a police officer, or even that I have any connection with the police. Or with you. It will make any information I got from Gail Gilles suspect, and put both our jobs at risk. And it might seriously endanger Charlotte."

Kincaid stared at her. "Damn it to hell and back. I sent you in there." He jammed his hands in his pockets, as if he didn't trust himself not to hit something. "*I* put *you* at risk."

"You couldn't have known. And I wanted to go. You just have to be prepared to throw everything you've got at the lovely Kev and Ter, once the Narcotics investigation is over."

"That could be months," he protested. "Narcotics won't give me a timeline."

"I don't think Narcotics would be so touchy if the operation wasn't coming to a head," Gemma said thoughtfully.

Kincaid continued his pacing. "Even if it's only days, every shred of evidence I have linking them to Naz Malik's murder is going to go cold. And there's something else. Azad told me that it was Kevin and Terry Gilles heading the mob that fire-bombed his restaurant. He didn't tell the police, maybe out of a desire not to make more trouble, or maybe from some sort of loyalty to Naz and Sandra. But if Naz knew . . ."

"Kevin and Terry might have thought that shutting Naz up would guarantee Azad's silence," Gemma suggested. "Or maybe Naz threatened to turn them in."

"Or it might be more complicated than that." Kincaid stopped at the desk and turned the paper back in his direction. "This piece suggests that Azad owns businesses that are less aboveboard than his restaurant. Low-rent housing for illegals, sweatshops. Maybe he didn't give up the Gilles brothers because Naz, or Sandra, had something on him."

"Tit for tat? You're assuming that Sandra would have protected her brothers?"

"No. I'm thinking that *Azad* might have assumed that Sandra would protect them."

Gemma shook her head. "I thought you'd pretty much ruled Azad out."

"Maybe I didn't look closely enough." Kincaid leaned across the desk and brushed a strand of hair away from her face. "And in the meantime, I want you to promise me you won't go near Brick Lane, or Bethnal Green, or anywhere in the East End." Although his touch had been gentle, his voice was grim. "Not until this drugs investigation is over with, and I have a chance to deal with Kevin and Terry Gilles."

No sooner had Kincaid walked out of Gemma's office than Melody walked in, carefully closing the door behind her. Her face was white as chalk. "Boss—"

"Melody, are you okay?" said Gemma. "Whatever is the matter? Sit down, for heaven's sa—"

"Boss." Melody stood at attention. Her crisp navy suit might have been a uniform, and she didn't meet Gemma's eyes. "Boss, I want to tender my resignation."

CHAPTER TWENTY-THREE

*I am very proud of my cockney background and have many
memories of my East End childhood. I wanted to record the
stories about that way of life before they were forgotten . . .
Many families have roots in East London or in similar
close-knit communities, and I wanted to preserve their
stories, too.*

—Gilda O'Neill,
East End Tales

"Don't be daft, Melody," Gemma said. "Sit down."

As Melody walked stiffly to the chair, she looked as if her limbs
belonged to someone else. She sat and nodded towards the paper.
"It's my fault. That story."

"What are you talking about?"

"My father. My father owns the *Chronicle*."

"What?" Gemma wondered if her headache was making her hear
things. "You're having me on. This isn't fun—"

"No. Oh, I'm serious, all right. I wish I weren't," said Melody.
"My dad is Ivan Talbot. *That* Ivan Talbot. The newspaper baron."

"But— But why did you never tell anyone?" asked Gemma, feeling thoroughly gobsmacked.

"Because I thought no one would ever trust me if they knew who I was. And they would have been right. None of this"—she prodded the paper with a scowl of distaste—"would have happened if it hadn't been for me."

"But surely you didn't deliberately—"

"Of course not. But when I saw Ahmed Azad in the club, I couldn't resist using the newspaper office to do the research. It was too easy, and it's not the first time I've used the *Chronicle*'s morgue when I needed information that I thought would help solve a case. I thought I could have my cake and eat it, too, more fool me. Because this time, I blew it.

"I thought my dad had gone for the day. I used his office, and he came back when I still had the file on Azad open. He saw what I was working on. And then"—Melody shook her head, as if astounded by her own folly—"and then I was stupid enough to ask him if he knew anything about Ritchie's club. That was all it took for him to put the pieces together."

"And he didn't tell you he was going to run the story?"

"You don't know my dad. Nothing is more important than a story. Nothing. I could kill him."

So that was how the paper had connected the police, the club, and Azad, thought Gemma.

"I should have known better," Melody went on. "I should never have trusted him. And you should never have trusted me."

"Melody, this wasn't a self-fulfilling prophecy," protested Gemma. "Maybe you shouldn't have done the research at the paper—"

"But this is just the tip of the iceberg, don't you see? You know what the papers are like, and my dad's is one of the worst. Oh, he wants a shred of truth to a story, but given that, he can spin straw into gold. If he knew I was involved in a sensitive case, he'd watch me like a vulture. And if anyone in the force knew my connection with him, they'd never let me near anything high profile. Didn't you wonder why I'd never applied for promotion? I couldn't risk it. I couldn't risk anyone taking an interest in me."

"Melody," Gemma broke in, "did it not occur to you that by leaking this story, your father might have been trying to sabotage your career? That he might have guessed you'd try to resign? I mean, really, this doesn't amount to all that much, except that it caused some ruffled feathers, and it humiliated you."

Melody stared at her. "No. But— Oh, God. I was even more stupid than I thought. He's never wanted me to do this . . . . He considers police work a waste of my very expensive education, and my intelligence, not to mention the fact that he thinks I should want to take over what he's worked so hard to build. And he's a persistent bastard, my dad, or he wouldn't be where he is." She frowned. "I just handed him the opportunity on a plate, didn't I?"

"Are you tempted?" Gemma asked, wondering what it would be like to be offered the kind of life Melody's father must lead. "To take over from him, eventually, I mean? I think most people would be. Power, position—and money. Your dad must be richer than— well, I don't imagine he worries about the mortgage or the grocery bill, to put it mildly."

"It's all on a relative scale," Melody answered with a bitter smile. "He has to worry about keeping up with his friends' private jets. But it's not really about the money for my dad. It's about what he can do, how much influence he has, how far he's come from snotty-nosed little Ivan Talbot who scrapped his way out of a Newcastle Council estate."

Gemma stared at Melody, bemused. She felt as if she was trying to fit together two photographic negatives, one over the other, that didn't quite match. "Talbot's a common enough name. I'd never have thought . . . But why on earth is your dad called *Ivan*?"

"My nan was reading Russian history at school when she got pregnant. She was a bright girl who raised a bright child, in spite of the obstacles. But"—Melody leaned forward—"I don't *want* to be him. I don't want his job or his newspaper. I would never be more than Ivan's daughter, no matter what I accomplished. Can you understand that?"

Gemma thought about her own father, about his constant disapproval of her choices, and his bitter disappointment that she had failed to fit into his mold. What might he do to scupper her career, if he had the power?

"And besides," Melody went on raggedly, "all I ever wanted for as long as I can remember was to be in the police. I grew up watching every cop show, reading books on how to be a detective . . . Dad thought if he sent me to the best schools, and university . . . that I would eventually grow out of it, that I'd learn to be 'normal.' But I didn't."

"And you're telling me that you would even consider letting him get away with this? I don't believe it." A desire to tell Ivan Talbot what she thought of him was making Gemma's head pound. "You are good at this, and I don't want to lose you. I don't want the force to lose you. I am not going to accept your resignation. And you—you're going to be much more careful from now on. No more research at the paper. No hints to your father about any cases, no matter how innocently given. Is that settled?"

"But—but how can you possibly trust me after this—"

"Because I know you." And in spite of Melody's dissembling, Gemma felt sure that she did. "What your father does is really no one else's business. And there is nothing that links you to this story"—Gemma tapped the paper—"other than your word and mine. And we're not going to discuss it again. With anyone."

There was a long moment in which Gemma and Melody looked at each other, and Gemma wondered if she had made the right judgment call.

Then Melody stood, giving Gemma a crisp nod. "Thank you,

ma'am. I won't disappoint you." Her round face was set with resolution. "And I can promise you something else. My father is going to pay for this, one way or another."

The rest of Friday passed uneventfully, but Gemma was still thinking about her conversation with Melody as she drove to Betty Howard's late on Saturday morning. She wondered how much her new knowledge would change her perception of Melody. Already she better understood both Melody's doggedness in pursuing an investigation and her personal reticence. And although she sympathized with Melody's desire to stand on her own merits, she thought it unlikely she would be able to keep her identity secret indefinitely. Gemma had kept her word, however, and had not told Duncan, but the omission niggled uncomfortably at her. She didn't like his taking the fall for something that had been her fault. It had been she who had taken Melody to Lucas Ritchie's club, starting the chain of events that had led to the story, but she couldn't see any other alternative.

It was already hot, and she hadn't felt like walking, although driving meant negotiating the jam on Portobello Road on market day. The boys had fussed about wanting to see Charlotte—Toby, in particular, was still coveting Charlotte's pencils—but they'd had their own activities.

Duncan had taken Toby to his Saturday football match, whispering as he left that there was nothing he'd rather do than sit in the sun in the park and watch a bunch of uncoordinated six-year-olds chase a ball, and Kit was meeting some school friends at Starbucks to discuss an out-of-term project. Or so he said—she suspected there would be good bit more gossip and music swapping than discussion, but she was glad to see him getting out a bit more socially.

She had just found a parking spot near Betty's flat when her mobile rang. Her heart skipped a bit when she saw it was her sister, although she had just talked to her mum that morning and Vi had said she was feeling fine.

"Hi, Cyn," she said, hoping as always that if she started the conversation on an upbeat note, it might stay that way.

"Mum said you're not coming to Leyton."

"I'm not coming today," Gemma clarified. "I told her I'd bring the boys tomorrow. They've got things on today, and I promised to see Charlotte—"

"Charlotte? That's this little girl Mum says you've taken in?"

"I haven't taken her in." Exasperation was beginning to make Gemma's head pound. "I arranged for her to stay with Wesley's mother, and I feel responsible—"

"You feel responsible for someone else's child and not your own mother?" Cyn's voice had risen over the sound of her kids, Brendan and Tiffani, squabbling in the background. "Will you two just shut it?" she shouted without covering the phone, nearly splitting Gemma's eardrum, and the noise level dropped momentarily.

Wincing, Gemma said, "Cyn, whatever is the matter with you? That's ridiculous. Of course I feel responsible for Mum—"

"Do you? You haven't seen her since she came home from hospital. She's so—so frail, and I don't— She seems old, Gemma, and I don't know what I would do—" To Gemma's horror, her ruthlessly unflappable sister sounded near tears.

"They've said it's the chemo, Cyn," Gemma hastened to reassure her. "Try not to worry—"

"And she asked me this morning about the wedding." Cyn's indignation had come back in full force. "What am I supposed to tell her? Have you done anything at all about making the arrangements?"

"I—I just haven't had a chance. I've been busy at work, and—"

"Right. It's always something, Gemma." Cynthia's voice had gone cold. "You don't care who you disappoint. I'm surprised Duncan puts up with you. And you know how much Mum is counting on this. You'll be the death of her if you keep on like this, you mark my words." The connection went dead in Gemma's ear.

"Cyn?" Gemma said. "Cyn?" Then, when it sank in that her sister had really hung up on her, she shouted, "Harpy," at the hapless mobile and threw it onto the passenger seat. It didn't make her feel any better.

With the things that had happened in the last few days, she had managed to put the wedding completely out of her mind. Now, all the weight of obligation came rushing back, and with it the nausea that had been nagging her since Sandra's brothers had cracked her head against the Escort's door. The interior of the car suddenly seemed unbearably hot and confining.

She got out carefully, fighting a wave of dizziness, and collected the holdall with Charlotte's things from the backseat. This time she looked round before she leaned into the car, but that made her dizzier.

Then, feeling oddly disconnected from her feet, she walked the few yards to Betty's building. As she went in and glanced up the stairwell, the climb seemed as daunting as Mount Everest. Slowly, gingerly, she made the ascent, stopping on each landing to ease the thumping in her head.

By the time she reached Betty's flat and Charlotte ran into her arms for a hug, she felt she was the one most in need of comfort.

Charlotte had finally been persuaded to let go of Gemma and settle down with her pencils at the small table in Betty's kitchen. She drew with grave concentration, while in the sitting room, Betty exclaimed over the clothes Gemma had brought.

"Her mama was that good to her," Betty said softly as she refolded a little pink skirt. "Oh, I don't just mean the clothes," she added. "But you can tell, with the little ones, when they've been loved. And I don't believe for a minute that this one's mama left her of her own accord." She added a neatly folded T-shirt to the skirt. "Not unless there was drink or drugs involved."

"Not on her mum's part, anyway," Gemma agreed, but when Betty gave her a questioning look, she merely added, "I'd have heard something by now, I think, if there was anything like that."

"Will she be all right if she goes to her granny?" Betty asked. "I do worry, and I haven't heard a thing more from the social worker."

"I know," said Gemma. "I'm worried, too."

The admission brought back her sister's hateful words in full force. Was she as selfish as Cyn had said? Should she be doing more for her mother and less for Charlotte? But how could she not do everything in her power for this child, who had no one else to protect her? And if Cyn was right, was she letting Duncan down, as well? Was he losing patience with her?

"Gemma, honey, you're right away with the fairies. Are you all right?" Betty was looking at her in concern, and Gemma realized she hadn't heard a word Betty had said.

"I'm sorry. It's just—" She couldn't begin to explain what was wrong, and especially not in front of Charlotte.

"Look, Gemma," said Charlotte, holding up her paper. She had drawn stick figures, the larger two red and blue, the smaller one yellow. They were a bit squiggly, but still recognizable as people. "That's a mummy and a daddy and a little girl," Charlotte informed her.

Gemma studied the picture with the seriousness it deserved. There were clouds, and a sausagey-shaped thing with legs near the yellow stick figure's feet. "That's very good, lovey. The little girl is yellow. That's a happy color. And is that her dog?"

"Georgy," Charlotte said. She still couldn't manage the *d* sound in Geordie. "I want to see Georgy."

"Maybe you can come over for a bit, this afternoon or tomorrow, if it's all right with your auntie Betty here." To Betty, she added, "The boys are quite smitten. As are the dogs," she added, summoning a smile. "Sid, I'm not so sure about."

"You should stay and have some lunch," said Betty. "I've made a cold salad."

"I'd love to," Gemma said, although the thought of food made the sweat break out on her forehead. "I'd better go, though. Toby has a football match, and I promised I'd take him to the art store for some pencils like Charlotte's afterwards." She stood and kissed Betty's cheek. "But I'll ring you, and we'll see about arranging a visit."

She gave Charlotte a hug, resisting the temptation to keep her in her arms, then waved as she let herself out of the flat.

The stairs, however, proved almost as daunting going down as they had going up, and when she reached the car, she got in and simply sat.

She felt overwhelmed, as if the pieces of her life were flying off in all directions, out of her control, and she couldn't summon the focus to hold them together.

Avoiding the tender bruise on her forehead, she rested her head on the hot steering wheel, trying to think. *Wedding . . . Mum . . . Charlotte . . . the Gilles brothers . . . Melody . . . wedding . . .*

Her mind whirled and she sat up, fighting another wave of dizziness. She couldn't sort it out, not the way she was feeling. She needed some sensible advice, and suddenly she realized who she *could* talk to. Putting the key in the ignition, she started the car and drove, not to Toby's football match, but to Kensington.

Doug Cullen had left home that morning with a list of flats and estate agents in his pocket. But somehow, instead of taking the District Line to Putney, he got on the wrong train and found himself at Victoria. The mistake was half habit and half absentmindedness. But as the reason for the absentmindedness was his mulling over of the business of the newspaper story, he decided to get off the train and go on into the Yard.

He was glad to shut himself in his office, quiet on a Saturday, where he could think it through properly. Something was not right about the whole thing. There was Kincaid's reaction, to start with. After his first surprise, the guv'nor had gone all quiet and nonchalant about it, and while he might have the clout to buck displeasure from above, Cullen had been in on the interview with Ritchie as well, and he knew *he* wasn't bulletproof.

How the hell had someone put together their visit—because that had to have been the "police investigation"—with Azad's membership in the club, something they hadn't known themselves?

Unless, of course, there really was another investigation . . . He picked up a pen and doodled on the message pad on his desk—names, interconnected with big swooping arrows. What if the club was somehow tied into the Narcotics investigation? But if he and Kincaid had been warned off, there was no way any other detectives were going to be going round asking official questions, so that idea didn't wash.

But Lucas Ritchie did have a connection with Sandra Gilles's brothers, through his friendship with Sandra. And if the brothers were dealing drugs, was it possible that Ritchie was running them? The club would certainly be a convenient front for money laundering, and some of Ritchie's clients might be investing in a bit of the action on the side.

But how did Ahmed Azad tie into that? He had never been accused, as far as Cullen knew, of having any connection with drugs.

The pen had leaked as he scribbled. Cullen tore the inky piece of paper into strips, staining his fingers in the process. He shuffled the strips, realizing he'd left something—or rather someone—out.

Gemma. Gemma had been involved in this case from the beginning, even before they'd been called in. And he knew her well enough now to be certain that she hadn't just walked away from it, especially after she'd helped arrange foster care for Naz Malik's daughter. But what could Gemma possibly have to do with Lucas Ritchie? The more he thought about it, the more certain he became that Gemma was mixed up in all of it, somehow, and he didn't like the idea one bit. But he needed more information.

Maybe it was time to take advantage of a favor owed him by a reporter on the *Chronicle*. These things were tit for tat—and Doug, like most detectives, had developed a list of contacts useful to both parties.

He picked up the phone, and after a few calls, managed to track down his sometime source, a veteran reporter named Cal Grogan.

But by the time he rang off, he felt more baffled than ever. Cal had assured him that he'd be more than happy to help, but the story had come straight from the owner's desk, and Ivan Talbot never revealed a source.

The square tucked away behind Kensington High Street was green and quiet, a residential enclave of elegant town houses. A few of these now housed businesses, including, on the ground floor at the end of a terrace, the café where Hazel had taken a job.

When Gemma walked in, she saw that the interior of the café was a clean, white space, with only a few tables, and fewer customers lingering over their lunches. Hazel stood at the back of the long, narrow room, stocking clean glassware on a shelf. She wore a white apron and T-shirt over tan trousers, and when she saw Gemma, she gave a radiant smile and hurried forward.

"Gemma! What are you doing here? What a lovely surprise."

"I'm sorry I didn't ring first. But I knew you'd said you were working today, and I just—I thought we could talk. Are you too busy?"

Hazel glanced at the remaining diners. "We're just finishing up the lunch rush. Then there will be a bit of a lull before the afternoon-tea crowd starts filtering in." She pointed Gemma to a small table at the front. "Have a seat and I'll bring you some tea. You can enjoy the view, and I'll be with you in a tick. There are some lunch specials left—have you eaten?"

"Just tea would be fine," said Gemma, avoiding the question.

"You look dreadful," Hazel exclaimed, examining her more closely. "What on earth did you do to yourself?"

"Oh, it was just something stupid that happened at work. I'm fine, really."

"Well, I suppose that's a better answer than 'I walked into a door.'" Hazel gave her an assessing, skeptical look, but brought her a cup of tea. When the last customers had left, she took off her apron and sat down beside Gemma with a cup of her own. "Coffee for me, I'm afraid. I need the boost to get through the rest of the afternoon."

"And this from the woman who used to drink herbal teas?" Gemma teased.

"Ah, well, another time, another place. Another person, really," Hazel added, with just a touch of sadness, but then she smiled. "And I've discovered I quite like coffee. I'm going to take full advantage of my few minutes' respite while Chef is out making an emergency-supply run." She looked much better than the last time Gemma had seen her, when they had talked under the Westway.

"I'm glad you're settling in."

"So am I. But at the moment, I'm more concerned about you. Is it your mum?"

"In a way." Gemma told her about the call from Cyn that morning.

Hazel frowned. "Well, no one would deny that your sister can be a bitch, but that's a bit over the top, even for her. You know she's jealous of you."

"Cyn? Jealous of me? But she's the one gets all the approval."

"Sometimes you are thick, Gemma," Hazel said with a sigh. "I suspect that's her way of making up for not having your life—your job, your partner, your children, your house. But in this case, I think it's more than envy. For all her bossiness, Cynthia is much more dependent on your mum than you are. I think she's terrified of losing her—as is your dad—and you've become a convenient scapegoat."

"But why would—" Gemma rubbed her head, trying to sort out her thoughts. "I don't understand why blaming me would make them feel better—and I feel like I'm just being stubborn, not giving them what they want." She swallowed, making an effort to steady her voice. "But this wedding has turned into a monster. I wanted it to be something special, for Duncan and me, and the boys, not some stupid spectacle in a cheap—or not so cheap—hotel. But if it means that much to my mum—"

"Darling, you are letting your father and your sister blow this all out of proportion. Your mother loves you. She wants you to be happy. And I think nothing would please her more than to see you get on with your life, by whatever means. And if you were thinking logically, you would know that your mother's recovery does not depend on your getting married in the Ritz rather than the register's office."

"No. I suppose you're right," Gemma admitted, feeling a smidgen of relief, and with an attempt at lightness, added, "Are you sure you shouldn't be practicing therapy again, rather than working in a café?"

"This suits me very well for the moment, and I mean to hold on to what I have," Hazel said firmly. "And you—you are not going to let your family spoil your wedding. You are going to do what feels right for you." Hazel patted Gemma's hand. "Now, promise me you'll go straight home and talk to Duncan. You can work this out between the two of you. That's what counts, after all."

But when Gemma arrived home, she found Duncan in the hall, looking as if he was on his way out, and his expression didn't augur well for a discussion.

"Where have you been?" he said, sounding irritable. "I've tried ringing you for ages. Toby and I wanted you to meet us for lunch. But when I couldn't get you, I made sandwiches, and now I've promised to take him to the art shop because you weren't here."

"Oh, no. My phone." Gemma remembered tossing it onto the seat before she went into Betty's, and that was the last time she'd thought of it. Had it fallen onto the floor of the car and turned itself off? "I think I might have lost it."

"You think?" He frowned at her. "What do you mean, you think? Either you lost it or you didn't."

"I can't . . . remember." The room wavered. She sank down onto the hall bench, knocking the dogs' leads to the floor. "I—I don't feel very well. My head's gone all fuzzy."

"Gemma?"

At least that was what she thought he said. His lips moved, but a buzzing sound rose like a wave, drowning the sound of his voice. Then his face receded to the end of a white tunnel and blinked out.

CHAPTER TWENTY-FOUR

It was seen as proper that you were married before you had a baby, and East End weddings were big social events. Even families without much money would try to put on a good 'do'.

—Gilda O'Neill,
East End Tales

The next thing Gemma knew, Duncan was stroking her cheek and saying her name, urgently. Then he turned his head and shouted for Kit and Toby.

She winced. "Ouch. Don't shout. It hurts my head."

"Gemma, are you okay? What happened there?" His face was inches away, his eyes intent.

"Just a bit dizzy," she mumbled. "I'm all right." She liked his hand on her face. It felt warm, and she pressed her cheek against it, closing her eyes against the light. But he tightened his grasp, using his other hand to turn her head.

"Open your eyes, Gemma. Look at me," he said sharply.

"The light makes my head hurt," she protested, but complied.

"Your pupils aren't normal." He sounded as if he was angry with her.

"I'm sorry. I didn't mean—"

The boys came thundering down the stairs, the dogs at their heels, barking excitedly at the commotion. The noise made Gemma's head feel like it was going to split open. She covered her ears, so that when Duncan spoke, his voice came through fuzzily.

"I'm taking your mum to hospital. Kit, I want you to look after Toby until we get back. I'll ring you."

"I don't want to go to hospital," said Gemma, pushing Duncan's hands away. "I hate that place."

"No argument." He slipped an arm round her waist and lifted her, and she found that in spite of her resistance, she needed the support.

"I'll start the car." Kit scooped the keys off the floor, where Gemma must have dropped them. She caught a flash of his face, white and frightened, as he went out the door.

"Kit, I'm fine," she tried to say, but it came out a thread of sound, and as Duncan started to walk her towards the door, the world began to go white and fuzzy again.

After that, she let Duncan fold her gently into the car, but she managed a smile at Kit as they drove away.

Then it was a blur of glass doors and gurneys and long, ugly corridors. Duncan stayed with her, holding her hand. At last they were through with scans and exams, and a young, female doctor came into the curtained cubicle to speak to them.

"The bad news is that you do have a concussion, Mrs. James," she said, and Gemma didn't correct her on the name or the marital state. "The good news is that there's no sign of subdural hematoma," the doctor went on. "But you should have come in sooner. Head injuries can be quite dangerous. Now, you're going to need to stay quiet for three or four days"—she must have seen Gemma start to protest because she said more firmly—"and that means bed rest. We don't want to see you back here. We'll give you something for the headache that will help the pain and reduce the swelling as well."

"But I can't——"

"I'll see that she stays in bed." Duncan's tone brooked no argument. He took down the doctor's final instructions, then rang Kit as she was being checked out.

Gemma made one last feeble attempt at resistance when he brought a wheelchair. "I don't need——"

"Hospital rules. It's the only way you're getting out of here."

She shuddered and let him help her into the wheelchair and then into the car. When he had climbed in beside her, she said, "I hate that place," and was mortified to find that her voice was shaky. "And I'm sorry you're angry with me."

He turned to look at her in surprise. "Angry with you? Don't be daft, Gemma. It's myself I'm angry with. I should never have let you go round with that lump on your head without having it checked out. You have an excuse because you weren't thinking clearly. I have none but stupidity. And believe me"—he gave her a dark look—"I'm going to make sure you do what the doctor said."

"But I promised I'd take the boys to see Mum tomorrow——"

"I'll take them, as long as you get someone to come and stay with you. Maybe Hazel or Melody. Or Betty." His voice had softened, and she saw the glint of a smile. "Otherwise"—he paused while he eased the car out into Ladbroke Grove—"you'll be running laps."

"Hazel's working. I'll ring Melody." She'd said it so quickly that Duncan gave her a suspicious glance. Gemma settled back in her seat, deciding she'd just have to make the call when he'd left her alone. Fuzzy headed she might be, but she wasn't about to tell him she had an ulterior motive. Not yet.

Melody arrived about ten on Sunday morning. Earlier, Gemma had got up, made the bed, put on shorts and a T-shirt, then been ordered back to bed by Duncan. She'd compromised by staying dressed and propping herself up on the bed with just a throw for a cover. To tell the truth, she didn't feel up to much, and had dozed off again when she heard the bell and voices in the hall.

Duncan called out, "Melody's here, and we're off," and a few moments later Melody came into the bedroom.

"Wow," she said. "This is lovely," and Gemma realized Melody had never been upstairs. Nor did she ever remember seeing Melody in anything as casual as the jeans and cotton print top she wore today, with her dark hair tousled and her cheeks pink from heat and sun. Even when Melody had come to their dinner party in the spring, she'd worn a white silk blouse and black trousers, an outfit that had seemed an extension of her uniformlike work clothes.

"It is, isn't it?" Gemma agreed. "I suppose there are worse places to be confined." She nodded towards the slipper chair in the corner. "Sit, please." Suddenly, she felt a little awkward in such intimate circumstances with this unleashed Melody who seemed so different from the woman she had thought she'd known.

But Melody pulled the slipper chair closer to the bed and perched on it, showing no hint of discomfort. "Columbia Road was brilliant," she said. "I want a garden. Or at least a patio or a balcony with room to plant things."

"But surely you've had a garden." Gemma, whose only previous experience with a garden had been a scraggly square of lawn at the house she'd owned in Leyton with her ex-husband, Rob, tended the terrace and patio garden of the Notting Hill house with much trepidation, and with considerable help from Duncan and boys.

"I grew up in a Kensington town house. With topiaries. My grandparents—my mum's parents—have a very formal garden in Buckinghamshire, strictly the province of the gardener, and my nan, my dad's mum, still lives in her council flat in Newcastle. She refused to move, no matter how much Dad bullied her." Melody grinned. "I always wanted to be like her when I grew up."

The words seemed to spill from Melody, and Gemma wondered how long it had been since she had really talked to anyone.

"I want a riotous garden," Melody added with a grin, "and now I know where to get things. I just have to figure out the how to manage the garden bit. And I apologize"—the smile faded—"for never having had you round, when you've been so kind to me, but there's not much to see in my flat."

"Well, I'll come whenever you like. But in the meantime, tell me about Roy. Did you speak to him?"

"Yes. He was a bit leery at first, but when I assured him I knew you, and I told him that Sandra's brothers were responsible for the attack on Azad's restaurant, he was furious.

"He said Sandra didn't tell him that she knew what they'd done, but he thinks it was the Sunday a week before she disappeared that he saw bruises on her arms."

Gemma sat up so fast it made her head pound. "Bruises? And he didn't tell me?"

"I've checked the dates. That would have been a week after the firebombing of Azad's restaurant. I'd guess either they bragged to her or she heard it from someone else and confronted them."

"Bloody hell," said Gemma, sinking back into the pillows. "That gives them a second motive for wanting Sandra out of the way. Maybe she threatened to shop them for that, instead of the drugs. Or as well as the drugs."

"Are you going to tell Duncan?"

Gemma rubbed her head. "I don't know. He'll be livid, but his hands are tied as far as the Gilles brothers are concerned. I don't think he could pull them in, even if he had hard evidence." She could see that Melody wanted to ask more, but she didn't.

Instead, she said, "Well, you'd better tell him, nonetheless."

"He won't be best pleased with me either, but I suppose you're right."

"Oh, I almost forgot." Melody reached for her handbag and

pulled out a small bakery box. "Roy sent this, for Charlotte. It's a lemon cupcake from a shop near his stall, called Treacle. He said it was her favorite."

Melody had excused herself before Duncan and the boys returned from Leyton. "Sunday lunch at my parents' in Kensington," she'd said with a grimace. "And my mum is famous for inviting unsuitable blind dates for me to her Sunday soirees." Her face settled into the expression Gemma had seen on Friday. "We'll hope she hasn't asked anyone else today, because I can tell you, it is not going to be pleasant."

For just a moment, Gemma felt sorry for Ivan Talbot.

When Melody had left, Gemma rang Betty and asked if Charlotte could come for a visit that afternoon, as an old friend had sent a treat for her. "And besides," she added, "I miss her."

She then had to explain why she hadn't come round herself, reluctantly relating the previous day's trip to hospital and the doctor's orders to take it easy.

She hadn't admitted to anyone how much that hospital visit had unsettled her. The memories of pain and loss associated with the last time she had been there were still too close, too shatteringly clear.

"Oh, I blame myself for not making sure you got that head looked at," said Betty, clucking a bit. "I could tell you were not feelin' yourself yesterday."

"I'm fine now, Betty, really."

"Well." Betty didn't sound entirely convinced. "I'll bring the little one round for an early tea, if you're certain, but only if Duncan and the boys are back to help look after you."

Kit had insisted on carrying her tea, giving Toby the task of bearing Charlotte's cupcake, carefully enthroned on a plate. What neither Roy nor Melody had foreseen, however, was that there were now three children and one treat.

"Why don't we get one?" demanded Toby. "Me and Kit should have a cupcake, too."

"Kit and *I*," Gemma corrected automatically. "And the cupcake was a special gift to Charlotte from a friend. You've had plenty of treats of your own."

"Don't be greedy," seconded Kit, handing Gemma her mug and settling on the end of the bed.

Charlotte had climbed up next to Gemma. "Wanna share," she said unexpectedly, and when Toby handed her the plate, she thrust it back.

When Toby reached for the cupcake, Gemma smacked his hand. "Go downstairs and get a knife, then. You'll divide it properly. And don't run," she called after him.

Toby returned, holding a table knife point-down as instructed, and, Kit having declined, the cupcake was ceremoniously divided in two.

"You're a good girl, Charlotte," said Gemma. "Toby should take lessons."

"You eat some, too," said Charlotte, holding her half up to Gemma, so Gemma cut off a tiny corner and nibbled it, then sipped her tea.

"I feel like the queen, being waited on in bed."

"The queen never stays in bed." Toby had dispensed with his half in two bites. "She's always out with her dogs and waving at people and stuff."

"I'll bet someone brings her tea in bed every morning," said Gemma.

"I wouldn't want to be queen," Toby declared. "It would be really boring."

"Well, there's not much chance of that, dopey," Kit told him. "And stop bouncing. You'll make Gemma's head hurt."

"Don't call your brother names," Gemma scolded, although she was touched by Kit's solicitousness.

But Toby was undeterred by Kit's teasing. "Charlotte could be queen, then, couldn't she?"

"She could," Gemma said, snuggling Charlotte a little closer. "But the job is highly overrated. I suspect she could do something much more fun."

"What's 'overrated' mean?" asked Toby.

Gemma sighed. "Never mind." It amazed her how quickly she got tired. "Let's read a story. Something for Charlotte."

"No. I want pirates," said Toby.

Kit rolled his eyes. "How about I read *The Count of Monte Cristo*? It has pirates, sort of." He had discovered an old copy of Duncan's on the bookshelf. The thin pages were almost translucent, and the smell of mildew that wafted from the book was so strong it made Gemma's nose itch. But Kit had developed an attachment to it, and Toby loved it, although Gemma doubted he understood much.

"I want the ships, then."

Kit nipped out and came back with a bounce of enthusiasm that almost equaled Toby's, book in hand. He curled up again on the foot of the bed and flipped through pages. "Okay. Here's a bit. 'Look out there! All ready to drop anchor!'" he intoned, then glanced up at them to make sure he had their attention. Satisfied, he went on. "'All hands obeyed. At that moment eight or ten seamen, who composed the crew, sprung some to the mainsheets, other to the braces, others to the ball'"—Kit struggled a bit with the word—"'the balliards'—"

"What's a *ball-y-yard*?" piped up Toby.

"I've no idea," said Kit.

Gemma's eyelids were starting to droop, and the discussion of sails and jibs passed by her. Charlotte's head was against her shoulder, and the child was humming to Bob, the plush elephant, and poking his black button eyes with cupcake-sticky fingers.

Then Toby, who had climbed up on the other end of the bed, said, "Who's Charlotte's friend?"

Gemma's eyes flew open. "Which friend?"

"The one who sent her the cupcake."

"Oh. His name is Roy, and he sells flowers at Columbia Market."

"Why is he Charlotte's friend? Could he be my friend, too?"

Sometimes Gemma wondered about the convolutions of Toby's mind, but did her best to come up with an answer that would satisfy him. "He was Charlotte's mum's friend, but I'm sure he'd be your friend if you met him."

Toby, however, was indefatigable. "Where's Charlotte's mum, then?"

Wide awake now, Gemma glanced at Charlotte and said quickly, "Toby, we discussed this—"

Charlotte looked up and said very clearly, "My mummy went away. My daddy went to find her."

"Did he— Ow!"

Kit had pinched Toby, and now they got into a scuffle. Kit wrestled Toby into an arm hold, still managing to grip the book in his other hand. "I think you need to go downstairs now, sport. I can hear the dogs calling you."

"They don't talk."

"Yes, they do. I'll prove it to you." Setting the book down, Kit wrapped an arm round Toby and, casting a conspiratorial glance back at Gemma, frog-marched him from the room. Gemma settled back, hoping that Charlotte hadn't been upset by the mention of her parents. But Charlotte had gone back to playing with Bob, seemingly unperturbed by Toby's questions.

Gemma wrapped one of Charlotte's curls round her finger,

frowning as she remembered something. Charlotte had said the exact same thing once before, that day at Tim's when Janice Silverman had told her her father was dead. At the time, Gemma had assumed it was a child's way of dealing with the idea of her father's death. But what if Charlotte hadn't meant it metaphorically, but quite literally?

What if Naz had told Charlotte that day that he was going to find her mother?

As Gemma mulled it over, Charlotte's breathing slowed and the plush elephant fell from her relaxed fingers. Very gently, Gemma tucked the elephant back under Charlotte's arm and brushed a stray strand of hair from her face. She eased herself down a bit into the pillows, taking care not to disturb the sleeping child, and closed her eyes. The late-afternoon light coming in the west windows seemed uncomfortably bright.

Drowsily, her mind went round and round, trying to make sense of the confluence of geography. Columbia Road, the center point, the vanishing point. Around it, like uneven spokes on a wheel, Lou Phillips's flat . . . . Naz and Lou's office . . . Gail Gilles's council flat . . . Pippa Nightingale's gallery. All within a veritable stone's throw, a five-minute walk of each other.

Were they connected by more than coincidence? Where had Sandra gone that day? If she had gone to confront her brothers, had it been at her mum's flat? If they had killed her, had Gail Gilles been a party to it, or at least an accessory after the fact?

And if Naz had come to the same conclusion, would he have gone to talk to them, alone, and allowed them to drug him without putting up a fight? There had been no mark of violence on his body.

And if any of these things were true, where did Lucas Ritchie come into it? Or Ahmed Azad?

No, Gemma thought, there was something she was missing, some part of the pattern she couldn't see. Sandra's decision to leave Charlotte with Roy Blakely, when she had only a few minutes before she was to meet Naz for lunch, had surely been spur of the moment. What had happened to Sandra that Sunday afternoon, between Fournier Street and Columbia Road? And there was something about Sandra's collage, the one on her worktable . . . Why did the girls have no faces? Why . . .

The next thing Gemma knew, Duncan was lifting Charlotte from her arms, and the room had grown dim. She reached out, making a little sound of protest, but Duncan said, "Shhh. Betty's here. Go back to sleep."

But now the space beside her seemed empty, and she felt oddly bereft. Voices drifted up the stairs, then the front door slammed— Toby's doing, no doubt. Gemma sat up, switching on the light against the dusk, trying to bring back the remnants of an interrupted dream.

The phone rang and she swore. Whatever it had been, the fragment of clarity was gone. The ringing went on. Duncan and the boys must still be outside talking to Betty, Gemma thought. She stretched towards the nightstand and picked up the handset.

When Duncan came upstairs a few minutes later, she was still crying. The tears had come unexpectedly, uncontrollably, when she'd hung up the phone, and she had been horrified to find herself sobbing.

"Gemma! What's happened?" He hurried to her and sat down on the bed, peering at her anxiously. "Are you all right?"

"Yes. No," she said, on a hiccup. "I mean, it's not me. That was Jack. Winnie's not doing well. They've admitted her to hospital. Enforced bed rest, and the baby's not due for another month." She wiped her cheeks with the back of her hand.

Duncan handed her a tissue from the nightstand and she blew her nose. "But she'll be okay," he said, "now they're looking after her."

"They've managed to stop the contractions, but her blood pressure's up . . . I can't bear thinking they might lose the baby—not

Jack and Winnie, after everything they've been through. And not after— Yesterday, the hospital—" She couldn't finish.

He pulled her to him gently and stroked her back. "Oh, love, I know," he said, and his voice was rough. "But try not to worry. Are you sure you feel all right?"

Gemma gave a strangled laugh. "I think this stupid head injury is making me daft. I never cry like this." She pulled away so that she could look at him. "And the worst thing is, it's not just because I'm worried about Winnie. Part of it is just because I'm selfish. I so wanted Winnie and Jack to be here for the wedding, and now it seems everything's gone wrong . . ."

He glanced away, his face very still. When he spoke, his voice was flat, colorless. "I understand if you don't want to go through with it, Gemma."

"No, no," she said, taking his hand and rubbing her thumb across the fine skin between his thumb and forefinger. "It's not that at all." He looked at her then, but she wasn't sure she could read the expression in his gray eyes. "The thing is . . ." She struggled to find the words. "I just want us to go on as we are. I don't want to *get* married. I want to *be* married. It's the *wedding* I can't cope with, and my bloody family. But I can't bear to disappoint my mum, and I'm so afraid . . . I'm so afraid she won't—"

"Oh, Gemma." This time he pulled her to him so tightly it hurt her head, but she didn't protest. His heart beat beneath her ear, and she thought she felt him tremble.

"I'm so sorry, love," she whispered. "I didn't mean to—"

"No, no. Don't you worry about anything. We'll sort something out, and I'll deal with your sister." His tone made her glad she wasn't Cyn. "If we have to, we'll take your mum with us and run away to Gretna Green."

"That would be very romantic," she said, managing a sniffled laugh.

"Well, I'm sure that as brilliant detectives, we can come up with some solution that will make you *and* your mother happy." He pressed his lips to her forehead. "And I—I don't care if we have a wedding on Mars. I just want to be with you."

Kincaid stood in the kitchen, trying to collect himself enough to make Gemma another cup of tea and something to eat—simple enough tasks—but he found he was staring at the refrigerator and the teakettle as if they were alien artifacts.

The house seemed unnaturally quiet—Betty had taken the boys home with her for a bit, saying she needed help with the frames for the costumes she was making, but had whispered to him that she just wanted to give Gemma a bit of peace.

But it was he who had been given the respite by the children's absence. It had allowed him to think, allowed him to admit for the first time, even to himself, how terrified he had been that he might lose Gemma, how afraid he'd been that she'd come to regret her impulsive proposal. He'd felt as if she were slipping away from him, and he hadn't known how to stop it.

When he'd gone up to get Charlotte, he'd stood for a long moment, watching Gemma sleep with the child beside her, and he'd realized that now he simply couldn't imagine his life without their oddly cobbled-together family. And then doubt had assailed him—he'd wondered if Gemma would ever be entirely willing to commit herself to them, or if there would always be some secret core in her heart that refused to yield.

And then she'd admitted, at last, how much she still grieved for the child they had lost. And she had cried. It meant, perhaps, that she could heal—that they could both heal, and that their loss would not separate them, but bind them closer.

But that thought brought him back to the problem at hand. What in bloody hell was he going to do about the wedding? He'd promised her he would sort it out, but he hadn't the foggiest how he was going to do it. Maybe Gretna Green wasn't such a bad idea . . .

The trill of the phone broke his reverie, galvanizing him. He lunged for it, hoping it hadn't disturbed Gemma, hoping it wasn't Jack with more bad news.

But to his relief it was Hazel, asking about Gemma. "I was worried about her yesterday," she said. "I've been thinking I shouldn't have let her drive home."

"And I was an idiot. I should have seen she needed to go to hospital. I should have insisted the minute I saw that bruise. She could have—" He stopped, unwilling to articulate what might have happened. Instead, he told Hazel that the doctor had ordered Gemma to rest for a few days, and then about Winnie and Jack.

"Duncan, are you sure Gemma's all right? Emotionally, I mean?" Hazel added, a bit hesitantly. "It's just that yesterday she seemed awfully worried about her mum and stressed about the wedding . . . Her sister—"

"Oh, I'm going to have a word with Cynthia. She's going to mind her own business or she's going to have to deal with me. But if Gemma and I get married in a registry office, without family—which seems the only manageable solution—and then Vi . . . gets worse, Cyn will have already convinced Gemma that it's her fault. But I'll be damned if I'm going to let Gemma's family bugger this. I just can't work out exactly what to do."

"It's difficult, yes," Hazel said slowly. "But I think I might have an idea."

CHAPTER TWENTY-FIVE

*A trio of Bangladeshi girls came up the street towards us,
chewing gum and smiling and chatting amongst themselves.
They were dressed modestly in long black coats, loose
trousers, and hijabs, but they also wore make-up and lipstick
and their nails were manicured and polished.*

—Tarquin Hall,
Salaam Brick Lane

The enforced idleness had not been as bad as Gemma had expected,
because either Betty or Wesley had managed to bring Charlotte for
visits every day, and Melody had kept her updated on work. Her
guv'nor had sent her flowers, and rung Kincaid to give him the mickey,
threatening to run him in on assault.

But by Thursday she'd been chafing at the bit, and after getting a
release from the doctor that afternoon, she charged into the office on
Friday morning with a zeal that had her staff groaning in mock dismay.

At least she hoped it was mock. By midmorning, Melody came in
with a sheaf of papers, reassuring her with a grin. "They're all bea-
vering away, determined to prove they haven't been slacking in your
absence. I think they missed you, boss."

"Not enough to solve these damned burglaries," said Gemma, glad for a break from the scrolling computer screen. Melody, she'd noticed, was wearing a bright pink T-shirt under her tailored black suit jacket, surely a sartorial statement of liberation. When they'd spoken on the phone during the week, Melody hadn't said anything about how her meeting with her father had gone on Sunday afternoon, and Gemma hadn't wanted to ask.

But now Melody nodded towards the chair and said, "Got a minute, boss?"

"Glad of it." Gemma blanked her screen as Melody sat down, giving her her full attention.

To her surprise, however, Melody said tentatively, "I was just wondering if you'd ever told the super what I learned from Roy Blakely about seeing the bruises on Sandra's arms the week before she disappeared."

"No. I meant to, but—there's been no word from Narcotics, and he hasn't been able to get any more information on the whereabouts of Kevin Gilles's mate's transit van on the day Naz was killed. He's even checked nearby furniture stores for a record of a purchase that day that matched the leather suite I saw in the flat, but no luck there either. And even that wouldn't prove any connection with Naz's death, only that they had the means to transport him."

"I wouldn't be surprised if the furniture *fell* off the back of a van."

"More than likely," Gemma agreed. "But there haven't been any reported thefts, so everything is circumstantial. And after"—she didn't want to mention the newspaper story—"and I hated for him to think I was meddling again," she amended. Absently, she touched the bruise on her forehead. It had faded to an unattractive yellow and she'd done her best to cover it with a little makeup.

"What about Charlotte's social worker?" Melody asked. "Did you speak with her?"

"She said even if Roy was willing to testify, it would still be an unsubstantiated allegation, and not likely to help in court. The next hearing is set for Monday, and so far Gail Gilles has apparently passed muster. I couldn't ask if she'd moved all the loot out of the flat."

"You're worried, then, about the hearing."

"Yes," said Gemma, although worry didn't begin to describe how she felt. The more time she spent with Charlotte, the less she could even bear to think about Gail Gilles getting her hands on the child.

"I've talked to Louise Phillips again, and she's willing to tell the judge that Gail's custody would have been very much against both parents' wishes. Still . . . there's no guarantee that will help if the judge is set on kinship care and Gail's toeing the line." She didn't know what else she could do that might influence the court, and she had begun to feel sick with anxiety over Charlotte's fate.

And although she didn't share it with Melody, she was also feeling a little uneasy about Duncan. She'd tried several times that week to bring up the subject of the wedding again. As she'd begun to recover from the effects of the concussion, she felt she'd been a bit overwrought about the whole thing, and that maybe she could screw herself up to do something that would please her family. But he'd breezily told her not to worry about it—she just needed to get well—and had promptly changed the subject. Had he decided she was an emotional basket case and changed *his* mind?

"Well," said Melody, "I don't know what I can do to help with Charlotte, but I thought this might be useful on the investigation front." Looking rather pleased with herself, she handed Gemma the top few sheets from the papers she'd brought in.

Scanning them, Gemma saw that the pages were a list of names. She glanced up at Melody. "What—"

"It's the membership of Lucas Ritchie's club. I told you my father owed me. Sometimes his connections are useful. And I told him that if he used this, or anything else he got from me, in a story, I would never speak to him again."

"He believed you?"

"I think so. My mum had a word with him, too, and she's the one person who can put the fear of God into him."

Gemma looked back at the sheets, reading through the list more carefully. There was Azad. Another name, Miles Alexander, seemed familiar to her, but she couldn't quite place it. Then she saw something that made her stop and check it again. John Truman, RCVS.

"There's a vet on this list," she said to Melody. "I wonder . . . The ketamine found in Naz Malik's system is a veterinary drug. Do you suppose this John Truman had any connection with Naz or Sandra?"

"One of Sandra's patrons?" suggested Melody.

"It's certainly possible." She thought about going to Fournier Street and looking through Sandra's studio again, but she had promised Duncan she wouldn't go there until some action could be taken against Kevin and Terry Gilles.

"Pippa Nightingale might know," she said aloud. She still had the number for the Nightingale Gallery stored in her phone. But when she pulled it up and dialed, she got a voice-mail recording. Without leaving a message, she clicked off. "Bloody voice mail." She tapped her finger on the phone while she thought.

After a moment, she announced to Melody, "I'm going to Rivington Street. There's no reason Kevin or Terry Gilles should be there. And I'm going to camp out on the gallery doorstep, if I have to, until I can talk to Pippa. Can you send a copy of this list to Duncan? I'll ring him once I've talked to Pippa."

"Where do I tell him I got it?"

"You're a crack researcher. Tell him you have your sources."

When Gemma reached Rivington Street, the gallery looked just as it had the first time she'd visited, and when she pressed the buzzer, the door clicked open.

This time, however, Pippa Nightingale stood at the top of the stairs, watching her as she climbed.

"Is there any news?" Pippa asked when Gemma had reached the top.

"No. I'm sorry. But I was hoping you could help me with something."

The same surreal monochrome works were on display in the long upper room, the scenes of snow and forest and nightmarish, enchanted creatures, all in blacks and whites except for the occasional shocking splash of red. Today Pippa wore red as well, a long, deep crimson dress, as though she dressed only to complement the art. She didn't invite Gemma into her office.

"Lucas said you went to see him." Pippa's voice was neutral, and Gemma couldn't tell if she approved or disapproved.

"Yes. He was very helpful," she answered carefully.

Pippa shrugged. "When it suits him. I wouldn't expect him to put himself out too much over Sandra's daughter, by the way. And I'm afraid I don't know anything that I haven't already told you."

"This is something else entirely." Gemma had realized on the way to the gallery that she couldn't very well show Pippa the entire list, not without more explanation than she was willing to give, considering Pippa's connection with Lucas Ritchie. "Do you know if Sandra ever sold works to a man named John Truman, a veterinary surgeon?"

"Truman? If Truman bought Sandra's work, it wasn't through me. That little snake. He used to be one of my regular customers."

Gemma thought she saw a hint of color in Pippa's pale cheeks.

"But he is a collector?"

"In a small way. Nothing too expensive." She frowned. "Although I had the impression that he liked to inflate the prices of the pieces to his wife. Maybe he needed to impress her."

Or cover up what he was spending on something else, Gemma thought. "Did he know Sandra?"

"He might have met her at an opening . . ." Pippa's eyes widened, and what Gemma saw in their ice-blue depths made her think that Pippa Nightingale's unusual physical poise was a mask for suppressed rage. Pippa walked to the window and looked out. "That bastard," she breathed, her back to Gemma.

"Truman?" Gemma asked.

"No. Bloody Lucas. Truman met Lucas here, at more than one opening. Of course Lucas would have recruited him for his club. It's just the sort of secret thing that would appeal to a little snot like Truman, and if Truman bought Sandra's work, it will be because Lucas displayed it in the club. John Truman never had any confidence in his own taste—he only bought things if someone he considered important had got in first."

"Do you think Naz would have known Truman?"

"Not socially, if that's what you mean. If he bought work from Sandra, he might have met Naz at some point, although Sandra did her best to keep her work separate from her personal life." Pippa turned, and the flash of anger Gemma had seen had been replaced with amusement. "You could ask Lucas."

Gemma knew there was something she was missing, some game between Pippa and Lucas Ritchie that she didn't understand, but she thought it revolved around Sandra. "I think I'd do better to ask John Truman," she said. "Do you know where I could find him?"

"Hoxton. His surgery's not far from the square, and he lives above it." She walked back to her office, checked a file, and wrote an address down on a note card stamped with the gallery name.

Gemma took the card and studied it, replaying her mental geography. "It's quite near, then."

"Oh, yes," said Pippa. "A Georgian house, like Sandra's, but butchered. I doubt Truman was inspired by the thought of the Huguenot silk weavers."

Gemma thanked her and turned to go, but as she reached the top of the stairs she turned back. "You and Lucas. You seemed quite angry with him. Will you stay friends?"

Pippa smiled. "If you want to call it that. He always comes back to me."

Gemma stood on the pavement just outside the gallery door as she pulled out her phone to ring Kincaid. He would need to pay an official call on this John Truman. Gemma had done as much as she dared. Any further action on her own and she would be seriously trespassing on a Scotland Yard investigation.

But she stopped, finger hovering over the keypad, as she thought about the implications of her conversation with Pippa. Had Sandra and Pippa become estranged, not because Pippa disapproved of how Sandra was marketing her work, but because a long-standing jealousy over Lucas Ritchie had come to a head?

Could Sandra have come here that day, from Columbia Road? Could Pippa have told her something, out of spite, that had made her run away? Or what if they had argued, and Pippa had killed Sandra?

Although Gemma could have sworn, on her first visit, that Pippa's grief over Sandra's disappearance had been genuine, theirs had obviously been a complicated relationship, and love and jealousy had brought about stranger things. But even if the slender Pippa had been able to kill Sandra, could she have disposed of her body—and so efficiently that it had not been found? And then killed Naz Malik? For Gemma was now utterly convinced that Sandra's disappearance and Naz's murder were connected.

She shook her head, staring absently at the front of the Rivington Street Health Clinic a few doors down. No, she was spinning theories out of air, and they wouldn't wash. Pippa's little display of spitefulness had been directed at Lucas, not Sandra. Truman, the vet, who was more than likely to have known Sandra, and who had easy access to the ketamine that had been found in Naz's system, seemed a more likely prospect. Maybe—

Gemma's speculations came to an abrupt halt. A young woman

wearing jeans and a T-shirt, her dark hair pulled up in a haphazard ponytail, had stopped in front of the clinic, glancing up and down the street before slipping inside. The profile had been familiar, although recognition took Gemma a moment, because the last time she had seen the young woman, she'd been wearing a head scarf. It was Alia Hakim, Charlotte's nanny.

CHAPTER TWENTY-SIX

Traffic in children has been going on for as long as mankind has been sinning and suffering. Josephine Butler (1828–1907) writes in her journals, pamphlets and diaries of the second half of the nineteenth century about seeing thousands (yes, thousands) of little girls, some as young as four or five, in the illegal brothels of London, Paris, Brussels and Geneva.

—Jennifer Worth,
*Farewell to the
East End*

Doug Cullen yanked the copy of Melody's e-mail from the printer tray on Kincaid's desk and stared at it. "Where the hell did she get this?"

"Let me see." Kincaid got up and took the pages from him. When he had read through the list of names, he said, "I'm not sure I want to know. It's called deniability, Doug. But this could prove very useful."

For all their digging, they had not been able to come up with anything dodgy on Lucas Ritchie or his club, and they had been warned off interviewing him again by powers higher than Kincaid's guv'nor.

"What I *would* like to know," Kincaid continued, "is what Gemma's up to. Melody was a bit cryptic when she rang. Something about the vet on the list . . ." He scanned the page again. "Truman, John. RCVS. Look him up, why don't you?"

Cullen did an Internet search and read off an address. "I would guess it's this one, in Hoxton. You're thinking a vet would have had access to ketamine? But did he have any connection with Naz Malik?"

"Worth talking to him." The staff at Bethnal Green was keeping a phone line available for calls from the public notice board. But as no new information had come in, there had been little else for them to do, and Kincaid had returned to the Yard. He was still thoroughly blocked from pursuing the one lead into Naz Malik's murder that had looked most promising: Kevin and Terry Gilles.

Now he grabbed his jacket, adding, "We've got eff-all else to go on with, and this case is getting colder by the minute."

Gemma's first response on seeing Alia's furtive entrance into the clinic was that the girl was in some kind of trouble. Needing contraceptives, or worse, pregnant. She didn't like to think how Alia's father would respond to either alternative, but she was certainly going to have a word with the girl and see if she could help.

Slipping her phone back into her bag, she walked the few yards to the clinic and pushed the entry buzzer. But much to her surprise, when she entered the small reception area, she found Alia not in the waiting area, but sitting behind the reception desk.

"Alia! You work here?"

"Miss—it's Miss James, isn't it?" Alia looked pleased to see her, then alarmed. "Is Charlotte okay? How did you— What are you doing here?" She dropped her voice, even though there was no one else in the room. "My parents didn't—"

"No, no, don't worry. Charlotte's fine, and I haven't spoken with your parents. I was just on the street and I happened to see you. Do your parents not know you work here?"

"I volunteer," Alia said defensively. "I don't work for pay. But no, they don't know. My dad, he'd go ballistic, like."

"Then why do you do it?"

"Because it's important. And because she did."

Following Alia's glance, Gemma turned and saw two of Sandra's collages on the wall above the slightly tatty sofa and magazine table in the waiting area. They were smaller works, but beautifully textured and colored, and in this room they looked like peacocks among sparrows.

"Sandra donated her collages?" she asked.

"Not just that. She worked here, too. She was really good at getting the women to talk to her. They trusted her, like. She said they needed a voice, didn't she?"

Voice and faces, thought Gemma. She studied the collages. One conveyed hints of shops in a tumble-down street, their windows filled with multicolored bolts of cloth. Women in fluttering sari silks and head scarves clustered in the doorways like bright jewels. In the background rose the now-familiar shape of the Gherkin, 30 St. Mary Axe, and a building like a shard of glass.

The other collage was darker, the feel more Georgian, the women's clothing suggested by bits of silk and lace, and all seemed to be engaged in some kind of manual labor. One scrubbed a doorstep, one hung up scraps of washing, one, glimpsed through a loft window, worked at a loom. And integrated throughout the piece were bits of paper covered with ink-blotted script, and scraps of old, yellowed maps.

Still gazing at Alia, she asked, "What do they mean, these pictures?"

"She didn't like to say. She said the point was, the piece would tell you a story, same as it did her, but you would hear it in your own way. For every person it was different."

Hearing the quaver in Alia's voice, Gemma turned. The girl's eyes were red. "You miss her, don't you?" she said gently.

"I thought she'd come back, see. She said I could do anything, be anything, and I believed it. But now"—she shook her head—"it's not true, is it, or she wouldn't never have left."

Alia looked as if she had lost weight since Gemma had last seen her, less than two weeks ago, and there were dark hollows under her eyes.

Gemma played a hunch. She sat down in the chair across from the desk so that she was close to the girl and on her level. "Alia, you knew about Sandra's brothers and the drugs. What else did you know?"

The girl's reaction was immediate. Her eyes widened, pupils dilating, her mouth tightening. "Nuffink," she said, her Estuary accent suddenly thicker. "Don't know what yer on about."

Gemma pulled her chair a little nearer. "You can talk to me. I won't tell your parents."

"If my dad even knew I was here, he'd kill me." Alia cast a furtive glance at the door. "Only reason the women who come in here don't tell is that they don't want nobody to know they was here either."

"There's a coffee shop down the street. Let me take you for something—"

"I can't leave. The regular girl's on lunch, and so's the doctor. There has to be someone here, 'cause of the drugs and things."

"Well, that's perfect, then. There's just the two of us. We can talk before anyone comes back. Don't the women mind seeing a doctor?"

"It's a lady doctor, miss. *He* don't come in to see the clients. He just oversees things, like."

"He?"

"Mr. Miles. But it's his own money that runs the place." There was a note of hero worship in her voice. "We give women advice about contraception, and sexually transmitted diseases and stuff, and what to do if they're pregnant." She was back on more comfortable ground, the stress gone from her voice, although she pronounced the clinical terms with studied nonchalance, as if she'd practiced.

"That's brilliant, Alia. I can see why Sandra cared about the clinic. But you were her special friend, weren't you? She told you things she didn't tell anyone else. You'd have known if something was worrying her."

Gemma could see from Alia's expression that she was wavering, and made herself keep quiet. The girl had wanted to talk before, in fact, had defied her father to come after them and tell them about Sandra's brothers. Would she have said more that day, if her parents hadn't been hovering? Or if Gemma had been alone?

"There was something," Alia said at last, with a glance at the door. "One of the girls that came in . . . afterwards Sandra was all quiet, like. Even at home the next couple of days, when I was looking after Char."

When Alia stopped, Gemma said very quietly, "But Sandra told you, didn't she? About what was bothering her. She needed someone to confide in."

"Yeah." Alia kept her gaze on her hands. "One day when Charlotte was asleep. Sandra said the girl that came in here, she was Bangladeshi, like, and just a kid. Younger than me. She was all crying, and Sandra took her into the little conference room.

"This girl, she told Sandra—she said that some man had married her in Sylhet, paid her father a lot of money. He got papers and he brought her here, but then he never let her out of the house. He—" Alia picked at her cuticle, her face suffused with red. "He did—" She met Gemma's eyes for a moment, then looked away. "If my dad knew I was repeating these things . . ." She swallowed. "This man, the girl said he did—did things to her. Then, when she—when she started her periods, like, he didn't want nothing more to do with her. He sent her to another man, who liked girls that little bit older, a man who didn't mind about . . . women's things. She wasn't supposed to go out of this house either, but that day she did. She was scared of what would happen if she got caught.

"Sandra asked her why she didn't tell no one, and she said because the man would do bad things to her. And even worse, she'd be sent back to Sylhet, where her family wouldn't have nothing to do with her and she'd be cast out on the street." Alia looked up at Gemma. "It's true. It's what my father would do. She'd be unclean, like, and it wouldn't matter that none of it was her fault."

"So what did Sandra do?" Gemma asked, trying to keep the horror from her voice.

"She told the girl to come back, that she'd help her work out something. But the girl never did."

Gemma took a breath. "This man, the one who brought the little girl in from Bangladesh. Was it Mr. Azad?"

"Oh, no." Alia looked shocked. "Mr. Azad wouldn't do nothing like that. He and Sandra, they were friends. No, this bloke, the girl never told Sandra his name. Just that he was rich, and white."

"And that's all you got out of her?" Kincaid said when Gemma rang him from the car and related her conversation.

"The regular receptionist came back from lunch. And I think that's all Alia knew. Except she did say she thought this happened two or three weeks before Sandra disappeared."

"And she was adamant that it wasn't Azad?"

"I asked her twice. She insisted that Sandra told her the girl had said the guy was white."

"Well, either the girl lied because she was afraid or . . . if she was telling the truth, that makes Lucas Ritchie the obvious candidate," Kincaid said. "Although there's nothing in the checks we've done that suggest he's ever been to Sylhet. And if he killed Naz Malik, he must have been able to teleport, because everyone at his niece's birthday party swears he was there the whole time."

"Back up a bit." Gemma had been thinking furiously. "Granted, Ritchie's club seems the perfect vehicle for moving on trafficked girls. But look at 'rich white guy' from the point of view of a girl who came from a village in Sylhet."

"Ah." Kincaid was following her. "That broadens the spectrum a bit, doesn't it?"

"Any male with a reasonable income would do. A professional, say. I think we should check out the vet, John Truman. Pippa Nightingale says he probably knew Sandra, and might very well have been one of her clients."

"You're thinking about the ketamine?"

"Yes."

"Maybe." Kincaid sounded only partially convinced. "But if the girls are passed on, there must be a network that allows it, some way that men who like little girls contact one another, some environment that makes them feel safe. And Ritchie's club would be the obvious place such an environment connected with Sandra Gilles. But I'll have to have something a lot more concrete before I can question him again."

Gemma realized she'd been hearing traffic sounds in the background. "Where are you?"

"City Road." There was the faintest trace of amusement in Kincaid's voice.

"You're already going to interview the vet, Truman."

"Spot on, Sherlock."

"Give me the address," said Gemma. "I'll meet you there."

The Georgian elegance of the terrace near Hoxton Square was rather marred by the shop at its end advertising "cheap booze." Gemma had no need to search for the address, as Kincaid and Cullen were already there and waiting for her in their car.

They got out and came over to her as she parked. "That was good timing," Kincaid said, opening her door. He brushed his fingers against her arm as he reached to help her out, a discreetly affectionate gesture. "A minute more and we'd have roasted."

Cullen gave her a smile that just missed being a grimace, letting her know that he was tolerating her presence because he had no choice, and the three of them walked to the door. The only indication that the house was a veterinary surgery was a discreet brass plaque beside the bell, bearing Truman's name and professional qualification.

Cullen rang, then held the door for them when the lock clicked open. They entered a hall, its style much grander than Naz and Sandra's entry. But like the Fournier Street house, there was a central staircase, and a reception room on the right that faced the street.

The woman at the reception desk—which looked as if it had started life as a Georgian dining table—looked up as they came into the room. Her expression was more puzzled than welcoming. "I'm sorry," she said, "but Mr. Truman sees clients only by appointment." She was middle-aged and well, if not stylishly, groomed, and her accent was posh enough to make well-to-do urban pioneers in the East End feel at home. Gemma doubted Mr. Truman ministered to many puppies and kittens from council estates.

The chairs and settees were formal, and the walls were hung with gilt-framed, dark-hued oil paintings featuring dogs, with the occasional cat in the shadows. Gemma thought she much preferred the cheap and cheerful posters and cluttered atmosphere of their veterinary clinic in All Saints Road. There was no sign of a Sandra Gilles collage, and she began to wonder if Pippa had been wrong.

Kincaid had shown the receptionist his warrant card, and she said frostily, "I'm afraid that's quite irregular. Mr. Truman can't see you. He's having his lunch, and his afternoon appointment will be here any moment."

"His afternoon appointment may have to wait." Kincaid's smile conveyed more threat than charm. "I'm afraid we will have to insist."

The staring match lasted a moment, then she got up, her mouth pinched with disapproval, and said, "I'll just see if he's finished his lunch."

"These paintings look the kind of thing you'd pick up at a market stall," Kincaid murmured in Gemma's ear as the receptionist left the room. "If he has a collage, I doubt he displays it for the paying customers."

They heard a door opening and closing nearby, and after a moment the receptionist returned. "Mr. Truman will see you in his office. Next door on the right." She dismissed them with a nod and turned back to her computer.

It seemed to Gemma that the woman's lack of curiosity at the advent of three police officers demanding to see her boss indicated a profound lack of imagination. Perhaps that was why Truman employed her.

Kincaid knocked on the door the receptionist had indicated, then opened it and went in, followed by Gemma and Cullen.

John Truman didn't bother to get up from behind his desk. A pudgy man, perhaps in his forties, he boasted thinning hair combed artfully over his scalp. He was straightening a stack of files, and his hands seemed unnaturally pale, the fingers sausagelike. His small mouth was pursed in an expression that managed to combine indignation with self-satisfaction.

Gemma found him instantly repellent. She couldn't imagine turning her dog or cat over to his care, and the thought of a child—

"This is very inconvenient," Truman said in a high, slightly breathy voice. "I can't imagine why you want to speak to me."

Gemma saw Kincaid's mouth twitch with annoyance. He wasn't much for standing on rank, but the man's behavior towards a senior police officer was appallingly rude. "It's Detective Superintendent Kincaid, Mr. Truman, Scotland Yard. And this is Detective Inspector

James, and Detective Sergeant Cullen. We understand that you knew Sandra Gilles. I believe you own some of her work."

"Sandra?" Truman looked genuinely shocked. "I have a collage, yes, in my house. They're very collectible. But what has that to do with you?"

"You do realize that Sandra Gilles has been missing for months?"

"Well, yes, but as you said, it's been months. I still don't see——"

"And where did you learn that Sandra was missing, Mr. Truman? Would that have been at the club in Widegate Street?"

Truman stared at him. His fat white fingers moved convulsively. "That's not—— How did you——I've no idea what you're talking about."

"Was it Lucas Ritchie who introduced you to Sandra?" asked Gemma. She sat, uninvited, in the chair in front of Truman's desk, leaning forward so that she encroached on his personal space as much as possible.

"Well, yes, but there's nothing wrong with that." Truman looked incensed. "I still don't see——"

Kincaid took up the volley. "Where were you Saturday before last, Mr. Truman?"

"Why on earth do you——I was in Spain, if you must know. It *is* August, and the last I heard there was no law against taking a holiday." Glaring at them, he added, "Are you the ones responsible for hounding Lucas Ritchie? I saw that piece in the newspaper. That sort of thing should be against the law."

"The newspaper story may have been in questionable taste, but I don't think it crossed the line into libel," Kincaid said pleasantly. "And I assure you we're not hounding anyone. We're merely doing our job, which is to investigate the disappearance of Sandra Gilles and the murder of her husband, Nasir Malik."

"Murder?" Truman came close to squeaking.

"Surely you were aware of that? Lucas Ritchie knew, and it seems to have been common knowledge at the club."

"I haven't been there much lately," Truman muttered, apparently losing sight of the fact that he'd been denying any knowledge of the place a moment before. "Maybe I did hear something, but it meant nothing to me. I never met the man."

"That's a bit unfeeling of you, considering you knew Sandra." Hands in his pockets, Kincaid had moved round one side of Truman's desk, studying the plaques on the walls. Cullen walked to the other side and stood, watching Truman. Kincaid and Cullen had learned, Gemma realized, that instant and silent communication required of partners. She felt a twinge of jealousy, quickly repressed. That was as it should be.

She caught an unpleasant whiff of sweat. They were succeeding, at least, in making Truman uncomfortable.

Kincaid turned from studying the certificates. "Conferences in Brussels, and Bruges, and Lisbon. And you were just in Spain, you say? You must like to travel, Mr. Truman. Have you ever been to Asia? India, perhaps, or Bangladesh?"

"What? No. Why would I want to go there? Those places are hardly civilized."

"Oh, I wouldn't say that. But some areas are very poor, and people will do desperate things to survive. Things like selling their children, for instance."

Truman stared at Kincaid. He was sweating visibly now, and had gone slightly blue around the lips. Gemma hoped he wouldn't keel over from a heart attack or a stroke right in front of them. "I've never been to Asia," he said. His tongue darted out to wet his lips. "You can check my passport."

"And the holiday in Spain, two weeks ago? Can you document that?"

"Of course I can." A bit of Truman's bluster returned. "I drove. I had my passport stamped getting on and off the ferry."

He was more comfortable accounting for his movements during the time of Naz's murder, Gemma thought, than he had been with the questions about Asia. And Kincaid's remark about the selling of children had frightened him badly. He definitely knew something dodgy.

Somewhere beneath them, a dog barked. "Mr. Truman." Gemma smiled at him. "I take it your surgery is downstairs?"

"Yes." He sounded a little wary, but relieved by the change in direction. "And there is a small boarding facility adjacent to the garden. The garden here is quite large, you know."

"You must have assistants," Gemma said, in a tone of sympathetic interest. The man was wearing a suit. Perhaps he traded his jacket for a lab coat, but she couldn't imagine him dealing personally with anything that might involve contact with blood or bodily fluids.

"Yes. Eric and Anthony. They're very good."

"Of course they are, or I'm sure you wouldn't employ them."

Truman had relaxed enough to glance at his watch. "And they'll be waiting for me to start afternoon surgery—"

"Do you use ketamine in your practice, Mr. Truman?" Gemma asked.

He stared at her as if a friendly dog had turned and bitten him. "Ketamine? It's not uncommon. It's a useful sedative." Puffing out his cheeks, he said, "Look, is this about drugs? I'm not stupid. I know ketamine is sold as a street drug, but if you're accusing me—"

"We're not accusing you of anything," Kincaid broke in. "But I'm assuming you keep records of use against supply."

"Of course I do."

"Then you won't mind if we have a look at them."

"I certainly would." Truman had regained his obstinate attitude. "You might as well accuse me of being a common criminal, and I won't have it."

"We could get a warrant," Kincaid said.

"Then I suggest you do it." Truman stood, and Gemma saw that he was a good deal smaller than he'd looked sitting down. His body seemed oddly proportioned, long in the torso compared to his legs.

Perhaps that was why he'd preferred to face them from behind his desk.

"But you will let us have a look at your passport?"

"I will not."

Kincaid shook his head. "That's most uncooperative, Mr. Truman. We have only to check with Immigration."

"Then I suggest you do that, as well." Truman crossed his arms, the stance of a man prepared to stand his ground. "And I won't speak to you again without a solicitor present. This is police bullying."

"I think you'll find it's not," Kincaid said, with a smile that would have made Gemma quail. "And you do realize, Mr. Truman, that the people who insist on solicitors are most often those who have something to hide."

"We've done nothing more than put the wind up him," said Cullen when they'd reached Gemma's car. "And given him a chance to falsify his drug records."

"If he's been selling veterinary drugs on the side, I suspect he'll have done that already," Kincaid answered. "And the amount given to Naz Malik would likely not be traceable. I thought he might slip and connect the question about the ketamine to Naz's death, as we've never released that information, but he didn't."

"Meaning either he didn't know or he's very clever," put in Gemma. "And I'm not sure I buy the very clever."

"He knew something about the girls," insisted Cullen.

"I thought so, too." Gemma unlocked her car and opened the door a bit to let the interior cool. "But if his passport's clean—"

"He could have traveled on false papers."

"I'm just not sure I see him as that enterprising. Or competent." Gemma gave a shrug of frustration.

Kincaid had been standing, gazing thoughtfully at the front of the house. "Truman ticks all the boxes. The connection with Sandra. The connection with Ritchie's club. The access to ketamine. But even if we assume that Sandra was onto him, either about the girls or the drugs, and that he was somehow responsible for her disappearance, we can't connect him with Naz. The pieces don't fit. There's something missing, and I'm damned if I know what it is."

CHAPTER TWENTY-SEVEN

"He may be a common policeman, but I have every reason to believe he is a fine young man and will make a good husband." [Sister Julienne]

—Jennifer Worth,
*Farewell to the
East End*

While Kincaid and Cullen returned to the Yard to begin the tedious process of checking John Truman's record with Customs and Immigration, Gemma went back to Notting Hill.

"We'll have to come up with something more solid to have any hope of getting a warrant to look at his passport," Kincaid had said, and although Gemma knew he was right, she felt frustrated and discouraged. They were so close to the truth, but she couldn't see how to move forward.

The more she thought about what must have happened to Sandra Gilles and what would happen to Charlotte, the worse things seemed. Everything they had was merely hearsay, speculation. No matter how convinced they were that they were right, they had no proof.

They couldn't talk to Alia again without risking her trust; nor could they interview Lucas Ritchie without presenting a very convincing case to Kincaid's guv'nor and the assistant commissioner.

She called Melody into her office and told her about her unexpected encounter with Alia and about their interview with John Truman. "The man's a complete slime. I know he's dirty—I'm just not sure how dirty. And if he really was in Spain, he couldn't have killed Naz, and we're back to square one—Sandra's brothers." She sighed. "But we couldn't have got this far without that list, and your help," she added. "Now, if I just knew what to do next . . ."

"I'll have another look at the list. Maybe there's something we've missed." Melody stood up and gave her an odd look. "Oh, by the way, Hazel rang you here. Your phone was off and she wanted to make sure you got the message. She wanted you to call her as soon as possible. Something about lunch tomorrow." Looking as if she were trying to suppress a grin, Melody went out.

What had got into Melody? Gemma wondered. She shook her head, which was aching again, but obediently dialed Hazel's number.

"What's this about tomorrow?" she asked when Hazel answered.

"I'm taking you to lunch at the Oriel Café," Hazel announced.

"Oh, Hazel, I'd love to, but I've said I'd go to Leyton, and anyway, I'm not sure I feel much like—"

"No, it's all set. Tell your mum and dad you'll come on Sunday. I've organized the day off tomorrow, and I've already worked things out with Duncan for Holly to play with Toby while we're out. It will be a treat for all of us, and you, darling, need a bit of pampering."

"But that's what I said last week—"

"Well, you had a good excuse for not showing, I should think. Now, really, I'm insisting. I'll call your mum myself if I must. I'll be round about eleven," she added, ringing off.

Gemma stared at the phone, bemused. Hazel could be a stubborn cow when she set her mind to it. Gemma found she was glad to see her friend more like her old self. And she was relieved, although she hated to admit it, to put off her visit to Leyton for a day. She was going to have to tell her parents—and more than likely her sister—that she still hadn't made plans for the wedding. She wasn't looking forward to it. Maybe a day out with Hazel would make it seem easier to cope.

When Hazel and Holly arrived on Saturday morning, Hazel examined Gemma's bruised forehead, then gave her a pat on the arm. "Much better. I'd say you're coming along nicely. But you've had a rough week, and we're going to make the most of our day."

Gemma was happy enough to get out of the house. Her whole family had been behaving oddly since the evening before; Duncan was preoccupied and seemed anxious to get rid of her, Kit was unusually serious and silent, and Toby kept breaking into hysterical fits of giggles over nothing. Gemma hoped he was just wound up over Holly's visit, and not sickening for something.

Hazel whisked her off to Sloane Square, insisting on driving rather than taking the bus or the tube. "We'll park in the garage at Marks and Sparks," she said, "and walk up the King's Road. It's a lovely day for it."

The Oriel Café, a bustling French brasserie, was a Sloane Square institution. They got a table by the window, and as Gemma sipped the glass of prosecco Hazel had ordered, she began to relax. Over their fish cakes and mussels, she told Hazel what she had learned from Alia the day before, and then about the vet, John Truman.

When she finished, Hazel's dark eyes were sober. "We know these things happen—have always happened, in some form or another, but that doesn't make it any easier when you actually confront them. That poor girl, whoever she was. And the others, because there must be others."

"On top of that, Charlotte's placement hearing is on Monday," said Gemma. Now that things had started spilling out, she didn't seem to be able to stop them. "I've rung the social worker again, but I haven't heard back. I simply will not let that horrible Gail Gilles get her hands on that child. I don't care what it takes.

"And, Hazel—" She paused, then blurted out the worry she hadn't been fully willing to admit, even to herself. "Last weekend, I told Duncan I was dreading the wedding. I tried to explain that it wasn't because of us. I thought he understood, but now he won't talk about it. I'm afraid—I'm afraid I've totally screwed things up." She gulped the last of her wine. When the bubbles went up her nose, she had an excuse for her watering eyes.

"Gemma." Hazel leaned forward and clasped her hand for a moment. Her touch was warm and comforting. "You absolutely cannot save the world single-handedly, as much as you want to. I don't see what more you can do about this case. Let Duncan get on with trying to find something more on this vet.

"As for Charlotte, try to have a bit of faith in the system. I know it's not perfect, but you haven't actually seen what social services can do. Let it go for a day or two, see what happens on Monday.

"And I'm quite sure Duncan understands about the wedding. In fact, he's probably relieved. After all, what man wants to get dressed up in a monkey suit and put on a show. Give him a bit of credit, too. Stop worrying." She pushed her glass aside and smiled. "And in the meantime, we're going shopping."

"Shopping?" Gemma thought about the children, the work she was still trying to catch up on, all the things that needed doing around the house. "But we hadn't planned—I wasn't—I shouldn't—"

"Oh yes, you should." Hazel waved the waiter over for the check. "Come on. We're going to Peter Jones."

"I need a new wardrobe after Scotland," Hazel told Gemma as she led her through the women's clothing collections in the Sloane

Square department store. "I'm not prepared for London summers anymore."

But she pushed things about on the racks with desultory interest, and didn't take anything to try on. Gemma followed as Hazel wove her way through the aisles. Then Hazel stopped and lifted a dress, holding it up as she admired it. "Oh, this is perfect."

It was a pale apple-green cotton, as fine as silk, with capped sleeves, a fitted waist, and a skirt that flared to the knee.

"It is lovely." Gemma touched it. "But I'm not sure it's really your color. You do better in bright things."

"I suppose you're right, more's the pity. However"—Hazel held the dress up to Gemma—"it certainly suits you." She inspected the tag. "And I think it's just your size. Come on, try it on."

"But I don't need a dress," said Gemma. "Where would I wear it? It's a garden-party sort of thing—"

"Of course you need a dress." Hazel gave her a stern look. "How often do you treat yourself to anything, Gemma? As for where to wear it, you'll just have to come up with an excuse. Make Duncan take you out to dinner or something." Hazel marched off towards the changing room, dress in hand, without giving Gemma a chance to argue further.

A saleswoman ushered them into the mirrored cubicle, asking if there was anything else they needed.

"Shoes," Hazel told her, giving Gemma, who had worn jeans and flats, a critical eye. "You can't try on this dress in those. And a sexy bra and knickers."

"Hazel, you've gone completely mad," Gemma protested. "I can't—"

"Just tell her your sizes."

Feeling giddy, Gemma complied. It must have been the prosecco they'd drunk with lunch, she thought. They were both a little mad.

Hazel carried on a whispered consultation with the clerk, and in what seemed a remarkably short time, the woman came back with some lacy wisps of underwear and a shoe box.

The bra and knickers were the same pale green as the dress, and each cream, open-toe shoe was adorned with a cream-colored, full-petaled fabric rose.

"I can't possibly—"

"Just put everything on." Hazel went out and closed the door with a snap. "Tell me when you're ready."

A few moments later, Gemma called out, "I can't do the zip."

Hazel and the saleswoman, who had been whispering again outside the door, came in together. "Breathe in," Hazel commanded, and pulled up the long back zipper. Then she stepped away and gazed at Gemma in the mirror. "Oh," she said on a sigh. "Oh, it's gorgeous."

Gemma stared at her own reflection. Although she would never have chosen the dress for herself, she had to admit it was beautiful. She looked—different. "It's—I feel like a princess." She smoothed the skirt.

"So you should. Now spin."

Gemma spun obediently. When the dress belled out around her, she laughed aloud. Then she peered at the price tag, and her spirits fell. "It's lovely, but I can't possibly spend this much on myself . . . This is ridiculous."

"No, it's not, and yes, you can. If you don't buy it for yourself—and the shoes, and the knickers—I'll buy them for you." Hazel glanced at her watch. "And you're wearing everything home. I've just realized I'm late picking up Holly. Can we just snip the tags off?" she added to the clerk.

"Hazel, don't be daft."

"I'm not. Duncan and the kids will absolutely love it. Wait and see."

It was only in the car on the way back to Notting Hill that Gemma said, "Hazel, that was the only dress in that color on display, and it just happened to be in my size. Not to mention the shoes were perfect. I'd almost think you picked them out beforehand."

"Nonsense. I just have good shopping karma." Hazel seemed very focused on her driving.

"You didn't buy a thing."

"Next time. This was your day."

When they reached St. John's Gardens, there seemed an unusual number of cars parked in the street, but Hazel was able to find a spot for her Golf. They got out and walked to the house, Gemma thinking, as she so often did, how much she loved the place. Just as they reached the door, Hazel said, "Oh, I forgot my phone. You go on."

Gemma opened the door and stepped inside. She heard a childish shriek, and a hum of conversation that fell suddenly still. Looking round, she saw that the house was filled with people.

She gazed in shock at all the familiar faces—in the dining room and sitting room, spilling out of the kitchen—all staring back at her with ear-splitting grins. Tim and Holly. Melody. Doug Cullen. Gemma's boss from work, Mark Lamb, and his wife, Diane. Duncan's guv'nor, Denis Childs, and his wife. Her sister and brother-in-law. Her niece and nephew. Erika, and Erika's friend Henri. Wesley, Betty, and Charlotte. And sitting stiffly on chairs in the dining room, her parents.

Hazel was behind her now, pushing her gently forward. Toby thundered down the stairs, shouting, "She's here, she's here!" He wore a white shirt and his school trousers, as did Kit, who followed him.

"What—"

Duncan appeared from the kitchen and came to meet her. He, too, was smartly dressed, in a suit she didn't recognize. But unlike the others, he looked anxious. Kissing her on the cheek, he said, "Hullo, love. You look absolutely brilliant."

"I don't understand," she said. "I didn't— What's going on? Has something happened? Is it someone's birthday?"

"No, it's a wedding."

"In our house?" She felt completely baffled. "Whose wedding?"

He met her gaze and held it. "Ours, love. If you're willing."

CHAPTER TWENTY-EIGHT

"Mothers and daughters always draw closer to each other as the years pass." [Sister Julienne]

—Jennifer Worth,
*Farewell to the
East End*

"But that's not possible." Gemma looked at Duncan in confusion. "It's not a legal venue."

"No. But it is possible to have a blessing. There's a humanist celebrant, a nice woman, waiting in the garden. Usually it's done the other way round, the civil wedding, then the blessing. But I explained that we were a little, um, unusual, and she agreed to come.

"We can have a ceremony, then next week we can go to Chelsea Town Hall and start the paperwork. Because that's all a civil marriage is—paperwork. This"—he gestured at their friends and family gathered round—"this is what matters."

Gemma suddenly realized that the house was filled with flowers—vases of roses and lilies and lovely things she couldn't name.

Following her gaze, Duncan said, "Wesley organized the flowers from the market this morning. Betty's cooking Caribbean food for after, and Wesley's going to take pictures. I organized the champagne—there's cases of it in the kitchen."

"And the cake?"

"I'm afraid we couldn't get a proper cake made in time. Wesley's bought loads of cupcakes from the bakery on Portobello."

Gemma started to laugh. "Oh, that's perfect, just perfect."

Duncan smiled back. He leaned over and whispered in her ear. "Is that a yes, then?"

She slipped an arm round his neck and whispered back, "What would you have done if I'd said no?"

"Had a hell of a party." He brushed his lips against her cheek, and suddenly she wanted him so fiercely her knees went weak.

"Hey, no snogging before the ceremony," Kit called out. "Let's get this show on the road. Everyone, outside."

"I take it Kit has appointed himself master of ceremonies?" Gemma said, reluctantly letting go of Duncan.

As the crowd began to shift towards the garden, Charlotte, who had been hiding behind Betty's skirts, ran over and wrapped her arms around Gemma's knees. "Ooh, look at you." Gemma lifted her into a hug. "You've got a new dress, too. Aren't you pretty."

"I'm da flower girl," Charlotte told her, giving her a somewhat sticky kiss.

"Oh, flowers." Gemma began to feel a flutter of nerves. "I don't have a bouquet."

"Yes, you do," said Wesley. He sounded uncharacteristically shy. "I had them make it at Tyler's. I hope it's okay." He handed her a spray of white roses and greenery, tied with a pale green silk ribbon.

"It's lovely, Wes." She saw that the dogs, who had joined the melee, had matching ribbons. She turned to Hazel. "And what would you have done if I'd refused to buy the dress?"

"I had confidence in my powers of persuasion. I spent all my off hours for a week finding that bloody dress. You were going to buy it or else." She pulled a lipstick and a hairbrush from her bag. "Here, touch-up time."

Gemma tidied up in the hall mirror, then turned to Hazel for inspection. "Do I look all right?"

Sniffing, Hazel gave her a quick hug. "Angelic. Now go."

"Cue the music," shouted Kit, and from the sitting room came the sound, not of Mendelssohn, which Gemma despised, but of a joyously ringing Bach prelude.

Then as she turned back to the room, she realized that the only people not smiling, and not moving towards the garden, were her parents. She went to them quickly. "Mum. Are you feeling all right? What is it?"

Vi looked up, her lips trembling, but it was her dad who spoke first. "It's not a proper wedding, is it? Not legal, like."

"We'll have a civil wedding in the register's office," Gemma explained. "As soon as we can arrange it."

"That's all very well," said her mum. "But there's no reception hall, is there? And what about the Rolls-Royce with ribbons and things? And, Gemma, your dress—you can't get married in *green*."

Gemma smiled, trying hard to hang on to her temper. "I'll tell you a secret, Mum. I'm not exactly entitled to wear white."

"Don't you be cheeky to your mother, miss." Her dad was scowling now, his color rising. "You've let down your mum and her friends, who were expecting a proper do. What are we going to tell people?"

She looked at them, then at the last of the other guests, trailing out into the garden. Duncan waited by the French doors. The Bach played on, a counterpoint to the happy murmur of voices. The scent of lilies came to her on the warm air. Her anger evaporated.

"I don't give a fig what anyone expected," she said firmly. "This is my day, and I'm not going to let anyone spoil it. I would like for you to stay and to wish me well, but that's up to you.

"Now, if you don't mind, I've someone waiting for me." She bent and kissed her mum's cheek, and after a hesitant moment, her dad's. Then she walked towards Duncan without looking back.

At the door, Wesley handed her the bouquet, and Duncan took her arm. "Rings." She pulled away in a last moment of panic. "We don't have rings."

"We do," Duncan assured her. "Toby has them. At least I hope Toby has them."

"You're very brave," she said, beginning to smile. A tide of joy was rising in her like a spring.

"Very brave or very mad." He looked at her, his face suddenly serious. "Or both. Are you sure, Gemma? Are you sure this is what you want?"

She glanced round at the expectant faces of their gathered friends, and at the children, who looked ready to burst with pride and excitement. "You did this for me. All of this. It couldn't be more perfect. And you"—she touched his cheek, then brushed back the wayward lock of hair that had fallen across his forehead—"*you* are exactly what I want."

Duncan took her hand and led her out into the garden.

CHAPTER TWENTY-NINE

Many Houses were then left desolate, all the People being carried away dead . . .

—Daniel Defoe,
*A Journal of the
Plague Year*

Somewhere between the second and third glass of champagne, Gemma kicked off her shoes.

The blessing had been short, simple, and beautiful, a celebration of their relationship as partners in life, and Gemma couldn't have imagined anything more perfect. The children had behaved with remarkable decorum, even Toby, and most of the guests had been a bit teary-eyed—as had Duncan and Gemma themselves.

Afterwards, Bach had given way to reggae, then eighties pop and sixties soul. The happy couple had been toasted, and they had all eaten, and drunk, and danced, and finally Gemma and Duncan had made a great show of cutting their respective vanilla and chocolate cupcakes.

Gemma's parents had stayed, and even seemed to enjoy themselves, although they'd picked at Betty's lovely Caribbean food. But by the cake stage, Gemma could tell her mum was beginning to tire, and they had left soon after.

Most of the other guests had followed as it began to get dark, including Hazel, Tim, and Holly. Gemma had walked Hazel to the door and hugged her.

"Thank you for everything. I'm glad you've come back. Although you are surely the most devious person I know—after Duncan."

"Thank you, I think." Hazel laughed. "Maybe I should think about becoming a wedding planner. Or a spy."

Now Gemma sat in the kitchen, rubbing her aching feet. Duncan and Betty were doing the washing-up, while Wesley, Melody, and Doug, the stragglers, clustered round polishing off a huge pot of tea Wesley had made. The children were playing in the garden with the dogs, and Gemma felt utterly, blissfully content. For the hundredth time, she held up her left hand and admired her ring.

It was Art Deco, a platinum band set with small diamonds. Henri and Erika had helped Duncan pick it out from a jeweler in the antique arcade on the King's Road.

"You can change it if you want," Duncan said, teasing her from the sink.

"No way." She wrapped her right hand protectively around her left. "You're not getting this off me for anything." He'd bought a plain white-gold band for himself, assuring her that it was all he needed.

When the doorbell rang, Gemma stretched and said, "I'll get it. Someone must have forgotten something."

But Wesley jumped up, flashing Duncan a conspiratorial grin. "No, I'll go. You rest your battered feet."

There were voices from the hall, then Wesley came back into the kitchen, his arm draped casually round a young woman's shoulders. A familiar tall, auburn-haired woman in surgical scrubs.

Gemma stood, laughing. "Bryony! What are you doing here?" Bryony Poole was their friend as well as their veterinarian. It looked as though Wesley had seen her more recently than Gemma, as there had been something definitely possessive in the way he'd guided her into the room.

"Congratulations." Bryony hugged Gemma and Duncan, then gestured at her blue scrubs. "I'm so sorry to turn up like this. I had afternoon clinic and couldn't reschedule. Wesley told me about the wedding the first of the week, but Gavin's on holiday in Spain, so there was nobody to take over." Gavin was Bryony's not particularly well-liked boss. "Have I missed all the fun?"

"No, nor all the champagne." Gemma poured her a glass from the bottle still standing in a tub of ice.

Bryony raised it to them before she drank. "To the happy couple."

"Holidays in Spain must be the thing for vets," Gemma said, sitting down and pouring herself another cup of tea. She told Bryony a bit about their investigation into John Truman's possible connection with Naz Malik's murder, leaving out Truman's name. "Would it be easy for a vet to set aside enough ketamine to stop a man breathing?" The vision of Naz Malik's body in the park brought the case back with a sickening jolt.

"Well, as little as a gram can be fatal. You can dissolve it—that's one of the reasons it's a good date-rape drug—but you might taste that much in a drink." Bryony swirled her champagne.

"There was Valium in his system, too."

"There you go, then. First you use the Valium as a relaxant, then you administer the ketamine as a dissociative. Same thing an anesthetist does before you have surgery."

"An anesthetist?" Kincaid turned from the sink.

"Yeah, sure," said Bryony, looking a little surprised. "Ketamine is best known as a veterinary drug, but anesthetists use it, too. It's just much easier for street dealers to steal the stuff from a vet clinic than a hospital."

Kincaid stood, hands dripping. "Anesthetist. Shit."

Betty turned, perhaps surprised by his language, but when Gemma saw his face, she held up a hand in a command for silence. She knew that expression all too well.

Wordlessly, Betty handed him a tea towel.

But Kincaid merely crumpled it, as if he had no clue as to what it was for, then tossed it away and wiped his hands on the trousers of his good suit. "Of bloody course. Why didn't I see it?"

"See what?" Gemma felt the world rock to a stop.

He looked at her, focusing on her face. "There's an anesthetist on the bloody list. Alexander. Doug and I met him at Ritchie's club. He came up and introduced himself. He was one of Sandra's patrons. And Ritchie said something about his sponsorship of a women's health clinic."

"Rivington Street," Gemma whispered. "Oh, my God. The clinic in Rivington Street." In her mind, the pieces began to fall together with dreadful clarity. "Alia talked about how involved Sandra had been with the work there, and then she said something about Mr. Miles not actually seeing the patients, because they were only comfortable with women doctors, but I didn't make the connection."

"Miles Alexander," said Cullen. "That was his name."

Gemma felt the blood drain from her face. "He works at the London. Mr. Alexander, the consultant. It must be the same man. He was the anesthetist on my mum's procedure. Dear God."

"We saw him the day of the postmortem." Kincaid started pacing and the others shifted a bit to give him room. "In the corridor by the mortuary, as we went to Dr. Kaleem's office. I knew he looked familiar. He must have been checking on Kaleem's results. Do you suppose there was something Kaleem missed?"

"Or maybe he was checking to see if there was anything *he* had missed," Cullen suggested. "Kaleem said he thought he remembered Naz's mobile phone being in a different place in the evidence bag, remember? And that day when he spoke to us in the club, was he trying to find out what we knew?"

"Maybe," Kincaid said. "Or maybe it was just plain bloody arrogance. Him deigning to play a little game with us."

"Wait." Melody had been listening intently, but now she shook her head. "You're making huge assumptions here."

"No, it all fits," Gemma said with a certainty that made her feel cold. "He knew Sandra, and probably quite well through their connection with the clinic. He bought her work. He had access to the drugs used to kill Naz, and the knowledge to use them. Lucas Ritchie's club would have provided a connection to Truman, and possibly others like him, if they shared an interest in little girls.

"The question is, what made Sandra connect the Bangladeshi girl's story with this doctor she knew, and probably trusted?"

Betty stepped forward, twisting Kincaid's discarded tea towel in her hands. "I'm not followin' all these things about girls and clubs. But do I understand that what you are sayin' is that our little Charlotte's mother is dead?"

"Yes." Gemma rubbed the sudden ache in her cheekbones and blinked back the prickle of tears. "I think I've always known that Sandra Gilles was dead. The question was always why, and how, and who."

"And the daddy," said Betty, "Mr. Naz? You think this same man killed him?"

"Charlotte told me that her dad had gone to look for her mum, but I didn't listen to her, not properly. Maybe Naz learned something that day. Maybe he went to talk to Alexander. Maybe he was fishing for information and didn't want to refuse when Alexander offered him a drink."

"That would explain where Naz was in those missing hours between the time he left the house and the time he died in Haggerston Park," said Kincaid. "If he went to see Alexander, Alexander could have drugged him and kept him in the house until it was almost dark—"

"And he could get him to the park," finished Gemma. She turned to Bryony. "How long would the fatal dose of ketamine have taken to act?"

"Not long. And it was probably injected, as it would have been difficult to get liquid down someone already incapacitated. It might have been a puncture mark under the tongue that your pathologist missed. Did your killer intend the death to look like a suicide?"

"If so, he should have moved his head into a more natural position, after he watched him suffocate." The thought of what Alexander had done made Gemma feel ill. "Maybe he thought someone was coming and cleared off a bit too soon."

Cullen had his phone out and was tapping the keys. Looking up, he said, "Miles Alexander lives in Hoxton. I've just checked the address. It's one street from John Truman. And a ten-minute walk from Columbia Road market."

Gemma saw it all, so clearly now. "What if, when Sandra left Charlotte with Roy that day at the market, she meant to pay a quick call on Alexander? She'd have assumed she'd be back in time to pick Charlotte up and meet Naz for lunch."

If this were true, she'd been right about Sandra having walked someplace not far from Columbia Road, but she'd focused on the wrong direction, south and east, towards Bethnal Green and Sandra's family, not north and west, towards Hoxton.

"She meant to be back for an ordinary Sunday lunch with her husband and daughter. Whatever she suspected, she couldn't have had any idea how dangerous he really was." Clamping down on the wave of fury that poured through her, Gemma looked at Kincaid and managed to say levelly, "Can we bring him in now?"

Kincaid frowned. "I think we'll have a patrol car pick up Alexander, on suspicion of Naz Malik's murder."

"But we don't have a direct connection between Alexander and Malik," protested Doug.

"Sandra is the connection. And there will be others—we just have to find them."

"Then why don't we get a team going door-to-door in his road?" Doug argued. "Maybe someone will have seen Naz, or Sandra, going into his house. That way we could serve a warrant, and pick him up at the same time. That would shake him up."

Kincaid shook his head. "If we start knocking on doors, even in plainclothes, I guarantee you Alexander is going to get wind of it. And if he does, he's going to get rid of all the evidence he can."

He stabbed a finger at them for emphasis. "I want more than evidence tying this bastard to Naz Malik's and Sandra Gilles's murders. I want him for human trafficking, too, and that means I want his computer, his photos, any little girls' clothing—all the things he's likely to have in that house that he could easily wipe or toss."

Thinking it through, Gemma said, "But if he is connected with Truman, we may have already blown it. Truman may have told him we were asking questions about Naz and Sandra, and the girls."

Kincaid rubbed a hand over his jaw and paced a few restless steps. "Maybe. But there's always the possibility that Truman might turn out to be useful. We'll bring him in, too—threaten to charge him as an accessory to human trafficking. If he really is involved, he's the sort who might be willing to roll over on Alexander to save his own skin. It's worth a try, and I want Alexander a lot more than I want Truman, the little tosser."

He glanced at his watch. "Doug, let's get a car on its way to Hoxton. And then get a team out. Let's see if we can find any neighbors at home who might have seen Naz or Sandra.

"Once we get Alexander out of the way, we'll have another team start going through his rubbish. We can do that without a warrant. It's Saturday—hopefully he'll have left something interesting in the outside bins for next week's collection."

He went to Gemma and looked down at her, putting a hand on

her shoulder. "I'm sorry, love," he said softly. "It's not quite what I had in mind for our wedding night. I'll ring you—"

"The hell you will." She gave his hand a squeeze and stood up. "Betty, Wesley, could one of you stay and look after the kids?" Turning back to Duncan, she added, "We'll spend our wedding night together one way or the other. I'm going with you."

Gemma stood in the corridor outside the interview room at Scotland Yard. Kincaid had gone to deal with the arrival of Alexander's solicitor, leaving her to stare through the window in the interview room door. She'd recognized Alexander instantly from that brief meeting in the hospital ward.

He looked as sleek and self-satisfied now as he had then, and more annoyed than concerned. And yet this man, she felt quite certain, had callously, remorselessly, snuffed out two lives, and put a child's future at risk. Charlotte's future.

How many other lives had he ruined? Children taken from their homes and families, raped, kept prisoner, and then . . . what? Abandoned like rubbish, castoffs for those who were willing to settle for soiled goods? Or put out on the street, where their only choice would be to earn a living as prostitutes?

When the uniformed officers arrived, Alexander had been hosting a dinner party for three other men, and the sergeant in charge thought he'd caught a glimpse of an Asian girl in the kitchen. He hadn't been able to go in, but he'd not allowed Alexander to talk to his guests alone before he'd ushered him out of the house and into the panda car.

Alexander had been delivered to the Yard, icily furious and demanding his solicitor.

But Kincaid's plan to play Truman against Alexander had failed. The team sent to Truman's house found it dark and shuttered, and although Kincaid had ordered a car to keep an eye on the house in case he returned, Gemma was afraid yesterday's visit had frightened the vet into doing a runner.

If only they'd realized, yesterday, who the real perpetrator must have been. Now, without Truman's corroboration, they might have to let Alexander go before they could convince a magistrate to give them a warrant to search his house and car.

Their best hope was the team led by Cullen, knocking on doors in Alexander's quietly respectable Hoxton Street. Melody had insisted—Gemma thought somewhat to Cullen's chagrin—on going along.

But it was late, getting on for midnight, and Gemma suspected they'd be more likely to get complaints from the neighbors than cooperation.

She rubbed her ring against the lapel of her jacket to polish it. The band was the only tangible reminder that the afternoon had not been a dream. She'd taken the time to change from her lovely dress into jacket and trousers. She didn't intend to face Alexander in her wedding finery, and face him she meant to do, no matter how long it took.

But would she have another chance to speak to him without a solicitor present? She looked up and down the corridor. There was no sign of Kincaid returning. Taking a breath, she opened the door and went in.

Miles Alexander sat at the table in his bespoke suit, studying his nails. He looked up at the sound of the door, then raised an eyebrow in an expression of mild interest.

"Haven't I seen you before?" he asked.

"I met you in hospital," said Gemma. "My mother had a shunt put in her arm. You were her anesthetist."

"A ginger-haired woman." He smiled, as if pleased by his recollection. "Leukemia. Not a good prognosis, I'm afraid."

The remark was deliberately, casually cruel.

Refusing to let him see that the taunt had hit its mark, Gemma smiled back. "Do you always have such a good bedside manner, Mr. Alexander? Or did you choose your speciality because the patients couldn't talk back?"

"Oh, aren't you the wit. I'm sorry, but I'm afraid I don't remember your name." Alexander seemed unperturbed. "Nor do I have to speak to you, although you do seem to be conscious."

"I can't question you, no. But I can *say* whatever I like." She moved a step closer, and wondered if she were imagining the metallic, slightly chemical smell of him. "You see, I know you murdered Sandra Gilles and her husband. And I don't intend to let you get away with playing God."

"Then I'd say you have a rather elevated self-image, and a very active imagination." Alexander smiled again, but she had seen the glint in his eyes, like the flash of a snake moving in the grass.

It was only then that she realized she'd been harboring the tiniest shred of hope that Sandra Gilles was still alive. She turned and left the room.

A few moments later, she was leaning against the corridor wall, her eyes closed, when she heard footsteps. She opened her eyes and saw Kincaid, alone.

"Where's Alexander's lawyer?" asked Gemma.

"Rethinking his strategy, I suspect. He said he needed to make a phone call."

"Why? What's happened?"

"Good news for us," Kincaid answered, but his expression was grim. "Doug and Melody came up trumps. Mr. Alexander's next-door neighbor came home after an evening out. She's a single mum, apparently, and was only too happy to talk about the odd goings-on next door.

"She didn't recall seeing Naz or Sandra. But"——he forestalled her disappointment——"she did tell them that she'd been worried about the young girl she'd seen in the house, sometimes looking out a window, a few times peeking through the open door when Alexander was coming or going.

"Once she stopped Alexander and asked if his little girl might like to play with her own daughter. He told her the girl was his housekeeper's child, and more or less to mind her own business.

"But the mum says she never saw a housekeeper. And not long after that, she stopped seeing the girl, too."

"When?" asked Gemma. "When did she last see the girl?"

"She said she was sure it was in May. Her wisteria had just finished blooming."

Gemma stared at him in dismay. "And she said *child*? Not a teenager? Not the girl who came into the clinic?"

"A little girl not more than ten or twelve, she told Doug. Asian, wearing traditional dress. I've rung the magistrate. We should have a search warrant by daybreak."

CHAPTER THIRTY

*The shadow of Christ Church falls across Spitalfields
Gardens and in the shadow of Christ Church I see a sight I
never wish to see again.*

—Jack London,
People of the Abyss
(1903)

Miles Alexander had, on the advice of his solicitor, refused to answer any of their questions. After a whispered conference with his lawyer, he had not reacted when told they intended to search his house. The solicitor, however, had looked distinctly uneasy.

Gemma thought Kincaid might provoke a response when he suggested that Alexander might find a night enjoying the hospitality of the Metropolitan Police a novel experience, one more comfortable than a night spent in a National Health Service hospital ward. But Alexander had remained bland as butter, with no more displays of the veiled viciousness that had marked his off-the-record conversation with Gemma.

Kincaid had left Doug Cullen preparing the request for a warrant, and Gemma and Kincaid had gone home and fallen into bed.

"We've made a real balls-up of this if we don't find anything," Kincaid said as Gemma turned out the light.

"We will. He's an arrogant bastard who thinks the rules don't apply to him—any rules. But he's not quite as clever as he thinks."

Duncan rolled over against her back. His voice already slurred with sleep, he threw an arm over her and murmured, "Wifey."

Gemma roused herself enough to poke him with her elbow and say, "Don't you dare call me that," but she smiled and pulled him closer.

"How are you going to stop me?"

"Oh, I can think of ways," said Gemma. She could feel the warmth of his hand on her belly, and snuggled against him. But his hand relaxed, and his breathing settled into a slow, regular rhythm.

She smiled and fell asleep.

As the sky began to gray, his phone rang. The sound was shockingly loud in the quiet room. "Oh, God, turn it off," Gemma mumbled groggily.

But when she heard his voice, she came wide awake, sitting up and pushing her hair away from her face.

"What's happened?" she asked when he rang off. "Did they get the warrant?"

Kincaid was already half out of bed. He leaned back and kissed her quickly. "A team will be waiting for us in Hoxton."

Gemma had washed her face and thrown on jeans and a light jumper, then checked on the children.

Betty had insisted on staying over, and had made herself a bed on the sofa. She'd put Charlotte in with Toby, and when Gemma peeked in at the two little ones, Toby had, as usual, thrown off the covers, and Charlotte was rolled up in the duvet like a little hedgehog, with just her curls showing.

Gemma stood, gazing at them, wishing with all her heart she

354 ~ DEBORAH CROMBIE

could protect Charlotte from any more harm—and from the truth about what had happened to her parents, if they should learn it. Then she sighed and closed the door.

The Georgian street in Hoxton seemed slightly later in period than Fournier Street in Spitalfields. The front doors lacked Fournier Street's ornate lintels, and the houses lacked the touches of eccentricity that made Fournier Street so appealing.

Here, the terrace was uniform, from windows and doors to trim work to bellpulls. Miles Alexander's house, however, was easily identified by the surrounding cluster of police cars, the SOCO van, and the open front door.

Doug Cullen was waiting for them on the pavement, and so, to Gemma's surprise, was Melody. Melody, like Gemma, had thrown on jeans and a cardigan, as the early morning air was still cool. She looked exhausted, but she had paper cups of coffee waiting for them. "Coffee shop round the corner," she explained. "I was desperate."

"What are you doing here?" Gemma asked her. "I didn't mean for you to get out this morning, after all the work you put in last night."

"Doug called me. And I wanted to be here."

Gemma noted with interest that Doug and Melody seemed to have advanced to a comfortable first-name basis, and that he had actually invited Melody's participation.

"Anything so far?" Kincaid asked.

"You were right, guv," said Cullen. "I had a look at his computer before forensics packed it up. Bastard didn't even have his files encrypted, but I suppose he thought he could wipe them if anyone came snooping round."

"And there *are* photos," Melody added, with no trace of her usual cheerful manner. "Albums of them." She hunched her shoulders. "Truman's in some of them, too. And some other blokes. We'll have to crop the girls' faces from the shots, so that we can show them to Alia, and to the lady next door."

"How many girls?" asked Gemma.

Melody shrugged and sipped her coffee. "Half a dozen, maybe. The last girl looked very young. Very pretty. The men were—" She shook her head.

"Any sign of girls in the house recently?" Kincaid asked.

Doug took over from Melody, but without his usual territorial defensiveness. "Not at the moment, no, but they've not got through everything yet. The interior of the house is recognizable from some of the photos, so apparently he used it for his . . . entertainment . . . on a regular basis. And the SOCOs found a pair of girl's knickers in the outside rubbish bin. They were . . ." Cullen seemed unusually hesitant. ". . . soiled."

"Blood?"

"And semen, they think. Maybe from last night's little soirée."

"Jesus." Kincaid looked as sick as Gemma felt. The fact that they'd seen these things before didn't make it easier. "His mates will have got the girl out after we had Alexander picked up. Bloody hell. We should have kept a watch on the house. I hope she's still alive."

Cullen nodded agreement. "I've got a call in to the sergeant who was in charge last night, to see if he can match any of the men he saw with the photos in Alexander's albums. Then we can start trying to put names to the faces."

"Lucas Ritchie may be able to help there. And I suspect he'll be glad to cooperate if he wants to hang on to any shred of reputation." Kincaid glanced up the road. A shiny red tow truck came round the corner and pulled up behind a new-model silver Lexus parked near the house.

"Is that Alexander's car?" asked Gemma.

"His pride and joy, looks like," Cullen answered, crumpling his empty cup. "But if he took Naz Malik to the park in it, the lab should be able to find traces of hair or fiber."

Kincaid nodded. "That would be a start, although it wouldn't prove that Naz was in the car the day he died unless they were found in the boot. And I don't see how he could have carried him out of the house and dumped him in the boot here. It wouldn't have been quite dark, and the car would have been in full view of all the neighbors. I imagine he walked him out as if he were very drunk, or ill, and put him in the backseat."

"Has there been anything in the house so far that links Alexander to Naz or Sandra?" Gemma asked.

"Not yet, but the SOCOs are working on it." Cullen sounded as if he took the failure personally, but Gemma hadn't really expected more. She was, in fact, astonished by Alexander's arrogance in leaving evidence of his trade in children in plain view.

A woman came out of the house next door and stood on her front step, watching them. She had a toweling dressing gown pulled tightly around her, as if she were cold. Her blond-streaked hair was pulled up with a band, and her thin face free of makeup.

"Is this the woman you talked to last night?" she asked Cullen and Melody.

"Her name is Anna Swinburne," answered Melody. "Nice woman. She seems very distressed by the whole business."

"Can't say as I blame her. I'll just have a word." Gemma walked next door. "I'm DI James," she said, holding out her hand. "I just wanted to thank you for talking to our officers last night."

Anna Swinburne's fingers were icy. "Is this because of me?" she asked, nodding towards the patrol cars and tow truck as Gemma released her hand.

"Well, at least in part. That's why—"

"Will he go to jail?"

Gemma looked at her a little more carefully. "I don't know. That's not up to us. It's just our job to gather the evidence."

"Well, I hope he does," said Anna vehemently. "I don't like him. I never felt safe with him next door."

"Was there any particular reason?"

"Oh, I suppose at first there was a bit of hurt vanity." Anna Swinburne smiled, and Gemma decided she was pretty in an intense sort of way. "I'm divorced. This was a new start, this house, and he was a nice-looking single man. But he made it clear he wasn't interested in giving me the time of day, and I was all right with that even if it was a bit ego dampening. But the more I saw of him—"

"Did he say something, or do something?" Gemma encouraged.

Anna shrugged. "No. He was just unfriendly, even for a Londoner. And . . . odd. I'm a television writer, so I work from home a good bit. He was always popping in and out at different times, sometimes just for a minute or two. I know he's a doctor, but I thought they kept more regular hours—that he'd be in surgeries all day or something."

If he'd been keeping a girl in the house, Gemma thought it quite likely that he'd been checking on her. It would have been a good way to keep the child too cowed to go out.

"After you stopped seeing the little girl, did he still pop in like that?"

Anna Swinburne frowned and pulled her toweling dressing gown tighter. "Now that you mention it, I don't think he did."

"And you never talked to her, the little girl?"

"No. Once or twice, when I saw her at the window on nice days, I waved to her. One time she waved back. But then all the landscapers were in and out, and after that I didn't see her again."

"Landscapers?"

"Oh, these houses have quite large gardens in the back. That's one reason I bought here, so my daughter would have a place to play. I don't know what he had done in his garden, but it must have been quite a big project."

"When was this?" Gemma asked, but she had a sinking feeling that she knew. Anna had already told Cullen and Melody that she'd last seen the little girl in May.

"May-ish, I'm sure. We had a warm spell, and I remember I could hear them working next door when I was sitting in my garden."

"Ms. Swinburne—Anna. We may have some photos for you to look at later. We'd like to see if you can identify this little girl."

The woman paled. "But I don't want to see—my daughter's ten. I don't want to think about—"

"It will be all right. It will just be the girls' faces."

Gemma thanked her and rejoined Kincaid. Cullen and Melody had gone to speak to the tow truck driver. "I want to go into the house," she said.

"I thought you would." Kincaid handed her the white overall he'd taken from the boot of the Escort. "I'll be right behind you. I just want to have a word with the SOCOs about getting those photos copied as soon as possible." The head of the crime scene team had just come out, carrying samples to the van.

When Gemma had slipped on her overall, she walked in slowly, studying the house. The decor seemed late Georgian, and was based, she guessed, on the period when they had begun to use gilt to reflect light. And although the rooms were laid out simply, as in the other Georgian houses she'd seen, the furnishings looked authentic, and of museum quality. The few pieces of contemporary art on the pale-stone-colored walls worked well, rather to Gemma's surprise.

The ground-floor rooms were the grand reception rooms, and in both sitting and dining rooms the elegant fireplaces served as focal points. But in the sitting room, the wall above the mantel was empty—a look at odds with the careful placement of furniture and artwork elsewhere in the house.

Gemma gazed at the room, and at the size of the empty space, and thought of the unfinished collage on Sandra's worktable. Had it been meant to go here?

That would explain so much. If Sandra had been working on a piece commissioned by Alexander, and had come to the house to get a feel for what her client wanted, and where the piece would go, she might have stumbled across something that made her connect the story she'd heard at the clinic with Alexander. Could it have been the little girl the neighbor saw, the latest of Alexander's victims?

But if so, what had become of the child?

Gemma went downstairs, and through a sleek, modern kitchen into the high-walled garden beyond.

The garden, like the house, was formal, with rows of neatly clipped hedges around the borders, and a paved courtyard with a fountain at its center. There were no flowers, and no color other than the green of the shrubs and the pale ocher of paving, gravel, and fountain. And although there were two stone benches, it was not a place in which Gemma could imagine spending time.

She looked down at the paving stones, so perfectly, newly laid. And she thought of Sandra's haunting, faceless girls and women, preserved forever behind the bars of their gilded cages.

CHAPTER THIRTY-ONE

"When you are on the streets in Brick Lane the interior spaces are external to you. There aren't many reasons to go inside the buildings and get into these private spaces that hold their time in a different way to street time, which is always contemporary." [Iain Sinclair]

—Rachel
Lichtenstein,
On Brick Lane

Doug Cullen came into Kincaid's office and laid an evidence bag containing a familiar-looking, gold-stamped leather folder down on Kincaid's desk. "Forensics just delivered Alexander's passport. Makes for very interesting reading."

"I bloody well hope so," Kincaid said, with feeling. It was Monday morning and he had been up most of the night. Miles Alexander had been singularly uncooperative, either sneering or silent, and Kincaid was tired and frustrated. "We'd better come up with something that will make the child-trafficking charges stick like glue, because we haven't got enough so far to sell the prosecution on a single homicide, much less a double one. And I do *not* want to let this bastard go."

He felt quite sure that if Miles Alexander walked out of Scotland Yard, he would disappear, just like his friend Truman.

He still had hopes that the lab would find fiber transfer that would place Naz Malik in Alexander's house or car, but even that might be too little and too late. Alexander could argue that Naz had visited him, or ridden in his car, at any time. What they really needed was to match Alexander with hair or fiber that had been found on or around Naz Malik's body. But the processing of trace evidence took time, and he doubted he'd get a result soon enough to allow him to keep Alexander in the nick.

"What about Gemma's project?" asked Cullen, his face schooled into a neutrality Kincaid was sure he didn't feel. "I hear the super's not best pleased at the expense."

Kincaid knew Cullen was less than enthusiastic about Gemma's suggestion that they excavate Alexander's garden. "Slow going. They've got the fountain moved and the pavers up, but apparently it's teaspoon digging from now on. They can't risk disturbing any evidence."

"If there's any evidence to disturb."

"Gemma's right, Doug," Kincaid said, his patience fraying. "If Alexander killed Sandra Gilles, he had to put her body somewhere, and the garden is as good a place to start as any."

He took Alexander's passport out of the bag and flipped through it, raising an eyebrow as he read. "Quite the traveler, I see. Regular trips to Thailand and Bangladesh, as well as visits to Spain, favorite holiday spot of his mate Truman."

Cullen pulled a chair up to the desk. "And quite the serial monogamist, too, if you believe the records." His face lit up with a self-satisfied grin. "I've been through the files. Every couple of years for the past decade, he's married a girl—supposedly of age—in Bangladesh or Thailand, then brought her into the U.K. Then after a year or two—I'd assume it's when they've got too 'old' for his taste—he files for divorce, in each case assuring the judge that he'll pay the girl maintenance so she won't become a burden on the state. Then the girl disappears from the system. Very neat."

"Any—"

Cullen cut Kincaid off. "The best part is yet to come. It's been the same court in every case, and the judge's name is on the members' list of Lucas Ritchie's club."

"And was his lawyer the same bloke who's representing him now?"

Cullen thought about it. "Yeah. As a matter of fact, it was."

"How much do you want to wager that the lawyer's name is on Ritchie's list, too?" Kincaid asked with rising glee. Shuffling through the papers on his desk, he found the list, then ran his finger down it until he found the name he was seeking. "Bloody hallelujah." Grinning, he looked up at Cullen. "Bingo. I thought his name sounded familiar. No wonder he's looked so nervous."

"If he's one of Alexander's playmates, he'll be thanking whoever he prays to that he wasn't in Alexander's photo album."

Kincaid glanced at his watch. "Speaking of the photo album, Ritchie should be at the club by now. It's time we took those photos round. I'll just—" His desk phone rang and he broke off to answer.

It was the receptionist informing him that a Ms. Louise Phillips was downstairs. "Have someone show her up to my office," Kincaid said, deciding he'd rather speak to her there than in an interview room.

"News travels fast," he said to Cullen, and a few moments later, a uniformed constable showed Louise Phillips in.

She looked better than when he had last seen her, as if she were beginning to pull herself together after the shock of her partner's death. But she still smelled of smoke, and her dark eyes were as intent as ever. Taking the chair Cullen offered her, she got right to the point. "I hear you arrested someone, a suspect in Naz's murder—an anesthetist named Alexander."

"Do you know him?" Kincaid asked.

"No. But there's something you should know. I'm here on behalf of my client."

"Azad?" Kincaid wondered if they'd been wrong to discount Azad's involvement in the child trafficking.

"Mr. Azad has been very distressed over Naz's murder. He didn't feel he could speak, however, as long as he was in the delicate position of facing charges himself."

"Are you telling me the Crown dropped its case?"

"Mr. Azad's nephew has returned. He no longer wishes to testify against his uncle."

"Please, enough of the lawyer-speak, Ms. Phillips," Kincaid said, exasperated. "What are you here to tell us?"

Phillips touched her bag, as if she were about to reach for a cigarette, then sat back in her chair with a sigh. "Look, it's like this. Azad's silly nephew got himself involved in a forced labor scheme in East Anglia. They promised him the moon, then kept him in a hut for weeks, except when they sent him and the others they'd recruited out to work in the fields. No decent food, little water, no lavs, no medical care—even after he suffered a bad cut—and absolutely no communication with the outside world.

"But day before yesterday, he managed to get away and thumb a ride back to London. He's thrilled to be back in his uncle's house, and now thinks washing dishes in the restaurant kitchen is heaven on earth. So he's not about to bite the hand that—quite literally—feeds him."

"I'm sure his uncle must be thrilled by his nephew's safe return," Kincaid said sardonically. "But I don't see—"

"Having heard about Alexander's arrest, Azad feels he may have had some degree of responsibility for what happened—although of course he didn't realize this at the time."

"Of course," Kincaid agreed, with no small degree of sarcasm.

"Look," Lou Phillips said again. She brushed at her lapel. "Azad's not a bad guy, really. Feudal, yes, but that means he takes care of his own. He's loyal to his friends and his family, and he would never condone child prostitution. He heard rumors going round in Ritchie's club. Maybe because he'd been charged with human trafficking, certain people let things slip. They were checking him out, he thought, to see if he was interested in abusing children.

"But Azad was disgusted. He told Naz about it. Then the day before Naz disappeared—the day before he was murdered," Louise corrected herself, "they had a row. The upshot was that Azad finally agreed to tell Naz the names of the people he thought might be involved. Alexander was one of them. But Naz must have made the connection between Alexander and Sandra himself."

"And then Naz went round to confront Alexander," Kincaid finished. "With disastrous consequences. You realize I could charge your client as an accessory. Or, at the very least, with obstruction."

Louise Phillips gazed levelly back at him. "I don't think you will. My client has only just realized the pertinence of his information."

Knowing he couldn't prove otherwise, Kincaid conceded with as good a grace as he could muster. "Would Mr. Azad be willing to testify?"

"Maybe," Louise said. "But first you lot have to make a case that will hold up."

Gemma nibbled a sandwich at her desk, trying to concentrate on shifting her neglected caseload. But between glancing at the clock and checking to make sure her phone was really turned on, she wasn't making much progress with lunch or work.

She'd left two messages for Janice Silverman, even though she knew that the family court hearing might have run behind schedule. She'd managed to refrain from ringing Kincaid, as she knew he'd call her as soon as he heard anything about the excavation of the garden in Hoxton.

When her phone actually rang, she dropped her egg salad and cress on her computer keyboard.

It was Betty Howard, and her warm voice sounded unusually harried. "Have you heard anything, Gemma?"

"No. I promise I'll call as soon as I do, but Mrs. Silverman may call you first."

"She's that unsettled today, little Charlotte," Betty said softly. "She didn't want to sleep in her bed last night. She wanted Toby, and she kept fretting for you, and 'the big man.'"

"The big man?" Gemma asked, puzzled. She cleaned the remains of her sandwich off her keyboard and tossed it in the bin.

"She means Duncan, but she can't say his name very well."

Gemma smiled. Naz Malik had been a small-framed man, so compared to her father, Duncan must seem large to Charlotte—and apparently comforting as well. Charlotte had become attached to him very quickly, but her trusting nature terrified Gemma as much as it touched her. The child had never been mistreated. How would she cope with Gail and her uncles?

"Oh, Betty, surely they won't place her with the family. At least not yet." She knew she was trying to reassure herself.

"Listen, Gemma . . ." Betty sounded hesitant. "I've been worryin' a good deal. Even sayin' the judge decides against the family, they may not place her with me. She's mixed race, and they may feel she'd be better off with a white family. And . . . truth be told, I'm not gettin' any younger, and I'm not sure I can give the child the best care in the long term."

Gemma felt as if she'd been kicked. "Are you saying you don't want her?"

"No, no, I'm not meanin' that at all," Betty said. "I'm just worried. I'd have to think hard about raisin' up another child—about what's best for her. She's special, this girl. She deserves more than I can give her."

"But, Betty, no one could do more—"

"Just you ring me soon as you hear somethin'," Betty interrupted, and disconnected.

Gemma stared at the phone, her head reeling. She'd thought that if she could protect Charlotte from her family, the child would be assured of care and a safe future.

But if Betty didn't take Charlotte . . .

It wasn't that Gemma didn't understand Betty's concerns. Betty had raised five children of her own, and the responsibility of another child at her age would be daunting.

Still, Gemma shook her head in dismay. She couldn't bear the thought of Charlotte vanishing into the care system.

When her phone rang again, and she saw from the caller ID that it was Kincaid, she answered a little shakily.

"You all right, love?" he asked.

"I'm fine," she said, knowing she couldn't begin to explain, not until she'd had a chance to think it through. "Have they found—"

"I've not heard anything yet. But I have a nice surprise for you. I've had a call from Narcotics. Meet me at Gail Gilles's flat in Bethnal Green. Soon as you can."

Melody had insisted on going with her. "I'm on pins and needles about Alexander," she'd said. "So I'm not accomplishing anything. And if it's something about Charlotte, I want to know, too."

As they drove, Gemma told her about her conversation with Betty.

"Her reservations are understandable," Melody said. "And she may be right about the placement issues. But you can't do anything until you know what position the court is going to take, and what's going on with Gail Gilles. You're sure Duncan didn't sound upset?"

"No. I'd almost swear he was laughing."

But when they rounded the corner into Gail Gilles's council estate and Gemma saw the police cars, lights flashing, her heart lurched. "What the hell—" she said, climbing out of the car.

Then she spotted Kincaid coming towards them. "What's going on?" she asked as they met. "Is someone hurt?"

"Well, yes," he said, his mouth twitching. "Terry Gilles is in hospital. It seems that Kevin and Terry got in a little scuffle with a gang of Bangladeshi kids. Kevin and Terry were moving in on a Bangladeshi estate, trying to sell their wares, and the kids didn't appreciate it.

"Terry got knifed, and he thought he was dying. A flesh wound in the side, but he bled like a stuck pig. Apparently he was also a little off his head, and felt a great need to confess. He gave the PC who rode in the ambulance with him the full monty, and Kevin didn't have time to do damage control." Kincaid broke into a grin. "I don't think you'll have to worry about Gail Gilles, or Sandra's sister or brothers, getting custody of Charlotte any time in the foreseeable future."

As Gemma watched, two uniformed officers came down the stairs, escorting Gail Gilles, who sported handcuffs along with her pink dressing gown and leopard-print slippers.

Gail, however, was too busy ranting at the officers to notice her observers.

"She knew about the drugs," said Gemma, although she hadn't much doubt as to the answer.

"She not only knew, she was holding for the boys. Not just a hefty stash of heroin, but cash. They found twenty thousand pounds, just where Terry said it would be, in a Manolo Blahnik shoe box.

"And according to Terry," Kincaid went on as Gail was helped, none too gently, into the back of a panda car, "the sister, Donna, was involved in a smaller way. They're still searching her flat."

Gemma shook her head, bemused. "If I were Terry, I'd be hoping they wouldn't put me in a cell with Kevin."

"Whatever happens to either one of them, it serves them bloody right." Kincaid's voice had gone cold, and Gemma knew he was thinking about her encounter with the brothers.

He turned to her and gave her arm a squeeze. "And now you won't have to worry about Charlotte."

Before she could answer, his phone rang. He excused himself to take the call, and when he came back all the levity had gone from his face. "They want us in Hoxton," he said.

The lower floors of the house had been cleared by the scene of crime team, so that Gemma, Melody, and Kincaid were now able to walk downstairs and through the kitchen without wearing sterile gear. Kincaid had told Gemma that Cullen had gone to speak to Lucas Ritchie, but was now on his way to the house as well.

Rashid Kaleem was waiting for them in the garden—a garden that looked quite different from the serene space Gemma had seen the previous morning.

The stone pavers had been levered up all around the fountain and stacked to the sides. The gravel that had lain beneath the stones had been carefully scooped into buckets and tubs.

The forensic excavation team responsible for the current state of chaos had set up lights and worked through the night.

"When they reached what looked like garden lime, they called me," the pathologist explained. He squatted by the pit, wearing the jeans and black T-shirt that Gemma thought of as his uniform. But his face and arms were streaked with dust, and his urbane charm seemed to have deserted him, although he gave Gemma a quick smile.

"The lads and the photographer have gone for a bit of a break," Kaleem continued. "And I've called in a forensic anthropologist. What comes next is more his province than mine."

"You've found her," said Gemma. And although it was what she'd expected, what she'd been all too certain of since she'd first looked at the garden, she felt a rush of grief that caught her by surprise. Sandra Gilles would not come home to her daughter.

"Yes, I think so," answered Kaleem. He rubbed his arm across his forehead, leaving more streaks. "There is an adult female body beneath the layer of lime. The lime slowed decomposition somewhat, but it's been a warm summer, so . . . the clothing is pretty well intact, however, and matches the description of the items Sandra Gilles was wearing the day she disappeared. The hair also fits Sandra Gilles's description—blond and very curly."

Gemma decided then that she was not going to look. She had seen Naz Malik's body. She wanted to keep her image of Sandra Gilles, the vibrant woman she'd seen in the photographs in the Fournier Street house, intact—for Charlotte's sake as well as her own.

". . . we will, of course, be matching DNA and dental records," Kaleem was saying as she dragged her attention back to him. "The victim was buried facedown, and it looks as though she received a blow to the back of the head. There's what appears to be matted blood in the hair, and a depression in the skull."

Kincaid stepped forward and looked down. His face was impassive. "He hit her?"

"Looks that way. I'd say when her back was turned. No guess as to the weapon without a proper examination."

"But—" Gemma tried to work out what had happened. "If she just came to talk to him, why did he take the risk of killing her, rather than just bluffing it out? Surely he could have covered his tracks up to that point—"

There were voices from the kitchen, and two suited forensics techs came out, followed by a photographer, and then Doug Cullen. Gemma noticed that one of the "lads" was female.

Kincaid and Kaleem moved aside so the techs could go back to work. "We're just going to remove a bit more fill, Doc," said the woman, who appeared to be in charge. "It seems to be quite soft beneath the body."

"I talked to the landscapers this morning," said Cullen. "The woman next door remembered the name on their van. This"—he waved a hand towards the fountain, now moved to one side—"wasn't the original plan. He was going to put in a fishpond, quite a deep one. They'd already dug for it, and delivered the pavers to go round it, but they hadn't taken away the earth that had come out of the hole.

"Then Alexander rang them the morning they were scheduled to concrete the pond and said he'd decided on something else and was going to do the work himself. They thought he'd just got a cheaper bid at the last minute, because he wasn't the type to get his hands dirty. But then he called them back a few days later and asked them to put in the fountain."

"So, he found himself with a body on his hands and took advantage of an opportunity," Kincaid said. "He had a hole, and the materials to fill it, and he needed to do it as quickly as possible—"

"Wait," interrupted Kaleem. He turned to Cullen. "Did your landscaper say how deep they dug? This body is actually quite close to the surface. If there's loose soil beneath her—"

Kaleem and the female tech looked at each other, then went to the edge of the pit and knelt, leaning down. The tech eased herself flat onto her stomach, and Kaleem steadied her while she seemed to be probing carefully in the bottom of the hole.

"Shit," she said, suddenly still. "Get me a damned bucket."

The other tech hurried forward and eased himself down flat as well, lowering an empty tub.

Kaleem watched intently as the female tech moved again, and Gemma heard the soft sound of earth falling into the plastic tub. Then Kaleem looked up.

"There's another body, lower down."

The two techs worked silently, easing soil from around the edges of the upper body. After a quarter of an hour, the woman said, "I think that's all we can do without disturbing the upper remains. But fortunately the lower body was a bit to one side, so I think you can get some idea of what we've got."

Kaleem knelt down again and peered in. "There's a hand and

forearm visible. From the size, I'd say they belong to a child. And there's hair. Long and dark. So I would guess, given the suspect's history, that this victim is female."

"Oh." Gemma drew in a breath as an added weight of sorrow descended upon her.

The little girl had stopped appearing in the window, not because she'd been passed on to another man, but because she had died.

"Was the girl there longer than Sandra, do you think?" she asked Kaleem.

"Can't say for certain without tests, but it looks like decomposition is a little more advanced. There's no lime over these deeper remains, however, so decomposition might have progressed more rapidly."

Gemma frowned. "Why no lime over the girl, I wonder?"

"Maybe the girl's death was an accident," Melody suggested. "He got too rough with her, or . . . well, anyway, whatever happened . . . maybe he just took advantage of the work in progress." She gestured at the garden.

"And then when it came to Sandra," continued Gemma, "he must have figured that what had worked once would work again. But he had to put her body closer to the surface, so he risked taking the time to get the lime. It was a Sunday, after all. He could have just driven to a garden center that afternoon. He wouldn't have buried her until after dark."

"It must have been backbreaking," said Kincaid, without the least trace of sympathy. "I'll bet we find he took a few days off work afterwards."

"But why didn't he bury Naz?" asked Gemma.

"He was running out of room. And maybe the lime hadn't worked as well as he'd thought." Kincaid shrugged. "Or maybe he just didn't want to dig up his pavers again. But whatever the reason, it was a bad decision. If Naz Malik had disappeared without a trace, we might never have learned what happened to Naz or Sandra. Or this girl."

"We found a pair of glasses, guv," said the female tech. "Almost forgot, in all the excitement. They were under the shrubs, covered with some leaf mold." She gestured towards the fill buckets, and Gemma saw a small evidence bag pushed to one side. She crossed the garden and picked up the bag, studying it. They looked just like the glasses Naz had been wearing in the photos on Sandra's corkboard.

"I'm certain these belonged to Naz," she said. "Do you think"— she hesitated, hating the idea—"do you think he left them deliberately?"

"If Alexander invited him out here for a drink—and I wouldn't be surprised if the idea appealed to him, the twisted bastard"— Kincaid grimaced—"then kept him here, drugged, until dark, Naz might have had periods when he was conscious enough to realize what was happening."

Cullen was shaking his head, not in disagreement, but in an expression that bordered on wonder. "Maybe that's what Alexander was looking for that day in the mortuary, when we thought he might have gone through Naz's effects," he said. "He realized he'd slipped up. But, my God, what a nerve."

The enclosed space of the garden was beginning to bake in the afternoon sun, and the odor rising from the pit was unmistakable. Gemma stepped back until she stood partly in the shade cast by the house. She looked up at the dark brick wall. "What we still don't understand is what brought Sandra here that day."

"They found a camera inside," said the tech. "In the bedroom nearest the bathroom upstairs. There were some girls' trinkets in a drawer, and a folded sari. The camera was tucked underneath, in the folds of the cloth."

Gemma imagined Sandra, driven by an impulse they might never understand, perhaps asking to use the loo, then darting across the hall for a quick look in the bedroom. Had she meant to take a photo of the sari, but tucked her camera beneath the silk when she heard Alexander coming?

"Were there any pictures in the camera?" she asked.

"I don't know, guv," the woman answered. "But I don't think they've sent it to the lab yet."

"I want to see it," Gemma said. She turned and went into the house, and Kincaid followed her.

While he went upstairs, she waited in the kitchen, listening to the murmur of his voice as he talked to someone on the upstairs search team.

When he came back, he held a small camera with gloved hands. "There was only one photo on the memory card." He held the camera up so Gemma could see.

She gazed at the bright square of the view screen. There was an arch of dark brick, and within it, a peeling poster. It was a street artist's fading work, so damaged that Gemma couldn't be certain whether it was a painting or a photograph.

It didn't matter. The young woman in the picture seemed to gaze back at her, unconcerned by her nakedness, her serene face innocent and as ageless as time itself.

CHAPTER THIRTY-TWO

In the old days there were angels who came and took men by the hand and led them away from the city of destruction. We see no white-winged angels now. But yet men are led away from threatening destruction: a hand is put into theirs, which leads them forth gently towards a calm and bright land, so that they may look no more backward; and the hand may be a little child's.

—George Eliot,
Silas Marner

"Why don't you sit down for a minute," Kincaid had said. "It's hot, and you look a bit done in." He'd fetched her a glass of water, then gone back into the garden.

Gemma had emptied the tumbler into the sink, then scrubbed it with soap and hot water before filling it again. It was stupid, she knew, and she was thirsty, but she didn't want to drink from Alexander's glass.

When Kincaid came back, she had rinsed it once more.

"I think I know her name," he said. "Cullen did some digging this morning. According to Immigration's records, the last girl Alexander brought in from Bangladesh was called Rani. He never divorced her."

"What about Lucas Ritchie?" asked Gemma. "Did he identify any of the men in the photos?"

"All of them. Cullen will get started on the warrants. Listen." He came over to her and took the glass from her hands, setting it in the sink. "There's not much else we can do here at the moment. I think, if we left right now, we might get to Chelsea Town Hall before closing."

Gemma looked at him blankly. "Chelsea Town Hall?"

"We have a marriage license to apply for, in case you'd forgotten."

"Oh, so we do." It seemed a world away from what she had witnessed in the garden—a world she suddenly wanted very much. She turned the ring on her finger. "I think that's a bloody brilliant idea."

Melody watched them go from the front step. She'd promised to drive Gemma's car back to Notting Hill, and had taken the keys.

Feeling a momentary pang of envy, she wondered when Gemma would see the light about Charlotte. Some people had everything, and were blind. But still, it wasn't her place to say—and it wasn't like her to be standing round feeling sorry for herself either.

The door opened and Doug Cullen came out.

"Oh, it's you," she said. "I understand you've been vehicularly abandoned. The super took the pool car. Do you want a lift?"

"Yeah. In a bit, if you don't mind." He stood beside her, gazing up the street, and didn't meet her eyes. "So is this going to show up in tomorrow's *Chronicle*?" he asked.

Melody looked at him, startled. "What?"

"You heard me. I did some research, you know. After the leak about Ritchie's club. It was blindingly obvious, really. It's just that no one ever thought to look.

"It's a common enough name," he continued, "common enough to pass unnoticed for a while, but how could you have thought that your identity wouldn't eventually come out? And to put Gemma at risk—"

"You're defending Gemma?" Melody's anger overcame her shock. "That's rich, since you're the one always trying to sabotage her. Admit it, you're jealous, and you have it in for me because I'm connected with her. So what are you going to do?"

Doug looked at her, his expression mulish. Melody glared back at him. Then, it came to her that the whole business was really stupid, and that she was tired of it.

"You're right," she said, her shoulders slumping. "It's not fair to Gemma, even though I've told her the truth. I should resign. I love this job, but I don't want to go on doing it like this."

"I'm right?" Cullen sounded surprised. "You'd really quit? What else would you do?"

"I don't know. I'm good at finding out things. I suppose I'd go to work for the paper. It's what my father's always wanted."

"But you didn't do what he wanted."

"No."

Cullen shifted awkwardly. "Look, I didn't mean—"

"Are you saying I should stay on, and have you hold the truth over my head?"

"No. Not me. But you should tell the guv'nor."

"You think I would ever be assigned to a major case again?"

"Well, if they discriminated against you because of who your father is, you could always threaten to take the story to the paper." He grinned suddenly, but Melody wasn't sure she found the irony funny.

"Seriously," Cullen continued, "you *are* good at what you do. And I suppose you were right. I have been jealous of Gemma, and of you."

"Doug, why?" she asked, and the use of his first name felt comfortable again. "You're a good officer, and Kincaid depends on you."

"Because I don't seem to have the talent for reading signals." He shrugged. "I'm good with facts, but I always seem to get things wrong with people. Foot in mouth." He looked away. "Like that night in front of the Yard. I was an idiot."

Even now, remembering his rejection made her flush with embarrassment. But she'd only suggested a drink, after all, and maybe he had just felt shy. Had she overreacted? And was it too late to make amends?

"You were," she agreed, but without rancor. "But that was ages ago. Do you think, if I talked to the super, that I could get on in this job?"

"There are times it might be helpful to have a friendly connection with the press. As long as the press knew where your interests lay."

"Loyalties, you mean," she said.

"Yeah. That, too. *Do* you know?" he asked, with a frankness she'd never heard from him.

"Definitely."

"Then maybe . . ." He rocked a little on his feet, and pushed his glasses up on his nose. ". . . if you gave me a lift, we could stop for a drink. Have a chat or something."

Melody laughed aloud. She felt a bit giddy with liberation. "What would we talk about?"

"I'm thinking of looking for a new flat."

"Well, that'll do for a start."

"You have sixteen days of official freedom," Duncan said when they left the town hall, having filled out the paperwork required by the Borough of Kensington and Chelsea for a marriage license. "In case you change your mind."

"I'd better not," she said, teasing. "Your mum and dad have promised to come to Glastonbury for Winnie's blessing. And Juliet's promised to come with the kids. Kit should be pleased." She took his arm. "It's cooling off. Let's walk down to the river, to celebrate.

"Winnie's doing well, by the way," she added as they strolled down Oakley Street. "I talked to her this morning." She didn't want to think about her mum, and whether she would be well enough in a few months to attend. Not today.

"You realize that if we go to Glastonbury for Winnie's blessing in the church, we'll be married three times," Kincaid said.

"Is that for luck, then?" she asked.

"I don't know about luck, but it should make it stick."

She punched his arm and he laughed, but when they reached the river, he stopped, his back to the railing, and looked at her soberly.

"Will you mind? About Winnie and Jack's baby?" he asked.

"No, of course not," she answered, but she knew what he meant. "I'm so pleased for them. Really, I'll be fine." And she realized, as she said it, that she was fine—that she was, in some indefinable way, healed, and that it was not a baby she wanted.

"But there is—" She struggled with the words. "I don't want you to think that it's not important to me to have a child of our own. But Kit and Toby, they're just as much ours as if we'd had them together. I can't imagine loving them any more, or any differently.

"And today"—she swallowed and went on—"when I knew what had happened to that little girl . . . to all those girls, I thought— If we could make a difference to one—"

"I know," he said, and smiled. "And besides, the boys need someone to keep them in line."

Steve Ullathorne

About the Author

DEBORAH CROMBIE was born in Dallas and grew up in Richardson, Texas, the second child of Charlie and Mary Darden. Her rather solitary childhood (brother Steve is ten years older) was blessed by her maternal grandmother, Lillian Dozier, a retired teacher who taught her to read very early. After a checkered educational career, which included dropping out of high school at sixteen, she graduated from Austin College in Sherman, Texas, with a degree in biology. Crombie then worked in advertising and newspapers, and attended the Rice University Publishing Program. A post-university trip to England, however, cemented a lifelong passion for Britain, and she immigrated to the United Kingdom, living first in Edinburgh, Scotland, and then in Chester, England.

After returning to Dallas and working for several years in her family business while raising her daughter, Kayti, a trip to Yorkshire inspired her to write her first Detective Superintendent Duncan Kincaid/Sergeant Gemma James novel. *A Share in Death* (Scribner 1993) was subsequently given Agatha and Macavity nominations for Best First Novel of 1993. Her fifth novel, *Dreaming of the*

Bones (Scribner 1997), a *New York Times* Notable Book for 1997, was short-listed by Mystery Writers of America for the 1997 Edgar Award for Best Novel, and was voted by the Independent Mystery Booksellers Association as one of the hundred best mysteries of the century. Crombie's following eight novels have been received with critical acclaim and are read internationally, particularly in Germany.

Crombie divides her time between England and her home in McKinney, Texas, where she lives in an early Arts and Crafts bungalow with her husband, two German shepherds (Hallie and Neela), and two cats. She is hard at work on the next Kincaid/James novel.

BOOK GROUP QUESTIONS

1. How does the clash of cultures found in the East End affect the characters in this book? Give examples of characters who are affected by the culture clash.

2. Why do you think the author made Sandra an artist? Why not make her a shop clerk or a bank teller?

3. What role does race play in this book? Who finds race important? Who doesn't? What do they do that tells you this? What is the author trying to say through these characters?

4. Sandra's work is about women in cages. What does Sandra do to liberate herself? Other women? Is this important work in your community? Why or why not?

5. Why is it important to Duncan that he and Gemma get married? Why is Gemma reluctant? Will marriage change their relationship?

6. Gemma is very worried about protecting Charlotte's innocence. How are Sandra and Naz innocent as well?

7. Contrast Naz and Sandra's marriage to the relationship between Tim and Hazel. Why doesn't Hazel believe she deserves a second chance with Tim?

8. Sandra grew up in a very dysfunctional family. How do you think she managed to create a strong family for herself? Who were her influences? What similarities do you see between Sandra and Gemma?

9. Melody drew on her father's contacts to gain important information about the case. Was it justified in light of the results?

10. How does Gemma bend the rules to help Duncan with his investigation? What does she risk by doing this? What does he risk? Are these risks they should have taken?

11. The addition of a child changes any family. Are there special challenges Duncan and Gemma will face because they chose to adopt a child rather than have one of their own? What additional challenges will they face because Charlotte is a mixed-race child?

12. How do the changes happening in the East End mirror changes in the broader society? Who will be the winners? What will be lost?

BOOKS BY DEBORAH CROMBIE

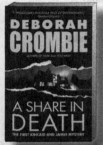

A Share in Death
ISBN: 978-0-06-053438-7 (MASS MARKET PAPERBACK)

"Great continuity, clever plotting, and hidden agendas all contribute to a successful novel."
—*Library Journal*

All Shall Be Well
ISBN: 978-0-06-053439-4 (MASS MARKET PAPERBACK)

"Crombie has mastered the genre of Agatha Christie."
—*Commonwealth Journal*

Leave the Grave Green
ISBN: 978-0-06-078955-8 (MASS MARKET PAPERBACK)

"The passages . . . are haunting, the mystery is intriguing, the characters are well developed and the solution satisfies. Stay tuned."
—*Publishers Weekly*

Mourn Not Your Dead
ISBN: 978-0-06-078957-2 (MASS MARKET PAPERBACK)

"Crombie keeps this series on its toes with her smooth procedural techniques and engagingly eccentric characters."
—*New York Times Book Review*

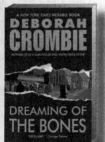

Dreaming of the Bones
ISBN: 978-0-06-115040-1 (MASS MARKET PAPERBACK)

"Crombie excels at investing her mysteries with rich characterization and a sophisticated wash of illuminating feminism."
—*Publishers Weekly* (Starred Review)

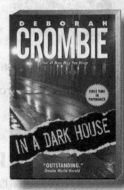
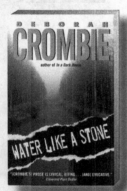